# HOUSE OF

*Maxym M. Mar*

Edira Brillwyn is a threadmender. She holds a rare, lifesaving power that can cure disease and heal injuries in the blink of an eye. But magic always comes with a cost, and saving anyone sacrifices a sliver of her own life. She's always kept her abilities hidden…until the powerful Fernglove family discovers her secret.

The Ferngloves are charming and beautiful, possess powerful magic, and don't take no for an answer—especially Orin, the head of these ruling elites. When Edira's brothers unexpectedly contract blight—an incurable virus killing people throughout the town, and an illness too strong for her to heal them both—Orin offers to help. Together at his estate they'll research a cure while Orin slows their sickness and Edira hones her magic. His kindness and honesty surprises Edira, as does her undeniable attraction to him.

But the other Ferngloves are suspicious of her power and may be more dangerous than the ever-present disease. The longer Edira stays within the confines of the Manor, the more the family's pristine exterior begins to crack—until Edira discovers a terrifying secret and must choose who she can save and at what cost…

**9781835413234 | 8th April 2025**
**Paperback & eBook | £9.99 | 384pp**

## PRESS & PUBLICITY

### Isabelle Sinnott
Isabelle.sinnott@titanemail.com

# HOUSE OF BLIGHT

**MAXYM M. MARTINEAU**

**TITAN** BOOKS

House of Blight
Print edition ISBN: 9781835413234
E-book edition ISBN: 9781835413241

Published by Titan Books
A division of Titan Publishing Group Ltd
144 Southwark Street, London SE1 0UP
www.titanbooks.com

First edition: April 2025
10 9 8 7 6 5 4 3 2 1

A CIP catalogue record for this title is available from the British Library.

Printed and bound by 4Edge in the United Kingdom.

*For those who constantly sacrifice in the name of others,*
*it's okay to save yourself first*

# PROLOGUE

When the stars were young and the sun was new, a woman of great power and strong mind met Death at a four-way crossing. Cloaked in shadow despite the high noon hour, he welcomed those who found their way to him, and he always afforded them the same opportunity: a path of their choosing.

"Successfully choose the correct path forward, and I will allow you to pass, turning my back to you and your kin. Choose incorrectly and walk with me now to your end," he said.

The woman studied Death with keen eyes. She was not afraid, but she knew there was magic in words. Her choice was not one to be taken lightly.

"What do the paths represent?" she asked.

With bony fingers, Death gestured to her left: "A fork in the road you missed in your youth." Then, directly before her: "The unchanged path, as most predict." To her right: "A future, wild and unseen." Death looked beyond her to the path she'd been walking: "And a past you cannot escape."

The woman pondered her options. She knew she was not the

first to meet Death on this road and surmised all paths had been chosen before. She glanced to her left. *To right a wrong or avoid a regret and start anew . . .* She narrowed her eyes. *Only to meet Death sooner.*

She stared past Death at the path ahead. *The unchanged path that led me to Death; the only prediction guaranteed to come true.*

She shook her head and gazed to the right. *Wild and unseen. Tragic and swift.* Grimacing, she regarded the path behind her, and she knew that if she turned back now, her feet would only carry her here again—the path she could not escape.

"Every path leads me to you," she said.

Death smiled. "Yes."

"I see. Then I'll return tomorrow." And with that, the woman left down the path she'd came, leaving a perplexed Death behind. When the sun rose, the woman returned. She asked Death the same question, received the same answer, and once again departed down the path she'd come.

This continued for a decade until Death's patience grew thin. "Your time is up." From the folds of his cloak, he drew a blade devoid of life and color, darker than the depths of night. The woman studied the weapon without moving, but there was a strange glint to her hardened stare that even Death could not miss. He gripped the weapon tighter and said, "Death comes for us all."

"Including you?" she asked, finally rounding her gaze to Death.

She was not the first person to ask such a thing, and she wouldn't be the last. Death once again hid his blade in his cloak. "There is death for me yet, but you are not it. You do not possess the power or the weapon. It is your fate to meet me here, and you've wasted enough of my time."

She nodded. "I understand. Grant me one final chance to say my farewells, and I'll part from the life I've always known."

Sensing a shift in her demeanor, Death allowed her this courtesy. When she returned the next morning, Death once again gestured to the roads. "Choose."

Without hesitation, the woman strode forward and unsheathed a dagger, a twin to Death's own weapon, and plunged it deep into his gut. "I know you, Death. I came into the world cloaked in your shadow when you stole my mother's life as I left her womb. You think I'm powerless? Far from it. I've been watching you for years, biding my time until it made sense for me to strike. You will not take me, too. The path I choose is yours."

Stunned by her revelation and grievously wounded, Death had no option but to concede. "Spare my life, and I'll spare yours," he said. She waited, her hand gripped tightly around the hilt of her blade. "Walk whichever path you please. You shall be . . . ever living." Slowly, so as not to draw the woman's blade farther into his own flesh, Death reached into the folds of his cloak and extracted a smooth stone of pure moonlight. "I cannot walk where there are no shadows. Stay within its glow, and you will never see me again."

"And for my kin?" She took the proffered gem while twisting her knife deeper. Instead of ruby blood, obsidian rivulets oozed down the blade.

Death hissed. "Split it. Search for more. All jewels of this nature are now bound by this promise, I swear to you."

"Good." She removed her blade and continued onward, down a path Death did not see, while pocketing the stone with a smile. And while Death lay crumpled in the crossroads, feeling bitter and cheated, he decided he'd allow the woman and her kin to feel safe for a time—long enough for all to forget the power of her bargain and everything she left out.

# ONE

I'd always found cemeteries a bit odd—they housed the dead, but the dead didn't need them. The dead didn't need anything. The very existence of graves, of coffins, felt like a living riddle. What was made for the deceased but comforted the living? A silk-lined box. It sounded like something one of the Evers would say, and while I had no desire to get involved with them, it was hard not to respect the power behind their words.

Or maybe I was drawn to the quiet graves because of the abundance of mugwort. That seemed far more likely.

Crouching before the nearest crumbling headstone, I drove my fingers into the soft dirt and uprooted the sage-green plant, minding the tiny white hairs covering the leaves. I tucked it into the overflowing burlap sack hanging from my hip and stood, brushing my hands along the fabric of my fitted pants. Most ladies of marriageable age favored satin skirts and low necklines, sumptuous frills and elegant lace trimmings. Perhaps if my station had been different, I would have, too. I had nothing against the artful construction of whalebone and ribbon, but when one rummaged through the dirt as often as I did, it was tiresome to change skirts frequently enough to remain presentable.

Plus, those ladies had families and coin that afforded them lazy afternoons sipping tea over gossip, whereas I did not. I would likely be plowing through earth right up to my final days, and I'd probably dig that grave, too. And even yet, that fate seemed preferrable to the alternative: spending time with Willowfell's elite for the chance of a marriage that would "save" me from my work.

I'd rather work for myself than work to be someone else's version of "suitable."

River birch trees clambered against the moss-covered stone wall rimming the graveyard, and I lingered in their shade a moment longer before navigating the path toward the flower-studded meadow. The spring air was thick with the scent of fresh linens, as the townsfolk strung up damp sheets and garments to take advantage of the cloud-free sky. I cut a glance toward the midafternoon sun. There were only a few hours left until my brothers returned from the nearby mines, and I was eager to brew a few tonics for tomorrow's market before they commandeered the kitchen.

Taking the right fork around a small hill, I came across the first crop of houses marking the edge of Willowfell. The quaint homes rimming the outskirts of town looked largely the same— the pearl-colored bricks were fashioned from stone found at the base of our closest mountain, and the hipped roofs were a dark shade of ivy to match the surrounding canopy of leaves. But perhaps the most unique custom of Willowfell was the construction of its doors. It was tradition for families to decorate them however they deemed fit. The Shatterlends' door was a mosaic masterpiece depicting a romantic embrace. Lazlo and his husband opted for a circular entrance with half-moon windows burrowed into the rich wood. The Hafters' was covered in iron handles.

Our door, though, was my favorite. The facade itself was simple, but the surrounding frame was something else entirely. Even now, as I passed by our neighbors' homes and found myself standing before my father's handiwork, I couldn't help but marvel at the intricate details. He'd taken a fallen branch from a nearby ash tree and carved an arch of interconnected roses and vines. He'd studied the flowers for weeks in order to capture even the most minor features. The thin veining in the leaves. The uneven crinkles in the petals. Buds blooming. Buds closed. Thorns of various sizes but precisely sharp. He'd polished it all to perfection, but he'd refused to stain it. For him, there was nothing more beautiful than the story told by the nuances in the grains of wood.

My heart twisted as I lightly fingered a petal by the bronze handle—my way of greeting him each time I returned home. My mother I kept with me at all times. Instinctively, my hand dropped to the front pocket of my pants, where I could feel the outline of an embroidered scrap of leather. She'd been excellent with a needle, often stitching designs into our clothes and crafting small toys for us with leftover fabric.

Years had passed since their deaths, and still I missed them so much I ached.

Once in the kitchen, I deposited my bag on the knobby, worn wood table and fished a heavy pot from the lower cabinet. After filling it with water, I lit the cast-iron stove. Heat bloomed outward in a drowsy bubble, cooking the space in a matter of minutes, and I tied my raven-black hair in a bun atop my head to keep the strands from sticking to my neck.

With deft fingers, I opened my bag and began sorting through herbs when my hand stilled. Something gold flashed between the muted greens and browns. At first I thought I'd picked up a coin in my foraging, but it was smaller than our currency and even more brilliant in its metallic sheen. Frowning, I drew myself closer, and the object—the insect—moved.

*Beetle.* My lips quirked up as it skittered across my knuckles. The edges of its outer shell were transparent, and two soft antennae twitched as it regarded me. Careful not to jostle the creature, I moved to the open window and let it crawl onto the sill. It stretched its wings as if preparing to fly, then stopped.

"It's all right," I murmured. "Take your time."

Just then, a hesitant knock sounded from the front door. "Ms. Brillwyn? Are you home?"

*Ms.?* I bit back a chuckle. One of the children, then, hoping a touch of respect would gain my favor. I was only twenty-five, and I'd never really cared for titles. That was something only the elders—or those hoping to become pinnacles of our quiet society—cared for. Ridiculous. I dusted my hands together and crossed the kitchen to the small foyer, sidestepping the worn stairs winding upward toward the bedrooms. When I opened the door, a boy with bleary, red-rimmed eyes looked up at me. He breathed heavily through his parted, chapped lips, careful not to inhale sharply as one hand precariously shielded his nose.

Sighing, I opened the door wider and leaned against the frame. "Toman, why am I not surprised?" I'd never met anyone in all of Glaes who injured themselves as much as him, and our country was rather large.

"Hi, Ms. Brillwyn." His congested voice trembled with the low whimper of a child hoping to avoid a scolding.

"It's just Edira. You know that." I tilted my head, trying to catch a glimpse of the injury he was hiding. "What happened?"

"Elbow to the face," he mumbled. I glanced over the top of his head to spy a discarded, filthy ball waiting for him at the edge of my garden. No doubt he'd been playing rough with his brothers and ended up here instead of risking an earful from his mother.

Stepping to the side, I gestured toward the kitchen. "Come on, then."

"Thanks," he said as he easily found his way to my table and sunk into one of the sturdy chairs. At this point, he could've claimed it as his own. I'd helped him and his siblings more times than I could count—all free of charge. Which was probably the *real* reason they kept finding themselves here. Mrs. Marlow was nothing if not shrewd. I really should've refused her sons altogether, but I loathed the idea of holding her children accountable for her snobbery. At least not until they showed signs of it themselves, and then I'd ignore their pretentious comments, too.

Dragging one of the opposite chairs across the creaking floorboards, I seated myself directly before Toman. "Let me see."

He hesitated, his caramel-colored eyes full of pain, and then slowly removed his hand to reveal a misshapen nose with dried blood caked around the nostrils. My brows arched toward my hairline.

"Does your mother know?"

His face blanched. "Are you going to tell her?"

"She's going to find out one way or another." With light fingers, I gripped either side of his grubby face and inspected the injury. The awkward angle, fresh, heavy bruising, and congested breathing were indicators enough. Broken. A prickling sensation spread outward from my chest and trickled toward my fingers, and I clenched my jaw to steel myself against the hidden surge of magic now flooding my veins.

And suddenly I was thrust into a memory of when I'd held Nohr's crushed leg in my hands just a few years ago. He'd come back from the mines with his femur split after loose rubble pinned him to the earth until Noam wrenched him free. Nohr was already unconscious when Noam dragged him back to our home and screamed for me in the foyer.

Threadmending hadn't even been a question then. Nohr never would've been able to work again if I hadn't healed him. He could've died. I'd tapped into my power as seamlessly as breathing and watched as his life threads unfurled, searching until I found the mangled fibers tied to the devastating injury that was his leg.

And then I'd poured everything I had into stitching them back together.

Of course, there had been a cost. There was always a cost when it came to my magic. For every ailment that I healed, every life thread I put back together, I'd sacrifice a few strands of my own and diminish my lifespan. As well as, to a somewhat lesser degree, suffer the physical consequences of the injury or illness.

Nohr's splintering pain had immediately become my own, and fires had ruptured from the bone in my left leg as tears stung the backs of my eyes. Heat flushed through my skin and left me raw. Every breath was a jagged, sharp exhale that stung, and I was a trembling mess coated in a thin sheen of sweat, until I finally finished my work and then collapsed beside my brother, letting the magic fade as I, too, succumbed to unconsciousness.

There was no way to know exactly how much of my life I'd sacrificed to save Nohr's leg. Threadmenders couldn't see their own threads. Why, I didn't know. My aunt, a threadmender like me, didn't either. But she speculated that the cost was scaled. Minor illnesses and trivial breaks? Possibly a few weeks. Major fractures like Nohr's leg? Several months at least.

I never dared to ask her how much of her life she thought she'd sacrificed to cure my mother of a winter illness that lingered far too long in her lungs. An illness that caused the townsfolk to avoid my family at all costs, barely offering condolences if they saw one of us in passing. I'd been young when it happened, but I still remembered how they refused to look directly at us. As if averting their eyes would somehow absolve them of acknowledging our pain.

But for Toman's nose . . . I forced myself back to the present, to the mild ailment at hand. I would not threadmend him. It wasn't worth it. Still, my power recognized Toman's need, and it flourished just the same, filling me to the brim with a near-unbearable tingling warmth. Fortunately, Toman had no idea I possessed such magic. And I had to keep it that way.

"Can you fix it?" he mumbled.

"I'm half tempted to leave it as is and teach you a lesson." I let my hands fall away and instead toyed with a sprig of lavender, giving myself a chance to squash the nagging pull of my magic. "Not to mention you'd acquire some of that roguish charm I hear is very attractive."

"Edira," he whined, dragging out my name. He searched my face for a moment, his gaze lingering on my hair before shifting elsewhere. My breath caught in my chest, and I resisted the urge to finger the black strand framing my cheek. I'd only just dyed it a week ago. A current of anxiety wove through me, but I refused to acknowledge it. I was safe. No one in town knew.

"Yes, I can fix it."

"Will it hurt?" An ache of fear gnawed at his vocal cords. That tiny mewling sound was like a royal doctrine I was obligated to follow, and I sighed. My lack of self-control would be the death of my pockets if I kept offering my services for free.

Of course, that was better than putting one foot in the grave by resorting to threadmending. I flexed my hand, fighting with the still lingering prickling in my fingertips. It didn't fully subside—and it wouldn't until Toman's injury was resolved or he removed himself from my presence—but it'd dulled enough for me to focus.

"Only a little. Promise." At that, I stood and made my way to one of the open shelves lining the walls of my kitchen. Jars and vials marked with my own handwriting clinked a quiet hello as my fingers maneuvered through them. After a minute of searching, I secured a small container with a corked lid and a vial with milky-white liquid: healing balm and numbing serum.

Before Toman could shy away, I'd tilted his head back and used a dropper to add the serum to his nostrils. The numbing agent worked quickly, and his face slackened as pain fled from his expression. A relieved smile tugged at his lips.

"Now to set it." I sank back onto my chair. "Are you ready?"

"Yes," Toman said, pulling my focus back to him.

"All right. Close your eyes."

Steadying myself with a deep breath, I cast away all thoughts of the day: the sounds, the smells, the sticky sensation of heat from the cast-iron range cooking away at my back. I stared only at Toman's misshapen nose. Again, my power called to me. Begged me to study the threads of his life, to find the frayed edges that needed repairing and stitch them together, but I pushed the impulse away and instead focused on the practical art of medicine.

I brought my hands to his face, pressing my thumbs on either side of his nose and pushing into the break. Toman gave a pained grunt—nowhere near as bad as it would've been had I not used the serum—as I realigned the bone, and then it was done.

"There."

With careful fingers, Toman tested his newly re-formed nose. "How does it look?"

I cracked a warm smile. "While I'm partial to suitors my age, I think you look rather dashing."

Boyish charm flooded his face. "Thanks, Edira. You're the best."

"I know. Here." I handed him the healing balm and watched as he opened the lid to inspect the heavy cream mixture. "Apply nightly to speed up the healing process and eliminate lingering pain. You'll be fine in a few days, but take it easy in the meantime. Understood?"

"Will do!" His grin was wide as he bounded toward the door. He was already down the walk before he turned to wave goodbye, and I sighed as I returned the gesture. He hadn't even bothered to clean the blood from his face.

*To be that carefree.* I shook my head, and my hair dusted along my cheek. A familiar swell of unease trickled through my stomach, and this time, I allowed myself to finger the loose strand. Still black. I rubbed the lock between my forefinger and thumb, only to frown at the dark film that began to smear across my skin. I needed to make another batch of dye to hide my telltale moonlit hair. If even a rumor of my power somehow spread throughout the town, the Evers would be at my door, and I'd disappear just like my aunt had, whisked away by the Ferngloves to cure gods only knew what until she likely passed from wasting so many threads of her own.

Swallowing thickly, I moved to the kitchen and set to work, splitting my focus between my remedies and the concoction for the dye. The afternoon quickly slid into evening as I tore at leaves, ground stalks, and brewed tinctures over the roiling heat of our stove. At some point, I paused to light one of the oil lamps clinging to the wall, and burnt-orange light bounced off the sludge-like surface of the cooling charcoal dye. I changed in my room into a thin nightgown splattered with ink-black stains and returned to the kitchen.

Careful not to spill, I angled my head over the massive pot and drowned my hair in the viscous liquid. I was fortunate to still have enough of a base coloring in my hair that the dye would likely set within the hour. Better than waiting for it to fully fade and having to sequester for the day so the townsfolk wouldn't catch me in the act. It was an exercise my aunt had done herself and taught me early to help keep my power hidden. Not everyone in my family was born with the power to threadmend, but enough had been blessed—cursed, really—that a handful of best practices had been passed down through the years.

A horrendous annoyance, to say the least, but a necessary precaution. Better to have charcoal-coated locks than be dead. Thank the gods I wasn't as vain as some of my tittering neighbors.

Satisfied with the thick layer of sludge now clinging to my hair, I twisted my locks into a tight bun. The dye hardened quickly, forming the worst kind of cakey, uncomfortable bonnet, and I returned to my remedies. As I counted vials and allocated herbs, I let out an annoyed groan. If I wanted to purchase enough flour and fresh meat for the week, I'd need to produce and sell at least a dozen more tinctures. Otherwise, we would have to dip into our reserves of dried venison to make it through. Before I could begin brewing another tincture, a heavy bell toll rang through the quiet evening air. The miners' shift was at an end.

Looking up from the ever-increasing number of pots piling high around me, I glanced through the open window. The golden beetle I'd freed was nowhere to be found, and the first smattering of stars winked back at me. Soon, Noam and Nohr would be home, and they'd want the kitchen to prepare supper. They'd willingly taken up cooking to grant me time away from the stove.

My fingers tapped against the wood-plank counter as I stared out the window, checking to see if they were already loping up the path to our home. Nothing yet. I sighed and began clearing what dishes I could. Willowfell had two mines nestled against the mountain—one for sapphires and one for garnets. Those without hefty inheritances or education were forced to toil away in their cool depths, which meant my brothers never had a chance to become something else. They'd been working since the moment their bodies could carry the weight of a pickaxe just to help us survive. The job wasn't easy. Or safe.

Of course, if they were lucky enough to unearth an everjewel, all that would change.

There was a loud grunt, followed by the door wildly swinging open and crashing against the wall. I rolled my eyes. Our father must have had the gift of foresight to create an ornate archway instead of a door.

"Any everjewels today?" I called without looking in their direction. It was the same greeting I offered every time Noam and Nohr returned from work—one that was always met with silence or groans of frustration.

The stones were rare and coveted by Evers. In my life, two workers were fortunate enough to find an everjewel. Both times, one of the Ferngloves, Evers living on the fringe of our town and owners of the mines, had left their manor to handsomely reward the laborer in person. Every prominent city or town stretching across Glaes had at least one Ever family to preside over the land. The Ferngloves came into Willowfell sparingly, but when they did, everyone always rushed to grovel before their immortal feet.

Except for me. I couldn't risk being discovered. Not by the very people who I'd long suspected were responsible for the disappearance of my aunt. She wasn't the only threadmender who'd vanished in recent years. Rumors had begun to spread throughout Glaes, thanks to traveling merchants who moved about our country and traded wares as well as gossip. Most townsfolk passed it off as an oddity and nothing more, but I saw what they refused to acknowledge: threadmenders went missing only in places where Evers ruled.

"Edira!" Nohr shouted, pulling my focus. I turned to find my brothers stumbling through the entryway, a limp body strung haphazardly between them like a loose clothing line. With gentle motions, they laid a young man on our weathered sofa.

"What happened?" I sped toward them, wiping my hands along my nightgown to rid them of lingering residue from my work.

Noam and Nohr exchanged a silent look. Their teakwood gazes mirrored each other down to the smallest of nuances. They shared the same slender build of boys on the cusp of becoming men, their labor in the mines threatening to usher them into adulthood all too quickly. Seventeen and they'd already endured so much.

"Is that Alec?"

Nohr ran his hand back to front through his cropped brown hair. A poof of dust clouded the space above his head. "Yes."

"He just collapsed," Noam muttered.

I peered closer. Beneath the caked-on dirt and soot, Alec was barely recognizable. A sweaty sheen had broken out along his hairline, turning the grime on his skin into a damp sludge. With a strangled moan, he shifted restlessly on the couch. My brows drew together as I scoured his trembling frame. Something was wrong, and the pull of my magic immediately flared to life. Warmth rippled outward through my limbs, and yet I saw nothing. No visible injuries, no broken bones or bleeding wounds. I rushed to the pot in the kitchen and dampened a cloth with leftover water, returning quickly to wipe away the layer of filth clinging to his face.

The moment I finally caught a glimpse of his skin, I dropped the rag.

"You brought him *here*? What were you thinking?" I couldn't take my eyes off Alec's sallow cheeks. Sprawling blisters climbed from his jaw to his forehead, and several had already ruptured to expose a sickening display of black mold and bubbling yellow froth. The edges of each lesion were rotted and brown like leaves withering in the presence of winter. My stomach clenched tight. The revolting odor of decomposing flesh and sour mulch bloomed from his skin, and I swallowed thickly to force down a gag.

Nohr's face went pale. "We didn't . . . I didn't . . ."

Tearing away from the couch, I yanked my brothers together and dissected every inch of their stock-still forms. The durable fabric of their work trousers was still intact, carefully tucked into leather boots. Their long-sleeved shirts were more grime than cotton, but thankfully they were free of rips. Pulling their hands upward, I inspected their gloves. Worn and in need of another round of weatherproofing, but again, securely intact. The rising concern in my chest slowed.

Diseased land had started to encroach on the areas surrounding the mines, but it wasn't an airborne affliction. My gaze drifted back to Alec, and I spied a small nick marring the space where his throat and jaw met. The risk of shaving was rarely the blade. A whisper of blight straight to the blood was all it took.

"We didn't know it was blight. We just thought he'd hurt himself somehow," Noam finally managed. Heavy tears cut pathways through the dirt on his face, and I looked away.

"I can't help him," I murmured softly, but Noam flinched as if I'd shouted loud enough to rupture his eardrums.

"You can try."

I pinched my nose. "There's nothing I can do. There is no medicine that can cure this affliction."

"Not medicine, but maybe something else." Noam refused to look at me. A cold chill swept down my spine, a direct contrast to the blooming heat radiating through my fingertips.

"No." My gaze flew to the open windows. A peal of laughter from kids playing in the fields outside carried in on a breeze. Townsfolk were still out. If they saw me . . .

Nohr followed my tight stare and sprang into action, quickly latching the windows shut and drawing the curtains tight. As if eliminating the possibility of someone witnessing my power was the only problem. Sure, I didn't want to be discovered, because that meant some brownnosing neighbor—likely an elder hoping to gain even more favor with the Evers—would alert the Ferngloves to my existence.

A sliver of anger wound through me. My brothers knew the cost to my magic. And still, they wanted me to try. To sacrifice a few years of my life for someone who wouldn't live to see tomorrow.

"It's not just about being seen. You know this," I hissed.

Suddenly, Alec bolted upright on the couch, his gaze locked on something far away. And then he laughed. Not a normal laugh—not the pleasant, rumbling sound of warmth from deep within his chest. But a maniacal laugh that bubbled from the depths of a clouded mind. One steeped in sickness. His eyes rolled to the heavens, showing white to the world, and his teeth gnashed together. The soft squirt of his canine puncturing his tongue sent gooseflesh rippling over my skin.

"Edira," Nohr said over Noam's sharp inhale, "please. He's our friend."

"And I am your *sister*." My throat bobbed as I stared at Alec. "I'd only be risking harm to myself."

My brothers' gazes dropped in unison. Before I could take another breath, Alec let out a pained cry as his body began shaking uncontrollably. His hands went to his arms, his fingers raking against the rough fabric of his shirt.

"Alec, we're here." Noam knelt beside him, mindful not to touch him but hovering close just the same.

Alec turned to Noam, unfocused eyes searching for something to anchor him to our world. He kept twisting his neck back and forth, craning it in impossible directions, until he spied me. He stilled as a glee-stricken smile pulled at his lips. "I see her. I can really see her. She's standing over there, and she's got the biggest grin I've ever seen. Annabelle."

"His sister. She died last year." Nohr grimaced.

"He doesn't have any other family," Noam added, voice terribly soft.

Alec wouldn't survive this. Again, I glanced at the drawn curtains. We were hidden from the outside world, and since Alec had no remaining relatives, there was no one to miss him or question his absence, save my brothers. I forced out a heavy breath. Slowly, I came around the sofa. Alec's gaze never faltered. He tracked every step of mine until I crouched beside Noam.

"Hello, Alec."

"You've got fire shooting from your fingertips. How'd you manage that? You don't look like you're burning. Can you come closer?" His voice climbed higher, words cracking as his grip on reality disappeared entirely. "I'm stuck inside this glacier and the heat would help."

I brushed my hands along his forehead for a moment, wiping away the film of sweat and dirt. He groaned as I nudged him to the side and edged onto the sofa, my hip bone flush with his. Unlike my brothers, I didn't have to worry about contracting Alec's illness. The only thing that could kill me was myself.

"Edira?" Noam's soft plea was a weapon straight to my heart, and my resolve wavered. No threadmender had ever been able to cure blight. Myself included. I wouldn't risk drastically shortening my lifespan by fully inviting Alec's affliction into my veins—not when there was nothing to be gained.

Alec's gaze locked on mine. "I hear my bones cracking. They're giant splinters caught in my skin, and I need to get them out."

My chest heaved. I'd lived through this exact scenario already with my parents, and even though I knew what would happen in the end, I couldn't bring myself to ignore him. "I'll ease his passing. That's all I can do."

It'd likely cost me a few threads, but I couldn't stand the look in his eyes. Or the weight of my brothers' pleas.

Energy hummed through me as I finally—*finally*—allowed my power to surge to the surface. Soothing warmth rushed over my skin, and while I couldn't see my eyes, I knew my normally dove-gray irises had been doused in an ivory light as brilliant as the full moon. As the world around me dulled, the threads of his life—invisible to all but me—began to unfurl around him.

They should've been a resplendent, glowing green, full of energy and vigor. Instead, hundreds of severed threads limply drifted about in his aura, each one of them dripping with black tar. When the sludge encased a strand in its entirety, it shifted to appear more like a rotted twig and then simply dusted away. All I could feel was pain. Fear. The real Alec was buried somewhere beneath this maelstrom of hysteria and despair, and I was the only one capable of giving him any relief.

Swallowing thickly, I willed my magic to flow outward. Moonlight ensconced my hands, my fingers. And I showered the tar clinging to Alec's dying threads with my power, but I couldn't wipe away the residue—or mend the fraying ends. Nonetheless, Alec sighed. My soothing energy flooded his body, calming the tremor racking his limbs.

A soft smile claimed his lips as he stared into my eyes. "Threadmender."

Quiet ringing started in my ears. "Yes."

"I never knew," he said. He hummed softly as his gaze shifted absently to the ceiling. It didn't matter that he'd pass in a matter of minutes—the fact that he knew my secret still sent my pulse racing. My eyes tracked the spreading blisters, now steaming as the blight cooked away at his meat and bones. At least he no longer felt any pain. I'd pay for it later, but between my brothers' pleas and Alec's trembling form, I couldn't bring myself to let him pass in agony. With one final surge of power, I thrust as much energy as I could over his body. Brilliant moonlight blanketed his form in earnest, and his eyes slipped closed. After three more shuddering breaths, his threads suddenly stilled and dusted to ash.

Capping my power, I released his grip and stood slowly as the world swayed beneath my feet. The backlash of easing his passing hit hard and fast. I hadn't even attempted to cure his blight, and yet I'd been close to Alec's affliction, scratched the surface of the illness and used my power to offer him comfort. And now I would suffer. A brackish substance flooded the back of my tongue, and I stumbled out the front door to vomit in the bed of morning glories. Everything *hurt*. My bones felt as if they'd splintered several times over, and my eyelids scraped like the tin scrubber I kept in the kitchen. Needles pricked at my skin, and I dug my fingers into the soft earth for purchase. My insides grew impossibly hot, as if someone were stoking a fire in the pit of my belly.

All this for simply helping. If I'd actually attempted to rid him of blight . . .

At some point, Nohr wrapped his arms around my trembling body, and he carried me inside. He'd already readied my room and peeled back the sheets, and he laid me on the quaint iron bed before tucking me in.

"Nohr," I managed to croak as black dots bloomed across my vision.

He crouched in front of me, lines of worry creasing his forehead. "We shouldn't have asked. I'm sorry."

I attempted to shake my head, but it came out as a weak twitch. "Don't touch him."

Eyes downcast, he nodded. "Okay, Edira. Just get some rest."

He didn't have to tell me twice.

# TWO

My head throbbed in time with my heartbeat as I dared to open my eyes. I hadn't moved an inch in the night, and that only seemed to compound the ache in my muscles. I should've coached one of my brothers into drafting a healing tincture before sleeping, but if my brain was muddled now, it was simply liquid before.

The last time I'd threadmended had been Nohr's leg. The time before, my parents. A chill crept down my spine. They'd both fallen ill at the same time and passed within an hour. I was only thirteen. I tried everything to save them, but I'd never used my powers in earnest, so I could only cradle their heads in my lap as they died. My gut churned, and I pushed that memory away. Reliving that horrific experience helped no one.

Groaning, I shifted in bed and pulled off the sheets. My arms screamed in protest, but I gritted through the pain and stretched toward the ceiling. A stiff crackling rippled across my scalp, and my fingers went to my hair. I'd never removed the dye, and one quick look at my pillow indicated I'd ruined those linens for good.

At least the color was set. As soon as I could manage, I'd rinse and dump the staining liquid somewhere unseen. Then after, a bath. I just couldn't fathom drawing one. My toes grazed the cool floor-boards, and I sucked in a breath as I stood up. The room spun only for a moment—long enough for my stomach to knot, but not long enough for me to call off my planned trip to market.

With slow, measured steps, I left my room and padded down-stairs into the kitchen to find Noam and Nohr already busy with the stove. My herbs had been gathered, tied, and hung from a series of wooden dowels along the far wall near my collection of rem-edies. The mess I'd left was gone, replaced by sparkling clean dishes drying before the open window. Eggs cooked in a frying pan, and coffee—fresh coffee—sat in a carafe in the middle of the table.

I'd never loved my brothers more. I was about to say as much when a prickling awareness teased the back of my mind and goose-flesh rippled over my arms. Turning toward the couch, I expected to find a decaying body waiting for me on the cushions.

I found nothing of the sort.

"I told you not to touch him," I said, my words quiet but sharp.

They both stiffened as they shared one of their signature glances, the kind only they could understand. "We wore our gloves and wrapped him in blankets," Nohr replied.

"We were careful. We just wanted to give you a break," Noam added a breath later.

My gaze traveled over their clenched jaws and drawn brows. The ghost of pain, of loss, still lingered in their puffy eyes, and I sighed. They'd gone through enough already. With an undignified plop, I fell onto one of the chairs and reached for the coffee. Nohr was there within seconds, pouring the life-giving sustenance into a ceramic mug.

"We should toss the couch," I muttered.

Nohr's eyes fell, his voice strained. "We can't afford it."

"We can't afford either one of you catching blight." I stared at the well-worn frame. The piece of furniture had sat in that exact spot for the entirety of my life and likely years before that. We could've done with a new couch, but Nohr was right. Money was tight. "I'll move the cushions outside for the time being and see what I can do about getting the whole thing reupholstered." I blew steam off my drink and took a heady sip.

Noam slid a plate of eggs in front of me before returning to the stove. "Mrs. Marlow might be willing to trade her services for some of your remedies."

I speared my breakfast with my fork and chewed slowly, eyeing Nohr as he dragged another large pot full of water and placed it atop the cast-iron stove. "I fixed Toman's nose yesterday. She owes me."

After that, Nohr and Noam joined me at the table and ate the rest of the eggs straight out of the frying pan. The quiet scrape of their forks' tines against the skillet filled our kitchen. None of us spoke. There wasn't much to be said, not really. Alec was gone. There was nothing more that could be done.

"We heated water for a bath," Noam said, twirling his fork against the pan. He'd ducked his head low while eating and now peered at me from behind the tops of his lashes. A peace offering for disposing of the body, no doubt. It worked. "I'll bring the wash-basin in if you're ready."

"Thank you." I blew out a breath as I stood. "Can one of you grab water for my hair?"

Nohr was out the front door and in the garden before I could blink. I wound my way through the small footprint of our house to the back door. One furtive peek through the curtains told me it was safe, and I slipped outside. I was thankful our home backed against the nearby woods, offering us a modicum of privacy for moments such as this. Dyeing hair wasn't exactly taboo, but it raised questions. Questions were the last thing I wanted.

After handing me a small bucket with fresh water, Nohr retreated inside. Gritting my teeth in preparation for the cold, I dunked my head in the liquid and watched as black ink swirled across the once-clear contents. Later, when time permitted, I'd lather on a different mask to bring the luster back to my matte locks.

Hair dripping down my back, I returned to the kitchen to find Noam and Nohr had brought in a tin tub and placed it before the stove. After they transferred the heated water, I sprinkled the basin with salts crafted for relieving aches and a few drops of oil to help soothe my mind. Noam wrapped me in a one-armed hug and pressed a soft kiss to the top of my head.

"Be safe," I murmured.

"I'd say 'you, too,' but not sure that applies to market," Noam said with a half-hearted smile. He was trying. Trying to forget what happened last night. Trying to move forward because we had no other option but to keep going. My heart twisted, and I hugged him tighter. Then I motioned for Nohr to join until I had both of them wrapped in my arms.

I would do anything for my brothers. I'd shoulder their grief and work myself to the bone just to make sure they had a chance at happiness. They were all I had left, and they needed me just as much as I needed them.

"See you tonight," Nohr said.

I gave them one last squeeze and then released them. They were gone in no time, and I blew out a sigh as I quickly undressed. I slid into the scalding water, not caring that it scorched my skin. I wanted to burn away the memory of the blight against my fingers, the scent of mold and decay from my hair, and the leftover residue of grime beneath my nails. I groaned and sunk deeper into the water. I would've soaked in the bath for hours, but I couldn't afford to miss market. So, when the pulsating ache in my muscles finally dulled to a mild discomfort, I eased out of the tub and returned to my room to dress for the day.

Part of me wished Noam and Nohr could go to town instead of me. Everyone liked them. They were generous and warm, and their laughter was the kind of sound that lingered in the air for what felt like hours. A beautiful, inviting thing. It wasn't as though people particularly liked or disliked me; I just couldn't get involved. Wouldn't. My friendships dwindled when my parents died and I had to step into the role of caretaker for my brothers, and I never bothered to rekindle them. Not when, years earlier, I'd seen the town elders notify the Ferngloves about my aunt's power. She was stolen from us the very next day. All because a child, one of Noam's friends, had peeked through our window to see if he was home. Instead, he'd watched as my aunt healed my mother's perpetual cough.

I didn't blame the child. He told his parents a curious, exciting thing he'd seen. I blamed the elders who reacted out of greed before even considering what it would do to my family to have our aunt ripped away.

Of course, the townsfolk didn't think it was "bad" to be employed by an Ever. My aunt was "blessed."

Grumbling wordlessly to myself, I braided my sable hair away from my face and wove in a few tiny white flowers from the baby's breath I kept potted in my room. Kohl above my lashes, mauve paint on my lips, a hint of rouge—good enough for market. I quickly slipped on a chemise and cotton stockings, fixing them in place with simple garter ribbons. My mother's corset thankfully still fit, and I secured the front fasteners before tightening the lace at my back. Then a soft skirt and matching burgundy bodice dotted with pearls and embroidered ebony flowers. The ensemble had been my mother's before she died. I'd admired it for as long as I could remember, but now that I owned it, the feel of it against my skin was both a comfort and a sadness.

Shaking my head, I slid my leather scrap into one of the skirt's hidden pockets and laced my ankle boots before heading down-stairs. I paused only for a moment to glance at the sofa. I'd take care of the cushions after market, but there was still the impression of Alec's long body pressed into the fabric, an outline of the person who used to exist. I hadn't known him well, and I thanked the stars for that small blessing.

Setting my jaw tight, I walked to the kitchen. It didn't take long for me to pack two leather traveling cases full of remedies. I carried all the standards: sleep aids, serums and balms for topical ailments, tinctures for digestion, oils for stress reduction, and, by far one of my most popular requests, performictum—a tasteless powder added to food or drink that when consumed resulted in . . . bedroom vigor. I also stored some of the more elusive concoctions in the hidden compartment that slid out of the back of the case, but I rarely ever needed those. Some referred to them as poisons. I referred to them as remedies for vengeance. Benign, but memorable.

After fastening the brass clasps into place, I grabbed the worn handles and made for the door. We lived on the fringe of town, which meant the walk to market was a good twenty minutes, and I had only thirty before the bell struck. The best spots were likely already taken. We weren't fortunate enough to own a carriage, and because the town itself was somewhat small, not many did. The elders, of course, had gilded wagons lined with plush cushions and attendants to drive the horses. But even they saved such extravagant means of travel for longer excursions to neighboring towns.

*They should've woken me sooner.* Noam and Nohr meant well, but their jobs didn't bring in the same amount of coin as my cures, and they relied on me to keep us going. The leather squeaked against my palms as I grasped my cases even tighter and set off down the main cobblestone road leading to the epicenter of Willowfell. I walked as quickly as my booted heels and laden cases would allow, passing other townsfolk already strolling toward market at a much more leisurely pace. The closer to the center of town

I got, the more densely packed the houses became. They crowded one another, trading open plots and fields for closer proximity to the shops and, perhaps more alluringly, the arch.

The twisted structure was taller than any shop in the square, but only as wide as a double-door entry. Barren tree branches with pale, smooth bark had sprung from the earth and knotted together. Several limbs at the highest point curled outward like antlers, and a variety of fowl often perched there but never nested. It was a gnarled passage for travel that only the Evers could use. Because when you possess magic, why bother arriving by carriage?

When the path opened wide to the circular courtyard where the market was housed, I cut across the center, giving the arch a wide berth, and began the arduous task of securing a spot. I would've preferred to spend another day rummaging for herbs than fight off other vendors for a prime location, especially when most of these dealers already owned the shops rimming the square. Tables were situated by the leaders of Willowfell in circles around the arch, rippling outward in perfect rows to press against the buildings.

The best spots, the ones nearest the arch, were already taken. I scowled at Milton's Apothecary, with its wooden awnings and glass doors, as I begrudgingly took a free table along the back row. Milton himself had already set up a display directly in front of the arch, and he'd made certain to claim a handful of other tables littered throughout the market to further push his half-baked remedies.

I could've outearned him in a day if I were willing to sell my threadmending services. I'd also be dead, but that was beside the point.

Still, there were a few folks who swore by my work and didn't mind the higher rates for better draughts—assuming they were able to venture three rows deep before spending their coin. The only table left was one directly to the right of Lysa's Confectionary, and I hoped the rich scent of freshly baked delicacies would be enough to lure people to my stall. Sighing, I gently hoisted my cases onto the sunbaked surface of the wooden table and undid the clasps. The doors unfolded with the release of the spring, and rows of balms and extracts jutted out in tiered drawers. The more popular cures I kept up top, ensuring their handwritten labels were easily visible.

As I went to adjust one of the vials, a faint droning met my ears before coming to an abrupt halt. A strand of hair had broken free of my braid and whispered against my cheek, and as I went to tuck it back into place, I paused. A golden beetle was inspecting the baby's breath wrapped within my dark locks.

"Hello again," I murmured, gently extending my pointer finger. "Are you the same little one from yesterday?"

It considered my finger as it adjusted its wings.

"Maybe you'll bring me luck. You're prettier than a gold coin," I said.

Then the town bell struck with a rolling gong, and the beetle took flight. It whirred about for a moment, as if the deep resonance disrupted its sense of direction, before settling on the trellis attached to the wall of Lysa's shop. With an irritated flap of its wings, it scuttled along the climbing ivy to shade itself beneath the leaves.

This first hour of market was a blur. There were the usual buyers who sought my wares out specifically, and we chatted amicably as I pretended to care about the latest town gossip. There were a few not-so-subtle comments about my age and lack of financial security, and how that was possibly why there weren't suitors lining up to ask for my hand. I gritted my teeth as I let them ramble on about the implications for my future.

And then Mrs. Marlow swung by to thank me for Toman's nose, agreeing to upholster our sofa free of charge under two conditions: one, I let the cushions and the frame air out for two weeks outdoors given the contact with blight—she'd mustered only a half-hearted frown and a feeble "That's terrible" when I explained what happened to Alec—and two, the new fabric had to be from last year's selection and not currently in fashion. I bit my tongue hard at that, hiding my disdain with a well-practiced smile. As the wife of one of the town's elders, her work as a seamstress, in her own words, was a folly she enjoyed but didn't need. It was a wonder she didn't parade around town in her carriage just for show.

By the time Mrs. Marlow swept up her layers of skirts and sashayed on to the next table, it was approaching noon, and my morning rush—possibly my only rush—was done.

"Of course I'm short," I muttered as I recounted the silver pieces I'd accrued from my transactions. Because why would anything ever go according to plan? Groaning, I rolled my head from side to side. Being an apothecary was a strange occupation. I never wished ill on anyone, but ill people were the ones who paid for the food on my table, and we'd finished the last of our flour days ago, never mind fresh meat from the butcher.

One or two sick people would be fine.

"Edira!" Lysa emerged from her shop carrying a silver tray full of frosted delicacies. Her cherry-stained lips were pulled wide in a genuine smile, and her periwinkle eyes sparkled as she extended the platter of confections toward me. "I noticed you didn't bring a meal with you today. Have a few."

A twisted pain grumbled through my stomach at her words. I'd been in such a rush to secure a spot I'd forgotten to pack any food for myself. "Thanks, Lysa. How's business?"

She beamed as she watched me pop a sugared tart into my mouth. "It's good. People love sweets." Or they loved her. Lysa was magnetic. Townsfolk flocked to her like moths to the flame, but instead of burning up their wings when they got too close, she simply kept everybody warm.

Or maybe it wasn't her at all but the fact that her father was one of the town elders and in good standing with the Ferngloves. No one crossed Lysa's family.

"How are your parents?" I snagged another treat, and she didn't object.

"Oh, you know how it goes. No rest for the town elders." She brushed curled honey hair off her shoulder as she scanned the crowd. "They'd rather me marry than run a shop, though."

That didn't stop them from purchasing her charming store for her. All the elders got a cut of the mines' profits—and it showed. From Lysa's callus-free hands to her pristine attire, she was ever the picture of perfection and wealth.

"Well, I'm thankful for your gift." I dusted crumbs off my lips before turning to my wares. My fingers traveled over the corked stoppers as I counted the vials.

"How are the boys? Noam?"

I noticed she didn't mention Nohr by name. Maybe she hadn't married because Noam hadn't picked up on her interest. Hard to do when he was in the mines all but one day of the week. And of course, Lysa's parents would object to her tying the knot with a lowly miner. They might even cut her off from their wealth and reclaim their shop. It had Lysa's name hanging from the copper plate above the door, but it most certainly was theirs. And then I'd have another mouth to feed in my home until she and Noam found a way to sustain themselves.

It was probably for the best that Noam didn't have a taste for sweets.

"They're fine. They're just—"

I never finished my sentence. A sharp crackle, like a log splitting beneath hungry flames, snapped through the air. The crowd fell silent as everyone turned to stare at the arch. A gossamer veil of magic unfurled from the antlers to the ground, fluttering like drying linens in a gentle breeze. The translucent, glittering surface caught in the sun, and suddenly the square was overcome with excited murmurs. An Ever was coming.

"Here we go." I grasped the edge of my table as I narrowed my eyes.

"What do you think they're here for?" Lysa gripped her tray and inched closer, just a toe away from joining the throng of thrilled onlookers.

"Early collections?" I chewed on my lower lip. Our wondrous mine barons typically visited Willowfell only at the end of the month to review what had been dug up from the bowels of our mountains. They'd make a big show out of appearing, perusing the local shops and spending more wealth in an hour than I managed to earn in a year. If the elders were lucky, the Ferngloves would stay for a meeting and some tea. I couldn't fathom what they discussed. I hardly cared.

"Maybe." Lysa's eyes shone with excitement. "What if it's a Waterstone? Or a Starglen?"

I sincerely doubted that was the case. The Waterstones and Starglens were Ever families who presided over two neighboring towns, each roughly three days' travel by carriage in opposite directions. I couldn't remember the last time one of them deigned to visit Willowfell.

"Oh, what if one of them is looking for a partner?" she asked in a breathy rush of hope.

My nose wrinkled. Apparently Lysa's fascination with Evers was the same as the rest of the townsfolk. I didn't understand it. How could they trust anything they saw? Evers *always* wore glamour. They were faker than Milton's remedies, and there were only whispers of what Evers truly looked like. Sometimes we'd get a rare glimpse of a bestial feature—scales, wings, horns—when they'd parade through town revealing small magics to charm and fascinate the townsfolk. But the true scale of an Ever's power?

Pure mystery. The Ferngloves were known to make the ground shake and flowers bloom, but I doubted that was the full extent of their magic.

To make things worse, Evers had a way with words. They could speak binding contracts into existence with only the slightest thought—and these magical vows had dire consequences if broken. There was a story passed down in Willowfell about a traveling vendor who made false promises to the former head of the Ferngloves. The charlatan lost his tongue the moment he tried to pass off fake everjewels as authentic stones. It was simply sliced off midsentence, no blade in sight.

While the townsfolk found all that power alluring, it was downright terrifying to me.

As if drawn by ropes, the veil parted like curtains and an Ever stepped into our square. I couldn't see them through the swarm of bodies and tables, but I knew they'd arrived the moment the glimmering sheet of magic disappeared, and vendors immediately began spouting their wares at abnormally loud decibels. Anything to grab the attention of an Ever.

A slow-moving chill dredged through my limbs, and my fingers instinctively went to my hair. Still black as night. Safe. But Evers were immortal and had dedicated their long lives to learning how to harness the magic of our world. If anyone was able to see beneath my disguise, it would be them.

It was the exact opposite of what I wanted.

# THREE

packed my first case in seconds. It was time to leave. I'd miss out on the afternoon sales, but the entire town was too distracted to shop. The likelihood of me peddling even one more tincture dropped the moment that veil appeared. I was willing to lose the few pieces of silver to avoid dealing with an Ever who only saw me for my magic.

I still remembered the day a Fernglove came to visit Aunt Rowena. I was only five and couldn't recall the words they'd exchanged, but I'd never forget her expression. It wasn't full of joy or excitement like the rest of the townsfolk. It was full of fear. She'd shut the door on the Ever's face with a strained goodbye, then offered a shaky smile as she knelt to the ground and grasped my shoulders tight.

*Keep dyeing your hair. Cure no one.*

I'd barely had time to grapple with her words. She'd only just healed my mother the day before, and that seemed like such a valid use of my aunt's power. One day she was there and the next she was gone. My mother took me with her to my aunt's house that morning to find it utterly quiet. She'd raced through the rooms calling Rowena's name, but my aunt never answered. My mother rifled through drawers and searched for clues with a frantic energy until she stalled before a small bookshelf in the living room. I'd never forget how still she went when her fingers grazed the binding of my aunt's poetry journal. It was pulled out a half inch farther than the rest of her books, as if it were begging to be read.

My mother had flipped it open, and a small note fell from between the pages.

*I love you and your family, Faye. This is not your fault. They've come back for me, but it will be okay. Keep Edira safe.*

My mother sank to the floor and clutched the paper to her chest, tears streaming down her face as she sobbed. I ran to her and climbed into her lap, and we didn't move for an hour. But after she'd wrestled with her grief, her guilt, she hid her emotions behind pursed lips and tore the note to shreds.

We never spoke of that day again.

Even if we had, if my mother had gone to the elders and demanded vengeance, nothing would've happened. Maybe they would've pitied her for a moment, but that sentiment would've quickly shifted to something more pandering.

*We were lucky an Ever chose her.*

*How fortunate for your family.*

*How do you know she didn't go willingly?*

And the elders would never admit their role in all this, or how they'd prospered from her disappearance. I couldn't prove it, either, but I knew. In my gut, I knew.

AFTER PACKING MY FIRST LEATHER case, I moved to the second.

"You're leaving?" Lysa asked, her attention split between me and the parting crowd.

"My remedies are of little interest to Evers. Plus, I've already sold enough today." *Lie.* In my peripheral vision, a flash of gold winked from beneath an ivy leaf. The beetle crawled forward a few inches, and its antennae twitched.

*So much for luck.*

Dropping my gaze, I began pushing in the drawers of my case when a hand with long, slender fingers adorned with polished rings touched my wrist. The motion was as gentle as checking for a pulse, and yet I couldn't help but flinch.

Slowly, I raised my chin. He was beautiful—all Evers were—but he exuded a sense of regality that demanded attention. No, adoration. Effortlessly wavy oak-brown locks fell to his shoulders and teased his square jaw. Keen green eyes framed by thick lashes watched me intently. As if the sun had decided freckles were simply too mundane for someone like him, his skin seemed to be infused with golden flecks.

It was absolutely unfair that anyone looked like *that*. Then again, he was glamoured. Maybe he looked like a toe beneath all that magic.

But the *clothes.* My mother would've been beside herself. He wore a paisley silk cravat tucked into an emerald vest trimmed in gold stitching. The sleeves of his fern-colored tailcoat were rolled and cuffed above his elbows, exposing corded forearms that had no business being that tantalizing.

He tilted his head, and his locks fell behind his shoulder, exposing an intricate sword tattoo along his neck. The masterpiece was awash with gray and lined in heavy black, the hilt adorned with a single ruby gem and framed by bone-white flowers with gray leaves. The blade itself was severed, the jagged edge dipping toward his collarbone. Insects of every kind swirled around the broken metal. Butterflies. Moths. Bees. Beetles. Where everything else was inked in graphite, the insects were an artist's palette exploding with vibrant color.

Fernglove. And not just any Fernglove, Orin Fernglove. Head of his estate and overseer of our mines' profits.

The same Ever who'd come for my aunt all those years ago.

"What do we have here?" he purred, dragging his fingers from my wrist to snare a vial and raise it to the sky. The off-white powder within shifted with the ease of sand.

"Performictum. I didn't know Evers needed help in the bedroom, but you're welcome to take it."

Something fierce shot through his eyes, and his smile hardened. "I can assure you I don't need it." With precise fingers, he slipped the vial back into place.

My blood cooled. "I didn't mean to offend."

I had, but more for his benefit than mine. I wanted him to know that I wasn't like the rest of the townsfolk who were over-eager to fall into his good graces. When I looked at him, all I saw were the faces of my brothers, slick with grime and soot. I saw their gnarled hands, their ragged bodies. I saw them toiling endlessly for just enough scraps to make ends meet.

Mostly, I saw my aunt's wide, panicked eyes. Orin might not have cared about my existence all those years ago, but I certainly had his attention now. I should've held my tongue or bowed my head, or better yet ran. But I just couldn't.

Beside the table, Lysa rolled her lower lip into her mouth as her gaze bounced from him to me. My slight hadn't gone unnoticed. The folks who'd gathered close to eavesdrop all stilled. If he left market without purchasing anything because of my words, I'd never hear the end of it. Not that I gave a damn about that. Their complicity cost me my aunt. So what if I cost them a handful of coins?

And then all at once a rolling laugh rumbled from the pit of Orin's stomach and the tension evaporated. The sound released the vendors, and they went back to touting their wares in the hopes he would eventually turn his attention their way. Even Lysa returned to her shop, and out of the corner of my eye, I saw her selecting some of her more artful creations to adorn her platter.

"No offense taken," Orin said, voice as smooth as syrup. He tucked his loose hair behind his ears, and an array of piercings winked in the sun. "Packing up? Let's see what else you have to offer."

"Are you in need of anything specific?" I studied the smooth planes of his face, free of wrinkles or scars. There were no bags beneath his eyes, no sag to his shoulders or hitch to his breath. Like all Evers, he was completely healthy. Annoyingly so.

"I'm not sure you offer it." His fingers dawdled over my remedies, but his gaze was locked on my face. "Perhaps it's something we can discuss in private."

I blinked. "Private?"

"Yes." His stare roved to my lips. "I've been to Willowfell many times, but I've never met you before. Why is that?"

He'd met me before, he just didn't remember. I'd always wondered if he'd dared to look around the room when he came calling for Aunt Rowena. If he'd noticed me wrapped in my mother's arms as we watched quietly from the couch. I hardly wanted him to recall my existence when it could've alluded to my hidden powers, but there was something about the way he continued to stare at my mouth that made it difficult to find words.

"I'm often away." I gestured to my cases, and his slow-moving stare finally shifted to my vials. "I forage for my own herbs and brew these myself."

"Such talent." The low murmur of his voice somehow blanketed out the sounds of the market. Once again, he reached for my remedies, except this time, his fingers hovered just above my hand.

"What's your name?" he asked.

"Edira," I said. No sense in trying to hide that. Someone in town would tell him if I didn't. "What was it you needed again?"

Without moving, he slowly peered into my eyes. "As I said, perhaps it's better discussed in private. Over tea?"

My heart hammered against my rib cage. "You want to have tea with me?"

"Why not?" His lips curled softly at the corners, the action so effortless and warm that it nearly chased away my looming fears. "I'm interested to hear what other quips might slip from that tongue of yours. *Performictum*." His laugh was low and heady. Then he gently rolled his bottom lip into his mouth as he glanced at my hair.

A familiar unease twined through me. I'd just dyed it. I was fine. He didn't know. Still, the ire fueling my "quips" waned as the weight of his words settled against my skin. I refused to be alone with the likes of him.

"Unfortunately, I don't have time. And in terms of tinctures or healing aids, I'm sure Row— your *threadmender* would be of better assistance than me." I speared my tongue with my teeth, trying to keep the lips he was apparently so interested in neutral and the rest of my words at bay. Calling my aunt by name would only heighten his curiosity and endanger myself.

A glimmer of shock temporarily coursed through his features, and then he let out a long sigh. "Rowena was a dear friend of mine. She was helping me with some groundbreaking work, even documenting the scope of her abilities in the hopes her magic could continue to help others after she passed. She died several years ago, which is precisely why I find myself standing before your stall."

A deep ache rooted in my chest, and heat pricked at the backs of my eyes. I fought to keep my breath even, to keep my tears at bay. While I'd expected as much, it still hurt to know she was gone. I'd always hoped that somehow, some way, I'd see her again. I'd clung to that hard, especially in the years following my parents' deaths, but I couldn't let Orin see how much his words affected me. She wouldn't want me to suffer her fate.

"I'm sorry to hear that, but if nothing here suits you, then I can't help you." I scooted the leather case out of his reach and fastened the clasps.

"I understand." He held my gaze for entirely too long. Something sorrowful, something almost *human*, passed through his eyes. "I'll find a solution more befitting to my needs, though I do hope our paths cross again."

"Yes, well, I should be going." Securing both handles, I lifted the cases and tipped my chin in the slightest show of politeness I could muster. "Good day."

Straightening, he tugged on the hem of his vest before brushing his hands along the shimmery fabric. He regarded me for a moment longer before shifting his focus to the trellis at my back, as if I didn't exist. "I certainly hope it will be." With only the barest movement of his head, he nodded once to himself.

I didn't dare respond. Instead, I turned on my heel and moved along the fringe of the market as quickly as I could without sprinting. But no matter how much distance I put between him and me, I couldn't shake the chill ravaging my skin. Or worse, the dangerous thought that his parting words—so soft and yet so full of unspoken threat—weren't intended for me at all.

## FOUR

The setting sun spilled over the quiet gardens flush with our home, and I reclined against the cool stonework at my back while stretching my legs out before me. Damp grass wet the fabric of my clothes, but I didn't mind. After depositing my apothecary cases inside, I'd immediately come here, to my mother's garden, to steady my nerves among the crocuses, daffodils, and rich maroon tulips. Bees lazily hummed from bud to bud, and I didn't flinch as one investigated the embroidered flower on my breast to see if it was ripe with pollen. It moved on soon enough, and I let out a tired sigh.

Aunt Rowena was gone. That knowledge brought a hollowness to my chest I hadn't anticipated, and I rubbed the space beneath my collarbone. In the very least, I'd done what she asked. I'd kept myself hidden. If I couldn't see her again, at least I could live the life she wanted me to have. Even if it meant foraging for herbs until I was a crone.

We had enough food to make it until next week's market, but that was it. I'd go back to the woods first thing in the morning to get a head start on replenishing my remedies. Maybe I'd unearth some morels I could use to barter with the butcher's daughter. We'd enjoyed the pleasure of each other's company a few times over, and I'd learned a thing or two about her tastes.

Still, I refused to make any sort of lasting connection. The townsfolk couldn't be trusted with the truth of my identity.

Lost in my musings, I didn't even register the town bell announcing the end of the miners' shift. It wasn't until I spotted Noam and Nohr sluggishly trudging toward our door that I realized the dusky sky was moments away from fading to night, and the droning hum of bees had long since been traded for the questioning chirps of crickets. Oil lampposts had been lit along the cobblestone path leading from town, and they cast long shadows behind my brothers. Body stiff, I rose to meet them.

"Any everjewels today?" I asked as we approached our home.

Nohr shook his head. "Maybe next time."

"And maybe I'll find a pile of lost coin while foraging for herbs." I thrust open the door and moved into the foyer, watching as the boys kicked off their boots.

"There's a dream." Noam slipped off his gloves and shoved them into the back pocket of his trousers.

I sighed. "Well, at least tomorrow you have the day off." My gaze roved across their grimy clothes and the thick layer of dirt caked onto their skin. Grief still clouded their eyes and tugged at their lips. They'd hardly had a chance to mourn their friend. "Go on, at least wipe some of that muck off. I'll boil water for your baths."

They nodded wordlessly as they lumbered up the stairs toward their shared bedroom, and while I was accustomed to their slumped frames after a hard day's work, I knew the weight pressing onto their shoulders had nothing to do with mining for gems.

I lit the stove and found the same pots they'd used to warm water for me. After filling them and placing them on the heat, I leaned against the kitchen counter and stared at the open window. With familiar ease, I retrieved my mother's leather scrap from my pocket and rubbed it between my fingers. After Rowena was taken, we never spoke of the Ferngloves. It was as if Mother was too afraid to even mention them in case it summoned them to our doorstep yet again.

*I'm safe. They don't know.* I squeezed my eyes shut as I pressed a light kiss to the leather. The flexible, textured surface was soft against my lips, and I breathed in the familiar, earthy scent before slipping it back into my pocket and opening my eyes.

As I went to check the water, my brothers' screams ricocheted through our house. I whirled in place as Nohr came rushing down the stairs, Noam tumbling close behind. Noam was strangely off-balance, his gait wobbly, his body keeled over, his free hand dangling loosely by his knee. His head lolled from side to side, and when I finally caught sight of his faraway gaze, I froze.

They were both shirtless as they'd prepared to bathe, which made it easy to spy the patchwork pattern of filth against their skin. And the slender line of red just above Noam's waistband.

A cut. Right where his shirt could've come untucked from his trousers during his work in the mines.

The curling edges of his wound were already shifting to a withering brown.

"No." It was all I could manage as an incessant ringing filled my ears. Needles pricked against my skin as the world shifted beneath my feet. It was too much. It couldn't be. A swarm of black consumed my peripheral vision, narrowing my focus to him. To that disastrous cut.

To the blight.

And then Nohr's knees cracked against the floorboards as he fell, and I thought it was a reaction to the same realization I'd just had. Except on his biceps I saw a long, puckered slice of red blooming with mold and yellow spores.

I screamed so loudly, so violently, that my head splintered in pain. I didn't even remember crossing our home. One moment I was in the kitchen and the next I was on the floor, cradling them in my lap as nonsensical babbling flowed like undammed water from their lips. Tears bisected my cheeks in heavy streams, and I pressed them closer. Sobs racked my chest, and I focused everything I had on the dormant power coursing through my veins.

*Please. Take me. Let them live.* My whole body was doused in moonlight, and the threads of their lives unraveled before my eyes. Frayed. Drenched in vile sludge. Petrifying into dust. An axe cleaved my heart, and I showered them with as much magic as I could muster.

*Threads are fickle things. If you can't coat them with your magic, you won't be able to stitch them back together.*

My aunt's quiet words filled my mind. She'd whispered them so softly, almost fearfully, as she'd splayed her palms wide over my mother's shuddering chest. Her wet, ragged rasps were a sound I'd never forget, but my aunt had chased them away. She had called on her power, doused her fingers in moonlight, and artfully moved them over my mother's rib cage, restitching what was broken.

I clung to my aunt's quiet lesson as panic climbed up my throat. With every inhale, I centered my power and willed it to bolster. To strengthen. And with every exhale, I focused on pushing more energy, more magic, to my brothers' threads. I needed to chase the blight away so that I could grip them tight and bring the frayed ends together again. If I could clear even a small portion of the damning black sludge, then I had a chance. I could save them.

It didn't work.

"Edira," Noam managed, turning his teakwood gaze toward me. He had the same eyes as our father—both in hue and in the identical cloudy haze I'd witnessed before he'd died. My insides knotted, and I wished I could do that to their threads. I needed to stitch them together, to tie them in such a way that they'd never come undone.

"S'okay," Nohr added, his hand weak against my thigh.

"No, it's not," I sobbed. I could've worked harder to keep them out of the mines, toiling away for elusive everjewels that rarely surfaced. I could've *done* more. Guilt rippled through me and fluttered like a current through the white light surrounding us. I didn't want to be alone. No one else in town knew the truth about me. I could never be myself around anyone, not really. What was I supposed to do without them? I needed them to survive so my existence had some purpose beyond secrets and death. I needed their smiles, their jokes, their constant warmth. If they were going to go . . .

I wanted to paint myself in the tar destroying their lives and disintegrate into soft loam with them. What good was it to be a threadmender if I couldn't protect my own family? My fingers ached as I mindlessly pressed tighter against their trembling bodies. The blight was everywhere, crawling over every thread, and my magic did absolutely nothing to stop its progression.

Another wail escaped my chest as I squeezed my eyes shut.

Pain had started to bloom through my limbs, and my vision blurred for entirely new reasons as the side effects of threadmending settled into my bones. Heat flushed my skin, and a vile, brackish substance coursed over my tongue. If I kept up this outpouring of power, it wouldn't be long before I faded. My heart squirmed. I'd rather slip away with them than watch as they left this world forever.

As I prepared myself to pull more of my magic to the surface, the front door banged open. The sound snared my focus, and my gaze snapped to the man—the Ever—standing in the dim light of my foyer. Orin surveyed the room in a breath and froze.

"You're a threadmender."

I glowered at him from my place on the floor. "What are you doing here?"

"I was hoping to convince you of dessert or a stroll since you didn't have time for tea . . ." His throat bobbed as his brows drew sharply together. "They have blight."

*Absolutely asinine.* I nearly laughed at the ludicrous notion of an evening walk with *him*, but instead I hugged my brothers tighter. A puff of yellow clouded around us as I accidentally ruptured some of the spores now dotting their arms. Pain clawed at my skin, and a fresh wave of nausea roiled through me. Time was not on my side. Or theirs.

"You should go."

Something flashed in his hardened gaze. "I have magic that can slow the progression, but I can't heal it."

"I know." I looked away to study the faces of my brothers. Their eyes had rolled to the backs of their heads and sweat dampened their hairlines. Bubbling splotches of black mold had formed in the creases of their elbows, the lines of their stomachs. They were rotting from the inside out.

"Work for me at Fernglove, and I'll stave off the blight." Orin stared not at my brothers but at me. A quiet sadness was etched into his gaze along with something else. Concern? Compassion? It felt so foreign when even my neighbors struggled to offer condolences each time my family faced loss. I was nothing to Orin, so why?

I swallowed thickly as I grappled with the grief rising in my throat. "I can't cure blight. Prolonging their fate helps no one."

"But maybe you could, with the proper instruction," he said, inching closer. "You don't have to die here. I can help you harness your power."

Unease trickled across the back of my neck. The light of my magic wavered. I was a waning moon heading toward a starless night, and even if I didn't drain every ounce of my power, I'd still find myself unconscious from the effort alone.

"Is that what you promised Rowena all those years ago?"

A flicker of surprise coursed through his expression, and his eyes widened. Understanding dawned in his gaze. "I remember you. As I said earlier, she was my *friend*." His voice dropped an octave as he lowered his gaze. "She was loved by all in my household. When I told her that we'd been working with threadmenders for years to rid the earth of this horrendous disease, she decided to help. We're close to finding answers because of her."

A lump formed in my throat, and I pressed my cheek against the crown of Noam's head. Rowena had given up a large portion of her life to save my mother from death. Who would I be if I didn't risk everything for my brothers?

Orin nodded toward the alabaster glow framing my body. "Don't expend yourself for no reason. Save your energy, your life threads." His words were so damn soft, his gaze too sorrowful. Slowly, he turned his stare to me. Pleading. He was pleading. Why? "Will you work with me? Like she did?"

*Keep dyeing your hair. Cure no one.*

My heart pounded in my ears as I recalled my aunt's warning. She couldn't have known that my life—my brothers' lives— would come to this. And yet, despite Orin's downturned lips and solemn eyes, I couldn't fully trust him. What would Rowena have done?

A flicker of gold pulled at my focus, and I watched as the beetle from earlier scuttled across the wooden rafters of my ceiling. Despite everything, despite the warring, roiling emotions colliding in the pit of my belly, that tiny glimmer was like a spark of hope. It wormed its way into the crevices of my mind, sprouting with the same ravenous appetite as the blight consuming my brothers, the last part of my family.

When Orin drew nearer, my hold on Noam and Nohr loosened. "I can't promise that you'll be able to cure them, but don't let them die without trying. I'll encase them right now in magic, I swear it to you. It'll control the spread of blight so you can let your own power go. Just say you'll work with me."

I was missing something. I had to be. Evers were master wordsmiths and rarely saw the raw end of a deal. I didn't want to end up like that tongueless traveling merchant, but what choice did I have? I knew I wasn't strong enough. Already my limbs were trembling, and sweat had dampened the collar of my blouse. I could keep going. Keep uselessly sacrificing my own threads, or . . .

"Please, Edira," Orin said. He reached for me but never actually made contact. He simply let his hand hang there, palm up to the ceiling, as his fingers beckoned softly toward him. "Let me help you."

Eternity passed in the span of seconds. Finally, I found my words. My resolve. "My brothers stay with me."

A look of pure relief filled his expression. "Of course."

"Then I agree."

A sudden chill ravaged my skin as a weight separate from the blight settled into my bones. Power thrummed through the air as the soft clink of a lock slipping into place filled my mind. Magic. I was bound to Orin's words, to his contract, and there was no escaping now.

The moment the vow solidified around us—invisible and yet somehow tangible, like metal links in a chain—Orin spread his arms wide. The ground trembled as thousands of minuscule green particles fell off his body in waves. The scent of the earth, of freshly bloomed flowers and pine trees and the rich aroma of soil, filled the room. And then he flicked his wrists, and the particles flew through the space to cocoon my brothers in magic. Power, heady and deep, rolled through the room. Orin had held true to his word, because once the magic had settled over Noam and Nohr, it solidified into a see-through casket and lifted them in the air.

Pain fled from my brothers' expressions as they fell into a deep slumber, and the blight creeping up their bodies halted altogether.

Safe. A gasp escaped my lips at the same time I capped my own magic. Noam and Nohr were alive. For now. Tears fell down my cheeks, and I felt my shoulders roll forward. I could save them. I could . . .

The aftermath of attempting to cure their blight—even to the smallest degree—hit hard and fast. Red-hot pain hammered into my bones as total darkness began to fill my peripheral vision. Sleep. I needed to sleep.

"Don't worry about your brothers." Orin crouched down before me and clasped his hands together. "I'll transport them immediately to Fernglove and ensure the magic remains intact. A few of my family members came to town when I didn't return home." He glanced over his shoulder at the open door, then turned his focus back to me. Concern tugged at his brow, and he inched closer. "Edira?"

The world tilted on its axis, and I toppled to the side. Before I could hit the floor, Orin was there. He cupped my head with his hand and eased me down gently. Light fingers swept away the sweat-slicked locks clinging to my forehead.

"Rest. We'll take care of everything else." His words were muffled and distorted as sleep tugged at my senses. I didn't know what I'd find waiting for me at Fernglove Estate, but I prayed that when I woke, I'd have the strength to survive my new role and eradicate the affliction that had robbed me of my family—and my future.

My HEAD KNOCKED AGAINST SOMETHING firm as a loud thud pierced the fog in my brain. One by one, aches started to register, and I cataloged the sensations without opening my eyes. Clammy skin. A deep pounding behind my forehead. A throb that racked my very bones and worsened as another peculiar bump jostled my body. My thoughts drifted back slowly, and I steeled against the queasiness of my stomach with a forceful exhale. I'd made an agreement with an Ever. Not just any Ever, but Orin Fernglove.

*My brothers.* It was a whisper, an echo of a memory, and my eyes flew open. But instead of the comfort of my living room, I found myself in the confines of a tufted carriage sitting opposite two young girls.

*More Evers.* Their dark hazel eyes were a stunning shade of hickory with flecks of clover green, and they perfectly complemented the tawny beige tone of their skin. One had loose blond curls that tumbled in a wave to her waist, whereas the other's hair was a deep brown and stopped at her clavicle. They shared the same severe jutted chin and full lips, and neither one of them spoke. Evers stopped aging in their mid-twenties, but these two couldn't have been more than sixteen, possibly seventeen.

"My brothers?" My words scraped against my throat, and I swallowed dryly.

"They're still alive," the blonde said as she tilted her head. "I'm Amalyss Fernglove. This is Tasia."

"Also a Fernglove," she chimed in a breath after her relative. They certainly looked alike, down to the way they dressed. Skintight sable pants with the reflective sheen of oil covered their long legs, and they each wore sleeveless blouses embroidered with silver stitching—Amalyss's in cobalt blue, Tasia's in a rich eggplant.

"Where are they?"

"Already at the estate," Tasia answered. "We've never had a threadmender bring their family before. That should be fun." Tasia's grin was cruel, jerking up sharply at the corners to reveal too-bright teeth with canines honed to fine points.

Amalyss's smirk matched Tasia's. "True, and your brothers are quite handsome. Maybe we'll get to keep them."

I should've encouraged Noam to spend time with Lysa. Her parents were far less dangerous than the pair of wolves sitting across from me, cackling as they shared a dark, private humor I had no desire to comprehend. I might have been employed by their family, but I would not allow them to frighten me. Not visibly, anyway.

"My brothers aren't playthings. Leave them out of whatever you're thinking." I glowered at them as I fought against the rising irritation in my chest.

Amalyss's and Tasia's smiles only stretched wider toward their ears. Leaning forward, Amalyss pressed one elbow onto her knee and cupped her chin with her hand. "You'll be fun, too."

We hit another bump in the road, and a wave of pain flared through my limbs, momentarily shifting my focus away from their predatory remarks. I prayed we were close to their estate. I'd never been to Fernglove, but I'd heard from a few lucky elders that it was several hours by carriage. I needed a bath and some balms . . . My shoulders sagged.

"I didn't get a chance to gather my things."

Tasia's tinkling laugh was as unsettling as her grin. "We grabbed your remedies in case you needed them."

"But nothing else," Amalyss added. "No need to invite blight into our home."

I couldn't imagine how any traces of blight in my house would've posed a threat greater than what my brothers carried, but I was just thankful Orin hadn't balked at the idea of me bringing them along. Otherwise I would have no way of knowing if Noam and Nohr were safe.

Or alive.

A rumbling gurgle rolled through my stomach, and both Amalyss and Tasia raised their brows in disdain. My hand pressed firmly against my belly, trying to quell the sound, but of course that did nothing other than alert me to the fact that my clothing had been changed. A dawning sense of frustration and anger thrummed beneath my fingers. One of these Evers had undressed me.

"My clothes?" I asked.

"As we said," Tasia murmured, her voice silky and full of threat, "we didn't need any extra blight in the house."

"Not that you had any fun garments to pick from." Amalyss's lips pulled together in a childish pout. Then she beamed. "Maybe he'll let us make you more presentable."

The absolute last thing I wanted was to be locked in a room with these two so they could dress me like a doll, curl my hair, paint my face—I didn't even know what Evers did to beautify themselves. Anything beyond their normal appearance hardly seemed necessary. Their skin was flawless, their hair glossy and nourished. I'd never seen an Ever even appear to be ill. Between their own brand of magic and their insistence on having a thread-mender on hand, they remained forever timeless.

Absently, I dropped my hand to my pants in search of my mother's leather scrap and froze. "What did you do with my blouse and skirt?"

Tasia leaned indolently against the window and stared at the passing trees. "We burned them to keep the blight from spreading."

Her nonchalance set fire to my bones, and I pressed my lips together to keep myself from screaming. I wanted to lunge across the cabin and smack the bored look from her expression. I'd been stripped of everything. My family. My home. My brothers were dying a slow, horrid death. I'd likely never see Willowfell again or the intricate flowered arch carved around our door. I didn't mind dying with the memory of those things, as I knew I couldn't hold on to them forever. But my mother I'd wanted to carry with me until the end. Until my magic gave out and I succumbed to death, saying goodbye to the short, cursed life I'd lived as a thread-mender.

And now that had been ripped from me, too.

"Oh, look, we've upset her." Amalyss studied my face. And then she laughed. "You're so easily wounded."

Tasia shifted her focus back to me. "Imagine how she'll react when we're forced to burn her brothers, too."

At that I snapped. I shouldn't have, but I couldn't help myself. I lunged toward her and cracked my palm against the soft skin of her cheek. An angry red welt bloomed across her blemish-free skin. Wide-eyed, she stared at me for the span of three breaths before reacting. And then she was on me, tackling me against the tufted bench to rake her pointed nails along the exposed skin of my neck and arms with the fury of a savage cat. Amalyss shrieked wordlessly, joining the hissing mess of limbs and fangs as we clawed at one another. I didn't know what I wanted to accomplish, just that the act of simply forgetting everything—the devastating sight of Noam and Nohr withering beneath my touch, the deal with Orin, the loss of my home—and giving in to anger was something akin to bliss. They ripped into my skin, slapped, bit, kicked, punched, until we tumbled into the door, and it sprung open, depositing us onto uneven ground.

The force of the hit thrust us apart as the carriage stopped, and I sprawled on my back to stare up at the dusk sky. The ground beneath my shoulders was uneven and damp, and the scent of wet dirt filled my nose. But before I could process anything else, Amalyss and Tasia pinned me in place. They jammed their knees into my shoulders, and a sharp cry scraped my throat as tears pricked my eyes.

Tasia lowered her face to mine, her pointed teeth barred and glistening. "Don't forget who you work for."

"Orin isn't the only one with power," Amalyss said. A surge of magic seemed to flow from the earth itself straight into their bodies, and their eyes glowed with the nocturnal sheen of wild animals. Everything about their features sharpened. Luminous feathers, like those of a hummingbird, pushed through their skin to line their cheekbones and temples, and Amalyss parted her lips to give her quickly elongating fangs extra room. The hairs on my neck stood on end as a crackling, electric sensation rippled over me.

"You need me," I sneered, ignoring the arcing pain lancing through my arms and the fear threading through my gut.

"You're wrong." Tasia's smile was a warning. "We could find another like you."

Before I could come up with some witty response, two strong hands drove into the collars of their blouses. They were yanked away in one fell swoop and tossed to the side with the ease of empty sacks. Still, Amalyss and Tasia were on their feet almost as soon as their backs cracked into the earth, and they rounded on the man standing over me.

"We were just playing," Amalyss whined. I was struck by the sudden childish tone to her voice, as if this had all been some minor misunderstanding that deserved nothing more than a slap on the wrist. The heady magic rolling off their bodies dissipated, along with the pregnant, suffocating swell of static.

"Besides, she started it," Tasia added.

"And I'm finishing it. Take the carriage back to the stalls, *now*," he said. He didn't bother glancing my direction, but that didn't mean I could drag my gaze away from him.

*For fuck's sake.* Textured, russet-colored hair fell across his forehead, teasing the tops of thick, angular brows in the same shade. Onyx dermal piercings, two above his left brow, stood out against his skin. He had a broad nose and wide, full lips that were downturned slightly at the corners, and I couldn't help but wonder what they looked like when he smiled. The amber hue of his eyes was closer to gold, but there was nothing warm about his expression. If anything, he seemed bored.

"Why? You were doing a fine job driving us." Tasia placed her hands on her hips.

The man took one step toward her, and she cowered. "Because you both just landed stall duty."

Tasia's mouth fell open. "Rorik, that's not fair!"

"We never clean stalls. We have farmhands for that," Amalyss practically begged.

"Now," he growled, gesturing to the carriage. I glanced past his hand to see the glossy black cabin was being drawn by two stags with ivy-laden antlers, glowing pale eyes, and mossy coats dotted with flowers. They exhaled forcefully, and mist curled upward from their wet nostrils.

Amalyss and Tasia turned on their heels, their gaits violent and rough. The carriage shuddered as they slammed the door closed and climbed up together to nestle onto the driver's seat. Once Tasia gripped the reins, Rorik sucked his teeth in a soft sound that spurred the stags back into motion.

"Are you going to get up?" He didn't offer his hand, instead opting to fold his arms across his chest as he finally looked at me. The action pulled his slate-gray shirt tight against his frame, and I trailed the line of his corded neck up to his clenched jaw.

"Yeah." I pulled myself to my feet, eyeing the retreating carriage as it followed a bend in the dirt road. "Thanks for that."

"You'd do well to avoid them." He turned without waiting to see if I'd follow and strolled down the path with languid ease. I hurried to keep pace, each of his long strides eating up the same distance as two of my own.

"I highly doubt that's possible," I muttered. The evening sky was quickly fading from lilac to indigo, and the long shadows of tall pines and spruce trees were already intermingling to shade the earth. A cool breeze rustled the underbrush and fallen leaves, and I rubbed my hands along my arms to spark warmth.

"Even so," Rorik said, bringing my focus back to him as we followed the same bend as the carriage, "avoid everyone from this family if you can." A muscle strained against his neck, but he kept his voice and gaze level.

I couldn't help but scoff. "You do know why I'm here, right?"

He paused and gave me the full weight of his molten stare. Then he grimaced. "You're here to fail at curing blight and then die. Only the gods know how long that will take."

I stumbled to a halt, frozen by his words. He regarded me for a long moment, searching for something—a weakness—and then he pursed his lips. Straightening his back, he jerked his thumb in the direction of the worn road.

"We're here."

Shifting so I could see around his broad frame, I gasped. Acres of gently rolling hills spread out toward the horizon, and the massive clearing was framed by a forest of densely packed trees. Fernglove Estate was the epicenter of it all, sitting proudly on a flattened portion of land. Manicured lawns stretched from the first building to where I stood, along with artfully trimmed hedges and an array of flower beds. I counted at least three structures immediately, though the primary residence held all my attention.

A river of babbling water wound from the woods to cross before the manor, and a solitary bridge of powder-green stone, wide enough for two carriages to pass side by side, connected the road to an open courtyard. The front of the manor was dominated by a pointed arch, and the pitched roof was trimmed in off-white wood. Limestone a shade lighter than that of the bridge made up the brick masonry of the sprawling establishment, and I lost count of the curved windows lighting up as the sky darkened.

It was breathtaking in its splendor but horrifying in its solitude. For despite its size, I struggled to find a single soul traversing the grounds. Everything was eerily quiet, save the soft chirping of insects welcoming the night. Unease crept through my veins. I wanted to blame it on the late hour, but I knew it was something else. I knew it like I knew my fate was a speeding course toward death that could not be altered.

Whispers of illness skirted through the air on the evening breeze, bringing a chill to my bones. Every Fernglove I'd encountered thus far was healthy and vibrant, a stark contrast to the suffocating presence of wrong that seemed to bloom from the near-silent estate. I couldn't see Death, but I could feel him. There were broken threads here, and my magic hummed in recognition.

"How many threadmenders have been here before?" I asked quietly, gaze locked on the looming mansion.

"Too many." Rorik's lips twitched as his stare hardened.

And they were all gone. Anger wormed through me, and I fisted my hands by my sides. "Of course. Gods forbid you face even the smallest ailment on your own."

At that, he laughed. "As if small ailments could bother us." He watched me closely for a moment, and then he strolled away. Without looking back, he spoke over his shoulder. "Welcome to Fernglove, Edira. May you live to see something else."

## FIVE

Walking through the double doors of Fernglove Manor was like stepping into an entirely different realm. The communal hall was colossal, with a polished double staircase that swept upward in a subtle curve. Dark hardwood floors spanned the entire layout, and ornate wrought-iron chandeliers draped in pewter crystals hung on chains from impossibly high ceilings. The oak-paneled walls were adorned with either rich oil paintings or stained-glass windows, and I found myself looking forward to the morning light just to see what colors would flood from the artful masterpieces.

I assumed all Evers had elegant estates, especially the Ferngloves with their ownership over Willowfell's mines. But this was opulent in a way I could never have fathomed, and yet . . . My gaze slanted to the rows of closed doors. Silence. Rorik strode past me, his booted feet thudding harshly against the floor. The sound reverberated endlessly throughout the hall, and again I was struck by the hushed emptiness of it all. I followed him without speaking, passing by credenzas laden with potted hyacinths of pastel purple, dusty rose, and ivory. Inhaling deeply, I expected a pleasing burst of fragrance to settle over me. Instead, I was met with nothing more than stale air and dust. My brows drew sharply together. Hyacinths were the very essence of spring, the perfume of the season. The whole floor should've been thick with their aroma.

"In here," Rorik said, his gait rigid as he strode through a set of open double doors.

We moved into a formal dining room, complete with a grand oak table that could seat at least twelve. A cream-colored lace runner embellished with forest-green leaves and bloodred roses stretched from end to end. Robin's-egg-blue plates fringed in gold rimmed the table, and a pile of food waited untouched in the middle. Rorik paused before a chair and gestured for me to sit. I hesitated at the threshold and tried my best to ignore the savory scent of herb-crusted chicken wafting through the air.

I couldn't help but think of the power these Evers wielded, of how my aunt had been whisked away or how the traveling vendor had lost his tongue. I'd entered willingly into a contract with Orin, but would that stop him or his family from making me more obedient? Subservient? Could they bespell my meal to make me comply without question? Perhaps the gossenberries, a vibrant yellow fruit composed of tiny drupelets, would make me susceptible to enchantments. The wine was likely just as dangerous, if not more.

Fear trickled down my spine. "I want to see my brothers."

"After you eat." Rorik braced his hands on the high-backed chair.

"I want to see them *now*."

One brow arched toward his hairline. "If you want to wander aimlessly around the estate in the hopes you find them, be my guest."

My hands curled into fists. "You won't take me to see them?"

"*After* you eat, someone will escort you." A belabored sigh escaped his parted lips, but there was an unmistakable edge to his words. "The others will join us shortly. I suggest you fill your plate before they arrive."

"How do I know it's safe?" I inched closer. My stomach ached with twisting hunger, but I couldn't risk consuming something that would leave me vulnerable.

"So many questions. Are you always this insufferable?" he murmured. When I didn't respond, he pinched the bridge of his nose. "It's safe."

Tension gathered between my shoulders, and I glared first at him, then the food. "Safe for you or safe for me? Tell me a truth that can't be twisted, and I'll eat."

"You want me to vow that the food is safe? Back the promise with magic?" He cocked his head in my direction, and the corners of his lips tipped up in a smirk. "Suspicious little mender. Maybe you'll survive us after all."

He released the chair to stalk toward me, and a devilish glint flickered through his golden eyes. Everything in me screamed to run, but I held my ground and clenched my jaw tight. As he paused before me, he slipped his hands into the pockets of his black pants and dipped his head close to mine.

"The food is safe for consumption and free of ensorcellment or poison." An earthy scent of moss and dirt accompanied his words, along with a flowing rush of coolness over my skin. Ever magic. Something about this power felt ancient, as if his magic was birthed from the land itself and would remain if his bones ever rested in the ground. Tension snapped between us as I held my breath, and he studied me for a moment longer before straightening. "Well? Will that suffice? I have promised it is safe. If my words were a lie, I would end up suffering the consequences in your stead."

At that, I blinked. I'd only ever heard of vows negatively impacting mortals. If that were the case . . . "Is it wrong to pray for accidental food poisoning?"

He chuckled darkly. "Keep those wits about you. Now, eat."

In a matter of moments, I was seated with my plate and goblet filled. "Can you at least tell me if my brothers are all right?"

Rorik ignored the food entirely and filled his crystal chalice to the brim with a deep red wine. "They're infected with blight. It's safe to say they're not all right, but they're still alive." He took a long pull from his drink. "You can thank Orin for that."

As if his name summoned him, Orin strode through the open doors with a wide smile. His brown locks were damp as if he'd freshly bathed, his tanned skin bright. Mirth filled his ivy-colored eyes, and he swept into the room as if he were hosting a party among friends.

"Edira, I'm thrilled you're awake. I can't wait to introduce you to everyone." He was dressed in lavish emeralds again, and the gold buttons along his vest winked at me as he took the seat at the head of the table. An attendant dressed in modest brown attire slipped into the room from a butler's door and immediately began filling his plate. After she poured him a hefty dose of wine, she disappeared.

"How many of you live here?" I draped a linen napkin over my lap and then clasped my hands together. Gods only knew what would cause these arrogant immortals to erupt, and I wasn't about to let poor etiquette be the first of my offenses as a new resident of Fernglove Manor. My stomach could wait.

"You've met my brother, Rorik, and our younger cousins, Amalyss and Tasia." His easy grin was genuine, and the tension between my shoulders loosened a fraction. "Aside from us, there are four additional family members and a handful of attendants who also live on the property."

Rorik said nothing as his brother spoke, but he draped a long leg over the arm of his chair and indolently leaned into the wooden rungs at his back. With listless eyes, he studied the rafters framing the ceiling. His apathetic posture had little impact on his brother's exuberance, though, and Orin continued on without interruption.

"We're also fortunate in that our lands neighbor those of two other Ever families: the Waterstones and the Starglens. Their children attend lessons here with Amalyss and Tasia under my guidance."

At that, Rorik snorted. "*Fortunate* is an interesting word choice."

Orin waved him off. "We've had our differences in the past, but it's imperative the youth are educated together so they can be better than we are."

Rorik dragged his attention away from the ceiling long enough to pin his brother with a stare and a smirk. "Did you say that when Flix stabbed you in the hand not two weeks ago? I must have missed that lesson."

Orin's answering smile was stiff. "You've missed many lessons, brother."

Harsh footsteps carried from the hall, punctuating Orin's and Rorik's words, and a woman breezed into the room. "Are you two at it again? Honestly." She leaned over me, not bothering to push back her sheet of blond hair and instead letting it smack into my face. With long, delicate fingers, she snared the wine carafe and poured herself a glass. Only then did she adjust her locks and slant her ice-green eyes toward me. With a quick dart of her tongue, she wet her lips. "Why, hello, dear."

A tingle shot through my limbs as I took her in, and I wasn't sure if it stemmed from fear or longing. This Ever was sultry—and it seemed like she knew it. Like it was a weapon she wielded with deadly efficiency.

Rorik went back to ignoring the table entirely, while Orin stood and opened his arms wide. "Seville, my dear sister."

She sauntered toward him, planting a quick kiss on either cheek before slipping into the chair to his right. Everything about

her was sharp: the tip of her nose, the edge of her jaw, the points of
her ears. She was hewn from diamonds, and her pale skin practically glowed with hidden light. While I knew all Evers wore glamour, she had mastered it to absolute perfection. She toyed with the
hem of her long-sleeved tailcoat, the color an identical match with
the wine in her glass, as she considered me.

I was suddenly too aware of the dull, false color of my hair
and my crumpled blouse. Of course I'd meet perfection incarnate
while looking like the carriage had dragged me to the estate instead of riding comfortably inside.

"Is this our new threadmender?" Her question was more of
a purr, and I fought the urge to shrink in my seat. Again, an attendant appeared and expertly picked from the array of displayed
food to make a plate for Seville. "We should've found someone
younger."

"Yes, this is Edira," Orin said as he returned to his chair. "And
you and I both know that her age has nothing to do with her
abilities."

Before Seville could add anything else, Amalyss and Tasia
bounded into the room, followed closely by two more Evers who
were undoubtedly their parents. The woman's honey-blond hair
was pulled tight in an artful bun, highlighting the same severe
chin as her daughters. But her skin was fair and dotted with
freckles, and her jeweled blue-green stare was sharp. The man was
impossibly broad with full lips and warm mellow-brown skin like
that of fall leaves. His eyes were a rich brown, their hue a deeper
shade than his daughters'. Without greeting anyone else in the
room, they sat together in a row and waited for their food to be
plated.

"Our aunt, Lydia, and her heartbond, Clesian," Orin continued by way of introduction.

My gaze lingered on Clesian and his quiet presence. *Heartbond.* Orin had uttered it with a soft reverence, and while I'd heard

whispers of the term growing up in Willowfell, I couldn't understand why the undertone of his voice hinted at the kind of awe and wonder reserved for miracles. Maybe Evers were slow to wed, and the idea of a spouse was both foreign and cherished.

"And last, but certainly not least, Mavis, our grandmother." Orin clasped his hands in front of him as the rest of the table—even Rorik—rose. I did the same, pushing away from my untouched plate to face the woman who waited in the opening to the dining room.

It was jarring to see such a youthful-looking woman be acknowledged as their grandmother. Not a single wrinkle dared to mar Mavis's rose-tinged fawn skin. Her round, doe-like eyes were brassy, her hair the color of wheat. It flowed around her frame like a tumbling wave to kiss the top of her waist. Her floor-length dress covered everything, but I spied the hint of a tattoo, a sword's pommel, teasing the edge of her neckline.

Immediately, I glanced at Orin, at the broken sword on his neck with the same pommel as his grandmother's. He moved around the table to take Mavis's hand and guide her to her seat beside me. She eased into it, her willowy frame trembling like dying leaves clinging to a branch. The others all glanced her way without directly looking at her, as if they didn't want to fully acknowledge the state of her weakened body. She sat limply in front of an empty plate, and no attendant appeared to fill it.

The moment she was seated, the family followed suit and began eating. Slowly, I took my place by Mavis and speared a small portion of chicken with my fork. It was as if a wall had been constructed around Mavis and me. No one spoke to us. No one looked our way. When they discussed house matters—like Amalyss and Tasia griping about mucking stalls—they did it with a sort of haughty superiority and underhanded malice that made me thankful I wasn't part of the conversation.

"You were out of line, Rorik. My daughters will not be expected to do such menial work." Lydia's upper lip curled in a snarl as she glared at Rorik.

He waved a dismissive hand in her direction, which only caused a fire to ignite in her already sinister glare. "Yes, of course, how dare I reprimand poor behavior. Gods know their parents aren't."

Clesian growled a low warning, and the metal fork he fisted bent from the pressure of his fingers. "Do not pretend to know what it is to be a parent."

"How civilized." Seville sighed with a pointed look to the ruined silverware. Then she drained her glass and signaled for more wine from the attendant.

"As if your manners are anything to make note of," Lydia spat. Beside her, Amalyss and Tasia kept their gazes down and their words to themselves. Smart.

Seville's smile stretched from ear to ear. "Oh, my manners are the least of your worries."

At that, Orin placed his palms on the table with a firm thud, and all eyes rounded to him. "Can't we just eat for once? Lydia, the girls will have stall duty for a week." When she opened her mouth to argue, he shot her a hard glare that had her lips forming a thin line. "Be glad it's not more. Seville, stop antagonizing."

"If you say so," she murmured into her now full glass.

The table fell into a strained silence, only the scrapes of fork tines drifting through the air. I knew before I'd finished dinner that I couldn't expect kindness from anyone outside of Orin. And possibly the matriarch, who'd been relegated to the same status as me. She hardly moved the entire duration of the meal, but there was something in her eyes that gave me pause. I couldn't place it, couldn't quite figure out what it was about her distant stare that blanketed me in unease. She might not have been involved in the family's mealtime quarrels, but something was happening behind her thick veneer of glamour.

"Girls," Lydia said by way of command, and her daughters stood abruptly in sync with their parents. "We'll be in our rooms. Don't bother us."

Orin raised his glass in acknowledgment, and they departed without a backward glance. The thick tension snapping through the air fizzled to an uncomfortable prickle, and I set my fork down on my cleaned plate.

"Don't pay them any mind," Seville said, voice as syrupy as her brother's. "They've been holding a grudge against us for decades. They didn't think it was fair for Orin to become head of the estate after our father passed."

"I see." It was the best I could muster. The last thing I wanted was to get in the middle of their decades-old drama.

"Yes, well, I'll do my best to uphold Grandmother's wishes." Orin glanced at Mavis.

I swallowed the unease clambering up my throat. "What's wrong with her?"

"I thought you were a threadmender. Can't you figure that out?" Seville's upper lip curved in disdain.

"I can activate my magic and look without needlessly sacrificing threads." I held her gaze without flinching. "But if you already know, why not just tell me?"

"Maybe you're just lazy," Seville drawled.

My brow twitched. "Hardly."

"Seville." Orin glared at his sister for a moment before sighing. His eyes fell, and he toyed with the rim of his glass. "Mavis is sick."

"With blight?" They were immortal, and yet Orin had made it a point to seek out threadmenders to rid the world of this deadly illness. If they were truly immune like me, why bother in the first place?

An uncomfortable, pregnant pause followed my question until, finally, he nodded.

I couldn't help my surprised snort. "Really? I always assumed you were immune." I glanced back at Mavis. "How long has she been sick?"

"Years." Orin swallowed thickly. "We still don't know how she contracted it—or how much time she has left. Months, at best."

Pursing my lips, I tilted my head toward her. She didn't acknowledge me at all. "Can she hear us? Speak?"

"I haven't heard her talk in . . ." His gaze lifted upward as his lips remained parted, as if counting silently, before finally returning his focus to me. "It's been too long. She hardly even moves on her own, likely to conserve what energy she has left."

My gut tightened. "You know I don't know how to cure this."

"Not yet." He braided his fingers together. "But I hope, with time, you'll learn. You'll have our vast resources at your disposal."

"Do any of those resources involve adding more years to my life?" I muttered, unable to keep the sarcasm from creeping into my words. If there was a means in this world to eradicate blight, someone would've found it already. Unless they had a way to grant me more time on this earth, more threads to sacrifice in my efforts to learn more about this illness, then their resources meant nothing.

"Don't forget about your brothers." Seville's eyes practically glowed as she stared at me. "You need a way to cure blight just as much as we do."

Low ringing sounded in my ears. She was right, of course. And if I did find a way to cure blight, Orin could simply command me to threadmend his grandmother under the terms of my employment before I even got to my brothers. I wouldn't have the power to say no. Even now, I could still feel the weight of his contract, as if his bargain had chained me to him and this place.

Understanding settled over me with a cold calm. This was the play all along. I'd known about finding a cure for blight, certainly, but not that I'd be mending an Ever who'd harbored the disease for *years*. What would curing something that persistent even do to me? Could I survive threadmending something like that *and* my brothers? I wasn't sure. But until I found out, I could hide in plain sight. No one knew what threadmending looked like. Only I possessed the power to see life's threads. Onlookers would only observe an outpouring of moonlight from my body as I worked, which meant the only proof of success came from ailments being cured.

I could wear a mask and plaster on smiles, move through Fernglove and play my role without ever breaking face. I could be demure. I could be brave. I could be smart or weak or arrogant or fearful. I could be anything. I could be *everything*. I would stitch whatever role I needed with sutures through my bones, and no one, not a single Ever from Fernglove or anywhere else, would be able to see the real me. I would bide my time, learn what I could, and then find a way to save my brothers.

Steeling myself with a breath, I turned my focus back to Mavis. "She shows no visible signs of blight. Glamour, I'm assuming?"

"The thickest." Rorik chuckled, and the hackles along the back of my neck stood on end.

Orin shot him a glare. "We afford her that dignity, so that she does not appear weak."

Everything about Mavis seemed weak. Focusing on the minute rise and fall of her chest, I tried to find the crack in her glamour, in the subtle shifts of movements. Maybe then I could pry apart the veil and gaze upon what lay beneath. But her mask was strong, and the only thing I succeeded in doing was sparking an ache behind my eyes.

"It will be hard for me to mend if I can't see the truth," I said, shifting my attention to Orin.

He studied me for a long moment. "When you're ready, we can discuss removing her glamour. Until then, we find it best to keep her condition hidden. Not to mention, our glamour acts as a bandage to keep her blight at bay, and we don't want to needlessly risk anyone else getting sick." He gestured to one of the attendants still quietly manning the wall with her hands clasped behind her back. If she was surprised by the news of Mavis's illness, she didn't show it.

"Gods forbid we taint her reputation," Rorik muttered.

"Mind your tone, Rorik," Seville snapped. She flashed her pointed fangs in a hiss. Rorik shrugged, then placed his empty chalice on the table.

"All right, you two. Seville, take Grandmother to bed." Orin stood and brushed his hands along his vest. "Rorik, do whatever it is you do—just not here."

Rorik stiffened in his chair, his golden eyes alight with an intensity that seemed steeped in history. "Edira requested to see her brothers. I was going to escort her."

"I'll handle it." Orin brushed him off with a flippant wave before coming around to my chair and extending his elbow. "Come. I'll show you the way."

Everything in me screamed to ignore his proffered gesture, but I wound my hand around his arm for the same reason I waited to eat: fear. I wasn't sure I could trust these seemingly innocuous acts of kindness. Even though they needed me to save Mavis as much as I needed them to keep my brothers alive, I couldn't let myself forget that I was now living in a den of monsters. They'd manipulated me into working for them, and they'd do it again without a second thought.

No, there were no kindnesses here. And the sooner I cured Mavis or died trying, the better.

"I'm sorry," Orin said quietly as we exited the dining room.

"For?"

"*That.*" He gestured limply over his shoulder, defeat tugging at his frame and making him seem almost vulnerable. The ratcheting anger in my chest dulled, and I let out a heavy exhale as he continued. "And for not immediately telling you about Mavis's blight."

"It's all right." Was it? I knew I'd been recruited to help cure blight, but I'd assumed it'd been some of the attendants who were infected. Not an *Ever*. I stared at the floor as we made our way to the foyer and climbed the stairs. A few steps groaned beneath our combined weight, and the quiet creaks filtered through the air and seemed to grow louder as they bounced off the near-silent halls. For a house so full of stuff, it was incredibly empty.

Orin's gaze flitted around, as if following the hollow sound, and he sighed. "Dinners like that never happened when my parents were around. Everything was so much easier back then."

A familiar pain simmered deep in my heart. "If you're the head of household now, was your father before you? Or your mother?"

His smile was wistful. "My father. He was an incredible person. If I turn out to be half the man he was, I'll be happy."

"I'm sorry he's not around," I said, though I wasn't quite sure why. Likely because Orin's voice carried a small, aching tremor of hurt that I knew all too well. It called to me and softened some of the fear still lingering in my bones.

Orin's smile was sad. "I'm sorry for your loss, too." He must have been referring to Rowena, but my heart faltered for a breath. I wasn't ready to share my parents' death with him. I hadn't talked about it with anyone. Who could really understand? Who could comprehend the guilt, the agony, of having the power to heal but being so utterly helpless and incapable when they needed it most? Orin watched me closely until we reached the far end of the hall. He paused before a set of double doors. "Your quarters are through here." He nodded toward the brass handles. "We have dinner as a family every evening. You'll be expected to attend. You may take your other meals however you please. Of course, if you'd like someone to dine with, I'll join you whenever you want."

"Well, if I find myself in need of dessert or a stroll, I know who to ask." I arched a brow as I repeated his earlier offer, and he grinned.

"The offer still stands." His gaze roved over me, lingering for a second on my clothes. Something raw and dangerous flickered through his eyes. "We did manage to bring a few of your things, but our attendants have taken the liberty of filling your wardrobe with additional garments."

A slow-moving heat climbed up the sides of my neck. "Should I even ask how you managed to secure my measurements?"

The curl of his lips was downright provocative. "I provided some of your clothes as reference. Pity it wasn't a more . . . hands-on assessment."

A playful spark lit his gaze, and words escaped me as heat rushed over my cheeks. Evers and their words. This was undoubtedly a ploy to unsettle me, to make me more amicable to his orders. And yet, the intrigue in his stare had me biting my lip.

Finally, he laughed. As he straightened, he removed his arm from mine, giving my body—and mind—space to process his words. "Someone will be by in the morning to assist you with whatever you require and go over your schedule for your work."

"My brothers?"

He pivoted toward another closed door on his right. "This is normally an attendant's room, but we had them placed in here. You may visit whenever you have free time."

My hand was already on the knob when I halted. "Thank you."

"Thank *you*, Edira." With gentle fingers, he caught a lock of hair lingering against my cheek. He rubbed the strands together, and a faint black film spread across his thumb and forefinger. Sadness flared in his eyes. "I can only imagine that you hid all these years because of us. I don't know what you've been told about Evers or what to expect, but . . ." He seemed to grapple with his words, swallowing twice before continuing. "At least you don't have to hide any longer."

A shiver crept over my skin, and his gaze trailed the gooseflesh down my neck. Without another word, he turned and strode

toward the stairs. I didn't linger in the hall any longer than necessary. The moment Orin began his descent, I bolted into my
brothers' room and shut the door behind me.

The ornateness of the space was subdued in comparison with
the rest of the manor, but it was cozy with a small hearth, a polished armoire, and a double bed with a simple frame. I didn't care
enough to marvel at any other details. My brothers were there,
encased in shimmering caskets and suspended in the air just
inches above the off-white sheets. Faint green mist coated their
bodies, leaving only their necks and pale faces exposed. They were
breathing—slowly—and most certainly alive. Their eyes moved
restlessly behind closed lids, and the first hints of blight—the fes-
tering black mold—lingered in the corners of their mouths. But
it wasn't devouring their skin. Yellow bubbles would blossom and
burst, but instead of spreading along their still visages, the fumes
simply plumed into the air and the mist suppressed it.

Slowly, I pressed my hand against the magical barrier of Noam's
casket. I hated that it felt like a coffin.

"Oh, Noam." Emotion thickened in my throat, and I forced
down a hard swallow as tears stung at my eyes. I moved around
the foot of the bed to place my other hand on Nohr's case. "Nohr.
I'm so sorry."

And that was all it took. One moment I was standing, my
arms shaking as I palmed the caskets holding my brothers, and
the next I was a heaping mess on the floor. Sobs racked my chest in
hard waves, crashing against my ribs and rendering my breath useless. At one point, I instinctively reached for my mother's leather,
only to come up empty-handed and fall into another spiral of erratic sobs. I was utterly alone. I had no ties to my home, save my
brothers. They were here, but they weren't really *here*. And I wasn't
convinced I was strong enough to save them. Pulling my knees
inward, I curled on the ground and wrapped myself in a ball. Be-

tween the dying fire in the hearth and the plush rug against my cheek, it was enough.

I didn't leave their sides. I never saw my room. I fell asleep at the foot of their bed and dreamed of carved wooden roses with embroidered leather leaves, somehow infested with blight and dripping in golden beetles.

My home, my heart, was infected, too.

# SIX

A curt series of knocks roused me from sleep, and I stared bleary-eyed at the door. For a moment, I couldn't recall where I was or how I'd gotten there. Decades had passed since yesterday. The stiff ache in my muscles from sleeping on hard ground, compounded by an unbearable crick in my neck, brought me back to reality, and I shoved myself into a sitting position just as the door swung inward.

A woman with soft curves and tightly braided chestnut locks stepped into the room. She had thin lips, smooth, round cheeks, and soft wrinkles that lined the corners of her walnut-colored eyes. The folds of her brown velvet dress swept against the floor as she moved, and she paused to slip her hands into the pockets of her white apron when she spied me.

"There you are." She clucked her tongue, giving me a once-over with the practiced disdain of a mother. "You're a mess. Come on."

Abruptly, she turned on her heel and left me to scramble after her. I paused long enough to cast a glance at my brothers and whisper a goodbye beneath my breath before closing the door.

*You may visit whenever you have free time.*

Orin's words filtered through my mind. I would be back. I wouldn't leave them alone, even if they had no idea that I was here with them.

Fortunately, the attendant hadn't gone far. She'd pushed through the double doors of my quarters and waited for me to enter before letting them click closed behind us. Rows of stained-glass windows bathed the large space in a rainbow of colors, painting the ivory accents peach and lavender and indigo. The attendant ushered me past an ornate bed, complete with a sheer canopy, to seat me before a white oak vanity. I stared at her through the reflection of the mirror. She pursed her lips in a tight grimace as she ran deft fingers through my knotted hair.

"Was the bed not to your liking?" she asked, yanking her hands away to inspect her coal-stained fingers.

"I just wanted to be near my brothers."

She scowled. "You're a room away. If you insist on sleeping beside them, I can arrange for a cot to be brought in."

I shook my head. "No, this is fine. Thank you."

She strode across my quarters to fling open a door. With an exaggerated sweep of her arm, she gestured to the attached room. "You're in desperate need of a bath."

"I can bathe myself." I stood, my body already protesting at the movement. Threadmending had left a lingering ache in my bones, and sleeping on the floor hadn't helped. I glanced about the room until my eyes snagged on my apothecary cases. Salts would help. Stiffly, I moved toward them and rummaged through the contents.

"That may be true, but my lord has instructed me to care for your every need." She gripped my arm and yanked me toward the bathroom before I could grab a remedy. "Ever-made medicine will be infused in the water. You'll find it more effective than anything crafted by human hands." She stilled, her eyes pointedly sliding to my fingers. "Perhaps it's not better than *everything*, but certainly this."

It was strange to be both coveted and hated for a talent I had no say in developing, and yet that's exactly how this woman gazed at my fingers. She strolled into the bathroom, and the lanterns clinging to the wall lit of their own accord. The copper washbasin—large enough to comfortably hold two people—began to fill. Steaming milky water swirled into existence until it reached the lip of the tub, and then all at once it went placid. My jaw hit the floor as I watched the room respond to her, but she barely acknowledged it.

*Magic.* I paused at the edge of the claw-footed tub. "How?"

"Everything in this house is attuned to the Ferngloves' magic. It does their bidding—and mine, too." She rolled up the sleeve of her gown to reveal the beginnings of the family's crest. "Attendants bear the mark as well."

Which also meant I could hardly function in this space without the presence of one of them at my side. Suddenly, the invisible chains of Orin's contract tightened around my body. "Is it safe?"

"How detailed would you like that answer? Nothing in this manor is safe, threadmender. But I can assure you that I will never be the one to harm you."

Noted. I inched toward the copper basin, but she snared my wrist between her fingers. Her grip was surprisingly strong as she tugged me to the side, forcing me to sit on a small wooden stool a few feet away. Tin buckets full of water waited near the legs.

"Hair first, bath second." She moved behind me to study my locks, then gave a disapproving scoff. "Don't want *this* mixing with the bathwater and staining your skin."

I sat quietly as she doused my hair and began the arduous process of removing the dye. I'd spent years using it, never once allowing it to fully fade and reveal the ivory shade that had claimed my locks. A familiar twinge of panic wrapped around my throat.

*I can't be seen.* My muscles tensed instinctively with every cool rush of water against my scalp. Black splatters dotted the floor as my most precious armor was stripped from me and cast to the side without a second thought.

*At least you don't have to hide any longer.* Orin's words rattled through my mind.

All I wanted to do was hide.

After wringing my hair for what must have been the hundredth time, the attendant had me undress and nudged me toward the tub. I went in quickly, eager to hide my body beneath the water's milky surface.

"This feels incredible," I moaned.

The attendant came around with a pitcher and tilted my head back, pouring fresh, warm water through my cleansed hair. The silky caress of the bath loosened my muscles, and I didn't fight as the woman sponged me clean and rubbed oils onto my skin. She hurried me along, wrapping me in a thick robe and toweling my hair before setting me back in front of the vanity. A small plate of food was already waiting for me, and I nibbled at toast and eggs as she combed through my damp locks.

I couldn't help but stare at my reflection while she worked. The last time I'd seen my hair, my true hair, I'd been a child. I hardly remembered the luster, the almost ethereal glow, that seemed to shimmer from the moonlit strands.

"What's your name?" I asked.

"Vora." She didn't look up as her nimble fingers twisted my hair into an artful braid.

"How long have you worked for the Ferngloves?"

"I've worked for my lord for years."

"By choice?" I bit back a snort. There had to be at least thirty attendants, if not more, working at the estate. Fulfilling every Fernglove whim, and for what? To simply be in the presence of society's finest?

She shot me a glare and gave my hair a final tug before brushing her hands along her dress. "You'll find that everyone came here by choice."

"That's debatable," I grumbled.

"You had a choice, and you'd do well to remember that." Angling her chin high, she looked down her nose at me. "Are you having second thoughts? Because I won't waste my morning getting you prepared if you're just going to waltz out of here by lunch."

"As if I could," I muttered. Leaving would mean condemning my brothers to death. It might have been my choice to accept Orin's offer, but it'd been a trap just the same. "Please continue."

She nodded toward the dresser. "There's an assortment of underthings in the top drawer. Take your pick." Then she pulled a cream-colored gown with embroidered rosebuds from the wardrobe and laid it upon the bed. I eyed the green lace along the hemline and thin shoulder straps. She flipped it over and loosened the strings, waiting for me to finish slipping on my undergarments. I stepped into the pool of fabric, and she pulled the straps over my shoulders before cinching the corset bodice tight.

I trailed my hands over my arms and the smooth expanse of my neck and upper chest. A wondrous thrill ran through me. I hadn't worn a gown like this in . . . well, ever. "Are all my clothes this ornate?"

"Ornate?" Vora folded her arms across her chest as she inspected the gown, then chuckled. "I imagine the family would find this one tame, but I do quite like it. Now, come along. Orin is expecting you."

My shoulders stiffened. "Asking me to begin work already?"

"Did you expect anything less?" She waited a beat before shaking her head. "Orin only tells me what he wants me to know. For now, I believe, he just means to check in on you."

"I'd hoped to spend some time with my brothers today."

"That will have to wait."

"Lovely," I said through a forced exhale. "Well, let's get this over with."

She placed her hands on her hips, studying my sour expression as if she understood my quiet frustration. "Take solace in knowing they feel no pain. And if you're successful . . ." She shrugged. "Then they will simply wake up and won't fret about how much time you physically spent by their sides."

Tension coiled tightly at the base of my neck. "One can only hope."

"Indeed." Something flickered through her sharp gaze. "Best not to keep Orin waiting."

"Thank you, Vora." I clasped my hands together. I imagined I wasn't the first threadmender she'd attended to, and I likely wouldn't be the last. At least it seemed like I could rely on her for the things I needed to survive. In this house, that was the most I could hope for.

She studied me for a long moment, a deepening crinkle forming between her brows. Then she made a beeline for the doors. "Be careful who you trust in this place, Edira."

Her quiet warning was such a stark contrast to the disgusted frown she'd shown me when I'd asked if she and the others worked here freely. A heavy, uneasy feeling settled low in my stomach, and I clenched my jaw tight.

She gripped the handles and pulled the doors open. "Let's go."

My feet wanted to root to the ground like the great trees of the surrounding forest, but I forced myself to join her and did everything in my power to bury my fears deep beneath the surface.

VORA DEPOSITED ME OUTSIDE OF Orin's study before excusing herself, and I was left to knock on the monstrous mahogany doors alone. They swung inward of their own accord, revealing a circular room with a high ceiling and polished rafters. Curved bookshelves

lined the back wall, and a heavy desk with gold foil inlays sat beneath an unlit chandelier. Sunlight poured in through an oversized window, and I spied the lush, rolling lawns sprawling from
one end of the estate to the other. Dense woods clambered against
the edges of the clearing, forming an impressive barrier between
the Ferngloves and the rest of the world. Orin looked out over it
all from his place on the window bench. With his back reclined
against an array of pillows, he'd propped an open book against his
knee. His fingers held his place while his gaze shifted from the
grounds to me.

A warm smile claimed his lips. "Edira."

A foreign tingle trickled through my limbs, and I wasn't sure
if it was awe or fear, but it was impossible to deny just how beautiful he was. Perhaps it was the way the sun caught on his tanned
skin, painting him a healthy bronze. Or maybe it was the boyish
curl to his lips or his relaxed, inviting posture, but his eyes were
alight with a curious glint I couldn't quite place. Intrigue? Mischief? Good or bad, I didn't know.

After a quick swallow, I found my voice. "Good morning. Vora
said you wanted to see me."

"Come. Sit." He sat upright and patted the tufted cushion beside him. "I trust you feel better after seeing your brothers."

*Better* was an interesting word, but I settled for a simple nod
as I dropped to the space he indicated. "How long can they survive
like that?"

"I'm uncertain. If they were Evers, I'd say a decade or so.
Humans . . ." After setting the book down beside him, he shifted
so his knees were angled toward me. "You're so much more fragile
than us."

"I'll work quickly, then."

He clasped his hands over mine. "Good. Now, there's the matter of making it official."

"Official?" I frowned. He had my brothers encased in floating coffins, minutes away from death without his magic, and he wanted something more concrete than that? I'd never leave them. I'd rather die trying to save them than walk away.

His grip on my hands slid to my wrist, and he shackled me in place with tight fingers. "Every member of Fernglove wears the mark. It's customary. Plus, at least in your case, it will act as a warning."

I bristled at that. "I hardly need the warning."

Orin blinked, genuine shock tugging at his brows. "Not for you. Gods, no. It's a warning to our neighboring Ever families. While we've established a tenuous peace, I wouldn't want them getting any ideas that you're available to work for them."

"I suppose branding me like cattle is one way to get the message across." I scowled but didn't fight his hold. I could live with a tattoo if it meant saving my brothers.

"It's for your safety. Not to mark you as property," Orin said as he gently thumbed my wrist. His gaze fell to the floor. "While I understand your hesitation, I still must insist."

"Is it permanent?"

"Yes."

With ease, he twisted my wrist to expose the pale skin of my inner arm. He dragged smooth fingers from the crook of my elbow down to my upturned palm. They danced across the lines of my future, and I wondered if he could see this moment etched in fate. After a breath, he moved his hand back to my inner arm and placed it against my skin.

"Are you ready?" he asked, voice low.

"I'm not entirely sure I have another choice."

His smile was timid. Soft. "I wouldn't do it if it weren't necessary."

I hesitated for a breath. We'd known each other for only a handful of days. And yet, he'd saved my brothers. He could have just walked away. But he didn't. He didn't even balk when I asked to bring Noam and Nohr with me to Fernglove. Orin had listened to my concerns and complied. I could do the same, at least just this once.

"Do it." I speared my bottom lip with my teeth, preparing for pain, and was instantly rewarded. Heat exploded from his touch, singeing my arm and imbuing the air with the scent of burning flesh. My body tensed as I pressed my eyes shut, and then all at once it was over. His hand was gone, the cool rush of air jolting against my raw skin. Slowly, I opened my eyes and looked down at my arm.

And there it was. The Fernglove tattoo. A broken sword detailed in an array of grays and blacks, framed by a horde of vibrant, colorful insects. It was horrifying. It was beautiful. It was a brand I could never escape. But considering my time on this earth was perhaps more limited than that of the Evers in this manor, I would wear it without complaint. Death didn't care about families or crests—it came for everyone just the same.

"Not so bad, is it?" Orin gently trailed one finger over the mark, and the last remnants of pain faded away.

I stared at the fresh ink, trying and failing to ignore the different, subtler heat brewing from his touch. "It's not absolutely horrid to look at."

Slowly, methodically, as if he were aware of every heightened nerve ending in my body, he raised my arm toward his lips, then brushed the gentlest of kisses against the blade. A trill of excitement raced through my limbs, and he smiled against my skin.

"There," he whispered. "The final touch."

"What do you mean?" Everything in me screamed to rip my hand away, to free myself of his strangely alluring grasp, but I couldn't. A prickle of magic settled like a fine layer of chiffon against my skin, and he looked up to meet my gaze.

"You now hold a sliver of my magic." His pupils seemed impossibly large as he moistened his lips. I didn't know what to make of *that* look. "I trust Vora mentioned how this manor works?" He flippantly waved to the chandelier above, and the lights flickered to life of their own accord. Or, perhaps, his.

I barely found the word to answer. "Yes."

"You cannot wield our power, but there's a trace of it in this mark. If you wish for light, it will come. Water for your bath, it will appear. Of course, you'll still have our attendants at your disposal, but I find, sometimes, privacy is needed."

I forced a hard swallow. "How thoughtful of you."

"I am a generous host." He smiled, his touch tender against the brand on my arm. Finally, he straightened, and the peculiar hold he had over me lessened. Largely because I found it hard to believe any Ever was *generous*, especially not a family that owned two mines yet likely never set foot in either. Images of my brothers' soot-covered faces filled my mind.

"If that were the case, I imagine the people of Willowfell would fare better. Especially the miners who make it so easy for you to maintain this lifestyle."

Orin looked puzzled. "The townsfolk . . . Is there not enough work? Or are they not receiving fare wages? I'll confess, most of my conversations are only with the elders, and they've never let on that anything is amiss."

"Well, that's not surprising. All they care about are their gilded carriages and lavish homes. They may as well be Evers." The jab left my lips before I could stop myself, and I stilled.

Orin, however, didn't seem to mind my insult. Instead, his gaze turned sad. "I take it the coin from the mines isn't being funneled appropriately. I'll speak to the town leaders and adjust our cut if necessary."

I didn't have the fortitude to school my shock. My mouth fell open, and it took me several tries to find the words to respond. "Just like that? But why?"

"Contrary to your very obvious opinion, not all Evers are

monsters." He released my arm to clasp his hands together. "We have funds to spare."

Of course they did. "Is that why you offer such large rewards when someone manages to find an everjewel? What are they to you?"

At that, Orin tensed. He looked away to some indiscriminate spot on the wall, as if recalling a lost memory. "Everjewels, while useless to humans, are special to my kind. They help keep us, well, us. But that's neither here nor there. Regardless, I'll hold true to my word and evaluate what's happening to the mines' profits."

That was news to me. We'd never been granted any explanation as to why the Evers paid such pretty sums for everjewels. Before I could pry further, Orin stood and extended his hand.

"Now, I do have a prior engagement commencing here shortly, but I have enough time to give you a small tour. If you're so inclined."

Considering I was liable to get lost in an estate this size, I couldn't exactly turn down his offer. Plus, I didn't entirely loathe the idea of spending a few more moments with him. Not after what he promised to do for my town. "Thank you."

"I hope you'll find it in you to trust me. I know you had no intentions of coming here, but perhaps fate intervened."

Slowly, I placed my hand in his. "Indeed."

"I, for one, am looking forward to our time together." His voice was low and pleasing, and that indignant spark lit in my chest again.

"Researching blight, of course."

Mischief filled his green eyes. "Of course."

As we left his study, I couldn't help but feel like I'd left a small part of myself behind. My inner wrist throbbed as we moved from room to room, his explanations of the spaces barely audible through the ringing in my ears. Orin was entirely too convincing. The old Edira would've yanked her hand away and rolled her eyes at his niceties. He was an *Ever*. The same Ever who'd come for Rowena.

The same Ever who'd called her a *dear friend*.

My chest tightened as we walked. His face was open, his smile wide. Everything about him was inviting. Had my aunt's own reservations softened in his presence? I couldn't say for sure, but I wanted to find out. Because when he looked at me, I saw nothing but boyish charm and hope. Hope that I would be the one to finish the work my aunt dedicated herself to. And while I knew hope was a dangerous thing, especially when it came to blight, I couldn't help the timid smile that toyed with my lips as he led me through his home.

# SEVEN

fter guiding me through the impossible labyrinth of rooms—
including a library, where we were to meet tomorrow to begin
our work—Orin brought us to a halt in the foyer. Again, I was
struck by the lack of aroma from the blooming hyacinths. Were
they fake? I inched closer to one and gently grazed the velvety
petals. The texture felt real, and there was a natural give and spring
to the leaves like any healthy plant, but still, no fragrance. When
I brought my fingers to the tip of my nose, all I got was a faint
whisper of mildew.

"Beautiful, aren't they?" Orin sidled up beside me and smiled.
"We change them out with the season."

"Their scent is off." I nodded at the overflowing display.

His brows inched together as he rubbed the back of his neck.
"Perhaps they've gone bad. I'll have an attendant check on that."

*Bad?* I glanced again at the bright petals, unable to find even a
dark spot or rotted leaf. I was about to say as much when a woman
breezed through the front doors without bothering to knock. Her
glossy hair fluttered behind her like a curtain, and the *color.* It was

stunning, like the depths of an ocean with varying hints of navy
and ultramarine that caught in the light. Her jeweled ruby-red
eyes quickly scanned the space until her gaze snagged on Orin.
A devilish smirk claimed her lips. Swirling, flowing ink wrapped
both of her biceps like churning currents, and her fingers dawdled
along the darkened cobalt lines as she crossed her arms. A young
woman and a boy accompanied her, and they sauntered into the
space with the same authority and haughty grins.

"Ossanna," Orin said, straightening to his full height. "You're
early."

"I didn't think that would be a problem." Her cunning gaze
slid straight to me. "Plus, I'd heard a rumor you managed to find
another threadmender. I wanted to see for myself."

"Word travels fast." He blew out his breath.

"It absolutely does." Ossanna slid a hand to her waist before
tilting her head toward the young woman on her left. "That aside,
Issa has been looking forward to today for quite some time. I could
hardly contain her."

Issa couldn't have been more than a few years my junior. Her
reddish-pink eyes—like blood paled by milk—and blue-black hair
stood out against her fair skin, but not as hauntingly as the stark
tattoo of angry currents wrapping around her throat. She dragged
her clawlike nails against her painted lips, smiling as she studied
Orin. The belt lazily draped about her hips quivered.

No. Not a belt. A tail.

It unraveled and twitched behind her as if she were a feline
preparing to snare a mouse. Her cunning stare drifted to me, and
she slowly assessed me from head to toe before letting out a quiet
chuckle. I narrowed my eyes, ignoring the swell of fear climbing
up my throat.

"Will your threadmender be joining us for refreshments?" Issa
asked.

"Edira. My name is Edira." The words were out of my mouth

before I could stop them, and all eyes rounded on me. An indignant heat simmered in my veins. "I may be employed by the Ferngloves, but I am not *his*."

Issa's smile was sharper than a blade. "Oh, I know."

"Edira, these are the Waterstones. Like us, they're Evers."

Obviously. I'd never seen a human with a tail. I shot Orin a glance. His expression was unreadable, save the tiniest of lip curls that felt wholly directed at me. He shifted subtly, inching closer to me without drawing more of the Waterstones' attention. It didn't seem like my words had offended Orin, but even if they had . . . The fear that had me carefully examining my etiquette during last night's dinner had evaporated the moment he'd branded me with his crest. I'd technically been claimed by the Ferngloves, but that didn't mean I liked being objectified as if I were a possession. At least Orin seemed to agree.

The young Waterstone boy pushed his way between the two women to frown at me. He shared the same hair and ruby-red eyes as Ossanna, and there were swirling tattoos around each one of his fingers. Twin horns, small and rounded as if they'd only just begun to grow, jutted from his forehead beneath his hairline.

"She seems like fun." His saccharine smile accentuated his harsh, impish characteristics, and I was reminded of the feral way Amalyss and Tasia had inspected me in the carriage. These Evers were impulsive. Brash. Did they all succumb to such wild, unpredictable whims simply to satisfy their own curiosity? For a moment of pleasure? Or maybe it was a side effect of their magic, of embracing more animalistic features and strengths.

"She seems boring," Issa remarked.

"Issa, Flix, that's enough," Ossanna said, though there was no forcefulness to her voice. Her focus returned to Orin. "Shall we?"

Orin plastered on a smile. "Of course. Amalyss? Tasia?" He pointed two fingers over his shoulder without turning away from the Waterstones. I jerked my eyes toward the winding staircase where Amalyss and Tasia stood completely immobile, their rapt gazes trained on us. I hadn't heard them approach, and yet Orin somehow knew they'd been there without even surveying the room.

"Yes?" Amalyss answered.

"Rorik is expecting Edira. See that she finds him."

"Of course," Tasia said. They descended the stairs with languid ease, pausing only to wait for me to join them by the front doors.

I blinked. "Rorik? Why?"

"I've asked him to help train you." Orin's features softened when he looked at me, and then he tipped his chin in a slight bow. "I apologize. I had planned on escorting you myself, but I do have some matters to attend to with the Waterstones."

"It's all right. Thank you for the tour." I allowed myself one furtive glance over my shoulder as I followed Amalyss and Tasia out. Orin's composure was perfect, a masterpiece of quiet joy and welcoming warmth as he amicably spoke with Ossanna. I quickly fell into stride beside Amalyss and Tasia without uttering a word.

They led me through an open courtyard as they chatted between themselves and traded gossip about Issa and Flix. I could only bring myself to pick up pieces of their conversation. My mind was still processing the fresh branding on my arm and everything I'd just witnessed with Orin.

We passed by the formal gardens, where neatly trimmed hedges surrounded ornate statues carved out of marble. There was even a small pond with a towering fountain sprouting from the middle of the blue-green depths. Lily pads floated lazily across the rippling surface, and fish with a kaleidoscope of colors drifted beneath the surface. I couldn't help but gape at the beauty of it all, at the azaleas rimming the pond and the artful walkways.

*If only Noam and Nohr could see this.* Curing their blight was an impossible task under normal circumstances. And there was the issue of Mavis, too. I chewed on the inside of my lip, and the sharp tang of blood squirted over my tongue. I winced. The thing was, even if I managed to cure *one* being of blight, I'd have to suffer through the aftermath of it. In that respect, it wasn't any different from mending a broken leg or curing a common cold. I would experience the side effects—to a lesser degree—of whatever ailment I mended, blight included, until my own threads severed. Each act ate away at my lifespan, and I wasn't sure I had enough years to save Mavis *and* my brothers.

And I knew whom I'd be expected to save first.

"You look pale," Amalyss said, tearing me away from my reverie. "Are we that scary?"

I almost reminded her that she and her sister had attacked me the first time we met. "No. It's just a lot to process."

"The Waterstones are nothing to worry about." Tasia scowled. "They come, they posture, they leave. Orin always handles them."

"The Starglens, too," Amalyss mused. She pointed to some indistinct spot on the horizon, as if I somehow possessed the kind of magic necessary to see what she was indicating. "They're our closest neighbors. Orin teaches their son, Briar, alongside Flix."

"And you two?" I asked.

Tasia shrugged her shoulders. "We attend sometimes, depending on the subject matter. We've been at it longer than Flix and Briar."

"What sort of things do you learn about?" While I knew I was here to study and eradicate blight, I couldn't deny the flicker of curiosity that flared to life in me. Evers had been around for centuries, even predating our town. I could only imagine the wealth of knowledge they possessed. And how unnerving it must've been for them to not understand how to cure a sickness that had the strength to take down immortals.

"Lots of stuff." Amalyss tipped her head thoughtfully. "Ever history, the different variants of magic, our ancient tongue—all stuff that's far beyond your comprehension."

"Typical," I muttered. "Where is Rorik?"

"Where he always is," Tasia drawled.

"What does he intend to do with me?"

"You ask a lot of questions." Amalyss ran a hand through her locks. "But I suppose we can't expect you to have the same deductive reasoning as the rest of us."

Anger flickered to life in my core, and I met her stare head-on, only to find they were both watching me with vicious curls to their lips. Waiting. Goading. A bigger person probably would've held their tongue. I had no such inclination.

"I wonder, is that haughty superiority an Ever trait? Or is it because you have sticks shoved up your asses and I can't see them through all that ridiculous glamour?"

They both stumbled, and their mouths fell open for a breath. Then their gazes sharpened as some of their glamour fell away to reveal the iridescent feathers shimmering along their cheekbones.

Tasia smiled, but her words were sharp. "Threadmenders can't heal themselves, right?"

A warning bell crashed in my ears, but I kept my gaze locked on the horizon. "Is that a threat?"

"That's for you to decide." Amalyss chuckled darkly before falling silent, leaving me with nothing other than their hungry gazes and my swirling thoughts. Their glamour returned to normal as we moved out of the gardens and onto the sprawling, manicured lawns. Wildflowers pushed through the soft dirt to add vibrant pops of orange, magenta, and indigo to the sea of verdant green. A lazy breeze ruffled the grounds. Beautiful, and yet quiet, save for the muted, inconsistent chirps of insects. We were heading for the tree line, and a single dirt path marked by moss-covered stones caught my attention. It wound into the depths of the forest before disappearing entirely in shadow.

*Run.* I could flee, but that would break my vow with Orin.

And I'd never run without my brothers, which meant I'd some-how have to sneak two floating caskets out of Fernglove unseen.

And then there was the obvious issue of the caskets them-selves.

*Work with me.* Orin's words rattled through my brain, and a heavy weight pulled at my wrists, my feet. Invisible chains tethered me to the Ever lord of this estate. What, exactly, did he have to do to maintain the magic keeping my brothers alive? Did they have to remain nearby? If I took them, would their life-saving tombs simply disappear?

No, I couldn't run. I would stick with the plan. I would learn. And if—*when*—I found a way to cure blight, then I would hide the results and save my power for Noam and Nohr. Mavis had lived long enough.

A faint smile tugged at my lips. No one would use me or my magic for their own gain.

For now, I would use them.

"We're here," Amalyss said as she and her sister came to a halt. She pointed toward a single tree that stood slightly apart from the rest, and I stilled. Its trunk was knobby and uneven, its bark a riot-ous whorl of whites and browns and blacks, and it was far larger than any surrounding tree. But what pulled my focus most was the hundreds of delicate bone-white flowers blooming from the highest twigs.

"I've never seen a tree like that before," I murmured, gaze transfixed on the strange mix of colors streaking through the bark. I was still a short distance away, not close enough to inspect the bi-zarre bumps and awkward angles of the twisted trunk, but I could see Rorik standing beneath it, staring up at the flowers with his back to us.

Tasia and Amalyss were quiet. Somber, even. They closed their eyes for a moment as if offering up a silent prayer, but when they looked at me again all traces of sadness were wiped clean from their expressions. Dark curiosity flickered in their identical gazes, and Tasia reached forward to drag her fingers over my cheek. My chest tightened as a chill crept down my neck.

"I hope he doesn't rough you up too bad."

Amalyss giggled. "But if he does, all the more reason for us to doll you up."

I scoffed. "Don't you have better things to do?"

"Not in the slightest." Tasia's grin deepened.

Amalyss peeked over her sister's shoulder, then locked eyes on me. "Come play with us when you're done." There was a heat to her words I couldn't place, and a fresh, floral aroma that came and went with the breeze. I cut a glance at the wildflowers nearby, lazily dancing in the wind.

"Sure." I hardly planned on seeking them out, but I was fine with letting them think I would indulge their fantasy. Never mind that I layered the word with enough sarcasm to suffocate any hope blooming in their chests.

They turned on their heels, high-pitched, grating laughter bubbling around them. Unease prickled along my arms and down the length of my spine, but I steeled myself with a quick breath before closing the distance between Rorik and me. My slippered feet padded against the ground, announcing my arrival with soft thuds that seemed to echo through the air. Rorik tilted his head and his shoulders stiffened, but he didn't turn to greet me. Instead, he waited until I stood beside him.

"What do you think of it?"

I followed his gaze to the delicate flowers above. Smoky gray leaves cupped the gossamer petals, and I opened my mouth to comment on their beauty when my words caught in my throat. My eyes narrowed as I studied the oddly jointed twigs branching off from the tree's limbs. Twigs with strange, knobby knuckles and rings of wrinkles, like skin that had solidified into bark. Those delicate flowers seemed to bloom from nail beds, as if the splayed twigs were actually fingers sprouting from elongated hands.

I jerked my eyes back to the base of the trunk and the strange twisting of weathered browns and pale beiges. Bile flooded my tongue. Legs of varying shades knotted and intertwined to form a thick base with twisted knees and bare feet sprouting roots into the earth. There were no heads, just bodies pressed together, and so many legs and arms and hands that I could hardly differentiate between all the extremities.

Fear slammed into my gut, and I took an involuntary step back. Dead bodies. That's what I was staring at. A shrine of death. And with that recognition, magic surged from my core and flooded to my fingertips. It took every ounce of control I had to keep my power from surfacing.

*Something is very, very wrong.* I caught the faint scent of decay on the wind. These people were gone, their threads longs since turned to ash, but I could sense the remnants of their lives in the sickening aura pulsing from the tree. A heady ringing filled my ears, and I felt the world tip beneath my feet. I didn't know when Rorik had placed his hand on the small of my back. All I knew was that everything was numb, the world a winnowing tunnel of gray and black, and then as everything slowly reoriented, the warmth of his hand grounded me enough to calm the rest of my senses.

"These are the remains of our ancestors. We don't use headstones or graves. We bury our kin at the roots, and a part of them lives on like this." As soon as the words left his lips, he folded his arms across his chest. The sudden absence of his hand's weight left me oddly uncomfortable, but I pushed that away as I braved another look at the tree.

"When humans die, we simply return to the earth, not actually sprout out of it. I've never seen anything like this." The world settled with every breath, and my power slowly receded. They were already gone. There was nothing to mend. And yet that scent, that undeniable pull to cure *something* . . . I couldn't shake it.

"Yes, well, we're not human." Turning his back on the tree, he finally looked in my direction. His gaze was a slow, scrutinizing crawl starting from the tip of my head down to my toes. He rolled his eyes. "Next time we meet, make sure you're properly dressed."

His condescending words were enough to chase away the last eerie chill still teasing my senses, and I scowled. "I'm sorry my attire doesn't suit your fancy. You'll be pleased to know I had absolutely no choice in the matter."

"As fascinating as that useless bit of information is, it still doesn't change the fact that I cannot help you train in a gown."

"If you think I can't stab you while wearing skirts, you're sorely mistaken." The words were out of my mouth before I could stop myself. Clenching my jaw tight, I swallowed the rest of whatever brewing retort lingered on my tongue. I was supposed to be learning something useful from this Ever, and here I was biting back before we'd even begun our first lesson.

Mischief filled his eyes. As he took a step closer, his lips tipped into a devilish grin. "You have a knife hidden in your petticoat?"

The heat racing through my veins shifted from indignant anger to something far more sinister. Something like desire. I hated it. "No."

"Pity." His nose was only an inch from mine, his breath a cool whisper against my skin. And then he stepped back with a barking laugh, breaking whatever hold he'd had over me, and flopped to the ground. Legs sprawled out before him, he leaned back on his elbows and looked up at me. "Sit. We'll work on breathing, then."

"I can breathe just fine." Still, I sat.

"We'll see about that."

For the first several minutes, Rorik simply watched me as we sat in silence. His heady gaze was locked on the rise and fall of my chest, and while I rationally understood he was not, in fact, staring at my breasts, I couldn't help the heat that clambered up my neck at the thought.

Which resulted in more erratic breathing. I shifted uncomfortably, chewing on the inside of my cheek.

He raised his brow, and his twin dermal piercings caught in the light. "You're fidgeting. A lot."

"You're staring right at my chest. What do you expect?" I shot back.

Heat flared in his eyes. "So I'm making you uncomfortable?"

"Don't take it as a compliment," I said as I folded my arms across my breasts. "Anyone would react this way."

"I'll take it however I want. It's delightful to know that I make you squirm."

"You'll just say anything that comes to mind, won't you?" I scowled at him and ignored the strange heat that bloomed to life at his words.

His gaze traveled to my face, a deep smirk already in place, and he chuckled darkly. Then he nodded at my arms. "Relax. I can't help you if I don't know what I'm working with. This is purely for knowledge's sake, though if you're interested in something more, we can discuss that later."

"Just be quiet," I growled, but I let my hands fall to my sides.

Rorik continued to recline on his arms, his partially unbuttoned shirt pulled tight across his torso to reveal a tantalizing sliver of skin. After a few more painful moments of his gaze locked on my chest, he sucked on his teeth in disappointment. "It's honestly a miracle you've survived this long." He stood and walked around me in a circle. Slowly.

"Perhaps I'd fare better at this ridiculous exercise if you'd actually tell me what you wanted." Rorik was dangerous, that much was obvious. It wasn't even the lean cut of his body, honed like a fine blade and ready for wielding; it was his words. His sinister tongue. The gleam in his eyes. And yet, maybe it was the Fernglove crest on my arm or the fact that I was here to help his family, but I wasn't afraid of Rorik. I was just irritated.

"Oh, I didn't mean you specifically. I meant all humans." Crouching next to me, he put one hand on the small of my back and the other on my sternum. I nearly shot to my feet, jolting beneath his touch, but his grip was firm. "So flighty."

"A little warning wouldn't have killed you," I seethed.

"It wouldn't have been nearly as fun." He chuckled, then coaxed my back to straighten. "You sit like an aged crone. Lengthen your spine. Relax your shoulders. Breathe through your stomach."

"What is the purpose of all this?" My heart thrummed rapidly, and I had the sickening feeling he could feel every unruly beat against his palm.

He let his hands fall away and stood, resuming his slow, circular path around me. "The power you have makes you weak. It drains you of life each time you mend."

"I'm aware," I muttered.

"Because breathing is instinctual," he continued without acknowledging my comment, "most never pay it a second thought. But if you can optimize your breathing, you can funnel more power to your magic and better harness your innate abilities."

"Do all Evers do this?"

He tsked. "We hardly need to."

"Of course, because why would you?" I tempered my irritation with a deep exhale that broke the rhythm I'd established. Rorik moved before I could inhale. One moment he was lazily circling me—like a predator so far above the prey he had his sights on that he needn't bother with stealth—and the next he'd crouched before me. With one swift movement, he jammed two fingers into the center of my stomach.

My ribs collapsed as what little air was left in my chest escaped in a rush. I keeled to the side and wrapped my arms around my abdomen, begging my lungs to inflate as a stinging pain spiderwebbed across my torso. Tears prickled against my eyes until, finally, my body shuddered and my gasps were rewarded with air.

"What the fuck?" My words were weak but sharp. Rorik didn't seem to care. The only movement he'd made was to drape his hands over his knees. He regarded me with a single brow raised and a sly twist to his lips.

"You need to work on your lung capacity. Physical training will help with that." He stood abruptly and cradled the back of his head with his hands. "There are a few ways we can achieve that. Running, combat training, or maybe you prefer exercise within the confines of a bedroom?"

My teeth gnashed together as I went toe to toe with him. Whatever minimal control over my emotions I had left fled with the breath he'd stolen from me, and I was filled to the brim with the fervent wish to smack him across the face.

"I would never sleep with you."

"Even if it paved the way for greater power?" He leaned closer, his words a whisper against my skin.

"*Never.*"

Something flashed in his eyes, and his devilish grin faltered for a second before he schooled his lips back into place. "Don't worry. The feeling is entirely mutual."

"You're absolutely vile."

"I know." His canines somehow sharpened, and my breath caught in my throat. Then he gently pressed his fingers against the same soft spot of my stomach. My body tensed in anticipation, expecting the harsh repercussion for once again demonstrating an irregular breathing pattern. But instead of a sharp jab, he applied gentle pressure. It was reminder enough, and once I'd gotten a grip on my wild breath, he pulled his hand away. "What a nuisance. I can hardly follow you around all day reminding you to breathe."

He inclined his head toward the leaves of the tree and let out a quiet, low whistle. At first I thought it was merely another expression of his disappointment, but then a faint movement caught my eye. A palm-sized, mothlike creature with pink and yellow fuzz fluttered down from the branches to land on Rorik's shoulder. It was unlike any insect I'd ever seen, with glassy blue eyes and spiral horns just above its antennae. Rorik bent to the ground to snag a blade of grass, and he held it before the moth. It willingly accepted his offering with a soft chittering.

"This is Ywena." Rorik didn't look at me. His attention was solely focused on the creature resting on his shoulder, and for the first time since meeting him, I saw a glimmer of something gentler. The ceaseless mischief in his expression was absent, the curl to his lips softer, more relaxed. The creases near his eyes were ones of joy, not scorn or frustration or anger.

"A moth?" I inched closer.

He snorted, and Ywena fluttered her wings. "She is as different from moths as Evers are from humans, but I suppose they look similar. She'll be your companion for the time being."

At that, Ywena took flight and erratically circled the crown of my head before perching against the crook of my neck. Her touch was silk against my skin, and if not for her size, I might have passed off her delicate grip as a lock of hair teasing my collarbone.

"Why?"

"She'll help you with your breathing." Rorik's gaze remained on her, that same warm expression still fully intact. If he dared to look at another being that way, Ever or human, I had no doubt they'd give in to his every whim. My pulse climbed higher at the weight of his gaze, on me but not *on* me, and my breath quickened.

And then a tiny shock jolted through me, and I yipped. It was gone as quickly as it'd appeared, stemming from the space Ywena had claimed and racing through to my fingertips. My eyes widened at Rorik's chuckle.

"Did she just shock me?" I asked.

This time, he met my gaze. No warmth. Just mischief and hunger. "Yes. She can detect even the smallest fluctuations in your heartbeat, your breathing, your emotions. So long as she's touching you, of course. And until I deem you skilled enough to breathe on your own, she'll be with you at all times. Understood?"

I tilted my chin downward, catching a glimpse of the picturesque creature now studying me with inquisitive eyes. "What if I crush her on accident? I don't want to hurt her."

For a long moment, Rorik simply stared at me. Again, he seemed to falter, caught somewhere between human and Ever, genuine and harsh, but he steadied himself with a firm shake of his head and displeased scoff. "Your concern is unnecessary. She's capable of protecting herself, and even if by accident you clipped her—which you won't—she's tougher than you could possibly fathom.

"But"—Rorik's expression turned dark, his gaze full of threat and promise—"if you intentionally harm her, I will ensure you experience the same level of pain. If not more."

I didn't know how I kept breathing, how Ywena didn't send an electric volt shooting through my limbs. I wanted to crumple under the weight of his malice, but I knew in my core I'd never do anything to deliberately hurt her.

"I'll keep her safe. I promise."

He watched my lips move, as if studying the words as they left my mouth to see if they rang true, and then shifted back to his normal, flippant self. With an indolent wave over his shoulder, he turned his back on me and strolled toward the manor. "Tomorrow, wear pants."

He never once checked to see if I'd follow. And at first, I didn't. The sudden release of tension hit me in a rush, and I exhaled so forcefully that Ywena had no choice but to send a tiny shock wave through my body. Which, of course, only set my breathing stampeding off in the opposite direction, and thus resulted in a series of back-and-forth shocks from my new moth companion until I finally composed myself. Only when I was certain I could keep both my emotions and breath at bay did I dare to make my way toward the manor. I wasn't sure what the evening would hold, but I was already bracing for a night full of *reminders* from Ywena.

## EIGHT

The tingling started the moment I walked through the doors to the manor. At first it was more like a prickle of awareness thrumming beneath my fingertips. I passed it off as Ywena's power swelling to a head, preparing to discharge if my breathing slipped. But as I spent the next few hours sequestered in my brothers' quarters, sitting at the foot of their bed and telling them about my day as if they could actually hear me, the sensation shifted to a nagging discomfort. It trickled down my neck, across my arms, to the small of my back. It was an incessant itch I couldn't scratch, and by the time I made my way down to dinner—where the Ferngloves were already seated and waiting—I was fit to claw my skin off.

"Edira," Orin said, pulling my focus from my untouched plate of food, "is something not to your liking? We can arrange for a different meal." The silent attendant was at his side before I could answer, her gaze locked on me and awaiting direction.

"Oh no, it's fine." I managed a meager bite of roasted meat before resting my fork against the platter. "I'm just exhausted."

Orin tracked my movements with cautious eyes. "Are you sure?"

"Yes." I dropped my hands to my thighs, fisting the fabric of my gown to keep my fingers from digging at my raw skin. Admitting something was wrong in front of the entire family felt like a trap. I could already hear Seville's scoff and feel the weight of Lydia's incredulous glare if I even hinted at weakness. But maybe . . . I chanced a quick look at Orin. He was still staring at me, his brows inching slowly together. If I discussed what I was experiencing with him alone, it might be all right. At the very least, he wanted me to be healthy. Safe.

"You pushed her too hard, Rorik," Seville drawled, then took a long sip from her goblet. "And what is with that ghastly creature tucked in her hair?"

Rorik twirled his knife between his forefinger and thumb. "It's necessary for her training."

"So long as it's not draining her needlessly," Orin said, his voice a hard warning. "You're to help strengthen her body so she can better withstand any possible side effects associated with mending blight. Nothing else."

Rorik didn't meet his gaze. "Tell me again what I already know."

"Rorik . . ." Orin's eyes flared with anger. "Don't harm her."

"Wouldn't dream of it," Rorik mused.

I highly doubted that. Perhaps this agonizing, ratcheting discomfort was a by-product of Ywena's power. She'd shocked me several times throughout the evening already. Maybe my body *was* simply exhausted. Or maybe it had nothing to do with Ywena's magic and everything to do with the Ever sitting before me. Had Rorik triggered some sort of reaction with his training? My hand fluttered to my stomach, to the space where he'd rammed his fingers and robbed me of breath. He could have enchanted me. I should have bound him with a vow before ever agreeing to his lessons.

"What exactly did your training entail?" Tasia leaned her elbows on the table. Her eyes lit with a strange eagerness, and her grin stretched wide as she watched me closely.

"Maybe it shouldn't have been . . . private." Amalyss licked her lips. Her stare bored into me with an intensity that caused the invisible prickling to shift to full-blown wildfire, and I abruptly stood up. Ywena didn't hesitate to shock me, but it barely registered against the raging heat flushing through my limbs.

Rorik let out a dark laugh, but there was an unmistakable tension lacing his voice. "Clearly by her reaction, any *private* training was out of the question."

Orin's hands turned to fists as he glared at his brother. Rorik sighed and raised his palms in mock apology.

"I didn't touch her beyond what was necessary, and certainly not in the way Amalyss is insinuating."

Orin considered Rorik's words for a moment before shifting his focus to me. All traces of anger were gone, replaced by a quiet concern that filled his eyes. "Did something happen?"

"No, nothing like that," I managed after a breath. "Sorry. May I be excused?"

"She's just adjusting to her new surroundings. Let her go." It was the first time Lydia had spoken about me, let alone to me. She sat quietly beside her daughters, and there was a similar, piercing intrigue to her stare as she regarded me with a wry smile. Clesian was silent, but he'd placed a thick hand over Lydia's.

"Of course." Orin continued to watch me. "Good night, Edira."

I barely dipped my head in a bow before bolting out of the room. With every step, the burn intensified. I rushed into my quarters and immediately drew a bath, hoping the water would chase away whatever strange ailment afflicted me. I filled it with salts from my apothecary cases and a tincture I'd crafted to aid with rashes. I doubted I'd had an allergic reaction to anything on

the grounds, but there were strange flora and fauna I knew nothing about. Maybe pollen from the white flowers of the Ever tree
had caused an adverse effect on my skin. After shucking off my
dress, I pulled my hair up in a loose knot and eased into the basin.
Ywena took flight until I settled, and then she nested in my hair
and resumed her practiced observance of my breath.

The caress of the water did nothing to abate the itch. As I gritted my teeth and willed the bath to do something—anything—the
agonizing burn shifted to a deeper pang that hammered through
my muscles. A wordless moan slipped from my lips at the same
time Ywena shocked me, and I flinched. Restlessness filled my
limbs, and I was out of the tub almost as quickly as I'd gotten in.
I dressed in loose clothing and paced in tight circles at the foot of
my bed. Orin would be finished with dinner soon. I'd go to him
the moment the house was quiet.

With a wordless huff, I moved to one of the windows and
pushed it open, welcoming the crisp breeze against my fiery skin.
Creeping shadows inched across the lawns from the surrounding
forest, and an owl made itself known with a single hoot as the
bloated moon eased into the night sky. In the distance, I spotted the Ever tree and its unruly, knobby limbs. The bone-colored
flowers shivered in the faint wind. Were the bodies sentient?
Could the limbs feel the presence of the world around them? Did
they shudder with the dropping temperature and encroaching
darkness?

Again, a low, unbearable sense of wrong threaded through the
night air, and my power threatened to come surging to the surface. But as I squinted harder at that tree—a harbinger for death,
really, not a monument—the stinging arcing through my limbs
sharpened, and I winced.

If it were possible for me to threadmend myself, I'd do it. I was
getting worse by the minute. An anchor had settled deep in my

core, and the attached chain was pulled taut through my limbs, as if it were tethered to some point beyond my grasp. I just needed to loosen the tension even a fraction.

An invisible, forceful tug rippled through me, and I straightened. Something pulled at my center, at that anchor in my pit, and I pivoted toward the bedroom doors. The moment I took a step, the pain dulled. I blinked, relishing the subsiding burn, as I considered the peculiar sensation. But I didn't move, and every second that ticked away brought back the burn until I once again stepped toward the door.

*I'm being summoned.* The thought hit me with such force, such recognition, that I knew it had to be true. I frowned. But why? If someone wanted to see me, why not simply knock on my door? Maybe they wanted something but didn't want to draw attention to their request. But who? I raked through my mind, recounting the day's events and trying in vain to figure out who needed me— and how they'd managed to ensnare me with this magical trap. I took another step and then stalled, my body trembling as I fought against the resurgence of symptoms. Even if I didn't *want* to go, I'd have to. Unease wound through my gut as I left my room in the direction of the insistent tug. Orin had promised I was safe. Hadn't he?

An invisible stare wormed its way between my shoulder blades as I walked, and I didn't know if it was my summoner or someone else within the halls. I whirled on my heel, but all I saw was a slip of something white, like a loose linen or sheet, fleeing around the corner.

I stared at the now empty space, trying in vain to push away the needling unease working through my gut. The flash of movement . . . My mind was playing tricks on me. I'd fought this summons for too long, and now the magic was toying with my vision. And yet, my throat tightened as I scoured the quiet hall. I believed in ghosts. Deeply. How could I not when I was one of the few who could see life's threads? Feel the leftovers of their presence when people did die? Nohr used to laugh at me for my staunch belief in the afterlife, often demanding proof and waving off whatever "feeling" I described. True, I'd never actually seen an apparition, but in an estate as old as this . . .

An angry tug stemmed from my gut, and I took an involuntary step forward. I couldn't focus on anything with this compulsion driving my movements. Ghost or not, I'd never know for sure unless I rid myself of this more pressing magic. Then maybe I could sleuth.

*As if you have an abundance of free time to go ghost hunting*, I scoffed at myself as I once again began to move down the hall.

The farther I went, the more restless Ywena became. She fluttered from the crown of my head to the crook of my neck, and her soft chitters were urgent. She'd hardly made a sound since becoming my companion, yet I knew that if I turned back the pain would resume. My only option was to play by the unfair rules set by these Evers.

When my feet carried me to a set of double doors across the manor, relief washed over me with the warmth of a summer rain. The pain was gone in an instant, and while my body sagged, my mind sharpened as I knocked gently against the wood.

"It's Edira," I said. "You called?"

The doors swung inward in a rush, and I stilled at the sight of Tasia. Warning bells crashed in my ears as I stared at her. My mind rioted at the idea of setting foot in her room, but my body wouldn't respond. No matter how much I begged my muscles to act, to sprint down the hall in the opposite direction and lock myself away in my quarters, my feet refused to budge.

Tasia smiled up at me. "Took you long enough. Come in."

This time, my body moved without question. I stepped over the threshold, and she closed the doors behind me. Two beds were pushed against opposite walls, and the center of the room was dominated by a massive marble hearth. Amalyss was lounging on a fur rug, her fingers lazily flipping through a book. She glanced up at me, backlit by a dying fire, and grinned.

"It's my fault," she said. "I wasn't specific enough." She closed her book and sat up, patting the space beside her. "Sit."

The pull in my core was immediate, and I was sitting beside her before I had time to even process her command. Unease prickled along my neck. Or maybe that was Ywena's restless legs tapping against my throat. Tasia joined us, and both she and Amalyss looked at me with rapt eyes.

"Specific?" I asked.

"We told you to come play when you were done, didn't we?" Tasia inched closer.

*Come play?* They'd requested I entertain them, and . . . Anxiety wormed through my gut. I'd said, *Sure*. Sarcastically. Sardonically. As if I would ever dream of agreeing to *this*. And yet here I was, sequestered in their room, and no one else in Fernglove was the wiser. My breathing hitched. Ywena was there with a shock, but it wasn't as startling as before. She was moving along my neck until she got a firm grip on my hair and began crawling toward the crown of my head. Then she took flight. Amalyss and Tasia watched with a mixture of curiosity and apprehension as Ywena fluttered toward the rafters . . .

. . . and then escaped through the open window.

It seemed even Ywena had no desire to test her luck with these two.

Tasia grimaced at her departure before shooting Amalyss a knowing look. It reminded me of those glances shared between Noam and Nohr, as if they were having a private conversation they didn't want me to hear.

"Seems our playtime will be limited," Tasia mused, her gaze still locked on the open window.

"Playtime?" My tongue soured. "What am I doing here?"

Amalyss gazed at my Fernglove tattoo. "You're here because we told you to come, and you agreed."

"Does sarcasm mean nothing to you?" I spat. "I did not agree to this."

"Oh, but you did." Tasia chuckled. "Magic doesn't care about intention—just the word itself."

"How do you think Orin will react when he finds out you've tricked me?" I glowered.

"He'll likely disapprove of all this," Tasia purred as she half-heartedly gestured between us, "but what have we *really* done? Nothing. You just proved exactly how inept you are, which helps no one."

Words formed and died on my tongue. All I could do was glare.

"Well, we haven't done anything yet." Amalyss's grin sharpened. "Though you are here to *play*, so . . ."

A glow lit in Tasia's eyes. "Show us your power."

Her words hit hard and fast, needling through my muscles with the swell of magic I had no hope of denying. I swallowed thickly as the itch brewed in my fingers. My body wanted to call on my power even though my mind did not. As I curled my hands into fists, my nails bit into my palms. None of this made sense.

"No. That's not a game."

"Maybe not to you." Tasia smirked as she moved closer. "Now, show us your power."

I tasted the magic in Tasia's words now, the fresh, floral scent coating my mouth. I'd smelled that unique, earthy aroma with Orin when he'd first bound me with his vow. With Amalyss on the lawns, I'd just passed it off as a common fragrance drifting through the grounds. I was a damn fool for missing it.

I exhaled forcefully and released my white-knuckled grip. "Why? What good does it do you? You must have seen thread-mender magic before."

"Certainly," Amalyss replied. "But we want to see it again."

I cut a hard glance at her before dragging my gaze back to Tasia. My fingers drilled into my thighs as they itched to begin working, to answer her command. Already the burn was settling into my bones, and I desperately wanted to rid myself of her control.

"Begin," she purred. The word was riddled with power that snapped against my skin. As much as I wanted to resist, I couldn't. Simply demonstrating my magic didn't exhaust my lifespan, though, so rather than risk incurring a more demanding order, I clenched my jaw tight and closed my eyes. My power surged forward the moment I called, rushing through to my fingertips and blossoming outward around my being in a shroud of ivory light.

When I peeled open my eyes and stared at Amalyss and Tasia, my lips parted and my breath caught in my chest. They had no life threads. None. I should have seen *something*. Anything. A cascade of twirling strands eagerly dancing about their frames, vibrant and full of color and life. Because they were alive. They were staring at me, eyes wide and mouths ajar, as they took in my power. They were the perfect pictures of awe and wonder. I narrowed my gaze. There was a softness to their features that hadn't been there before, as if something gossamer had been delicately layered over their bodies. Their hazel eyes were muted, their once-lustrous hair now somehow faded. My brow furrowed as I leaned toward them, and I swore I caught glimpses of small, silvery filaments weaving through their locks.

A sense of knowing settled quietly over me. Glamour. The magic was stitched into their bodies, preventing me from seeing what lay beneath. It was both incredible and horrifying, because while their impressive power granted unblemished appearances, it also masked the beauty of their life threads. Of their true, glimmering essences.

"Your glamour," I murmured, studying every inch of Amalyss in hopes of finding a crack in her magic. Nothing. "Has a thread-mender ever seen anyone here without a veil?"

"Mavis." Amalyss tipped her head to the side as she marveled at my moonlight-drenched fingertips. "But only when they attempted to cure her. You can imagine how that turned out."

"Why? What's the point?"

Amalyss smiled daggers. "Who wouldn't want to be flawless if they could? Once you've mastered glamour, it's as easy as breathing. We hardly even notice it anymore."

But I noticed it. The strange fabric of magic coating their bodies. What was odder was that in some places, it appeared to be disintegrating. Just small pools of thinness here and there across their arms, their legs, their chests. Maybe they weren't as practiced at holding it together as their elders.

Tasia looked at me head-on. "Your power is beautiful."

"Thank you." The sincerity of her words softened the lingering anger in my bones. The pale light covering my body dwindled, and I was about to fully cap my power when Tasia's hand darted out and gripped my arm. A glimmer of fear coursed through her eyes.

"Don't." Then she ducked her chin. "Not yet."

"Tasia," Amalyss whispered. She gently grazed her sister's shoulder. "It's all right."

"I just . . ." She scratched at her arm, at one of the thin points in her glamour. "I want to experience threadmending. I'm curious to know what it *feels* like." Tasia skewered her bottom lip with her teeth and dropped her eyes to the floor. Everything in me stilled. In that moment, Amalyss and Tasia didn't look like Evers. They looked human. Like Noam and Nohr, eyes full and glistening with unspoken emotion. The sight of them chilled me to my core.

*Be careful who you trust in this place.* Vora's words surfaced in my mind.

"What if"—she absently picked at her arm—"I cut myself earlier. You can't tell now because I've glamoured it, but I'd like you to mend it."

"Tasia," Amalyss hissed. Her eyes darted to the window where Ywena had fled.

Warning bells crashed in my head. The insistent pull from the girls' earlier demands had begun to fade, as if I were nearing the end of the bargain's power. If I could just *play* a little longer without actually healing, maybe I could persuade Tasia to change her mind. I'd only just begun training with Rorik to strengthen my body, and I hadn't even started with Orin. I was no better off than my days in Willowfell, and I didn't want to needlessly sacrifice threads before the real work began. While I knew curing a simple cut would likely shave only a few hours, perhaps a day, off my life, it wasn't a risk worth taking. Not when I might need all the days, hours, and minutes I had just to cure my brothers.

"Don't Evers heal on their own?" I asked.

"We do. Much faster than humans, too." Amalyss pointedly stared at her sister, though Tasia refused to look her way. "And we have medicine for things as small as cuts. Tasia, it isn't worth it."

"That's precisely why I want to see it, feel it. It's so miniscule, it should hardly cause any uproar," she retorted.

I fidgeted, trying to find a way around her resolve. "We should clear it with Orin first."

As I hoped, this gave Tasia pause. But only for the briefest moment before her expression shifted to one of hardened disgust and anger. Her lips curled as she practically spat her words. "I'm tired of following Orin's rules. They've gotten us nowhere."

"If I threadmend without his knowledge—"

"Do it. Now. And then we'll be done *playing*." Tasia's words stung with the tang of magic, and my body shuddered. My power practically crawled out my throat as I gripped the rug for purchase.

"I can't with your glamour," I wheezed. "I need to see the threads."

"Tasia, you *mustn't*." Amalyss's voice jumped an octave as she glanced between us. "If Orin finds out . . ."

Tasia ignored her completely. "I'll only remove the glamour on my forearm. That should be enough."

She trailed her fingers lightly over her inner arm, as if pinching an invisible scrap of fabric, and then cast her hand to the side to leave her arm exposed. My eyes dropped to the unfettered scrap of tawny skin and the shallow cut peeling apart. Between her command and the sight of the wound, my power fully came to a head—and with it, so did a few of Tasia's life threads. They snuck out of her gash and danced in the air, and I gasped at their splendor. I'd never glimpsed an Ever's energy before. Where humans' threads were a vibrant green, Tasia's were a startling aquamarine infused with glittering diamonds. They were nearly blinding to watch, but there was a darkened gray hue to one's base, right where it stemmed from the wound.

"Your glamour isn't completely gone," I said, peering closer.

"It's hard to isolate such a small patch," Tasia muttered, and I glanced up to see sweat had dampened her brow. But her gaze was resolute, and she thrust her arm forward. "Mend me. Now."

There was no sense in denying her. Pushing as much energy as I could to my fingers, I began the process of threadmending. Cupping my hands around the fraying strand in question, I began to douse it in magic so that I could grip it tightly and stitch it back together with my power.

I pinched one tattered end and reached for another when the pain started. Just a flicker of uncomfortable heat where the cut would've been on my own arm. But quickly that heat bloomed and flushed from my neck to my face. A tremble started in my hands, and I stared at the quivering thread skewered between my forefinger and thumb.

This was a cut. Nothing more. I should've experienced some minor discomfort, perhaps followed by a healing, prickling itch and a mild headache from expending my power. But this? My body tensed. I could barely think through the heat in my veins.

"How did you get this cut again?" I asked.

Her wide eyes bounced from my trembling hands to my dampened hairline. Amalyss had gone still, her mouth slightly parted, and her face paled before she yanked her sister away, taking Tasia's threads along with her. Adrenaline left me in a cool rush as gooseflesh rippled over my skin.

Fear shone in their eyes for several breaths, and their gazes traversed the length of my body over and over as if searching for answers. Some hint of weakness? Sickness?

"Why did you stop me?" I hadn't cured her, and yet I couldn't shake the underlying spread of pain that still trickled through my limbs.

A flicker of relief raced through Tasia's expression, and she sighed.

"Wasn't it obvious?" Amalyss shot her sister a glance. "Our Ever magic was too strong for you to handle. A cut shouldn't have affected you that much." She nodded curtly toward a lone bead of sweat sliding down my temple.

I studied every inch of their haughty expressions, but all traces of concern were wiped clean from their faces. Dread was a sink weight in my gut, and I stilled. "No previous threadmender has been able to cure *anything* for you?"

Amalyss flicked her hair over her shoulder and let out a smug tsk. "Well, Orin seemed to have such high expectations for you, so we thought you'd be different. Clearly, we were wrong."

Panic set my heart racing. Everything was a game to these Evers. Their intentions, the truth. Now I had to consider that Ever threads were that much harder to mend? I was rash to think the process would be the same as that for human threads. Ever magic tainted *everything*.

Pushing myself to my feet, I fisted my hands by my sides and took a step toward the door.

"We're done here," I spat. But just as I went to grasp the handle, the world shifted on its axis and I stumbled, barely catching myself on an end table laden with candles. Exhaustion from mending had settled deep into my muscles, and already my body was longing for bed. It didn't matter how much I wanted to find Orin and hang these pretentious shits out to dry for their actions. I'd have to wait.

Or maybe not.

The door swung inward, and I barely stepped out of the way before the handle clipped my arm. Which of course caused me to stumble over my feet and go tumbling toward the floorboards, only to have an arm quickly slide beneath my waist.

"Edira," Orin said, eyes stricken with concern. He quickly helped me stand as his gaze roved the length of my body. "Are you all right?"

"Amalyss. Tasia. What have we here?" Rorik leaned in the open doorway, his shoulder propped against the frame with Ywena fluttering about his head. Malice filled his words as he stared at the girls with a sardonic, tense smile, and the whole room went still. Both girls shifted their pleading stares to Orin.

"Orin, we didn't—"

"Please, you have to understand—"

"Silence." Orin never met their gazes, instead looking only at me. The quiet ire in his cold voice sent a chill racing down my back. "Rorik, deal with them and then send for Vora. Immediately."

"My pleasure." A dangerous glint flashed through his amber eyes. He didn't bother to look our way as Orin placed one hand on the small of my back and steered me out of the room. We didn't speak as we moved through the halls. I wanted to step out of his grip, but with the world swaying gently and my feet heavier than normal, I knew his sturdy touch was the only thing keeping me upright.

And the last thing I wanted was him scooping me off the floor. Again.

It wasn't until he reached for my door that I found my voice. "I can take it from here."

His shoulders rolled forward, but he didn't release the handle. "Please. I want to hear what happened from you—not them. I only know what Ywena shared with Rorik."

"Then you know enough." I tried to brush him off and force the door open myself, but a flare of dizziness had me freezing in place. At least I didn't fall.

"Edira." He ran a hand over his face, and when he let it fall away, all I saw was remorse in his eyes. "Please, I just want to make sure you're all right."

I didn't know if it was the weight of recent threadmending or the sadness in his deflated frame or some combination of both, but I didn't have the strength to resist. So, I let him open the door. As he helped me slide between the sheets of my bed, Vora rushed into the room with a wooden tray and a glass full of a thick liquid I didn't recognize. She took one look at me and cursed beneath her breath. After setting the tray on the nightstand beside me, she forced the cup into my hands.

"Drink."

"What is it?" I asked, tipping it to the side. The viscous liquid slowly moved over the ridges of the glass's quilted design, leaving behind smears of ruddy green in the pattern.

"Medicine. Now, drink." Vora didn't need magic or bargains. Instead, she shot her hand out to grasp the bottom of the cup and force it to my mouth. My lips parted more out of shock than agreement, but that was enough. The revoltingly sweet, cloying liquid slid over my tongue. It tasted of apples, clove, and some other foreign substances I couldn't place, and my stomach clenched in disapproval. I was about to push it away when Vora's sharp glare made my hand pause midair.

"Force it down. It'll help." Without prompting, she added, "I promise it's safe."

My taste buds would've argued otherwise, but she didn't give me the opportunity to respond. Instead, she kept the glass flush with my mouth until I relented. I swallowed a large gulp and then exhaled to cut the harshness of the flavor. A shiver crept down my neck and across my arms, and I gritted my teeth. Vora set the glass on the nightstand and then dusted her hands over her apron.

"Be sure to finish it. Every drop," she said.

A strange, delightful numbness trickled through my limbs, and the exhaustion lingering in my muscles lessened. I cut a glance at the syrupy concoction. What I would've given to know how she made it. I could've sold it for a fortune to the townsfolk.

"Thank you, Vora." After dragging an armchair to the foot of my bed, Orin had watched us in silence, the perfect picture of remorse and concern. His elbows were braced against his knees, and his hair was tousled over his searching eyes. "That will be all."

She pressed her lips into a fine line before nodding and meeting my gaze. "I'll check back in later. There's a mild sedative in the drink that should kick in shortly and help speed along recovery. Rest." Her skirts billowed around her as she strode out of the room, and the door clicked firmly shut behind her.

Alone. I was alone with Orin in my bedroom. I shifted uncomfortably beneath the weight of his somber stare. He swallowed thickly, and I couldn't help but track the bob of his throat.

"Tell me what happened." It wasn't a question, and yet his voice softened with a plea.

Tipping my head back against the headboard, I recounted the day's events: my walk with Tasia and Amalyss, how they'd asked me to "play." The subsequent, insatiable tug that had started some hours later and how it eventually led me to their doorstep. And then I told him about Tasia's cut. At that, he stiffened, his lips curling in a harsh show of displeasure. It only lasted for a moment before he fell back into guilt and blew out a heady sigh.

"You have my word that Amalyss and Tasia will not trick you into a bargain again."

"Or anyone else in this horrid place?" I couldn't keep the bite from my response.

His shoulders rolled forward as he deflated. "All I want is for you to be able to move and act freely within our estate—not be bound by evervows."

It didn't escape me that he didn't answer my question. Not really. "Evervows?"

"That's what we call them. Magical bargains that have dire consequences if reneged by either party."

At least I hadn't lost my tongue like that unfortunate traveling vendor.

"Like the one you and I share," I said bitterly. I'd willingly agreed to his terms, but the very thought of those icy, invisible chains binding me to him set my teeth on edge. "I'm mad at Tasia and Amalyss, but even more so with myself. I should've known better than to trust I'd be safe here."

"Edira," Orin said through an exhale as he scooted his chair closer. "I don't want you to feel that way." His eyes dropped to the crest on my arm, and his face twisted with a mixture of anger and frustration. "You're part of Fernglove. I can't believe they would go against my word. You could've been hurt."

"Is it true what they said? About me being too weak to cure an Ever?"

He wrung his fingers together. "Yes. For now. That's why I wanted to work with you to help develop your abilities. You mustn't threadmend any of us again without my knowledge, do you understand?"

His harrowed expression was a match to the emotions brewing in my chest. I hadn't known the whole story when I'd agreed to work with him. *For* him. How many hidden truths would I discover in the days, weeks, to follow?

"How did they even manage to trick me into a vow?" I sighed.

"Vows require both parties to agree, and unfortunately, magic doesn't pick up on intent. From how you explained it to me, your agreement to their request was enough." He shifted in his chair, but his gaze never left mine. "You can tell if an Ever is trying to invoke a vow by the swell of magic and usually a scent specific to that Ever family. For us, it's an earthy, floral aroma."

I had noticed it; I just hadn't paid it any mind. Because of course the telltale for their magic would be the literal scent of the surrounding world. Super identifiable.

"Lovely," I muttered. "I can't do the work you want me to do if I'm constantly reexamining every conversation I've had in this house."

"You won't have to," he said swiftly. "Within the hour, everyone will know of Tasia and Amalyss's mistake—and not to try anything like that again. I promise."

I held his stare for what felt like minutes, studying every nuance in his expression in search of deception, and found none. He leaned forward, pressing his forearms against his knees, and ducked his chin slightly. Hope. That's what made his lips part and his breath catch. He wanted to make things right.

The way he looked at me . . . I could hardly stand it. I reached for my glass, giving my hands, my thoughts, anything else to focus on. With one swift movement, I drained the last of my repugnant tonic.

"How do I know they'll listen?"

The veins along his neck strained against his tanned skin, and his nostrils flared. "Because I will *make* them." He clenched and unclenched his jaw. "No one is to harm you, Edira. I don't care how they're related to me." Magic flared around him as if in response to his rising emotions, and with it came the aroma of tilled earth and the heat of summer rays.

My breath caught in my chest. The fierce conviction in his stare couldn't be denied, and my fear slipped away. It was strange to feel so protected after I'd spent my life hiding from Evers. From him. Slowly, I nodded. "Okay. I believe you."

His power receded with my words, and a small, relieved smile dared to tug at his lips. "Thank you."

I shifted farther down between the sheets. Not because Orin's lingering gaze brought a flush to my skin that I didn't want him to see. But because with the absence of magic came a chill, and I needed to warm myself.

I cleared my throat as I tossed a quick glance to the ceiling. "I should rest."

Orin was on his feet in a breath. "Of course. Good night, Edira."

And with that, he reached for my hand to place a gentle kiss on my knuckles. A soft tingle spread through my fingers, but I didn't have a chance to fully revel in the sensation before sleep dragged me under.

## NINE

My dreams were fitful and fleeting, until I found myself once again in the cemetery outside Willowfell. Dappled midday sun filtered through the trees overhead, and I was lying on the ground between my parents' graves. The grass was soft, the breeze peaceful and full of the scent of wildflowers. I had one hand over my mother and the other over my father, and everything was just so *calm*. I was among the dead, and they didn't judge or demand or manipulate me to get what they wanted. I was simply existing.

But as I rolled grass between my fingers, the blades turned to mush and the ground trembled. The lush scenery decayed rapidly to gray as the earth came alive, shifting and squirming with golden beetles and soft yellow loam. A tomb opened up beneath me, and I fell into blight. Into decaying limbs and hollow eyes. Into a vat of disease that ate away at my skin. Into a stench-ridden catacomb with shredded Ever life threads wildly lashing about like withering vines. They snared my wrists and legs, dragging me under.

Rotting soil filled my mouth as I screamed and succumbed to the certainty of death.

My eyes flew open with a sharp intake of breath, and my body went rigid. Fernglove. I was in Fernglove. My pulse hammered against my throat, and I was thankful, at least, that Ywena was not nearby to shock me. I'd dealt with enough Ever antics for a lifetime. My body was ready for a break.

A thin slice of sunlight cut through the curtains, and I peeled off the sheets and clambered out of bed. I made my way to the bathroom, grabbing my apothecary cases as I went. Technically, I didn't need my tinctures. Vora's concoction had worked wonders to alleviate my pains, but my remedies gave me comfort. Some semblance of control. So I drew a bath and added my favorite salts for relaxation.

After, I toweled off and dressed quickly, not bothering with a gown. Instead, I opted for pants and a loose blouse before immediately visiting my brothers. Relief sang through me at their unchanged state. I still had time. Not much, but enough to stir hope.

A soft knock preceded the quiet groan of hinges from the door. "Edira?"

I turned to find Vora standing in the open frame, her brows scrunched together in worry. I let my hands fall away from Noam and Nohr.

"How are you feeling?" she asked, voice low.

"Good. What was in that drink? I might need to steal that recipe from you," I said with a smile.

"Maybe I'll teach you," she said. "But for now, you should eat. I've set up breakfast in your room."

I followed her into my quarters without complaint. She tugged my hair into a braid while I devoured eggs and fruit, pausing only to sip coffee between bites. The window above my vanity was open, and I studied the sleepy lawns. Early-morning light bathed the lush fields in a soft glow, and the vibrant gardens were empty, save for the marble statues manning the coiling pathways. The fountain centered in the middle of the pond was showering the water in a fine spray, and the countless droplets shimmered like falling diamonds in the sun's rays. Yet, the stunning scenery wasn't enough to hold my focus. My gaze traveled right back to that damn tree.

A chill crept down my spine as I cleared my throat. "What happened to Amalyss and Tasia?"

Vora's hands stilled against my scalp. "They're being adequately punished for their actions. They won't try that again."

"What kind of punishment?" I asked.

"It doesn't concern you." She let her hands fall away and then reached around me to secure my empty plate. "That said, I strongly recommend you avoid the family until things have settled."

My brows drew together. "Why?"

Vora sighed. "Lydia and Clesian are not pleased with Orin's decision to admonish the girls . . ." Her words trailed off, leaving plenty of space for me to interpret the danger lying in wait somewhere in this gods-forsaken estate. No doubt they blamed me for whatever Amalyss and Tasia were now enduring at Orin's hand. "He's ordered everyone to give you space, but most of the family is quite good at skirting his word."

"As evidenced by last night," I said with an eye roll. "Speaking of Orin, do you know where he is?"

"He told me to bring you to the library," she said as she made her way to the door. "Shall we?"

"Unless you know of another way to earn my keep outside of threadmending."

Vora snorted. "Follow me."

We moved through the quiet manor until we reached a cavernous room packed with weathered tomes. The sheer curtains framing the countless windows were drawn open, allowing light to fill the rafters and catch on the crystal chandelier draped from the ceiling. A tufted sofa was positioned before a polished coffee table and two armchairs with matching cream-colored fabric. A stack of slim books was arranged on the table, along with a pile of blank papers and ink pens.

"He's just finishing an appointment. I'll let him know you're ready after I drop this off," she said as she balanced my empty breakfast plate in her hand. She exited quickly, hooking a left once she crossed into the hall. As she disappeared, I breathed in deep, savoring the faint scent of worn leather.

Dust motes floated in the beams of sunlight, and I waved my hand through the air as I eyed the space. We didn't have many books at home, but the few novels we did own I'd read more times than I could count. I moved to the stack of books on the table and dragged my fingertips along the thin spines. They were more like journals than novels, but beautifully crafted nonetheless. I lifted the first one off the pile, marveling at the ivy-green cover and gilded pages. There were no markings to be seen, but when I flipped open the weathered journal, I spied a single name in neat handwriting along the top of the page.

*Rowena.*

My fingers hovered over her familiar scrawl as a weight dredged through my gut. This was likely the last piece of my aunt left in this world. And while I knew I'd eventually have to turn the page and learn about her time here at Fernglove, for a moment, I could simply stare at her name and pretend that she still existed—that the life we once shared in Willowfell still existed.

My heart hammered in my throat for what felt like hours, until a quiet yet insistent cough forced me to look up. Orin stood a few inches away with a drink tray in hand. Twin mugs with faded blue flowers painted onto the ceramic were filled with tea, and a small dish of sugar cubes sat beside them. With a smile stretching from ear to ear, he placed the tray on the table and sidled up beside me.

"I see you found what I wanted to review with you." Then his gaze drifted to Rowena's name, and his expression sobered. "She was an impressive threadmender."

"I know." I swallowed thickly before sinking to the sofa. "I miss her."

Orin sat beside me and offered me a mug of tea. "I hope her journal, along with all our previous threadmenders' journals, will help you refine your talents. They've learned many things about the scope of their magic over the years."

I accepted the drink and took a slow sip, surprised by the delightful blend of jasmine and orange blossoms. The warmth of the tea settled me, and I trailed a finger along Rowena's journal. "Thank you. These are . . . invaluable."

"I imagine so." Orin pressed his mug to his lips. "I can't fathom having a magic that is a detriment to practice."

*Cure no one.* My aunt's own words. I wondered if I'd find that warning again outlined in her entries, but Orin was right. Part of the reason threadmenders knew so little about developing their talents was because the risk was often not worth the reward. We shared small learnings with each other, passed down from one generation to the next. But nothing would compare to *this*. I eyed the stack before me again as a seed of hope bloomed in my chest. I could do this. I could study the methods they'd developed and learn from their failures. Here, their whole job had been dedicated to perfecting their magic. It may have cost them their lives, but maybe I didn't have to lose mine.

Orin watched me closely, his tea forgotten in his hands. After a beat, he set it on the tray and shifted so his leg just barely grazed mine. "I've read all of these myself, but I do think they'll mean something different to you. I can only imagine the power they describe." He looked at my hands then, a kind of rapt curiosity filling his expression.

I gripped the mug tighter as I tried in vain to ignore the wild desire to ignite my power, just to see if he'd marvel at my glow the same way he did that day in my house. "It's probably best if I read them myself first."

"Of course. I'm here to support you however you need." He leaned closer, and I tilted my head toward him. He was no more than a breath away. I inhaled deeply, hoping to catch a sliver of his scent, but came up empty. There was nothing but clean air and the faint aroma of the library.

"I'm sure I'll need your help after I get through these." I thumbed the binding of Rowena's journal before nodding to the others. "You know the magic of your kind better than any thread-mender."

His hand absently skimmed the side of my thigh. "Consider me an open book, then."

My traitorous heart was thundering madly in my chest, and I briefly wondered if he could hear the damn thing cantering about. I hoped not. I didn't even fully understand why I was inching toward him, why it felt good to be near his warmth.

"Thank you for this, by the way." I held Rowena's journal between us, effectively drawing his focus to the pages. "I've thought about her all these years, and now it's like I get to see what her days were like. What I missed."

Orin placed his hand over mine. Pressed it tight against the journal, against a piece of my family. Our fingers nearly threaded. "I'm sorry you didn't get to say goodbye."

"Me, too."

For a while, neither of us spoke. We sat there, fingers becoming more intertwined with each passing breath, and simply basked in the comfort of shared silence. I didn't understand why he was looking at me with such care. Why my own pulse kept ratcheting with each minute that scraped by. It wasn't until he cleared his throat that I realized I'd leaned in far too close, and I straightened as a heat overcame my cheeks.

Orin tracked the crawling blush across my skin, and want

flickered to life in his gaze. Still, his smile was gentle. "Take your time. For now, I'll give you a few days to read these without interruption. You can resume physical training with Rorik later, and I won't distract you any further."

I removed my hand from his and busied my fingers by flipping aimlessly through the journal's pages. "I'll let you know if I need anything."

"Please do." Orin stared at me for a moment longer, letting his smile wash over me fully, before standing and straightening his shirt. He left without another word, and it was all I could do not to collapse on the cushions.

*What in the Ever-loving hell was that?* A groan simmered from my chest, and I closed my eyes. Orin defied every preconceived notion I had about Evers. Every. Last. Thing. I hated him for it, and yet, at the same time, I didn't. Because here I was, holding a piece of my family's history that I never knew existed.

Opening my eyes, I righted myself on the sofa and flipped Rowena's diary open to the first page.

Before her days as a threadmender, she'd been the town's poet laureate. She had been prolific and eloquent, and her cozy home— now property of the town elders—was packed with books and journals full of her neat handwriting. When she'd left us, I kept a few of her smaller memoirs for myself. But this journal was the last thing she'd penned.

I forced myself to swallow my grief and slowly began to move through her dated entries. Her work was formal, her prose stiff. It was so different from what I was used to seeing from her, and I realized that while she may have agreed to help find a cure for blight, she took no joy in it. Still, I read every word. Every detailed explanation of Evers' threads, their movements, their strength and resilience. She'd also built on methods for mending based off the earlier threadmenders' journals, and while I planned to read those as well, I couldn't help but appreciate her meticulous instructions.

The only page that lacked any detail was the final entry. It contained only one word.

*Mavis.*

A dull ringing settled low in my ears.

"Aunt Rowena," I murmured to myself as I traced her handwriting. The page was dated fifteen years back. Orin had said she'd died several years ago, but *fifteen?* My heart twisted. Her life had been cut drastically short. Had she known that attempting to cure Mavis would result in her death? Tears welled in my eyes as I stared at the name. She hadn't managed it. I'd known as much, given the situation I was in, but seeing that entry . . . that solitary word . . .

A fist clenched my heart tight as I gently stroked the page. A sudden, sharp pain sliced through my forefinger, and I winced as I dropped the book in my lap. A bead of blood welled to the surface of my skin along the neat slit. Glancing down at the open journal, I spotted a small, jagged fragment of paper jutting from the center binding.

*A missing page?* The evidence of the rip was almost imperceptible, just the barest scrap to indicate a page had been there at all. There were no ink splatters or notes of any kind that had bled across its surface, and since it was sandwiched between Rowena's last entry about threadmending techniques and the final page with Mavis's name, there was no interruption in her train of thought. If not for the cut now dulling on my finger, I never would have known it was missing.

I flipped through her journal to see if anything else had been removed, but the remainder of the binding was intact. Had she torn it out? Or someone else? A ghostly chill crept down the length of my spine. I could ask, but what good would it do? Would they even tell me the truth? Did they even notice?

"Strange," I muttered. Wiping away the droplet of blood on my pants, I set her book beside me and reached for the next journal. I had four more to browse, four more chances to glean any additional information about blight or the Evers' threads. But as I spent the next few hours sifting through the threadmenders' memories, I couldn't help but think of the missing page from Rowena's diary and that single, damning word.

*Mavis.*

# TEN

Two days passed in blissful solitude. The only Ever I encountered was Orin as he occasionally checked in on my progress, but it seemed like the rest of the family had, in fact, heeded his warning. Even when I took breaks or strolled the grounds to clear my mind, I passed by only attendants going about their duties. I wasn't required to attend family dinner. What the Ferngloves were doing or where they were, I didn't know. I didn't much care. The journals held all my attention.

Unfortunately, I moved through them quickly. Despite the years the threadmenders had spent at the estate, their diaries were lucky to exceed fifty entries. All of them. I'd started taking notes on my own, jotting down ideas and methods to try first. One of the earliest threadmenders had penned an idea for cutting versus stitching, and that gave me pause.

Isolate the affected life thread with your nondominant hand.
Then focus your power to the palm of your dominant hand.
Will it to take the shape of a knife or scalpel, and then aim

the sharp end at the base of the thread. Go for a clean cut to create neater ends in the life thread and reduce the chances of unnecessary fraying.

I'd yet to test slicing away at someone's strands, Ever or human. Would the pruning help or hurt? Would they die like a withered plant too far gone, or would new growth sprout, free of infection? Perhaps it would, but that wouldn't eradicate the disease that seemed to stem from somewhere deep in the body. Pruning might temporarily alleviate their symptoms, but one unknown remained: me. If I endured the actions of what I inflicted, would I survive healthy strands being cut away from my core? Or would I propel myself toward death that much faster?

The former threadmender didn't explain in detail, but his final entry was illuminating enough: *Don't cut.*

Another threadmender, the one before Rowena, had the idea to somehow pinch threads while utilizing his magic, but for what purpose, I couldn't tell. He'd left a sketch in his journal illustrating a forefinger and thumb holding a thread that had been shaped into something like a needle. It was his final entry, and a ghostly chill ravaged my skin. I hoped he hadn't tried it only to die in the process. But . . . I underlined the idea and made a note on my papers. Perhaps.

By the second morning, I'd set their journals aside and turned to the surrounding shelves. A few of the threadmenders had mentioned reading other books for inspiration, but they'd left little notes about the texts themselves outside of the titles.

"Where are you?" I murmured, squinting at the spines as I inched along the bookcase. Dusty, old tomes with gilded leather and worn bindings were packed neatly on the shelves, many of which had obscure titles or were stamped with ancient sigils I had no hopes of deciphering. But finally, I found the three books that had been mentioned in the journals: *A Collection of Rare Flora*,

*Sloan's Guide to Curses and Poisons*, and *Fable or Fact: A History of Evers*. Returning to my seat, I started with the latter after a quick glance at the tome's contents revealed the passages were at least written in modern tongue.

The very first entry was a short myth involving Death and a woman whose words were full of magic. She'd become Ever after escaping his clutches, and both her and her kin were granted eternal life. Apparently, blight didn't give a damn about Death's promise. Mavis was still dying, despite being a descendant of the original immortal woman.

I flipped through the chapters and made notes of what to revisit until I reached the end. The last portion of the book was reserved for a sprawling lineage chart that spanned several pages, complete with the names and locations of Ever families.

*So many.* I lost count of their ancestors, of the hundreds of branches in the chart that all somehow tracked back to the first Ever centuries ago. Their origins were ancient. Some offshoots seemed far removed, and the majority of families did not have a crest above their names. But those that did were penned in a bolder, larger font as if to give the family more weight. Importance. Power.

Within Glaes's borders, only four families were inked in that manner: the Ferngloves, the Waterstones, the Starglens, and a fourth I hadn't heard of. The Embergraves. Frowning at the name, I flipped back through the pages hoping to find details about any of the families present, and yet nothing. I hummed wordlessly to myself, making a mental note to ask Orin about it, more out of curiosity than anything, when my gaze drifted to the passage I'd stalled on.

The First of our kind spent decades understanding the nature
of fire, even going so far as to bathe in the flames until her
skin no longer charred and the power took root in her veins.

There, she learned how to extract heat from within and ignite sparks from her fingers. In an effort to strengthen her powers, she searched the world for rare creatures that possessed magic similar to that of the original stone—and was greatly rewarded. She embedded parts of ancient beasts into her being and gained additional strength and power in return.

Because of this, Evers are born with fantastical traits of their own. And while our magic derives from the original Ever, it manifests differently for each family offshoot, some stronger than others.

Maybe that's why the Ferngloves were bolded and marked with a crest. They were simply stronger. No doubt that's what made their threads so resilient. Thumbing through the pages, I paused when I discovered one of the corners had been neatly folded. It was so firmly creased, pressed entirely flush with the text, that I'd almost missed it. Frowning, I scanned the page.

Heartbonds are formed when two Evers agree to share their intrinsic magic with each other. When this happens, a ribbon of magic—visible only to the pair in question—will appear and wrap around their arms. Once accepted, it becomes a permanent, invisible bond between the two. This cannot be reversed, and even upon one Ever's death, the former partner will continue to have access to that wealth of power for their own use. As such, this level of power sharing and commitment is revered and only to be undertaken after careful consideration.

I was so engrossed in the description that when I heard the soft creak of the wood floors announcing someone's arrival, I didn't bother to immediately look up. If Orin was back with more tea, I'd gladly take it—and ask him to stay and clarify more about the nuances in their power. Pressing one finger to the worn page, I held my place as I glanced at the doorway. And then froze.

"So this is where you've been hiding." Lydia's voice was cool, her gaze sharp. Thinly veiled ire sparked in her blue-green stare, and I knew without a shadow of a doubt that she was the last person I wanted to encounter. My heart rammed against my chest as I set my book down on the coffee table.

"Hello, Lydia."

She took a deliberate step forward. "Do you know what my children are doing at this particular moment in time?"

Warning bells crested in my ears. "No."

She reached the edge of the sofa. "They're paying for your mistake."

"Mistake?" Irritation flared in my voice. "They tricked me."

"And that's within their right. You are property of Fernglove." She gripped the lip of the couch, and her nails scraped against the wooden frame. "Explain to me how it's fair for you to sit here and leisurely read while my daughters have been locked away until my dear nephew deems it appropriate to release them."

My blood ran cold. "I didn't ask for that."

She inched closer, and I stood, backing away from her until I bumped into one of the bookshelves. Her haughty chuckle seemed to hang in the air. At that moment, Vora rounded the corner of the hallway and came into full view of the open library. She took one look at Lydia, and her grip on the serving tray she carried tightened. Turning on her heel, she left without offering to help, a flurry of skirts billowing after her.

Great.

"You're under Orin's protection now, but if you cause even a modicum of discomfort for either one of my daughters again"— she closed the distance between us, her tense frame vibrating with malice—"I will not hesitate to hurt you."

"I am not responsible for their actions," I seethed. My hands formed fists by my sides, and my back stiffened. "And if you threaten to harm me again, it won't be just your daughters suffering through discomfort."

"How dare you." She hooked my chin with one finger and yanked it upward. She wasn't even taller than me. It was all a show, all a move of power. And it made the anger churning in my veins spike even higher. "Foolish mortal. You're utterly incapable of harming me."

My hands itched to prove otherwise, but I never got the chance.

"Careful, Aunt Lydia. Wouldn't want Orin finding out you've been pestering our threadmender." The amused drawl filtered through the room, and Seville stepped into the library. She sauntered around the couch and then parked her hip against it, crossing her ankles and smiling wryly at my predicament. "And right after he permitted you to visit Amalyss and Tasia, no less."

If Lydia was angry before, she was downright furious now. She jerked her hand away and swiveled sharply in place to glare at her niece. "Seville. Your presence is wholly unnecessary. As usual."

Seville gasped and lightly draped her hand over her mouth. "Auntie, my goodness. Is that an age spot I see? You should get that checked, darling."

A sharp hiss scraped through Lydia's teeth, and she instinctively placed two fingers along her seemingly clear cheekbone.

"One day you and your brothers will learn your place. Assuming I'm kind enough to let you stick around."

Seville laughed. A brittle, callous sound. "Be off now, Auntie. Return to your heartbond and your ill-behaved children."

Lydia opened her mouth to respond, then slammed it shut. Something malicious flashed in her eyes, and she held Seville's gaze for a heated breath before storming away. When Lydia's retreating footsteps faded, Seville let out an exaggerated sigh.

"It's any wonder her daughters acted out." She shoved off the sofa and looped an arm loosely about my shoulders. "Come, come. Orin will want to hear about this."

I allowed her to guide me down the hall while she aimlessly chattered about things I clearly had no ability to contribute to: the awful shade of Lady Starglen's newest gown and the peculiar quietness of her son, the horrid design choices of the Waterstones' foyer. Nothing was pleasant. I doubted Seville found anything other than herself to be beautiful.

When we arrived at Orin's study, she didn't bother to knock, instead waltzing in as if it were her respite and not her brother's. Orin sat behind his desk bent over stacks of paper and lightly twirling a pen between his fingers. He glanced up at us and stilled when his gaze met mine.

"Did something happen?"

"Just Lydia voicing her concerns about the treatment of her daughters." Seville abandoned me for a candy jar nestled on a shelf. She selected a ruby-colored morsel and popped it into her mouth. "I took care of it."

"I see." Orin's gaze never left mine. "Seville, will you give us a minute?"

"Sure thing." She snagged another candy before heading for the exit. "I'm expected at the Waterstones', anyway."

"Please see me when you return."

She offered a flippant wave over her shoulder as she disappeared. Orin set aside his pen and braided his fingers together. "Did Lydia harm you?"

"She's an absolute nightmare, but no." I sighed. "I'm fine."

The tension left his shoulders, and he offered a dry smile as he gestured to the empty armchair across from his desk. "My aunt is difficult, to say the least."

"I'm not sure that's saying enough," I muttered.

At that, he laughed. "No, you're right. She's downright abhorrent, but I try not to push her too hard. When my parents passed, she expected to inherit the estate. Instead, it fell to me, and it's been a bit tumultuous navigating that relationship ever since."

Sinking into the armchair, I clasped my hands in my lap. "How did they die?"

"It's . . ." He swallowed thickly, his eyes downcast. "I still have trouble discussing it."

I could relate all too well. A ghost pain flickered through my chest, and I instinctively reached for the pocket of my trousers hoping to find my mother's leather scrap. Of course, I came up empty, and the ache in my heart deepened. "I understand."

"My father was brilliant, though. A truly intelligent business-man." He reached for a miniature golden hourglass near his pens and turned it over. Fine sand began to trickle into the empty base. "Always stressed the value of time and the importance of words. He fell in love with my mother the moment he saw her."

The sprawling lineage chart bled to life in my mind. "Was he human? Or from a different Ever family?"

"He was an Ever, though his family had little magic. Mavis thought he was only after my mother for our power." His eyes darkened as he glowered at nothing, but after a breath he brushed it off with a slight wave of his hand. "Anyway, my mother's grasp on our familial magic was stronger than Lydia's, so she became head of house until she passed. Lydia assumed she would take over, but because my parents were heartbonds, my father still possessed all my mother's abilities."

I watched the sand fall as I marveled over his words. "Ever magic is fascinating."

He grinned. "Glad you think so. But enough about me. I'll speak with Lydia. I'd already told her not to seek you out, and she clearly went against my word." Orin leaned back in his chair and cupped the back of his head with his hands.

"Don't worry about it," I said. "She was just concerned for her daughters. They're being punished?"

"Amalyss and Tasia have never respected my authority." He blew out a sigh. "But Lydia makes it sound far worse than it is. They are being confined to a room with fewer luxuries than their quarters, but they're not in a cell or anything."

"Pity," I said.

Orin's lips jerked up in the corners.

*I'm interested to hear what other quips might slip from that tongue of yours.* A warm blush crawled over my cheeks as his words from market filled my mind. I couldn't help but wonder if it was just my quick wit or my tongue he was curious about. As if hearing my thoughts, his gaze dipped to my lips.

"That aside," he murmured as he came around the desk to lean against the corner. One of his legs brushed against mine as he adjusted. "I am curious to know how your research is going."

"I've made a few notes for different methods I'd like to try when the time comes, but . . ." My mind rewound to my aunt's journal. Did he know about the missing page? What if it was nothing? A torn sheet used for note-taking much like I'd been doing for the past few days. I doubted he—or anyone else for that matter—had taken anything from the journals. They wanted me to succeed just as much as I did.

"The journals are informative," I said finally. "But I was hoping for more details about their work with Mavis's blight specifically."

"Not all of them had the chance. A few had been threadmending before they joined us, so their lifespans were already shortened." He'd spoken softly, and his smile turned tired. Sad. "And the one or two who did . . . Well, I didn't make documenting their experience mandatory. In hindsight, I should have made it part of our agreement to aid future threadmenders in their efforts."

Despite myself, I hated the way he looked so defeated, as if he'd failed somehow in the face of this strange illness. Ultimately, I was glad he hadn't forced the threadmenders to relive what was likely the last few moments of their lives. So instead of fixating on something we couldn't change, I offered him a teasing smile. "Going to make an amendment to our terms of employment?"

"No." The hint of a grin tugged at his lips. "I have faith there will be no need for future threadmenders after your work with us."

I was suddenly too aware of the heady beat of my heart. Of the hushed tone of his words, of the closeness of his body. He reached out with one finger and lightly grazed my hair. It was only a whisper of a touch, and yet my body thrummed with electricity. I couldn't help but study the planes of his face and the depths of his eyes.

I steadied myself with two breaths before continuing. "Your faith in me is unwavering."

"I'm certain you'll be able to help us."

"Us?"

"Mavis is part of our family." He lifted a single shoulder as his hand fell away from my face. "Curing her would most certainly help all of us. We don't want to see her like this anymore."

His voice was soft, his eyes downcast. He seemed so vulnerable. Real. I didn't know how to process his emotions when I'd spent my whole life convincing myself that Ferngloves were nothing more than self-absorbed Evers.

"Mavis's glamour," I finally managed to say. "Can you remove it?"

"Will it help?"

"Yes."

"I . . ." He was breathless and his cheeks flushed. Why was he breathless? He wetted his lips and shifted closer. "Before she fell ill, Mavis was very proud. She didn't like to appear weak, and when it grew too taxing to maintain her glamour, we elected to do it for her." He absently tapped his fingers along his leg as he stared into nothing, as if reliving a memory I wasn't sure I'd ever be privy to. "Stripping it from her when everyone in this manor has the power to flawlessly sustain that magic . . . Something about that feels wrong. I don't want to hurt her."

Gently, I angled toward him. Not because it was instinctual. Not because I wanted to soak up his heat. But because something in his tone gave me pause. "What about your glamour, then?"

"Mine?" He blinked at me.

"Yes. You said everyone here uses it. I read that your bodies are a product of ancient beasts being embedded into the first Ever."

Orin's brows flicked up in surprise, but he didn't interrupt me.

"I'm curious to know what that looks like, if that magic somehow is responsible for your threads being so unusually difficult to work with."

He hesitated for several breaths, his endless gaze peering directly into my soul.

When he didn't respond, I leaned in closer. I needed . . . *wanted* him to trust me. I didn't dare examine why. Softly, I asked, "Is there a reason you're hiding, too?"

"Oh, I'm not hiding." His smile grew impossibly wide, and a flush of power rippled around his frame and heated the small space between us. "I've always just found that a more demure appearance is easier for mortals to digest."

Orin dropped his veil like a slow-moving sheet falling to the earth in the wind. It fluttered and rippled until it faded away, and then he was there. Unfiltered and raw and heart-stopping in every sense of the word.

Four bone-white horns sprouted from his forehead and wrapped his hair like a crown. His ears elongated, along with the points of his nails and teeth. Glistening emerald scales lined his temples and disappeared into his hairline, and I caught a hint of more peeking from beneath the collar of his tunic. A thin tail that ended in an arrowpoint unfurled from his waist and fell to the backs of his calves.

"Orin." It was all I could manage.

His grin deepened. "See what I mean?" With light fingers, he grazed the crown protruding from his forehead—fitting for the head of his household.

"Courtesy of the first Ever, right?" I stared at the horns, fighting the urge to reach out and touch their bone-like surface.

"I love that you read our history." Pure joy lit in Orin's eyes. "What else do you know?"

"I only got through a handful of passages before Lydia rudely interrupted me."

"You're correct, though. Those original modifications, if you will, were for bolstering her abilities. As her descendants, we get slivers of that ancient power to boost our familial magic. For Ferngloves . . ." He twirled his fingers in a circular fashion, and the air warmed like it'd been kissed by a summer sun. The fragrance of wildflowers and rich soil filled the study, and a faint shimmer of green particles bloomed above his palm. "The earth answers to us, as well as its creatures. But it takes decades to master that kind of skill."

I stared in awe at the magic collecting in his hand. "And other Evers?"

"Our powers are tied to our bloodlines. But even within families, we all present differently. Seville has the most beautiful wings, whereas I have none. It's just how the power chose to mark us. Some Evers like to flaunt their unique appearance. Others feel more inclined to walk with mortals rather than look down upon them."

I laughed, thinking of the way Seville and Lydia would forever consider humans "less than," regardless of their perfect glamours.

"May I?" I stood and reached toward the cluster of emerald scales peeking out of his hairline. Something heated flashed in his gaze, but he nodded and pressed his lips together. I grazed their slick surface, and a trail of gooseflesh rippled over my arms at their cool kiss. We fell into silence as I moved from one feature to the next, quietly studying. There was a definite thrum of magic that vibrated outward from his being, and it didn't seem like something he could simply shut off. It had to be affecting his threads, too. It was all so foreign and captivating, and the power rolling off Orin in heady waves was intoxicating.

Orin stared at me the entire time, longing coloring his eyes something fierce. My heart hammered against my rib cage as the world seemed to slip away. We were in our own private bubble of shared breaths and unspoken words, and something was happening. Something I wasn't sure how to comprehend and certainly didn't want to acknowledge.

My fingers brushed his lips, and he stiffened beneath my touch. "Curious what those can do?"

Heat bloomed across my cheeks as I stared at his chest. "I'm not adverse to learning."

Slowly, his hands went to my waist. "I shouldn't be surprised. You were the one who mentioned performictum."

At that, I laughed. "I probably have some stowed away in my cases."

"Hardly necessary." His grin stretched wide, and I marveled at the beauty that was him. I searched his face, lingering on every unique feature and display of Ever magic. He was so open. It was strange to feel breathless at the sight of him, knowing everything he wanted from me. How he was fine with ushering in my death at the expense of saving Mavis. And yet, I understood. Saving my family, caring for my brothers, was all I'd been doing for as long as I could recall.

I'd never wanted to see someone's life threads so badly.

Without warning, I summoned my power from the depths of my body and willed it outward. Orin's eyes grew wide as his gaze shot to my now glowing fingertips, and all at once his glamour slammed back into place. The sudden wall barricading his magic .

was a forceful, cold sting, and I jolted, just as a loud knock hammered into the door.

My hand remained frozen over Orin's chest, and he clamped it tight before pressing a kiss to my knuckles. "I apologize. I sensed someone coming and reacted without thinking."

Was that all? I struggled to find words but capped my power and nodded. Half-baked thoughts skittered through my mind, forming and disappearing like a faint breeze.

"Come in," Orin called without breaking my gaze.

The door swung inward with far too much force, and Rorik strolled into the room. He took one look at our joined hands and rolled his eyes.

"Rorik. To what do we owe this pleasure?" Orin asked.

I broke away immediately. A wry smile pulled at Rorik's expression, but it felt stilted, and his eyes were cold. Even the ease with which he leaned against the doorframe was a pretense, a picture of nonchalance that wasn't quite right. Ywena was perched on his shoulder, and her wings fluttered once as her antennae twitched.

"I came to return Ywena to Edira," he said. "It's been three days. Seems I'm the only one concerned about her resuming training."

Orin straightened. "We were merely discussing her needs."

He barked out a laugh. "Of that I have no doubt."

"Did the Starglens accept?" Orin asked, ignoring his jab entirely.

"Yes. I still think it's a foolish idea, by the way." He sauntered toward the desk and braced his hands on the back of the armchair. "Not safe in the slightest."

"Noted." Orin tipped his head toward me. "Edira, would you give me and my brother some privacy, please?"

"Of course." I quickly skirted around Rorik. As I did, Ywena took flight and found her home against the crook of my neck. The familiar tickle of her feet sent goose bumps down my back.

"We'll pick up where we left off tomorrow." Rorik smirked as he met my gaze. "You know, with our individual training. Don't forget your pants. Again."

Heat threatened to tinge my cheeks pink at the same time Orin stiffened.

"One of these days, Rorik, I'll pin you to the ground beneath my boots, and you'll pray I'm wearing a skirt so you at least see something nice before I spit in your face." I spun on my heel and made for the door. "See you tomorrow."

I didn't bother to turn and examine Rorik's expression, instead smiling to myself as Orin's robust laugh followed me out.

# ELEVEN

From my quiet window bench in the library, I watched Orin hold lessons for the Ever children. Blankets had been arranged on the pristine lawns of the courtyard in a semicircle around a slender tree with emerald leaves and budding pink flowers. Dappled sunlight filtered through the branches, and Orin leaned against the trunk as he peered at an assortment of papers in his hands. Amalyss and Tasia shared a woven tapestry, and their gazes were downcast, their hands firmly clasped. It seemed they were no longer confined to their "cell."

With them sat two additional Evers: Flix, whom I recognized from the foyer, and a young boy with eyes the same shade as the first fringes of dusk. His blue-black hair was deeper than the night sky. On his neck was a smattering of indigo dots and thin lines that connected in the shape of a constellation: the family crest of the Starglens. With practiced ease, he manifested tiny stars that danced about his fingers in strangely beautiful patterns. Flix did the same, summoning a swirling orb of ink-black water that churned angrily in his palm. He was the only one who dared to reveal a sliver of his true form. His horns were proudly on display, his locks expertly parted around them.

*It's hard to isolate such a small patch.*

The ghost of Tasia's words sent a chill down my spine. She'd been so reluctant to let go of her glamour, and yet Flix had enough control to display his horns. Was he stronger than them? Or something else? Centering myself with a breath, I called on my power. Magic thrummed through my veins and a soft glow began to emanate from my body. I knew my eyes would be doused in the same light, granting me the ability to see life threads.

Normally, anyway. But with Evers, there was always glamour. And glamour hid *everything*.

Just as it had been with Tasia and Amalyss, each Ever seemed to be coated in a thin gossamer fabric that softened the outlines of their body. Immediately I focused on the space where Flix's horns had punctured through the magic. They were clear and free of glamour, a glistening black that seemed to throb with power. And right at the base, where the magic veil was layered, I caught a glimpse of a wayward thread that had somehow snuck through. It should've been as vibrant as Tasia's and yet was a leeched gray.

*The base of one of Tasia's threads had looked like that, too.*

"Edira."

I startled and immediately recalled my power. And with Ywena once again nestled in her favorite spot, I received a fresh jolt of electricity to go along with my erratic breath. Jerking my head toward the entrance of the library, I spied Vora standing in the open doorframe with her brows arched toward her hairline. My pulse slowed, and I blew out a breath.

"Vora. Did you need me?"

"Shouldn't you be training with Rorik?" she asked with a pointed nod toward Ywena.

"I know it will help." I sighed as I stood, ignoring Vora's disapproving glare. "But can't someone else teach me?" I cast one last glance through the window. Orin looked up then, as if somehow my gaze had summoned his, and a warm smile claimed his lips. A flicker of heat twisted through my stomach. He tipped his chin ever so slightly before shifting his focus back to Flix, and the heat in my belly threatened to move to my cheeks.

"No," Vora said, her words sharp. "Now go before you make Rorik mad."

"Fine." I turned on my heel and made for the front doors without bothering to see if she'd escort me. My emotions steadied as I trekked toward the sacred tree where my training was held. Nothing like a little light torment to make the afternoon pass quickly. I glowered at nothing, thinking of Rorik's snark and hoping I really would get the chance to stand over him one of these days. At the very least, I hoped his methodology worked to improve the length of my lifespan. Maybe I'd eventually be strong enough to hand him his ass.

Rorik turned as I approached, and his gaze immediately dropped to my pants and boots. He smirked. "Prepared to step on me?"

"Always," I said as I folded my arms across my chest. "Believe it or not, I actually want to get better at mending. Even if it means spending time with you." I came to a halt, and Ywena crawled over my shoulder to nestle more closely against my neck.

"Good, because spending your days researching or in Orin's study is useless if your body isn't ready."

"At least he's helping me." I scowled.

"I see, so you find *my* time pointless." His smile deepened to something sinister. "That hardly seems fair, considering we've only had one lesson."

"Ywena has only shocked me once since you brought her back." I placed my hands on my hips and settled into my stance. "I think we can move on to something a little more productive."

Heat flashed in his eyes. "How interesting that *you* think you have the appropriate knowledge and skill set to tell *me* when we need to shift our training." He stepped toward me, halting just inches from my body. My breathing didn't falter. Not once. He dragged his gaze from the steady rise and fall of my chest to Ywena and, finally, to my face.

"Well?" I prompted when he said nothing. He looked down at me as he brought his face closer, as if testing the effectiveness of his proximity on the steadfast cadence of my breath. I focused on inhaling, on drawing in every possible ounce of air, and forcing it out with measured calmness.

"If you think you're ready for something physical . . ." His voice was gravelly, rough, and it damn near ruined my perfect control. He seemed to notice, too, and something unreadable raced across his expression. Then he chuckled darkly. "Run."

"What?"

Rorik was a feral creature in that moment, and I swore his glamour slipped, if only for a breath. There was a flash of something iridescent, something otherworldly and possibly beautiful, but his predatory smile—complete with sharpened canines—stole my focus entirely. Ywena shocked me as soon as my breath caught, and that tiny jolt spurred me into motion. Without thinking, I ran. I sprinted toward the trees marking the edge of the back lawns as Rorik's laugh filled the air like a storm. He was everywhere and nowhere—I glanced over my shoulder to find he'd disappeared— and I failed miserably to maintain control over my breathing. Every inhale and exhale was accompanied by a shock from Ywena, and before I knew it a deep pang spurred in my sides.

*For fuck's sake.* I tried to breathe through it as I found the small path winding into the depths of the forest. I flew over the moss-studded stones and bolted down the dirt trail, but roots had puckered the soft soil to create a path laden with obstacles. The toe of my boot caught on one and I went tumbling forward. My

hands smacked into the ground, the rough scrape of bark and jagged stones cutting away at my flesh, and I rolled to my side.

*Real graceful, Edira. Just great.* With a sharp wince, I flexed my
battered hands and forced myself to slow down, to settle. Gingerly,
I eased to my feet and tried to get a grip on my wild breath so
Ywena's incessant jolts would subside.

"How did you get through that unscathed?" I muttered to her
as I glanced at my shoulder. She fluttered her wings only once in
response.

A twig snapped in the distance of the wood, and I jerked my
head toward the sound. The dense thicket of trees was impossible to pierce. They clambered around like giants, their long
limbs covered in leaves that blocked out almost all the daylight.
The ground was nothing more than pools of darkness, and a
low ache simmered behind my eyes as I strained to see. The trail
was desolate—just a strip of soil and stone stretching into the
shrouded abyss. A thin mist had bloomed from somewhere deep
within the bowels of the forest, and it rolled over the earth like
a wet exhale. A chill swept through on a rattling breeze, and the
hairs on my neck rose. The sun had all but disappeared, as if it
were afraid of the darkened, fingerlike shadows inching across the
ground to snare my ankles.

The woods were a living, breathing monster, and I'd stepped
into the belly of the beast. All I could hear was my ragged breath,
my pulse thundering in my ears, and the soft chittering from
Ywena as she activated her power again and again. I winced with
every prick, yet it wasn't enough to chase away the looming para-
noia.

A wet breath teased the skin behind my ear. "You're slow."

I jumped so high I smacked the top of my head into Rorik's
jaw. I hadn't even heard him approach. He cursed and took a step
back as I tumbled to the ground. Ywena shocked me—of course—

and I let myself fall flat on my back as I stared at a patchwork blanket of limbs and leaves. The creeping shadows skittered away with my panic, and the suffocating darkness was suddenly gone. The sunlight was still weak, but not nearly as powerless as before, and I blew out an angry sigh. I'd let my mind get the best of me.

And Rorik.

"You can fuck right off," I said to Rorik between breaths. I wanted to revel in the satisfaction of hitting his stupid jaw, but my head was throbbing from the impact, whereas he was already crouched before me, smirking as if it'd never happened.

"Unfortunately, I can't." Then his gaze dipped to my hands. He snared one before I could blink and then swiped away a stray bead of blood with his finger. "You're incredibly clumsy." Then my mind completely stalled as I watched him dip it into his mouth. He snorted. "Weak, too."

"As if you can taste that," I spat.

"Maybe I can," he said with a sinful grin. I couldn't tell if he was teasing or not. "When you can run around the estate three times without Ywena shocking you, we'll move on to the next drill."

"Three times?" I raised a brow at him as I finally stood.

"You're woefully in need of conditioning." He turned back down the path, leading us toward the quiet, sun-drenched lawns outside of the estate. "We can't have you passing out when you threadmend. Which will be soon."

I frowned, remembering the concern that had lit Orin's eyes at the thought of me mending Tasia's small cut. "He doesn't want me to try and cure anything until I'm ready."

Rorik snorted. "And I'm sure you know my brother better than me. What, a little glimpse beneath his glamour and suddenly you think you're special?"

"At least he believes I can do it," I said as we rounded the last bend of the trail. "Will I start with Mavis?"

Rorik said nothing for a long moment, instead waiting until

we'd crossed the threshold of the dark woods. "No. Most likely an animal. Some of our beasts have become infected as well. They'll be good practice."

"Better to practice on them than the likes of you," I grumbled.

At that, he laughed. "I would never let you practice on me. Not mending, anyway."

My lips curled in disdain. "As if I would entertain the idea of anything else."

He rolled his eyes. "But you would with Orin? You do realize all Evers are the same beneath the veil."

"How do you mean?"

"Arrogant and selfish, as I'm sure you're aware." He brushed a stray pine needle off his pants, casting a cursory look at the Ever tree as we passed. Likely every ancestor of his was just as vile, but it wasn't nice to speak ill of the dead . . . out loud.

So instead, I rolled my eyes. "Too bad I have no hopes of curing arrogance."

"Nobody's perfect," he said with a shrug.

"As an Ever, I suppose you're the forefront on that opinion," I said.

Rorik gave me a sidelong glance. "I'm dying to know what slight against my kind you're going to deliver next."

I couldn't help but smirk. "You all are so obsessed with glamour, with hiding any semblance of imperfection. Of course an Ever would be the one who most innately understands the concept of never being able to achieve it.

"What I don't understand," I continued when all he did was snort, "is why. Why hide the features that make you unique? That speak to your power?"

"Because it's a pain to display those but keep everything else under wraps."

"You're immortal. Why hide what doesn't age?"

"Not all magic is pretty," he responded, voice low.

He stared straight ahead, thin lines creasing between his brows and lips pressed tightly together. I doubted there was a single blemish on his skin that could compare with a mortal scar, but I knew nothing about the ramifications of the first Ever infusing magic into her bones and passing those traits off to her kind. I tilted my head slightly, itching to call on my power and see if there was any way to pierce his veil. To get a glimpse of what lay beneath. He caught me watching and grinned.

"Enjoy the view?"

"There's not much to look at." *Lie.* Ywena shocked me at the twinge in my pulse, but I fought to keep my expression even. Somehow, I imagined Rorik still knew. Something akin to desire flickered through his eyes.

"Time for drills." He folded his arms across his chest. "We'll let up when the sun sets."

True to his word, Rorik ran me through a series of exercises, each one leaving me more breathless than the last. From balancing on one foot with my other knee raised to my chest, to lying on the ground and cycling my legs, he pushed me through it all. Ywena shocked me the entire time. There wasn't a single moment where my breath was steady, and by the time the sun edged toward the horizon, I was a mess of shaking limbs and sweat.

Rorik chuckled as he tipped his head toward the evening sky. "That's enough. Dinner should be ready soon. Shall we?"

I barely had the energy to grumble a response. We walked the rest of the way to the manor in silence, the only sound marking our approach the crunch of grass beneath our feet. When he opened the doors to the hall, however, we were met with a swell of heated words spoken together in a rush. Rorik tensed immediately, and the soft ease of his stance disappeared. He scowled as he strolled forward, leading us into the crowded dining room where the rest of the family sat before empty plates and full goblets.

"Finally. Now we can eat." Seville reclined in her chair and flicked her hand over her shoulder. An attendant stepped away from the wall and moved about the table, effortlessly filling plates before returning to her station.

"Rorik. We were beginning to worry." Orin looked between us as we sat.

"I highly doubt that," Rorik said. He grabbed his glass and took a heavy pull. "What was all the commotion about?"

"Your reckless brother has just informed us that he plans to invite the Starglens and Waterstones to the silver fete," Lydia said, practically hissing. If she'd been glaring at me instead of Orin, I might have shrunk under the weight of her affront.

The silver fete. The exhaustion from my training fled, and I straightened in my chair. Never in my wildest dreams would I have fathomed I'd be anywhere near it. The Ferngloves hosted it once every twenty-five years, and only the elite townsfolk of Willowfell were permitted to join. It was a multiday affair full of revelry. Receiving an invitation elevated one to the upper echelon of Willowfell society, and many scrambled at the opportunity to get in good with the Evers. I glanced at Orin, but he'd already shifted his focus back to Lydia.

Beside her, Clesian gripped her hand tight. "You've yet to tell us your reasoning." His rich, smooth voice was pleasing and heady, despite the tension clearly riddling his frame. Beside him, Amalyss and Tasia sat silently with their gazes fixed on their plates.

Orin sighed. "We need to keep our households allied."

"I fail to see why," Lydia spat.

"Well, you are shortsighted," Seville purred.

"Enough," Orin said, just as Lydia abruptly stood. Her chair scraped angrily against the floor, and an attendant quietly came to her side to scoot it back into place. Lydia slowly sank to her seat without even bothering to check if the chair had been replaced.

Once she'd aimed her gaze back at Orin, he let out a long sigh. "It is vital that we continue to work with other Evers in case new magic is discovered."

"You mean in case our threadmender fails," Lydia said.

I stilled in my chair. None of them looked at me. I was there, and yet I wasn't—just as important as the attendants who flitted around them, but as voiceless as the matriarch who once ruled this house. My gaze slanted to Mavis. Sometimes it was hard to remember she even existed. That faraway stare. The absent way her lips remained parted as if she were about to speak.

Orin grimaced as he reached for his glass. "I have every faith Edira will find a way to cure blight. But as a failsafe, yes. We don't know how much time Mavis has left. Imagine if the Waterstones or Starglens unearthed a new method for curing her ailment and we were none the wiser."

Silence followed his words, everyone's attention riveted to the matriarch—the apparition—beside me. After a full, weighted minute, Lydia dared to speak.

"I'm surprised the Starglens are willing to attend. It's any wonder they even allow Briar to join your lessons."

"We will *not* drag the past into this." Rumbling anger colored Orin's voice. Or maybe it was his magic, because at the same time as the words left his lips, a drying heat as intense as the summer sun cooked the air, and the ground trembled. Everyone at the table stiffened. Orin flexed his hands, as if trying to call the magic back into his body, and the tremors subsided. Then he sighed. Rubbing his temples, he met his aunt's gaze. "It's time we set aside petty squabbles and find a way to deal with blight together. There will be no more arguing about the fete. The date and time have been set."

Rorik leaned back in his chair so the front legs lifted from the floor. He cupped the back of his head and sneered, but his stare turned flinty. "When?"

"A week's time," Seville said as she twirled her fork across her plate. The scrape of metal raised the hairs on my arms. "Everyone"—she dragged out the word as she pinned Rorik with a pointed stare—"is expected to dress accordingly."

His lips thinned in a deranged, stiff smile. "Clothing is the least of my concerns. What of Edira?"

The sound of my name jolted me, and Ywena consequently sent a shock arcing down my arm. If anyone noticed, they didn't say anything. They were too focused on the nearly visible thread of distaste stitched tight between the siblings.

"What of her?" Seville took a small sip from her goblet.

"She'll attend, of course," Orin said.

"You've lost it." Rorik chuckled, and that small action eased the tautness of his frame. He let the legs of the chair fall back to the floor as he snagged his glass. He drained its contents in one fell swoop. "Why would you put our threadmender in harm's way?"

"Are you suggesting we can't look after our own?" Orin asked.

Rorik's answer was quick. "Look what happened just a few days ago under your watch."

Amalyss and Tasia appeared as though they wanted to melt into their chairs, and they glanced at me through the tops of their lashes for the briefest of moments. Lydia slammed her palms against the table, rattling the dinnerware, while Clesian let out something resembling a growl. Seville laughed, but each cackle felt more like a threat and was just as frightening as the others' outbursts.

Orin shot daggers at his brother with his eyes. "Edira—"

"Is a person, not an object, and can speak for herself." I reached for my wine and took a long drink, steadying the rising irritation in my chest. "I'll go."

Finally, they looked at me. I held my ground under the weight of their scrutiny, softening only a touch when I met Orin's stare. He exhaled quietly—a relieved, soothing thing—and his lips lifted in a grateful smile.

"It's settled then." He never looked away from me.

"Right, well . . ." Rorik rotated the stem of his empty goblet, then reached over and snagged Clesian's untouched glass. He cradled the cup with his fingers as he stood and made for the hall. "I have more interesting things to do."

With Rorik's departure signaling the end of a dinner that never even began, Lydia, Clesian, Amalyss, and Tasia followed suit. Seville stalled long enough to force down some fruit before coming to Mavis's side and gently escorting her from the room. Which left me alone with Orin.

He didn't touch his food. "I didn't anticipate that to be so . . ."

"Hostile?" I offered. I nibbled at a piece of bread, suddenly too aware of the way the crumbs clung to my lips.

"Hostile is sort of our default setting." His shoulders sagged as the last of the tension stiffening his frame dissipated. "Still, it's hardly acceptable."

I set aside the bread and reached for my spoon, dipping it in my soup to twirl the broth. Orin watched without speaking, but his eyes said more than enough. Frustrated. Defeated. It must've been difficult to keep his family together with the prospect of Mavis's death, by a disease that shouldn't have affected her at all. Blight was an affliction they were wholly unprepared for. The need to comfort him swelled in my chest until I couldn't hold my tongue any longer.

"One time, when we were young, Noam got into an argument with a neighborhood kid over some bunnies." A small smile tugged at my lips as the scene replayed in my mind. "There was a burrow with a mom and a few babies, and this kid wanted to flush them out so he could trap them." I let the spoon fall against the side of the bowl as I stared at the swirling broth.

"Noam wouldn't stand for it. He told the kid to go trap something else, to leave the family alone. And this kid just started hitting him." I sighed as I propped my chin in my hand and glanced over at Orin. "Noam never fought back. He just sat there and took it."

Orin had gone completely still, his eyes locked on me. "What happened?"

"I happened." I chuckled. "Usually Nohr was the one who always stepped in, but he'd gone off to help Dad with something, and I saw the whole thing through our kitchen window. I tried to break them up. Or maybe I didn't try as hard as I should have; I just remember being so angry. I saw Noam's bloody face, and I couldn't think of anything else.

"I managed to pull the kid off Noam, but instead of letting that be the end of it, I went after him. I wailed on him like he wailed on my brother, until my knuckles were red and aching. That's when Nohr and Dad rounded the corner and saw us and put a stop to it all."

"You beat him?" Orin's brows raised in shock.

"Me." I leaned back in my chair, a sad smile teasing my lips. "I wasn't exactly sorry, either. He'd hurt Noam, and that was enough for me. I guess what I'm trying to say is that I get it. Hostility, that is. It's hard not to feel that way when family is involved."

"And the boy?" Orin was looking at me with an emotion I couldn't place. It was both terrifying and exhilarating, and my pulse quickened in time with my breath. Ywena jolted me in response, and I adjusted in my seat as I regained control of my emotions.

"He was fine," I said, a creeping bitterness coloring my words. "Even so, my mother was less than pleased. And it wasn't like I could use my threadmending abilities without being discovered, so I couldn't fix his injuries. Not that I would have, and she certainly wouldn't have asked that of me. But she had me make a salve with her and tortured me by cooking my favorite meal—rotisserie duck with the most amazing orange marmalade—and not letting me have a single bite. Instead, I had to deliver the medicine and food to the boy and his family."

Orin laughed, a deep rolling sound that reverberated through my bones and straight to my heart. "Was the crime worth the punishment?"

"I'd do it again in a heartbeat if it meant defending my brother." I shrugged and pushed away from my meal. "Plenty of ducks in the world, only one Noam."

The corners of Orin's eyes crinkled with his smile. "They're lucky to have you."

"I know," I said quietly. "I just hope by the time we make it out of this mess, I'll still have a few years left to spend with them."

"You will." Reaching over, he grasped my hand. "I've never met someone as determined as you."

Orin's gaze hammered into my soul, and I found myself leaning toward him. Seeking comfort from his touch. He'd disrupted everything from the moment I met him.

He swallowed thickly. "I hope you understand me orchestrating the fete is not due to a lack of belief in your abilities."

"No, I understand the need to exhaust all avenues." I gave his fingers a reassuring squeeze. "Though I am curious: Is this the first time other Ever families have attended the silver fete? I know it's *the* social event for the townsfolk. I don't really know much about it other than that."

"There used to be more Evers, but we've lost touch with some over the years."

My mind wound back to the bloodlines detailed in *Fable or Fact: A History of Evers*. There were so many families detailed across those pages, it wasn't hard to believe that they couldn't keep up with them all.

"What happened with the Starglens?" I asked.

At that, Orin grimaced. "That is an age-old feud I'd rather not drag you into. All that aside, I do have a request to make." His expression softened, and he smiled as he ran his thumb along my knuckles. "The tailor. Seville will take you tomorrow and have them make you a few dresses fit for a queen. You can pick any style, of course, but . . ." He seemed sheepish. Boyish. It was impossible to look away. "For the first night, maybe something green?"

I grinned. "Are you asking me to dress to match you?"

"It's a thought."

"I'll keep that in mind." It didn't matter that green wasn't my favorite color, or that I'd never attended a fete before and would likely make a fool out of myself. Orin had woken something in me that was warmer than hope and just as terrifying. He made me want to think beyond the immediate future, to ponder the possibility of a life—no matter how short—with someone else. Someone like him.

It was a tantalizing thought, so I clung to it as I walked to my room after wishing him good night. The soft, warm feeling was almost enough to stave off the tingling sensation of watching eyes that always seemed to occur when I hit the top of the stairs.

Almost.

A shiver raced down my spine, and I turned in place only to catch a glimpse of brassy hair fading into nothing. My heart hammered against my throat. Somehow, I kept my breathing in check as I inched toward the fleeting image. The walls seemed to close in on themselves as I moved. They formed a winnowing tunnel ushering me forward. The thick carpet runner beneath my feet swallowed all sound, so that the only thing I heard was my thundering heartbeat. Or maybe it was the house's demanding pulse.

*Come.* Beat.

*Follow.* Beat.

*Find me.* Beat.

Anxiety and curiosity vibrated through to my fingertips, but I couldn't stop. Not until I neared the end of the hall and almost ran face-first into Lydia.

"What are you doing?" she sneered. "Forget how to find your room already?"

"No," I said quickly. All at once the nagging sensation of eyes dispersed. Lydia raised an incredulous brow as I absently brushed my hands along my arms. "I thought I saw someone."

"Yes, how entirely *strange*." She placed her hands on her hips. "Especially considering the number of people who actually live here."

Her condescension was thick, and rather than try to argue, I simply turned away. "Right. Night, Lydia."

"Lady Fernglove," she called to my back, not bothering to hide the malice in her words.

I clenched my jaw tight as I picked up the pace and made it safely back to my room. Lydia's disdain aside, I could've sworn I'd seen something. Rather, something had seen me—and it'd been watching me from the moment I'd set foot in this manor. The lines of the Fernglove family tree sprawled through my mind. Maybe an ancestor spirit still lingered in these halls. I shivered. Regardless of its origin, I'd somehow snared its attention, and there was little I could do to change that.

# TWELVE

The next morning, I woke with the sun, well before most of the household even dared to leave the comfort of their beds. Rather than wait aimlessly for my day with Seville, I dressed and moved through the quiet halls toward the kitchen. Shortly after, coffee and biscuit in hand, I headed for the library. I'd left the journals out on the table, and it took me only a few moments to settle on the sofa and reclaim my aunt's diary. Again, I pored through every entry. Again, I fingered the remains of the missing page while I stared at Mavis's name. I didn't know what to make of any of it. It could be nothing. It could be everything.

An hour passed until the sharp clack of heels against the floor-boards disrupted the stuffy quiet of the library, and I glanced up to find Seville sauntering toward me. She yanked the journal out of my hands and held it a few inches from her face. Her eyes softened, lingering on my aunt's scrawl.

"Ah, Rowena. My favorite threadmender." She snapped the book shut and handed it back to me. "She had a beautiful way with words."

"You wouldn't know it from her entries here." I set the journal on the table. "Did she share other writings with you?"

"Some things here and there," she said with a dismissive wave. "I don't particularly feel like discussing it right now."

"Ah, yes. Seville's agenda or no agenda," I murmured.

"A bit brazen this morning, I see." She leaned against the back of the couch and braced her hands on the polished frame. With a wicked grin, she dipped her lips toward my ear. "Glad you're getting the hang of things."

Gooseflesh rippled down my shoulder, and I scooted out of her reach. "I'm guessing by your presence it's time we visit the tailor?"

"Yes." She flipped her lustrous hair off her shoulder, then straightened. Her stare shifted to my neck. "Probably best if you leave that thing behind."

*Thing?* I followed her gaze to Ywena, who'd given a strange huff in response. She fluttered her wings and practically flattened herself to my skin.

"She's not a *thing*. And I doubt Rorik would be fine with it," I said.

"Good thing I don't answer to him." She then waggled her fingers at Ywena in a shooing motion. "Go on. We'll be trying on clothes, so there'll be no place for you to perch anyway. Tell Rorik if you must."

Ywena hesitated for a moment, her antennae twitching madly, and then she took off. She fluttered through the shafts of light spilling from the windows until she reached the foyer and then drifted out of sight.

A devilish grin tugged at Seville's lips. "He'll just love that. Off to Willowfell we go."

"Willowfell?" A heaviness settled in my stomach.

"Where else did you think we would go? Some of our attendants are skilled with needles, but not to the extent we're looking for." Her thin brows inched together as she studied me. Then her face relaxed and her lips curled into a wicked, knowing grin. "You don't want the townsfolk to see you with me. With an Ever."

"No." *Yes. No. Maybe.* I couldn't really parse the emotions coalescing in my gut. For years, I'd been vocal about my disdain for Evers and their antics. Walking through Willowfell with one at my side would feel like the obscenest of hypocrisies. And I wasn't even by Seville's *side*. Not in that sense, not as an equal. But as an employee. It didn't matter that I'd had little choice in the matter. I wasn't even certain anyone in town knew about my whereabouts or what'd happened the evening my brothers succumbed to blight.

Of course, there was also the obvious truth that no one, not even the families I grew up with, had known I was a threadmender. Anxiety knotted tight in my gut, and I fingered a strand of diamond-white hair. I'd left it down, and it billowed over my shoulders with the languid movement of water. They'd know in an instant what I was.

"No time to be so melodramatic. We're leaving. Now." Seville's slender hand found my wrist. We were through the front door before I fully collected myself, and only then did she release her hold.

When we hit the courtyard, I paused before the turn leading toward the stables. It would be an uncomfortable few hours sitting by Seville, but there didn't seem to be a way around it. "Are we not taking a carriage?"

Seville kept walking forward, not bothering to adjust her pace. "You've got our magic in you now. No sense in wasting time when we have a faster means of travel. Plus, the stags have blight. Better to let them rest until Orin decides you're ready to cure them."

Upping my pace, I rejoined Seville at her side as we made our way to the front gates. "Do you know when he wants me to try and threadmend them?"

"I don't think anyone knows what Orin wants." The words were so calm, so easily delivered, that had I not been looking at Seville I would have assumed she was simply being flippant. But there was a subtle twitch to her brow, the slightest pursing of her lips. She caught me staring, and her expression shifted back to a more familiar smirk. "Except perhaps you."

"I don't know what you mean." Heat crawled over my cheeks.

"Sure. We've lived for a century and still can't recognize the signs of longing. How *quaint*," she said as we passed through the open gates and came to a halt at the bridge. Instead of crossing, Seville pointed to a smooth, rectangular stone of white marble. It came up to her waist, and she gently laid her hand on its polished surface. "Our lands are rich with currents. This ley line will take us to the center of Willowfell." She extended her other hand for me to grasp.

"Lovely." I eyed the seemingly harmless structure, happy to let Seville's prodding about Orin fall to the wayside.

Seville snared my arm and yanked me close. "Hold tight."

She gave me no other warning. Magic snapped to life around us as a swirling faint green portal appeared. The mist seeped into the air around the column until it enveloped us entirely. Sweltering heat battered my body, and my heart thundered in my ears. It was like standing in direct sunlight with a fresh burn: aching, twisting discomfort. Yet the longer it went on, the easier it became to handle, and I managed to catch sight of a twining current of green that slipped beneath our feet. It slid around us like a fast-moving river, ushering us through time and space to deliver us to new shores. And then it was over, the magic evaporating in a rush, and we were standing beneath the arch in Willowfell's town square.

"It gets easier with time," Seville said as the gossamer veil from the arch dissipated around us. Glittering particles of dust showered the ground around our feet. I remembered what it looked like from the other side, to be set up at a stall and marvel at the sudden display of magic. Now, I felt like a spectacle.

Because of course it was market day. And all eyes were already on us.

Gods, I wasn't prepared for the swell of emotion that gathered in my throat. The clover-strewn cobblestone beneath my feet. The rows of tables manned by vendors of every profession. The scent of freshly baked confections wafting from Lysa's shop. Artfully decorated cottages with unique doors to suit the owners. A sudden pang sprouted in my heart as I thought of my own home and the delicate entryway my father had carved. And, of course, there were the people themselves, all clustering together in awe as their gazes bounced between Seville and me.

A few stares glazed right over me, but then the whispers started to race through the stalls and built with each passing breath.

"Is that Edira?"

"She's a threadmender? Since when?"

"No wonder her remedies worked so well."

My jaw clenched as their curiosity swelled. I'd spent years perfecting my disguise, hiding the truth of what I was for the chance at a somewhat normal life. Even if I survived the Ferngloves, I could never be normal again. Not here. The town's collective surprise lasted for a few more pregnant moments before their awe shifted toward Seville, and they started touting their wares. Seville shot me a wayward glance and then grinned, looping her arm through mine as she guided us toward the nearest stalls.

"Shall we browse a bit before trying on gowns?" she asked.

She'd spoken clearly, and yet her words were muffled, pulled through cotton in my ears as I struggled to sift through my emotions. "I'd rather just get this over with."

She paused before a stall selling handmade glass figurines. I recognized the owner, who gaped at me without speaking for several breaths. After a forceful series of blinks, he turned his focus to Seville and aimlessly gestured toward his wares. Her careful stare cut between him and me, and she moved away from his table with nothing more than a nod.

"It appears I'm experiencing a first," she said.

"What do you mean?" I asked.

"You're outshining me." She flipped her hair over her shoulder. I couldn't tell if she was annoyed or intrigued, but the sly twist to her lips and pointed arch of her brow ratcheted my already heightened nerves. "I can't believe you were able to hide your true nature from them for so long. You're as practiced as we are at wearing glamour."

I didn't have a chance to respond. Lysa's father, the primary town elder, parted the crowd and came to a halt before us. He shared the same honey hair and periwinkle eyes as his daughter, but their similarities stopped there. Where Lysa was generous, Mr. Erikston was greedy. Even now, as his gaze tripped over my revealed appearance, I could practically see the gears turning in his mind. My mother had long suspected that he'd been the one to out Rowena's existence in exchange for coin. To him, I was likely nothing more than a missed opportunity.

Still, he didn't bother to address me and instead turned to Seville. "Lady Fernglove," he said, and dipped his chin low as he spoke. "We can't thank you enough for adjusting the taxation on the mines." As he straightened, he beamed at her with too-white teeth. "Rest assured, our increased take has gone toward furthering the town's development, as mandated."

I couldn't keep my mouth from falling open. Seville handled the news with far more grace. "Of course. I'll give your gratitude to my brother."

"Anything you wish is yours. Free of charge." Mr. Erikston gestured wide to include all the stalls, as if he oversaw all their profits. To a degree, he probably did.

"That won't be necessary. I'll pay as I always have," Seville said.

"You are as kind as ever. My family and I look forward to seeing you at the silver fete." He bowed slightly, just enough to show respect but not so far that he couldn't keep his eyes locked on her.

"Of course, but until then, I would like to resume my shopping." Seville turned her back on him without waiting for his answer, leaving me to stare wide-eyed at his retreating form.

Orin had said he'd look after the people of Willowfell; I just hadn't expected him to follow through. I'd expected some twist of words that would leave him the benefactor of the promise, and yet I could see a bit of polish to the town that was lacking before. New tables free of splintering wood. Heavier coin purses among some of the patrons.

A quiet ringing settled in my ears, and the warmth in my chest blossomed. I had no problems admitting my attraction to him— at least inwardly—but this was dangerous. This felt emotional.

"Ah, here we are." Seville's eyes snagged on a brick storefront with oak shutters and large bay windows full of mannequins. The crowd parted as she strolled forward, making it easy for us to find ourselves in front of Mrs. Marlow's shop. My gaze lingered on the windows for a moment, and a flash of something brilliant stole my focus. At first I thought it was nothing more than the sun's reflection on the freshly cleaned glass, but then a small beetle appeared from behind the leaves of the climbing ivy on the wall. A golden beetle.

A faint smile teased my lips. Despite the creature not bringing me good fortune during my last venture to market, there was something welcoming about its presence. It soothed the rattled emotions brought on by revealing my status as a threadmender, and the tension in my shoulders eased. Seville paused for a moment, her hand on the bronzed handle of the shop door. For the briefest of moments, her gaze shifted to the insect. Then she chuckled to herself as she breezed into Mrs. Marlow's store. My brows crawled together as I followed in her wake. She was planning something, and I had the feeling I'd bear the brunt of whatever *humorous* endeavor it was.

A bell tinkled as we pushed open the door, though the announcement of our arrival was unnecessary. Mrs. Marlow was already standing in the entryway with a wide, ecstatic smile and bright eyes. Like the rest of the townsfolk, she faltered for a beat as she took me in. Wringing her hands, she dipped into a low bow.

"Welcome back, Lady Fernglove," she spoke to the floor, but her giddy voice carried the same fervent desire as everyone outside. After a moment, she righted herself and gestured to a small dais positioned before three floor-length mirrors. "I'm assuming you're here for the fete? I do have some premade gowns, but I can clear my agenda if you're looking for something bespoke."

"Likely the latter." Without looking my way, Seville gestured with two fingers. "What do you think, Edira? Has she ever crafted anything original for you?"

Mrs. Marlow shot me a pleading look. I had no doubt she'd tailored custom creations for the more well-to-do townsfolk, but the most I'd seen out of Mrs. Marlow was unfinished off-the-rack fabric.

I wondered if she would have offered more, had she known I was a threadmender.

"She was going to reupholster my couch," I said with a shrug. "Not sure if she got around to it, given I left shortly after that agreement." A strange sense of satisfaction brewed in me at her dropped jaw. Seville looked at me with a raised brow and a slow-moving smile.

"Well, adorn me better than a couch." Seville stepped onto the pedestal and stared at herself in the mirror as Mrs. Marlow flew into action. She bustled through the shop, selecting bolts of brightly colored fabric and a selection of garments from one of the racks toward the back. I couldn't recall the last time I'd seen her move so quickly.

"Why was she going to repair your furniture?" Seville asked. She studied me through the mirror, and I did the same, angling to catch her reflection.

"Payment for fixing her son's broken nose."

Seville stilled. "Threadmending?"

I held her gaze for a long moment. "No. Just proper care and some balm."

"Have you ever threadmended before?" Seville scowled at herself in the mirror. "Such inexperience. I hope Orin's not wasting his efforts on you."

"Twice." I hovered by the window, catching sight of the beetle's underside. "I tried to cure my parents when they had blight."

I didn't know what prompted the words to slip from my mouth, and I stalled at their sound. Perhaps it was being back in Willowfell after everything I'd learned, everything I'd seen. Perhaps it was the fear that if I didn't figure this out, I'd be burying my brothers beside my parents' graves in a matter of months. Weeks, even.

Seville was a statue. "When?"

"I was thirteen."

The long-buried memory began to unfold before my eyes. It'd been snowing, flurries blanketing the earth in a thick layer of white. The fire in the hearth had been crackling and warm, and I'd curled by it with a quilt while my brothers played in their room.

My throat bobbed as I searched for words. "My mother was afflicted first. She was making us lunch. She dropped something, and my father went to check on her. The next thing I knew, they were both sitting on the kitchen floor babbling nonsense."

Mrs. Marlow returned to hold a strip of fabric near Seville's exposed neck, and she dismissed the seamstress with a brusque "Shoo." Then, much softer to me: "That's horrible."

I nodded. I hadn't understood much about threadmending then, just the few lessons I'd held on to from my aunt. But I saw my parents' wild, sickly threads. Felt the cool whisper of death. I remembered screaming. I remembered shaking them and begging for their lives as if that would've been enough to fix their condition. I remembered rushing to my brothers' room and barricading the door from the outside so they wouldn't see.

And then I remember running back and tapping into my power, only to fail.

"I obviously couldn't save them. Expending that kind of power without any semblance of control . . . I passed out. When I woke, their bodies were already decomposing on the floor." I'd never forget the sight of black mold and rot and putrid mustard-yellow spores sprouting from their chests. I'd wrapped them in rugs and dragged them to the graveyard myself. I didn't have to bury them. The blight had done that for me. Later, when I'd recovered, I'd gone back and erected simple headstones where their bodies had disintegrated. It'd done nothing to alleviate the hollow ache in my chest, but it'd been *something*.

Silence filled the quiet shop, and even Mrs. Marlow kept her distance. The townsfolk, of course, knew how my parents had died, but the details I'd never shared. I looked back to the window and relished the warmth of the sun. The soft rays chased away the chilling memory, and I rubbed my hands along my arms.

"And the second time?" Seville asked.

That memory was easier. "Nohr. Ten years later. Broken leg."

Seville regarded me for a long moment down the length of her straight nose, then scoffed. And yet there was still a touch of sadness, of understanding, that she couldn't fully mask in her eyes.

"The tailor's kid's broken nose, your brother's leg, Tasia's cut." She ticked off the occurrences on her fingers one by one. "You have a soft spot for children."

I lifted my shoulder. "Perhaps."

"Keep that to yourself around Evers. Next thing you know, you'll be a broodmare. Children are rare among my kind. Our magic is picky like that." She waved Mrs. Marlow back over and inspected a fresh batch of gowns before letting out a disappointed sigh. "But some mortals have been known to get pregnant with an Ever child."

Color leeched from my face as I stared at her through the mirror. "I wouldn't live long enough to see them grow. I don't want to experience that."

Seville watched me for a long moment. "Fair enough." Then she stepped down from the platform to saunter toward me, leaving Mrs. Marlow to fuss after her. When she was only mere inches away, she folded her arms beneath her bust and settled her weight into one hip. "Seems like it'll be bespoke attire for both of us. None of those gowns suited me. Go on, it's your turn."

"I'm sure I'll be fine with something here."

She grinned. "But Orin won't."

Her small chuckle filled my ears, and I bit back a heated curse. It was always something with her. What did she think was going on with Orin and me? We hadn't even *kissed*. Not that I didn't want to. I silenced a groan as I stepped around Seville. She sunk onto a low settee by the window and reclined like a goddess with her legs stretched over the tufted fabric. With a small wave, she gestured for me to move. I looked between her and Mrs. Marlow, who did nothing but tightly grip the hem of a sky-blue gown.

Stepping onto the dais, I stared at myself in the mirror. "I suppose being here with you is better than with Tasia and Amalyss. They wanted to dress me like a doll the first time I met them."

"In case you haven't figured it out already, I am by far the *best* Fernglove." Seville cradled her head with one hand and draped the other across her stomach. Then she glanced at Mrs. Marlow. "Bring me some tea and draw the curtains. Edira is being fitted for undergarments as well. Something black and lacy."

I whirled on her without stepping down from the platform as Mrs. Marlow practically vanished into thin air. "For fuck's sake, is this really necessary?"

"It is necessary. For fuck's sake specifically." She let out a dark chuckle, but there was no mirth to her expression. "Don't fight it."

"Why?"

"Because if you are going to find a way to survive this mess, then you'll need all the help you can get." She glared at me, and even still, she was beautiful. Remarkable.

I swallowed thickly as I stared at her. "It doesn't matter what I wear, so long as I do my job."

"Your job. Is that what you've been doing with Orin?" With practiced ease, she unbuttoned the top of her silk blouse to reveal a hint of something satin and trimmed in lace. It was only a shade darker than her skin, giving the illusion that she was revealing much more than she actually showed—and I wondered if that wasn't Seville in a nutshell. She'd perfected the image, the glamour, of want and desire, and no one really knew what she hid beneath it all.

A slow-moving heat flushed my face. "What are you doing?"

"That's a lovely hue." Her gaze targeted my cheeks, and my stomach squirmed. "The best thing about silk and lace is how disarming they can be. They're a type of armor, in a way." Her words were smooth as syrup, her motions flawless as she redid her button and reclined against the settee.

And still, I was frozen. "You hardly need armor."

Mrs. Marlow returned at that point with a silver tray arranged with tea and sugar, and she placed it before Seville, reaching behind her to draw the beige curtains closed. Then she moved to me and began to free my torso of clothing. My mind spun as I stared at Seville. Her words, her thoughts, were impossible to follow.

Tilting her head in my direction, Seville regarded Mrs. Marlow as she measured beneath my bust. "Everyone needs armor. But more importantly, you need what this particular type of armor gives you."

"And that is?"

Seville waited until Mrs. Marlow excused herself in the pursuit of fabric. Once she'd shuffled away, Seville leaned forward and served herself tea. "The freedom to look without being seen."

A cold chill raced down my spine. "What?"

"I quite liked your aunt," she continued, ignoring my question entirely. "I dare say I considered her a friend."

In the subdued, warm light of the shop, I felt strangely exposed, and it had little to do with my lack of blouse. I fought the urge to cross my arms over my chest, to hide the simple linen undergarments and bare skin.

"Why did you bring me here, Seville?"

She took a long sip of her tea before leveling me with a sharp look. "We used to trade letters unbeknownst to the family."

*She had a beautiful way with words.* Seville's reminiscing from early rattled through my mind. "Now you feel like talking about her?"

"Of course." She smirked, but it didn't fully reach her eyes. "My agenda and all."

"Why?" I dragged out the word, trying in vain to unearth her intentions.

"Because I feel like it." She barked out a laugh. "Why else would I do anything?"

"No, not that." It was impossible not to glare at her. "Why did you and Rowena exchange letters?"

"Ah." The curve to her lips became softer, gentler. She looked away at the space behind me, and her fingers dawdled over the lip of her cup. In the span of a breath, she was gone—lost in some memory that caused her body to slacken. I wondered if this was the real Seville. Pensive. Amorous. She was bathed in a gauzy, romantic light with her blond hair spilling over her shoulders.

Seville didn't need to try so damn hard to be beautiful. Because this version of her was the very definition of ethereal, and I couldn't find the gall to speak.

After that solitary beat that seemed to last an eternity, Seville straightened. She flipped her hair back, and the veneer she always wore—exquisite, yet remarkably cold, especially after what I'd just witnessed—slid over her expression.

"Why do you think we spoke privately?" Her gaze raked over me, and mischief lit in her stare. "Why do you and Orin spend time alone?"

My lips fell open at her insinuation, and I went rigid all over. My aunt and *Seville*? Seville giggled and pushed herself into an upright position. "Gods, your face. Relax." She waved off my reaction as if it were nothing more than a bothersome fly. "Tell me what you know about power sharing and heartbonds."

"Power sharing and heartbonds . . . ?" The whiplash of her words made my head spin, and I tossed up my hands in frustration. "How do you expect me to keep up with this conversation?"

"By providing me with your rapt, undivided attention."

Mrs. Marlow returned at that point with several options of varying colors and textures, which was a reprieve as I was afforded the excuse to look at something other than Seville's painted-on grin. I desperately wished I could call on my power and somehow see the threads of her words, figure out all the hidden things she was weaving into her little tales.

"Well? Go on, then. Tell me something," Seville prompted.

"I don't know much. Just that the effects are permanent," I said as I trailed light fingers over an emerald-green bralette hemmed with silver thread. I hadn't spoken to anyone in the house about heartbonds yet, but I hadn't forgotten about that dog-eared page from their history tome. Maybe the same person who had marked it was responsible for the missing page from Rowena's journal.

"Indeed." Seville's keen eyes shifted to the fabric in my hands, and she pinned Mrs. Marlow with a quick glare. "I said black. Or better yet, gold."

"Gold?" Mrs. Marlow snatched the garments from my grip and cradled them against her chest. "That's not a hue I carry. I would have to have a bolt specially dyed, and I'd need ample time to construct something from scratch. It would be costly."

*Gold.* The color of riches and royalty. The color of crowns. For a moment, I glanced at the window and imagined being able to peer through the fabric at the world outside, at the golden beetle hiding between the ivy leaves. Maybe I had been marked for something more. Seville clearly had made me part of her plan, because while her questions were wild, her thoughts scattered, her gaze had never felt more meaningful.

"I'll pay it," Seville said, effectively breaking me from my reverie. "In the meantime, I suppose it's fine to fit her with some of your existing options." With uncanny swiftness, she secured the teapot and refilled her cup. "She'll be needing something to wear immediately, so your *lesser*-quality creations will have to do."

I bit my tongue at Seville's nonchalant dig. Mrs. Marlow, however, was much better at schooling her indignation into place. She didn't flinch—only smiled and left to return to her racks in search of something Seville would deem suitable.

Seville dragged a lazy finger along the rim of her cup. "Did you know that some Ever families have stronger magic than others? Abilities specific only to their kin? Control over the elements—I met someone years ago who could summon stars that dusted into diamond-like particles. It was beautiful."

An image of Briar sitting outside during lessons cradling a cluster of stars flooded my mind. "Like the Starglens?"

"Yes." She went impossibly still. Her lips were sealed tight, but there was something fiery in her gaze, something that begged for recognition. I couldn't fathom what. She let me feel the full weight of her stare and that sole word for a breath, and then she tapped her wrist for effect. "The same goes for us Ferngloves. These unique powers live in our blood. The only way for that magic to be passed on is to bear children—which I mentioned is rare—or through a heartbond."

Her words seemed to hang in the very air as I turned them over. Again, I couldn't help but notice the quiet reverence in her voice at the mention of the bond. But there was an undercurrent to her tone, a low heat that matched the intensity of her stare. A warning. Or . . .

An opportunity. Something in my mind clicked like a lock releasing, and suddenly the quiet sounds of the shop were too sharp, the light too harsh. My breath caught in my chest.

"Has an Ever attempted to form a heartbond with a human?"

"Not that I'm aware of." Seville didn't move an inch. "There's never been any power to share, so why give something freely when we stand to gain nothing in return? We prefer consorts and save the bonds for other Evers."

"But if there was power to share . . ." I let my words fall away as Mrs. Marlow returned with a brassiere made of sheer slate-gray fabric and black stitching that formed intricate swirls. Seville stood and took it from her, shooing her away with one stern look. She came up behind me and pinned the straps to my shoulders with her fingers, allowing the fabric to loosely drape against my chest.

"Careful, Edira," she murmured against my ear, and gooseflesh rippled down my neck. "Speak it into existence and it just might happen. And it cannot be undone."

For a moment, all I could do was stare at myself in the mirror, at the armor Seville had expertly selected.

She was helping me win over Orin. That's what this was all about. Because if I could convince him to form a heartbond with me, I would gain access to his powers. Maybe his brand of magic could bolster my own. Maybe that was why no one had managed to cure an Ever of blight, because it required a level of magic that no threadmender had possessed.

*Or he could use you for your power.* A shudder raced through my limbs. I had no reason to believe he would. He'd held true to every single one of his promises, including allocating extra funds for the town. This preconceived notion I'd formed about Evers—Orin never fit into the mold.

Seville chuckled quietly. "I think you've had enough lingerie. Time to find you a gown."

Without adding anything else, Seville turned and took the lingerie with her as she sauntered toward Mrs. Marlow. Over the dull ringing in my ears, I vaguely heard her demand for a selection of dresses to determine what style suited me best, but all I could think about was the lengths Seville had gone to in order to orchestrate this disjointed conversation. Pieces of it were clicking into place slowly, but there was still something just beyond my grasp. A pivotal fragment of information just begging to be recognized.

# THIRTEEN

The next day was the first time I made it around the manor once before being shocked by Ywena. It was two laps short of what Rorik demanded, but it was better than I'd ever done, and I couldn't help but smile to myself as I sunk to the ground before him. He leaned against the ancestor tree—it didn't have a name, so I decided upon one myself—with his ankles crossed and scowled.

"That wasn't three laps."

I wished one hand would dislodge itself from the trunk and smack that self-important look right off his face.

"Thank you for that astute observation." I rolled my eyes as my breathing slipped, and Ywena didn't hesitate to send a tiny jolt of electricity through to my fingertips. I'd grown used to her reminders, and while they didn't exactly hurt, they certainly pulled my focus. "I hit my limit. If I'd kept going, Ywena would've shocked me before the next bend."

"Then you should have run to the next bend," he said.

"You're insufferable, you know that?" I folded my arms over my knees and glared up at him. "I'll try again in a minute."

He dragged out a sigh as he tilted his head toward the branches. Leaves fluttered in the gentle breeze, and a butterfly with bright blue wings and sable markings lazily followed the current to land on a withering flower. Rorik's expression softened as he spied the creature. Instinctively, my fingers trailed over the crest inked into my forearm.

"Why insects?" I asked.

He raised a brow. "What do you mean?"

"Well, they're not exactly appealing. I mean, I don't mind them, but most people shy away from them."

"What makes you think we care about being appealing?" He raised his hand and extended a single finger to the butterfly. It considered him for a moment before floating to his knuckles.

I snorted. "Are you kidding me? If you didn't care about that, you wouldn't bother with glamours."

Surprisingly, he chuckled. "Point taken. As for why insects . . ." His amber eyes softened. "They're plenty appealing. All the colors and variations. But more importantly, they're strong. And they adapt exceedingly well."

"How do you mean?"

The butterfly took flight, and he tracked its path with his eyes. "Most of the insects around here are infected with blight, yet they live on. In fact, they thrive. Blight seems to have altered their biology, but instead of killing them, it allows them to feed on diseased plants. Life is wonderfully resilient."

"It's a shame there's no magic for tapping into that adaptation," I said as I watched the butterfly disappear into the tree line.

Rorik folded his arms across his chest. "Orin's tried, of course. Nothing has worked."

Images of Orin's body, stripped of glamour and enhanced with otherworldly magic, filled my mind. "What do you look like beneath your glamour?"

"Your obsession with seeing beneath our veil is tiresome." He straightened, and his scowl returned.

"You know, some insects shed their skin. You should try it." I stood and brushed loose grass from my pants. "At least Orin trusted me enough to show me the beauty of his magic."

"Beauty?" Rorik's laugh was dark. "I see. Well, I'm sorry I'm unwilling to make myself attractive for your benefit. I'll leave that to Orin."

I clenched my fists. "Orin showed me his true self because he trusts me."

"You're a fool." Rorik glowered as he inched closer. "It just means he doesn't think you're a threat."

Irritation bloomed in my chest, and I took an indignant step forward. His breath skated against my skin, and I ignored the involuntary gooseflesh that traveled down my neck. "And what about you? Is that why you won't reveal yourself? Do you think I'm a threat?"

Something like desire flashed through his eyes, and he faltered for a breath before masking it with a smirk. "I don't find you threatening. I just don't think it's worth my time."

"Is that right?" My words were deadly calm. I'd never once in my life aimed to be threatening. Well, maybe *once*. Back when I fought a kid for Noam's sake. Maybe also when I slapped Tasia in the carriage. Maybe a few other times. Regardless, there was something hot and angry that always seemed to linger beneath the surface when it came to Rorik. I didn't need him, and yet I wanted him to think I could do this. I wanted to be a threat, whatever that meant, to him. To the blight infecting his grandmother and my brothers. I wanted to be strong enough to take it all on.

"Not in the slightest." His grin was wicked. Again, I longed to slap it right off his face.

So I tried.

I moved fast, pulling my hand back and swinging it wildly through the air with the hope of meeting his cheek in a resounding crack. But as quick as I thought I was, Rorik was faster. Worse yet, he was smooth about it. He barely leaned back, just enough to avoid the arc of my swing, and the momentum of my wayward hand knocked my entire body off-balance. I went toppling into his broad chest with an undignified grunt.

And then he started laughing.

The deep rumble barreling from his chest shook my entire body. With my erratic breathing and my nose buried in his shirt, I expected to smell something. But nothing filled my nostrils, not even a hint of salt or musk to indicate he'd been baking beneath the sun. Fucking Evers having to be perfect. I pushed away from him hard—*so hard*—and yet he still didn't falter. Instead, he keeled over, hands on his knees, and laughed at the very earth.

"All right, enough of that," I seethed. Ywena was shocking me endlessly, but her consistent jolts did nothing to distract me from the burn ravaging my cheeks.

When Rorik finally righted himself, he swiped at one of his eyes as if chasing away a stray tear. "Next session, we're moving on to strength training. That was pathetic."

"Asshole," I hissed.

He lifted a shoulder, a smirk still toying with his lips. "Happy to be one."

"You won't be laughing when I actually do punch that grin so hard you lose teeth."

"I would love to see you try," he murmured, voice gravelly and dark. For a long moment, neither of us spoke. Neither of us moved. He simply stared at me with an intensity that made my skin flame and my pulse race. Electrical currents rolled down my limbs in waves, courtesy of Ywena, but I didn't care. I couldn't seem to escape Rorik's gaze. I was being scrutinized from head to toe, and yet . . .

"Run, Edira. Three laps." He laughed as he folded his arms over his chest. "Don't make me chase you—unless, of course, you prefer that kind of play."

I spit at his feet before taking off, trying in vain to ignore the heated blush that had crawled over my cheeks.

In the days leading up to the fete, I got only one chance to swing at him again. We'd warm up with running—rather, I'd warm up with running, and Rorik would watch me from his place beneath the tree—and then he'd push me to every limit imaginable for hours on end until my body gave out, and I'd return to the manor to research. My muscles screamed and buckled with the new exercises as he made me carry stones while doing simple things like balancing. He also made me punch the air endlessly until my shoulders burned and my arms shook. Anything to better my chances of success, he'd said through a laugh. And of course, I was expected to breathe evenly throughout it all, which I failed to do every time.

"Who can manage this bullshit?" I grumbled once after falling to the ground in a heap, my hair an unkempt mess and my blouse plastered to my skin with sweat.

"I can," he mused with a raised brow. "Now do it all again."

I'd cursed loud enough for a set of nearby attendants to balk as they set up some outdoor furnishings for the upcoming fete.

Throughout it all, Rorik insisted we continue our training. It was somewhat of a relief, spending my days outdoors away from the chaos within the manor, and I wouldn't have been surprised if Rorik felt the same. With each passing day, the perma-glare carved into his expression grew sharper and deeper, and he rarely spoke save to bark out orders or correct my form. Beyond those curt directions during our sessions, he opted for silence at meals and then disappeared altogether. He was a brooding harbinger of malcontent, and I had no idea why.

That is, until the day before the fete when I finally managed to make it through a round of weighted lunges without my breath faltering.

Rorik studied me intently as I came to a halt before him, sweat pouring down my brow and my skin flushed with heat, but the rise and fall of my chest was steady. Even. My lungs screamed with every raw, burning breath, but I didn't cave.

And Rorik actually smiled. It was still devilish in the most dangerous way, and yet there was also a sliver of pride to his expression. "Good. You've earned your chance."

"My chance?" I asked, allowing my shoulders to roll forward.

"Hit me," he purred, voice tantalizingly dark.

"Are you a masochist or a sadist? It's impossible to tell." I rolled my neck from side to side. Yet I couldn't deny the trill of excitement that spurred through my limbs. Maybe I was a little bit of the latter.

His eyes flashed with heat. "Both."

"What a horrid combination." I'd gone still as I stared at his flawless face. I pictured it with ease. The way I'd cock back my arm, the tightness of my muscles, the sting of skin on skin as my hand connected with his cheek. I moved instantly, rearing back with the hopes of becoming the threat he wanted me to be . . . and met nothing but air.

At least this time, I didn't fall into him. Glaring at his haughty smirk, I regained my balance quickly and fisted my hand by my side. Just like before, he'd easily leaned out of my trajectory. Now, though, he dipped his chin low so that he was no more than a breath away.

"Everything you do is painfully obvious."

"And everything you do is painfully annoying."

This time when I went to smack him, he didn't back out of my space. He simply snared my wrist before it could make contact and held it an inch away from his cheek.

"One chance per accomplishment, Edira."

I curled my fingers slightly, and the tips of them grazed his smooth skin. He froze beneath my touch. Two could play this game. If I couldn't punch him, then at least I'd irritate him to no end. I longed to ghost my fingers along the length of his sharp cheekbone, to trail over the dermal piercings hammered above his brow. But before I could bring my fingertips farther along his jawline, he cast aside my hand with a scowl, taking an exaggerated step back.

A satisfied grin stole across my expression. "At least I got rid of that damn smile somehow."

Heat flared in his eyes. "That's enough for today. Can't have you worn out for tomorrow's events."

He strode across the lawns without a backward glance, leaving me behind. I didn't try to catch up. I was done running to or away from that bastard. Rorik was a wild card that I didn't know how to play. But I didn't care. Couldn't. Because night was here and the fete was tomorrow, and my body throbbed from all the work I'd put it through. Nothing was more important than sleep, so I put his confusing antics to the side and eased the front doors open.

Just down the hall, two attendants were busy rearranging a multitude of flowerpots on the credenzas in preparation for the festivities. Final touches, I assumed. Seville's theme for the fete was "grandeur," which made me laugh out loud when I heard her mention it to the staff. She'd orchestrated everything down to the varying perfumes she selected so each room would house its own unique scent.

*The flowers should have done that.* I eyed the overflowing pots. The nagging reminder that something was off with the flora was inescapable. With their backs to the front door, the attendants hadn't noticed me slip into the house, and their whispered conversation carried through the near-silent foyer.

"I can't believe Dagas is attending. After Lorelai, I assumed they'd never set foot here again." Her brown hair was swept up into a sloppy bun, and she adjusted the silk scarf along her forehead to keep loose strands from falling into her eyes.

The other attendant, a woman with short black hair, nodded her agreement. "She did pass rather quickly after, well, you know."

Dagas? Lorelai? I paused at the bottom of the stairs, curiosity outweighing my desperate need for sleep.

"Not the first time, either." The brunette took a step back and surveyed her work. "Still, I'd rather work here than for the Starglens. I've heard their home is atrocious."

Just then, sharp heels clacked against the floorboards, and the women straightened as if lightning had struck their spines. I stiffened with them, knowing full well who was likely rampaging through the manor at this hour in four-inch pumps.

"You two!" Seville came into sight from the opposite end of the hall, and she glared at their frozen forms. "I demand to know who set out the glassware for the Ever meeting. I specifically requested our crystal stemware—the set with the diamond inlay. Retrieve them now and make sure the kitchen knows to serve wine from the reserves when we meet with the Waterstones and Starglens."

"Of course. Right away," the brunette said, and both attendants scurried away without a backward glance.

"The incompetence." Seville pinched her nose, and then without bothering to look my way, she said, "Get to bed, Edira. I swear to the heavens if you have bags beneath your eyes tomorrow, I will riot. We did not spend a fortune on gowns for you to look like death warmed over."

A heat flamed my cheeks, and I grasped the banister as I glared at her. "You should get some sleep, too."

"As if anything in this world could make me look less than flawless." She let her hand fall away before she turned on her heel. "Go. I have work to do."

And with that she was gone. I grumbled at nothing as I climbed the stairs to my room. I wouldn't have to worry about bags or harried appearances if I could wield glamour, too. But I obviously couldn't, and the fatigue from training was already settling deep into my muscles. Still, I couldn't help but think about the attendants' hushed gossip. This fete, it seemed, was truly vital for putting old feuds to the side.

I only hoped diamond stemware counted for something when it came to the Starglens.

THE NEXT MORNING, I LOUNGED in bed and revisited the Ever texts I'd pulled from the library. I nibbled on scones and sipped coffee, more than content to let the day slip away, until Vora breezed into my room and announced it was time to get ready. I groaned at the stiffness in my body, but relented when she bribed me with a steaming bath, complete with rosewater and lavender. Of course, it was over entirely too quickly, and before I knew it, I'd been whisked away to an oversized dressing room where Amalyss and Tasia were already waiting. They sat side by side on cushioned, low-backed chairs while two attendants twisted their hair into artful updos. When I stalled in the doorway, their quiet conversation halted.

"Come on. We don't have time to dally." Vora nudged me in the back as she guided me toward the third open chair. We were surrounded by ornate mirrors and glass trays full of perfumes and balms and oils. The room was thick with colliding aromas, and I struggled to parse one scent from the next. Tea and coffee had been arranged on end tables near each chair, and Amalyss delicately set down her cup as I approached.

"Good afternoon," she said. Beside her, Tasia nodded but didn't meet my gaze.

"Afternoon." I took my seat, and Vora immediately got to work, combing through my damp locks. Ywena abandoned my shoulder to temporarily perch on Vora's, giving her the chance to style without interference.

Strange. I'd never seen Ywena with anyone outside of Rorik, and yet she'd effortlessly settled against the crook of Vora's neck, all without the attendant even blinking.

For several minutes, none of us spoke. There were a few mumbled comments from the attendants as they traded ideas for our appearances, but aside from that and the gentle clink of fine ceramics, there was nothing to abate the ever-growing tension between Amalyss, Tasia, and me. I would've been content to sit silently and listen to their aimless conversation, but they wouldn't even speak to each other. Amalyss and Tasia were still walking on eggshells, as if even the sound of their voices would invoke Orin's wrath. And he wasn't even here.

"So." I cleared my throat, and they both tensed. "Are you excited for the fete? What color are your gowns?"

They shared a private look before Amalyss dared to speak. "The fete should be fun. My dress is blue."

"Mine is violet." There wasn't even a hint of excitement in Tasia's voice. "What about yours?"

"Green." Or some variation of it, at least. I'd largely left the design up to Seville and Mrs. Marlow.

"Green?" Amalyss raised a brow. "Interesting. I pictured you in silver."

"Or gold," Tasia said. Amalyss cut her a hard glance as she curled tense fingers around the arms of her chair.

"Does it matter?" I asked.

A pregnant pause hung between us. Then, finally, Amalyss blew out a breath and released her vise grip. "Typically, partners dress to match. It's an Ever custom for these sorts of things. And Orin always wears green."

"Yes, he asked that I wear it. I saw no reason not to." A lightness bloomed in my chest at the thought of Orin. We hadn't declared ourselves as anything—partners or otherwise. But I couldn't help thinking of my conversation with Seville. About heartbonds. Tilting my head, I glanced between both girls. "Your parents are heartbonds, right? When did they decide to make that commitment?"

Tasia's and Amalyss's attendants excused themselves as they went to plate us a light snack, but Vora remained behind. Her hands stiffened against my scalp, and she gave my hair a firm tug that felt wholly unnecessary. I frowned at her through the mirror, but she only clenched her jaw as she returned to her task.

Tasia finally looked at me, and I was struck by how soft her gaze had become. "They met around fifty years ago, but they declared themselves as heartbonds after twenty years of dating. It's not something Evers take lightly."

"Because of the power sharing, right?" I asked. This time when Vora scraped my scalp, I winced.

*Be careful who you trust.* Right now, her words felt like a warning for her own actions.

Amalyss cast a wary glance at Vora. "Yes. The theory is that you become stronger together."

"But if two Evers decide they no longer want to be heartbonds, it doesn't matter." Tasia picked at the hem of her silk robe, same as the ones Amalyss and I wore, as she spoke. "The bond remains even if they both agree and go off to find other partners."

"Which means they always have access to each other's powers," Amalyss said.

"And you two? You're their children. Do you have both your father's and your mother's powers?"

"Father comes from a small Ever family with weak ties back to the first Ever. It's typically the more dominant power that's passed on." Tasia opened her palm to reveal a faint green glow, similar to the one that Orin summoned in his private study. "It's why we're still considered Ferngloves."

"Beyond power, though, there's also the emotions to consider," Amalyss mused, but she had an almost dreamy look to her expression. "Can you imagine? Being able to feel what your partner feels, sharing your truest desires with nothing more than a thought? You don't have to be in love to form a heartbond, but if you are . . ."

Tasia's exhale was soft. "Apparently there is no feeling like it. That's how Mother describes it, anyway. It must be bliss."

*Bliss.* I mulled over their words as the attendants returned with tea sandwiches and fruit. The girls picked at grapes and berries, and with each passing breath they relaxed. Their smiles came easy; their conversation shifted to lighter, more mundane things. And they often asked me questions about human customs, and for the first time since coming to Fernglove, I actually felt welcomed. Between attempting to cure Tasia and this conversation about dresses and heartbonds, I'd gained an ounce of trust.

My heart twisted with a familiar ache as my mind wandered to my brothers. These were the conversations we'd have over meals. I hadn't realized how much I'd missed that sense of family and togetherness. I visited Noam and Nohr every night, finding what little solace I could in their even breaths. Hours would pass as I fixated on their blight and hoped, prayed, I'd be strong enough to stop its slow-moving progression. I'd been so focused on their survival that I'd buried the need for true familial connection deep. But now, as Amalyss, Tasia, and I finished our snack and our dresses were brought in, I couldn't deny the budding joy in my chest.

As Tasia and Amalyss squealed over their dresses, running light fingers over the folds of fabric, it suddenly made sense to me why Orin insisted the silver fete go on as planned. His family could sit and fixate on the blight eating away at Mavis until she'd rotted away, or he could help them take solace in the little things. In the beauty of a new gown, in the joy of togetherness. The warmth he'd sparked in my chest grew. He was more caring than I'd realized, more perceptive about his family's needs. He wanted them to enjoy every moment they could—and it felt like he wanted that for me, too, despite our working arrangement. Perhaps *in* spite of it. Grinning, I pushed out of my chair and joined Amalyss and Tasia before our dresses, eager to soak in their excitement.

Yet, as I met Vora's gaze through the reflection in the mirror, all I could see was fear and dread. The stark, chilling contrast between her and the girls was enough to root me to the ground. Her stare held a warning that I couldn't comprehend, and before I could excuse myself to ask her questions, Amalyss and Tasia had looped their arms through mine and were guiding me toward the changing screen. They dropped their robes in one fluid motion and stepped into their gowns, shimmying them up their bodies far enough to cover themselves before seeking the attendants' help.

*You're allowed a moment.* It was a small, quiet thought, but insistent nonetheless. I stared at my dress without moving. Vora's eyes were still burning into me, even through the safety of the screen. Maybe she thought this fete was as ludicrous as Rorik suggested. Maybe she wanted me to get back to training. An indignant flame of irritation sparked in me. All I did was work for them. If Orin went to the trouble of creating this event for us to enjoy a break from reality, then I was entitled to that joy, too. I didn't want to think about my brothers dying upstairs. About my shortening lifespan or my contract with the Ferngloves. Tonight, I wanted to be Edira Brillwyn of Willowfell.

I stepped into my gown and stepped out of my responsibilities, giving over fully to the giddy swell of excitement permeating from Amalyss's and Tasia's bodies. Vora said nothing else as she laced the back of my corset, and it wasn't until she stepped away that I dared to look in the mirror.

"Edira," Amalyss said, coming to stand beside me. Her sky-blue dress was dotted in tiny crystals that winked like stars. Tasia's dress was the same, but in a richer deep violet that felt almost celestial. Together, they were the progression from dusk to night. And they were stunning.

Tasia grazed the airy fabric of my skirt. "You look beautiful."

I stared at myself in the mirror. "I look like a garden."

Both girls laughed, and then Amalyss smiled. "No, you look like an Ever."

The corset bodice hugged my curves in a way no article of clothing had ever appreciated my body before. The boning was made to look like vines and stems that crawled toward my breasts and bloomed with delicate pale pink flowers that bordered on white. Strips of green fabric with appliqué leaves draped over my shoulders and moved liked the long strands of willow trees in the wind. The skirt fell to the floor, but it was featherlight against my skin. There was, undoubtedly, a certain earthy beauty to it, and since the layers of chiffon were all dyed in varying shades of green, Orin would be happy. And I would not acknowledge the thrilling sensation that wound through me at that thought.

"Come. Let's finish your cosmetics. The silver fete awaits." This time when Vora met my gaze, she'd schooled her conflicting emotions in place. I returned to my seat while she painted on makeup, and the attendants did the same for Amalyss and Tasia. Once finished, they lingered by the door, seemingly waiting for me to join them.

Vora brushed a translucent powder over my skin as a final

touch, and she leaned closer under the guise of inspecting her work. Her fingers lingered on the crest on my forearm.

"Be careful."

And then she straightened, plastering on a smile that didn't reach her eyes. I stared at her for a long moment, uncertain what to say, until Ywena fluttered off her shoulder to return to the crook of my neck. The gentle feel of her limbs was reassuring, and I nodded once.

"Shall we?" I stood and crossed the room to Amalyss and Tasia, and together we made our way through Fernglove Manor toward the fete outside.

# FOURTEEN

Seville had outdone herself. The back lawns had been transformed into a scene out of a book. Gossamer canopies
stretched across the space like low-hanging clouds, and chandeliers covered in glittering crystals hung from the wooden rafters
of the structures. The gardens had been dressed in twinkling tea
lights, the fountain adorned with lilies and floating candles encased in glass. Tables overflowed with an abundance of food, and
there was upbeat music from a quartet stationed near an actual
fountain of wine. A short distance away was a makeshift dance
floor with shined wooden floorboards arranged in a perfect square
beneath a pergola draped in ivy. Amber orbs cradled by vines hung
at varying heights, and a magical glow hummed from their centers
to cast the space in a warm light.

All at once I understood why the townsfolk always fell over
themselves just to speak with an Ever. This unbridled revelry and
beauty . . . They wanted to drink it in.

*I* wanted to drink it in.

Amalyss and Tasia immediately strolled toward their parents when we approached, and while I'd gained their favor, I couldn't say the same for Clesian and Lydia. Rather than test my luck, I wandered to a table laden with beverages. An attendant was quick to hand me a glass with a polite nod before busying herself with other patrons.

"Thank you," I said. The pleasing taste of dark cherries and herbs coursed over my tongue as I took a sip and strolled aimlessly toward the throng of people. I recognized a handful of elders and their families, and I was stunned to see them dressed so ostentatiously. Mrs. Marlow must've made a fortune from all their attire. It was so drastically different from what they normally wore. Every possible hue and shade from the rainbow were displayed in their fine clothing, and a few of them had gone so far as to add feathers, wings, or ribbonlike tails to their attire, as if they were trying to make themselves look more like Evers. Still, they didn't move with the same animalistic grace as the immortals. A handful of townsfolk had taken to the dance floor, but most lingered by the food and drink.

My mouth parted when I saw Lysa standing beside her father. She was wearing a silken champagne gown with ivory rosebuds lining her frame, and it clung to her every curve. A wreath of flowers sat atop her curled hair. Her gaze met mine, eyes widening temporarily in shock, and then a grin split her face and she rushed toward me.

"Edira!" She threw her arms around my neck, sending Ywena in a flurry to the top of my head, and hugged me tight. "I've missed you!"

My hands fluttered aimlessly for a moment until I settled with a light pat between her shoulders. "Hey, Lysa. How are you?"

"I'm wonderful. The silver fete. Can you believe it?" Lysa released me, and she watched with awe as Ywena returned to her usual perch. "What's it been like? You have to tell me *everything.*"

"It's been fine." I didn't really know what else to say, but I did understand her curiosity. The townsfolk didn't visit Fernglove without invitation. Outside of the silver fete, their knowledge of the manor and its inhabitants was limited.

"Did Noam and Nohr come with you?" Lysa asked as she glanced past me to the house. "I was hoping to see them tonight."

The lingering taste of wine soured in my mouth. She didn't know. I guess I didn't expect her to—it wasn't like I'd shared their condition with Mrs. Marlow while I was in town, and it wasn't the Ferngloves' place to discuss my family's problems. And I wasn't sure I wanted them to. Tonight was supposed to be a breath. A moment for me to escape the horrid predicament I'd found myself in. I didn't want to think about blight. I wanted to just . . . be.

But a part of me softened at her question. Here she was, dressed like a goddess and poised for an Ever to claim as theirs—no doubt as her father intended and likely hoped for—and she was asking about my brothers. About Noam.

"They're traveling overseas." I plastered on a fake smile. "An old family friend reached out and invited them to join him. He's a traveling merchant."

"Oh." Her eyes fell. She snagged her lower lip with her teeth for a moment, then turned, securing a glass of wine from a passing attendant. With one easy movement, she drank half of it, then cleared her throat. With a bright smile, she said lightly, "I expected there to be more Evers."

I thought back to the bloodlines and Orin's call for a more peaceful way forward among the Ever families. "Maybe there will be more next time."

"That would be something to see," she said with a dreamy sigh. "My grandparents remember a time when all sorts of Evers came and stayed with the Ferngloves for the fete. But I assume drama between immortals lasts lifetimes. My father says the feuds between the houses are catastrophic." Eyes alight with joy from

sharing gossip, she took another quick sip of her wine. "I personally think that's why so many townsfolk are here. Obviously this
is my first fete, so I can't compare. I'm just grateful for the opportunity."

I scoured the crowd until I spied Briar standing near Flix
and Issa, his gaze locked on the night sky. Perhaps the Starglens
would be the first of many to set aside old disputes. But before I
could chat more with Lysa, her father called for her, and she gave
me another tight squeeze.

"I'll come find you later. Or tomorrow! I have a different gown,
you just *have* to see it. This is so exciting!"

I smiled to myself as she strolled away, only to be halted by the
son of a different town elder. Normally Broderick would've been a
perfect suitor for Lysa—he was tall with dark hair and handsome
brown eyes. Freckles dusted his broad nose, and twin dimples burrowed deep into his cheeks. But he wasn't an Ever. I doubted Lysa's
father would let her linger for too long.

Taking another long sip of wine, I turned back toward the
clearing reserved for dancing. A breath skated along the shell of
my ear, followed by a whisper full of heat. "Enjoying the view?"

I spun around to find Rorik bent over, a devilish grin pulling
at his lips, and he chuckled darkly as he straightened. Of course,
Ywena shocked me, which only deepened his laugh as he watched
me adjust. I was about to open my mouth and chastise him for yet
again scaring me instead of saying hello, but the words died on my
tongue.

Rorik was *sinister*. There was no other word for the dark
beauty that he exuded. He was mostly dressed in liquid-black
clothing that shifted like water when he moved, but all the edges
were trimmed in golden thread that shined as bright as polished
metal. The cuffs of his sleeves were folded over, and the underside
of the fabric was gilded silk that was as reflective as mirrors. His
burnished hair was dusted with golden foil, and smears of gold

paint had been dragged across his cheeks, halting just before his lips. He'd even swapped the onyx dermal piercings on his brow for shined gold.

His attire was alluring, but his Ever features . . . Gods. Sable horns with sharpened points had pushed through his forehead, just beneath his hairline. His eyes were beetle black without a trace of white to be found. But what stole my focus were his wings. They were massive, sprouting beneath his shoulders to fall to the backs of his heels. The outer shells were black, but the insides were a resplendent gold, and they twitched twice as I marveled at their captivating sheen.

He was danger incarnate. Even the way he loosely cradled his crystal goblet, as if he couldn't be bothered to hold it properly, felt alarming. Like at any moment he'd crack it against a stone and use the broken shards as weapons.

What I would have done to him if I didn't loathe the time we spent together.

"Dance with me," he said after draining the rest of his wine. His lips were stained from the ruby-red liquid, and I couldn't help but fantasize about what they'd taste like.

"Is that a command?" I asked, all too aware that my voice was unnaturally hoarse. I brought the rest of my wine to my lips and forced it down with a long swallow. His gaze dropped to my neck, and he grinned.

With one finger, he grazed the hollow of my throat. "I would never force you to do something you didn't want to."

I stilled as I fought to keep my breath steady. "You're drunk."

"Will you dance with me?" His voice was more like a predatory purr.

As he extended his hand, all I could do was stare. Rorik had *never* offered me his hand. He'd jabbed my stomach to alter my breathing, and straightened my back to adjust my posture, and teased me with his nearness, but never a gesture like this.

His tone softened. "If you say no, I'll leave."

This time, there was a burn to his words. A promise steeped in magic. It was subtle, much like the quiet vow Amalyss had placed on me, but with none of the vile intention. So I placed my hand in his. "Okay."

He took my glass and set both our stemware on the tray of a passing attendant before guiding me to the floor. A few of the more practiced couples were already twirling together in complicated patterns I didn't recognize, trading partners and moving with an artful confidence I didn't have a chance of replicating. Unlike the elders and wealthy townsfolk, I'd never had the luxury of lessons or soirees where I could learn even the most basic steps. I couldn't fathom why Rorik wanted to dance with me.

"I don't know any dances." I hesitated at the edge of the floorboards, and Rorik halted as he glanced down at me. "I'm liable to smash your feet with my heels."

His wry smirk did wondrous things to my fluttering heart. "Is that an excuse so you can harm me without recourse?"

"Hardly." I eyed the spinning pairs before us. "But if that's your concern, you can step on my feet every time I step on yours. A toe for a toe."

"Oh, Edira." He draped one of my hands about his neck before wrapping his arm around my waist. With his free hand, he threaded our fingers together. "The only pain I'd ever intentionally inflict on you is the agony of making you wait to feel the pleasure of release."

My mouth fell open as he took off, spinning us with an effortless grace. Heat ravaged my cheeks as his words played on repeat in my mind in tune with the beat of the music. Apparently, he didn't consider jabbing me in the gut as "pain," because his words hinted at something deeper. I couldn't keep myself from pressing closer to him, from wanting to feel the form of his hard muscles beneath his clothing. I didn't know how my feet kept up with his. I wasn't sure they ever did. At one point, I registered that he'd lifted me slightly in a twirl so my toes skated above the earth, and then he never placed me back down. Not until he dipped me low before bringing me back flush with his chest.

He chuckled at my shocked expression. "Have I snared your attention?"

*Indefinitely.* "No. I was just shocked you knew how to dance so well."

"Dancing is a form of training, you know." He nodded to Ywena, who'd crawled to my sternum and unfurled her wings to flatten herself against my cleavage. I knew he was staring at her and not my breasts, but I couldn't help but blow out a shaky breath. She shocked me, and I bit my bottom lip to steel myself. Rorik's eyes immediately riveted to my mouth, and the hunger in his stare was magnified by a sudden, reflective sheen of gold that passed across those ink-black pools.

"Keep breathing," he said, voice guttural and low and so damn tantalizing.

"You, too." I couldn't help myself. I had no idea if he was keeping control or not, but the reaction I got out of him was worth it. His fingers dug deep into my hip and a husky growl escaped the back of his throat.

"Tell me a lie, Edira. A good one." He spun me out in time with the music before slowly pulling me back to him. "Tell me I'm beautiful."

I snorted. "You want me to compliment you when you haven't even acknowledged my appearance? Such an Ever thing to do."

"Of course." He dipped me low again, his mouth just inches from mine. "Why be anything other than what you expect me to be?"

Ywena must've shocked me at least twice, and his heated gaze drifted to her fluttering wings before shifting to my eyes with a look of pure desire. He held me there for what felt like an eternity, neither of us daring to speak. I feared he'd keep me caged in his arms all evening if I didn't respond. Part of me didn't want to.

"You are stunning."

He stared at me as my words washed over him. "Truth or lie?"

"Which is more dangerous?" What was I even saying? Doing? I'd had only a glass of wine, and yet I was intoxicated. Drunk on him and his presence, unsure of how to proceed but loving the thrill of not knowing what was going to happen.

He pulled us back upright, slowing our pace to an intimate sway, as his lips brushed against my cheek. "You look like a garden."

At that, I burst out laughing and didn't even try to keep my breathing even. Shocks jolted over me as I gripped Rorik tighter. "I said the exact same thing."

Leaning back, he released my hand to trail his fingers along my side. Longing coiled tightly inside me, and I pressed into his touch.

*Stop. Stop, stop, stop.* Not to him, but to myself. Gods, I didn't want him to stop. I wanted to stop wanting it, and yet I couldn't.

"Regardless, you are beautiful."

My throat dried as I fought to keep control of my emotions. "That's the first nice thing you've said to me."

It was hard to decipher what emotion coursed through his pupil-less eyes, but that reflective golden sheen passed over them again as he inched closer. When he was only a breath away and Ywena was shocking me to the ends of the realm, he dragged a thumb along my jaw until reaching my chin. Then he angled it up.

"Rorik." Seville's sharp voice broke his hold over me, and I backstepped out of his reach. He didn't move. Instead, he blinked at the space where I used to be. And then a flood of anger raced through his expression, so volatile and threatening that my breathing stopped completely. It only lasted for a moment before he hid it all beneath a cool veil of indolence. Straightening, he turned to face his sister.

"Yes?"

"You know better than to steal the first dance. Plus, Jules is looking for you." Seville glared at Rorik as he shrugged and offered a flippant wave.

*Steal the first dance.* Had it all been a power move? Really? It didn't feel like it had, and yet I knew the Evers loved their games. A sinking coldness trudged through my limbs.

"Fine, fine. I'll entertain her. Take care, Edira." He sauntered away like a predator who'd grown bored of his prey, never looking back to see if I'd fled.

Seville groaned as she pinched her nose. "Fucking idiot." Then, to me: "Orin is looking for you."

"Rorik didn't do anything," I said once I found my voice. "I'm fine."

I wasn't, but she didn't need to know that.

She narrowed her ice-green eyes as her gaze raked over my body. It was as if she could hear my lie. In the twinkling light of the magicked chandeliers, her stare glowed with power. Her skin was as radiant as ever and infused with diamonds—a perfect complement to her ethereal wings that shimmered like glass. Her bloodred gown was draped about her curves in the most tantalizing way, and a slit from hip to foot exposed her right leg. A lacy garter dotted with garnets wrapped around her thigh, and her Fernglove tattoo was inked beneath it as if she'd sheathed the thing and could draw it at a moment's notice.

Seville scoffed as she adjusted the plunging neckline of her dress. "Even if he didn't physically hurt you, he shouldn't have touched you."

"I'm not a possession," I bristled, not caring that I turned a few heads as we went. "You all seem to forget that."

Seville glowered. "Be that as it may, there are things at play tonight that you cannot fuck up. And Rorik . . ." She hissed, more to herself than to me as she maneuvered around a pair of drunken dancers. "I don't love either of my brothers, but I know which one not to piss off."

Glancing through the crowd, I spied Rorik towering over an Ever I could only assume was Jules. Like all of them, she was flawless, and she leaned against the trunk of a tree as she inclined her head toward him expectantly. Rorik's grin was feral, and he dragged a thumb over her lips before pressing his mouth to hers.

I quickly looked away, surprised by the flicker of annoyance in my chest. So much for him calling me beautiful. I suppose that was a safe truth. Beauty was relative, and he was relatively occupied with another version of it.

*The only pain I'd ever intentionally inflict on you . . .* I cut off the thought before it could do more damage.

Orin's deep laugh rose above the gathering of people, and Seville stopped to give me yet another once-over. She was still muttering under her breath about Rorik's stupidity. I wanted to ask more, to understand this strained family dynamic that was so starkly different from the one I shared with Noam and Nohr. But I doubted Seville would give up any information willingly, and a crowded fete was hardly the time to pry.

Especially not when everyone parted to let Orin through.

Seville excused herself, planting a quick kiss on his cheek before disappearing into the throng of bodies. Orin came to a standstill, rapt gaze caught on me.

"Edira." He swallowed twice, his eyes wide and full as he took in my appearance. "You look—"

*. . . like a garden.*

"—beautiful."

It was the third time I'd been called beautiful since donning my dress, and maybe that's why it felt like the compliment didn't hold as much weight. Or maybe it was because I'd delighted in the shared surprise that came with Rorik likening me to a garden. It was such an abstract comment that felt so wildly synchronous.

But no. I was done letting him invade my thoughts and play with my emotions. Not when another with much more grace and kindness was focused solely on me.

"Thank you," I said with a smile.

Mirth filled Orin's gaze. His ivy-green tailored suit was a perfect complement to my gown, as well as the emerald scales framing his temples. He'd styled his oak-brown locks to fall around his horns, truly as if he were wearing a bone diadem. I remembered the first time I saw him, I'd thought he was regal. I'd had no idea quite how magnificent he was. His tail darted behind him as he moved toward me, and he offered me his hand. I took it without hesitation.

With delicate fingers, he tucked a loose strand of moonlight-white hair behind my ear. As his gaze shifted to my collarbone, he grimaced. "Ywena, fly back to your master. Edira has no use for training tonight."

Her reluctance was palpable in the way she nestled closer to my skin. And I wasn't sure why, but that only served to irritate me further. It was hardly her fault that Rorik was such a colossal ass, but at least for tonight I wanted nothing to do with him. Still, I couldn't—wouldn't—dream of hurting her.

"Go on." I gently nudged my finger beneath her limbs, and I swore to the gods that she actually huffed. I blinked as she took off, likely to find Rorik. Eventually, she'd have to come back. But for tonight, I was blissfully free.

"Now that that's settled, what would you like to do?" he asked.

"I could go for a drink," I said, suddenly parched.

"Certainly." He effortlessly steered us through the crowd without failing to greet those around him. He was magnanimous in his presence, calling each person who approached by name as if they were longtime friends instead of distant acquaintances. When we secured our drinks, he even made a point to thank the attendant before returning his focus to me. The warmth of the wine was beginning to linger in my limbs, and I reveled in the pleasure that came with it—and Orin.

"You're nothing like I expected," I said. The words were out before I realized, and I pressed my glass to my lips to keep anything else from accidentally spilling out.

"Oh? Well, I hope that's a good thing." Orin smiled. "I know the circumstances in which we met were less than favorable, but I'm not a monster, Edira, despite some of my more animalistic attributes."

"I quite like the horns." I should've just kept drinking. Talking was dangerous.

His grin deepened. "Good to know."

Heat flushed my cheeks, and I averted my eyes to instead stare at the throng of people growing more riotous by the minute. They twirled beneath the chandeliers, sweat glistening in the flickering light, with drunken smiles stretched wide across their faces. Ignorance was bliss. So was wine.

Orin took a careful step closer, and the heat of his body against my side was a wonderful thing. "Care to dance?"

"Won't your guests be expecting you? I'd hate to keep you from your duties." I nodded toward a cluster of onlookers neither dancing nor eating, but precariously loitering as if they were waiting for Orin to move so they could determine how to interject.

"They can wait." He placed a warm hand on the small of my back as he brought his lips to my cheek in a gentle, chaste kiss. "You're the only one I care to entertain right now."

Gooseflesh raced down my spine, and I rolled my lips together. Perhaps there was some benefit to looking like a garden when it meant being paired with the god of earth himself. No one would dare trample me. That realization brought a sense of power I'd never felt before. Here I was, surrounded by all sorts of important people, and I was the one who was untouchable.

This time, I led Orin to the floor designated for dancing. I didn't care that I didn't know the steps or that my movements weren't as fluid as his. Because I held all of Orin's attention, and that was a power no one else had the hopes of attaining. His smile was wide, his body warm and safe. I loved that we could move together without trading ridiculous words or me worrying about my breath. About his breath. We were one. Just a tangled mess of limbs and laughter as I botched dance patterns and he saved me from falling. It was the most fun I'd had in years.

When the song ended and we were both breathless, we moved to the outskirts of the floor near tables laden with food and drink.

Orin's hands found my shoulders, and I reveled in the warmth of his touch. "Shall we go again?"

"I just need a minute," I managed. Orin nodded as he grabbed a chalice full of wine and drained it in one easy swig. His lips were stained a flush pink, and my fingers burned to brush against the soft opening of his mouth. Standing on my toes, I leaned against his chest and reached my fingers up to swipe away a bead of wine from his lip. "You left some behind."

He tensed beneath me, his heart hammering into my body, and then his teeth gently snared my finger.

"Oops," he murmured, still not releasing his grip.

A soft gasp pushed through my lips, and I was about to give in to the strange carnal desire I felt toward him, when an annoyed throat-clearing crested over the din of the partygoers.

"Orin, pleasure to see you."

He released my finger and glanced over the top of my head. Annoyance flickered through his eyes, but it was immediately replaced with a wide smile befitting the evening's host. "Ossanna. My apologies for not greeting you sooner."

I turned to find the striking Ever, drink in hand. She looked the same as she did that day in the foyer, right down to the mischief in her ruby-red eyes.

"The others are waiting." Her gaze slanted to me. "Shall we?"

Orin's hand shifted to the small of my back. "We were just on our way."

"Excellent." She turned, the swish of her blue-black hair cutting through the air, and she crossed through the throng of people without an ounce of hesitation. Dancers turned, irritation lancing their features, but they swallowed their retorts the moment they spied who'd cut in front of them. No one dared to confront her, and instead they went back to their revelry without objection.

"Best we get this over with." Orin sighed, and with a gentle push, he steered us around the crowd in the same direction as Ossanna. "Then, maybe after, we can finish what you started."

I glanced past him at the lawns, at the twirling bodies and mirth-filled gazes, and for a moment my eyes wandered back to the tree where I'd last spotted Rorik. He was nowhere to be found— and neither was Jules—but I couldn't focus on that. Orin's words had filled me with something else entirely. I wanted to laugh like I had, to pretend like there was nothing more than tonight and this moment. All I wanted was to fall into the same merriment as the rest of the revelers. And I didn't care who provided it.

"That sounds lovely."

And I meant it.

# FIFTEEN

On the outskirts of the fete sat a collection of ivory tufted chairs with ornate wooden feet. Most of them were occupied. Orin made quick work of introductions, confirming that the Evers sitting before me were in fact the prominent members of the Starglen and Waterstone families.

Issa and Flix flanked their mother's chair and stared at me with fang-clad grins, but there was no one else seated with the Waterstones. Ossanna hardly seemed to mind. If anything, she struck me as the type who thrived off total control. I doubted she was keen to share whatever power her name granted.

And then there were Zelyria and Dagas Starglen, aunt and uncle to Briar, the young boy who attended Orin's lessons, and joint heads of their household. If Briar had parents, they weren't mentioned. Still, he stood behind their chairs, unmoving and impassive as ever. But instead of looking to the night sky like he had been earlier, he aimed his gaze solely at me. The weight of his unblinking eyes was unnerving. The longer I held his stare, the more my stomach tightened.

When I couldn't stand it any longer, I shifted my focus to Orin and Seville. Rorik's chair was empty. Amalyss, Tasia, and their parents were still lingering within the fete, though I occasionally caught Lydia glowering in our direction.

"Thank you all for coming," Orin said. An attendant had swung by the moment he'd arrived and brought wine for those seated. At least they'd remembered the diamond-inlay stemware, per Seville's demands. Orin took a small sip. "Let's keep this brief and enjoy the evening, yes?"

"Wouldn't want to steal you away from your prize." Ossanna's eyes glistened with trouble in the low light of the moon. Removed from the fete as we were, the nearest magicked lantern was several yards away and did little to illuminate our surroundings. Of course, I doubted these Evers noticed. With so many bestial parts on display, I would've bet my weight in coin that they could see in the dark. Still, the night was dotted with blistering stars and a half-moon—enough for me to detect the desire and curiosity in her expression.

Orin merely raised a brow. "Alone again, Ossanna? I can arrange for some available suitors, should you be interested. I know plenty who admire the Waterstone name."

She laughed. "I'm surprised you don't offer the same to your sister."

"As if I need Orin's help." Seville took a heavy drink from her glass before pinning Ossanna with a heady glare. "You should be thankful my brother is willing to help at all."

"Indeed I am." Ossanna's grin deepened. "My daughter deserves only the best for her future."

My throat dried at her words, and suddenly I was aware of the lack of drink in my hand. I didn't like the tension that snapped between Ossanna and Orin, despite his calm facade. He sighed and shook his head once, but I didn't miss the way his fingers tightened around the arm of his chair.

"Let's leave that discussion for another day." He shifted his focus to the Starglens and dipped his chin by way of greeting. "Thank you for joining us. It's been too long since our families came together like this."

Zelyria considered him for a long moment. Her indigo eyes were endless, the dark shade of her hair like a black void that seemed to suck in all color. She and Dagas both shared the same constellation pattern as Briar, and it stretched across her face in an intricate dance that highlighted her soft features. When she spoke, her voice was surprisingly low. "Some more than others."

Just then, a tinkling laugh followed by a heated, guttural growl broke through the faded din of the fete at our backs. Rorik sauntered toward his empty chair with Jules clinging to him like an article of clothing. She whispered something in his ear before swiveling her head toward the gathering. Violet eyes framed by impossibly thick black lashes bounced from one body to the next until she noticed me. Her star constellation was more like diamonds dripping down her temple, but it signaled her family ties just the same.

"You're late, as always," Seville drawled.

Rorik effortlessly flopped into his chair, pulling Jules onto his lap with him. "I'm nothing if not consistent."

Gods, I hated him. I wished I'd lied to him. I didn't know what caused it—his presence, my anger, or Orin's steady comfort—but I shifted closer to Orin's arm. And even though he didn't meet my gaze, he made sure I knew he was there. With the lightest touch, he grazed my wrist with his pinkie. That subtle action was enough to steel my emotions, and I turned my attention back to the group.

"Daughter," Dagas said, leaning forward to brace his elbows on his knees. "We missed you at mealtime."

She didn't even miss a beat. "I was eating something else."

I nearly choked on my breath at her words, and I turned away to cough.

*I need a fucking drink.*

"Edira?" Orin asked as his eyes found mine. Nothing but concern filled those beautiful green irises. They dipped to my throat, and then he glanced back at the Starglens to where Briar continued to stand. "Briar, can you fetch her something to drink, please?"

Briar waited for Zelyria to nod her agreement, and then he was gone, silently ghosting through the crowd like an apparition.

"Thanks," I mumbled, as I forced a scratchy swallow. Absently, I rubbed the hollow space above my collarbone before letting my hand fall to my side.

Finally, Rorik looked at me. His glassy eyes suddenly sharpened, and the redness of his cheeks and ears faded to a more pallid shade. "You're missing something."

The rest of the group fell silent as they rounded their gazes on him.

"I'm not." I wasn't sure what the etiquette was for a situation like this, talking back to an Ever in the middle of what felt like a very important—and strained—meeting, but Rorik didn't exactly come across as favored. If anything, his family barely tolerated his existence. I doubted the Waterstones or Starglens, aside from Jules, cared much for him at all.

"Ywena. Where is she?"

"I sent her back." Orin placed a hand on mine, and Rorik's eyes briefly targeted the action. "If she's not with you, then that's your responsibility."

"Ywena?" Ossanna cocked her head to the side, and I swore her grin touched her ears, as if the possibility of conflict could contort her expression to the extreme. "Another consort for the evening?"

"I can assure you, the only one he's been occupied with is me." Jules's disdain was palpable, and she sank farther into Rorik's arms as if to claim her space.

A strange and foreign heat flickered to life in me, and I deigned

Rorik the briefest of scowls. "I assume Ywena noticed you were occupied and chose to stay away. Smart of her, if you ask me."

I didn't know what Rorik was trying to tell me with his eyes, and I didn't care to try to find out. Instead, I looked away, relieved to see Briar coming through the crowd with a drink in hand. I'd take his creepy, intense stare over Rorik's gaze any time.

"My, my, Rorik," Jules purred as she leaned across his body to peer more closely at me. "Someone is jealous."

"Enough." Orin's heady voice carried enough authority to silence even the quiet chirping of insects, and he stood abruptly. "Jules, if you'd be so kind as to join your family, I'd like to speak with my brother. Privately."

Apparently even Jules knew better than to cross Orin. She let out a belabored sigh, but she didn't fight otherwise. In a few short steps, she was at her parents' sides. Without a word from Orin, Seville assumed the role of host and abandoned her chair to engage the Starglens and Waterstones in small talk. Orin didn't even wait for Rorik to stand. Instead, he gripped the edge of his collar and practically yanked him to his feet. Rorik snarled in answer, baring his fangs and extending his wings. Orin didn't react. He only shoved him a few feet away, and the two of them stormed off toward the nearby tree line.

"That was eventful." The quiet lilt of Briar's voice was so subdued I would've mistaken it for the night breeze if I hadn't glimpsed him nearing the group. Turning to face him, I accepted his proffered glass of wine and took a heavy sip. The familiar taste of dark cherries flooded my mouth, along with an herb I couldn't quite place. It carried a deep heat and was almost slimy in texture. The sensation settled onto my tongue like a weight, and saliva formed in earnest as my brows drew together.

"Where did you get this?"

"The table." He gestured to the same space where I'd gotten wine before. But as each breath passed, a purling, sticky warmth seeped into my bones. My lips started to tingle as a funny, light feeling invaded my limbs, and all I wanted to do was laugh. Raising my hands before my face, I studied the odd shapes of my fingers and giggled. I must've said something, because Briar actually grinned. And then his form shifted, revealing batlike wings and endless rows of pointed fangs, and somewhere in my mind I knew I should've been scared, but the only thought that managed to surface was how hard it must've been for him to eat without skewering his lips.

He looped his arm through mine, and we skipped away. Laughing. Twirling around dancers. Moving through the crowd until we broke free on the other side of the fete. We kept going, running through the moonlit fields of lush grass and into the densely packed woods. The trees welcomed us with open arms, their limbs stretching out to finger my hair as I ran. It was so different from the time Rorik chased me into the bowels of the forest. There was no haunting darkness. No echoing, rattling breath. The creeping chilled mist was now a soft, balmy breath against my skin. I wasn't worried or afraid. I was free.

"Keep up! We're almost there." Briar's voice was like a song, and I longed to hear every note. To follow him to the ends of the earth if he willed it. The world spun around me as I tripped over clouds and stars, until finally I landed on the ground in front of a knotty, worn tree trunk. I grimaced at the scrapes on my knees, the tears in my gown. There was no pain, just an uncomfortably warm and tacky sensation.

"Briar," I managed, my words slow and full of hope, "can I take a bath? I'm covered in sap."

"That's not sap. That's blood." A giggle threaded through his words as he stared at me with glee.

My answering laugh was too loud in my ears. "Oh. I see." I didn't, but I was already moving on, focused instead on the cut-off trunk before us. "We're here?"

"The ley line." His fingers lightly trailed over my Fernglove crest, then wrapped in mine. "Normally humans can't travel it, but you've got Ever magic in you."

"Like with Seville," I mumbled. Lazy images of me posing on the shop's dais in lingerie filled my mind. It'd been such a *lovely* outing. No doubt this one would be, too.

"You've traveled this way before?" His grin was impish. "It won't feel the same. You're too incapacitated."

Then he palmed one particularly knobby section of the bark, and the trunk bloomed like a wooden flower, opening to the night sky. Out of its center rose a swirling orb of faint green mist. Giving my fingers a squeeze, he leaped into the strange sphere and yanked me in with him.

The oppressive weight of ancient, otherworldly magic battered into me with the force of stormy waters. An unbearable ringing crested in my ears as my limbs trembled. My skin was being peeled from my bones inch by inch, and my insides were becoming shriveled and twisted like the ingredients I kept in my apothecary jars. I screamed, and my lungs were shredded as magic raced down my throat. Beside me, Briar only watched in sick fascination. And just when I was about to claw my eyes out from their sockets, the energy halted.

Briar stepped out of the ley line with practiced ease, his booted feet meeting solid ground in a place I didn't recognize.

I fell to earth on all fours and hurled.

"That's it. Get it all out." He rubbed my back, and I retreated from his fingers.

"You drugged me." The rough rasp of my voice made me cringe. That foreign herb in my wine I couldn't place. He'd slipped me something. My bones creaked as I craned my neck upward to glare at him. "Why? Why did you do this?"

Instead of answering, he clamped one clawed hand around my wrist and yanked me to my feet. Stars danced across my vision, and I cursed. Briar didn't wait for my body to settle, and instead he forcefully dragged me across an open stretch of mulch and filth toward a monstrous, lone hill covered in swaying reeds. The last dregs of tainted wine made me clumsy, and I hobbled behind him as I tried in vain to rid myself of his iron grip. With every shaky breath, my throat burned. I wanted to fight harder, to pull away from this impossibly strong Ever, but it took everything in me simply not to fall with each uneven step. The ground was muddy and slick, and it gave way beneath my feet as we edged closer to the looming mound.

When we reached the base, a cavernous maw came into view. Withered roots ran along the dirt ceiling and stretched to the ground like gnarled teeth. Lichen coated the packed walls, showering the space in a faint green glow. Once we crossed the threshold, we made our way to the back of the cave, and Briar pushed aside a sheet of brittle ivy strands, revealing a narrow corridor that plunged deep into the earth.

"This way." With another tug, he set us down the spiraling path. At first, there was nothing but packed dirt all around us. As the lichen died off, so, too, did the light. Briar kept moving. Whether familiarity or magic helped him navigate the cave, I couldn't say. But it wasn't until I slipped and nearly pulled him down with me that he seemed to realize a need for light.

With his free hand, he summoned a cluster of stars that hung about his fingers. Their blistering glow illuminated the path with ease, and he continued onward without losing his grip on my arm. The air cooled as we descended farther into the ground, and eventually the path beneath our feet shifted to stairs made of something akin to black glass. The walls transitioned to the same material, and the path opened into a large, circular room. An enormous hole was cut out of the ceiling, and moonlight poured through the opening to drench the space in a soft glow. Thousands of winking specks shimmered from the depths of the onyx walls and floor, as if I'd stepped out into the night sky itself. Directly beneath the opening stood a decaying tree with knobby limbs and bone-white flowers.

*That's the same type of tree as the Ferngloves'.*

A chill swept down my spine. "What am I doing here?"

Briar didn't answer as he let his power recede. Then he shoved me toward the tree, and I stumbled over the worn roots that'd erupted from the strange black earth. Something caught my arm before I could fall, and as I craned my neck toward my elbow, my stomach plummeted to my feet. An arm had unwrapped itself from the base of the tree, and disjointed fingers had gripped me tight. And then three more limbs were suddenly peeling away from the trunk. In less than a breath, I was snared. I'd been flipped around so my back was against the now writhing bark, and the limbs snapped at odd angles as they locked me in place. My brain rioted at the eerie feel of leathery skin rubbing against my exposed shoulders, and I yelped as a finger scraped along the length of my neck.

Alarm bells crashed in my mind. The last effects of the wine had finally ebbed, and I strained against the tree's hold. A weighted groan—like a mixture of creaking branches and breaking bones—cut through the ringing in my ears. I was trapped. Trapped in an Ever's lair with absolutely no power to break free. No one to help me. No one to come to my rescue. I'd never longed for Ywena's presence more than in that moment. She'd saved me before—flown off to get help when I'd been tricked by Amalyss and Tasia. But now, I was utterly alone.

Straining against the branches, I buried my fear behind a hard glare. "What do you want from me?"

"Your help." Briar tilted his head as if it were odd I'd even bother to ask such an obvious question.

His furrowed brow only fueled my anger. "With what?"

"Threadmending."

*Fuck, not again.* "I can't."

"Sure you can." He pursed his lips. "At least you can try."

"You can't make me." I struggled against the tree's hold, but I didn't gain an inch. "I won't make a bargain with you. I refuse." At least Tasia and Amalyss had taught me something. Already my ears were straining, searching for any hint of power behind Briar's words that would signal the telltale magic of an evervow. I wouldn't fall for that again.

"There are other ways of *persuading* you," a low voice called from the depths of the cavern. Zelyria emerged from a hidden corridor, followed closely by Dagas. Jules was nowhere to be found.

"We're not above tactics that involve more physical reminders of why you'd want to listen to our suggestions." Dagas strode forward and came to a halt before me, peering closely as he inspected my face. "It's true, we Evers often forget we are so much more than our words."

Zelyria sauntered up beside him and leaned her head against his shoulder. "We don't wish to hurt you."

"I'm having a hard time believing that." My eyes narrowed as I tried to piece together a plan. And failed. I could scream, but what good would that do? Even drunk on wine, I'd been coherent enough to glean that there was nothing else around this burrow. The Starglens lived a three days' ride from Willowfell, if this was even their home. I couldn't be sure how far we'd traveled. My breathing turned shallow as adrenaline flooded my system.

*How do I get out of this?*

"I said *wish*. Not that we wouldn't hurt you, if it came to it." Zelyria straightened and then beckoned for Briar. He came without hesitation and stepped into her open arm. She folded him against her side. "Briar lost his parents to blight. They're the ones holding you now."

The hands gripping me tightened like shackles. "I didn't realize other Evers had caught it."

Zelyria blinked, her expression surprisingly soft and tinged with remorse. "Oh, my dear, how you've been wronged. I am truly sorry we are adding to that grievance."

My stomach churned as the limbs anchoring me to the tree tightened around me. "I don't understand. You're not sick."

"According to who?" Dagas raised a brow.

"Orin would have told me."

"Would he? Why?" Dagas asked. "Does he frequently share the details of other Evers' households with his employees? Or are you something more?"

Words formed and died on my tongue. We weren't anything, and yet I'd assumed if he knew . . . No, he couldn't have known. Otherwise, he would have shared that knowledge with me, if only to help me understand how to combat the blight in Mavis.

"We're all sick," Zelyria said as she watched me closely. "That's why we're here."

All of them. Zelyria. Dagas. Briar. I could hardly focus on their words. The arms were still tightening, and fingers had untucked from the trunk to press into my sides. My skin crawled as bile soured the back of my tongue, and I forced myself to focus on my breath, to center myself any way that I could in the hopes of finding a means to escaping this horrifying nightmare.

*Lengthen your spine. Relax your shoulders. Breathe through your stomach.* I let Rorik's words surface in my mind as I pictured his steady hand on my back.

"Even so, I can't cure you. I don't know how."

"And yet, you're going to try." Dagas's words were full of heat and threat, and all at once their glamours dropped. My mouth fell open as I stilled in the tree's grasp.

I didn't even need to call on my power to see the illness—they'd wiped away every ounce of magic, every meticulous layer of glamour, to reveal the absolute truth of their shared condition. They were dotted with dozens of rupturing pustules and gaping wounds. Their lustrous hair was now patchy and brittle, and their frail bodies were so withered and decrepit it was a miracle their clothing remained in place. The bright colors of their bespoke attire were so at odds with their ashen complexions and grotesque sores. Skin sloughed off from Briar's cheek as he watched me, and Zelyria absently brushed it from his shoulder. Everything about them was horrifying. Sickening. But nothing was more gut roiling than the stench that wafted from them in heady waves.

They couldn't have much time left.

"The others . . ." My mind was spinning, replaying every interaction I'd had with an Ever, until one memory bled to the surface of my mind. It'd been so trivial, and yet . . . Seville had laughed at a blemish hidden beneath Lydia's glamour. Seville could see everything beneath her aunt's veil. Nothing was hidden from view.

Which meant that the Ferngloves must have known about the Starglens' sickness.

"They knew," I managed after several steely breaths. "Orin knew."

Zelyria blinked. "I told you, we're *all* sick."

All sounds deafened at her words and heat stung at the backs of my eyes. All of them. Not just the Starglens or the Waterstones or even the Ferngloves. All Evers. Every. Single. One. The fringes of my vision dimmed.

"No," I murmured. "That can't be true."

"Our glamours are difficult to pierce. They're carefully layered sheets of magic. The more you peel back, the easier it is to rip apart the whole thing and discover the truth." Dagas folded his arms across his chest. "It would be simple enough to trick you into thinking you'd seen it all, when in reality, you likely only scratched the surface. Even our lands are filled with the disease."

Orin in the study. His body on display, his beautiful enhancements and unparalleled power.

And then another truth hit me like a kick to the stomach. Not a single member of Fernglove smelled of anything. Their scents were as absent as the hyacinths' in the foyer, because everything was masked beneath countless layers of glamour.

To hide the stench of blight.

I wanted to vomit. I'd been tricked into believing Mavis was the only sick family member, but it was the entirety of Fernglove. And even if I managed to find a cure, I'd never have the lifespan to save them all and my brothers.

But none of that mattered. Not now, as I faced down a family who was already out of time. I could see the panic in their eyes, in the desperate, hungry way they focused on the magical shade of my hair.

Hours ago, I'd thought myself untouchable. Now, I knew how wrong I'd been.

And I wasn't strong enough to stop them. My gaze cut to the opening in the ceiling and the night sky. With a subtle shift, I pressed against the unforgiving tree limbs. I had no chance of escaping, either. I looked back at the Starglens. At Zelyria, Dagas, and Briar. Jules was still missing. Was that her angle all along? To distract Rorik so her family could steal me away? But then certainly Orin would notice. He'd have to.

I just needed to keep them talking and pray that, with enough time, the Ferngloves would become aware of my absence—along with the majority of the Starglens—and come to my aid. I didn't want to be anywhere near Orin after what I'd discovered, but he was the only one capable of saving me in that moment.

"You must know that I can't cure blight. Not yet. Otherwise, the Ferngloves would be healed," I said.

"You'd also be dead." Dagas shrugged. "Your body wouldn't be able to sustain that many rounds of magic. Better to take you before that happens and have you expend your talents on us."

My heart hammered in my ears as they inched closer. How could I prolong something they'd been dying to acquire? Images of Tasia and Amalyss surfaced in my mind, their desperate ploy to get me to threadmend. They'd been terrified. Both of dying and of Orin's wrath. They'd hardly spoken to me for fear of repercussions. Maybe the threat of Orin's power would terrify the Starglens, too.

"Orin will come for you." I forced my voice to remain steady, to lace it with as much heat and promise as the Ferngloves often wielded when they spoke down to me.

It didn't work. "A risk, of course," Zelyria said.

"But if you manage to cure us . . ." Dagas reached forward and wrapped my hair around his finger. "No one at Fernglove could stop us."

Panic clawed at my throat. "But Orin—"

"Deserves to be punished!" Dagas roared. The tree responded to his words, tearing into my gown and impaling sharpened, fingerlike twigs into the soft skin of my sides. Pain splintered from my stomach, and the warm, sticky heat of blood dribbled down my legs. A scream burned through my lungs as I writhed in place.

"A life for a life." Dagas's eyes burned with rage. "It seems fair, after Lorelei. He cherishes you like we cherished her."

Lorelei. The name rattled through my brain. She was the Starglen the attendants had mentioned while arranging flowers for the fete. "What happened to her?"

"Dagas"—Zelyria gripped her partner's arm tight—"we will get our justice, but only if we take care of ourselves first. Don't take your anger out on the threadmender."

Dagas forced out an exhale, but the ire remained in his gaze. "Fine. Cure us, then, threadmender. And we'll tell you whatever you desire. Consider it a vow."

"I can't cure you," I wheezed. "I can't."

"Try," Dagas commanded, and the twigs burrowed deeper into my sides. White-hot agony arced down my legs, and I shrieked as my vision swam.

*Breathe.* But I couldn't. I couldn't focus on anything other than the digging of fingers beneath my skin, pulling at muscles and worming between tendons as blood spurted over my gown. I pressed the back of my head against the tree as my vision darkened. Deeper and deeper the fingers went, entrenching in my limbs as if I, too, were destined to become part of the bark. I knew I was screaming—I could hear it in my ears—but it sounded so distant. So separate from me. I could hold out and die or threadmend and die. The choices weren't really choices, but at least one would buy me some time. If I could deceive them long enough, then maybe there was still a chance I could be saved. The idea of relying on anyone else to come to my rescue burned me to my core, but I was running out of options.

Igniting my power, I brought my focus back to the Starglens. All at once the tree halted its advance, and relief sang through my bones as the writhing limbs pulled back a fraction. Dagas, Zelyria, and Briar stilled as they stared at my moonlit eyes.

"Your threads." My voice was raw and coated with agony, but I steadied my breathing as I took in the limp strands of their lives. All of them. Only a few, virulent aquamarine threads remained. The rest were soaked in tar and lifeless, waiting for their final moments before solidifying and dusting to ash.

"I need my hand." I tilted my chin slightly toward my pinned arm. "Just one."

Dagas and Zelyria looked at each other briefly, and then they nodded. With the flick of his wrist, Dagas commanded a branch to peel back, and my arm was blissfully free. Ignoring the urge to groan in relief, I flexed my hand and held it out before me. The white light ensconcing my fingers grew sharper as I beckoned to their life threads. The Starglens' strands reached for me in earnest, begging for me to help them, to rid them of the sickness eating away at their existence. I knew what would happen if I tried to pick away at the blight. I also knew what would happen if I did nothing.

Shifting in the tree's hold, I winced as some of the sharper fingers curled beneath layers of sinew and skin. "How long?"

"As long as anyone else," Zelyria responded. Her gaze was locked on my raised hand. "It's hard to say exactly when."

Orin had so much to answer for. The thick tar coated every strand, and there were no fraying or torn edges for me to stitch back together. And merely trying to wipe the black liquid away was futile. Severing their life threads altogether would be just as fruitless.

Gingerly, I extended a finger to one of Briar's soaked threads. The Starglens watched with rapt focus, despite being unable to see what I could. It was the only blessing in this horrific scenario. I could feign threadmending for a time without actually doing it, and they'd be none the wiser. Still, they'd grow impatient.

Briar's infected thread hesitated before my fingertip, then slithered over my hand to gently wrap around my wrist. I wasn't even attempting to cure him, and I could feel it. The blight. Nausea hit my stomach hard. A pain separate from the tree's barbs pulsated through my body, blossoming from the space where his thread rested against my skin. A headache hammered behind my eyes. Betrayal was a hot knife slicing through my gut. It felt the same as when I'd attempted to mend Tasia's cut.

The Ferngloves were quick to convince me it'd just been the nature of their immortal threads that made mending difficult, but they knew. They knew blight lingered beneath it all.

"Well?" Zelyria asked. Breathless. Hopeful.

"It's . . ." I didn't have words. Instead, I stared at the sludge now dribbling over my forearm. It hissed as it met my skin and turned to steam. Blight—or any illness, for that matter—had never been able to infect a threadmender. Evers used to be the same. It was the only similarity we shared. So why had I adapted when they remained woefully exposed?

*The insects around here are infected with blight, yet they live on. In fact, they thrive.* Rorik's words crept from the recesses of my mind. Other creatures had figured it out, too. But how?

A bestial roar so loud and violent ruptured the night, and my thoughts fled as hope sped through my veins. Rorik dropped through the hole in the ceiling and slammed into the ground. The polished stone spiderwebbed beneath his feet from the impact, and he raised his head to glower at the Starglens. His impossibly black eyes were flooded with malevolence, and his wings snapped angrily in the air behind him. A snarl ripped through his chest, and he took an aggressive step forward. Dagas's face went pale at the sight, and both Zelyria and Briar shrunk into his shadow.

Before Rorik could strike, a dangerously quiet voice crested from one of the many hallways. "Oh, Dagas. What have you done?"

"Orin." Zelyria pressed Briar tight against her body.

Orin emerged from the corridor, his face eerily placid. I pressed my back against the tree, not caring that the action caused the fingers to dig deeper into my muscles. Unfettered rage filled his strained gaze as he glared at the Starglens. It was the first time I'd felt my insides go cold at just the sight of him.

"You don't deserve her magic," Dagas said, but his words faltered.

Rorik stiffened as his stare shifted to me. For a moment, he looked only at my face, and then his gaze traversed the length of my body, bouncing from wound to wound as his hands fisted by his sides. He snarled, revealing too-sharp teeth as he returned his focus to Orin and the Starglens.

"You'll gain no mercy from me," Orin said, calm voice doing nothing to hide the rage behind his words.

Without waiting for them to respond, he strode forward and gripped the arms of the tree tight. The limbs snapped beneath his grasp, and the sickening crunch of splintering bones filled the small room. He ripped the arms clean off the trunk, and ash-gray filaments dusted around us as he tossed them to the ground. The remaining limbs retreated before Orin could forcibly remove them, and he caught me as I slumped against his chest. Blood wept freely from my unobstructed wounds, seeping into his clothes.

The sight only made him growl. "I leave it to you, Rorik. Dispose of them."

In the span of a breath, Orin had swept me into his arms and was striding toward the exit.

"You will pay for this!" Dagas shouted. "You cannot keep—"

A wet gurgle, followed by a sudden splash, cut him off. Peering over Orin's shoulder, I barely caught sight of what happened. One moment Dagas was speaking, and the next Rorik had his hand through Dagas's throat. Rorik was lethal. And when he extracted his hand, he brought Dagas's larynx with it. Blood flooded in a rush from the gaping wound at the base of his neck, and his lifeless body slumped to the floor.

Rorik dropped the remains of Dagas's voice box beside him. He pivoted to Zelyria and Briar. Their screams reverberated through my ears, and I squeezed my eyes shut as I buried my head against Orin's chest. Still, nothing could drown out their pained cries. Or their pleas. Or the whimpering. Or the horrifying silence that followed.

"Edira." Orin's words were soft, his hold gentle. "It's okay, Edira. I've got you."

A sob racked my chest, and I nodded. It was all I could muster, but Orin didn't ask for more. Instead, he raced toward the ley line, not bothering to look back at the monstrous burrow we'd left or the bodies that now made it a crypt. I didn't even complain when we stepped into the gut-churning ley line that ushered us back to the outskirts of Fernglove Manor. I didn't berate him for the secrets or the truth of his blight. I couldn't. I didn't have the strength. I simply clung to him and let him carry me back to safety and away from the nightmare I'd endured.

# SIXTEEN

I didn't rise from my bed until early afternoon the following day. Vora was there as always, but for once she didn't chastise me. She said nothing as she helped me bathe and dress, and instead looked at me much like my mother used to when I came home with bruises. Worry. Sadness. A sliver of pride for defending my brothers. I didn't know what Vora saw in me now, but I was grateful for her silence. She brought me food and redressed my bandages, then excused herself with a nod.

Sinking into the tufted lounge at the foot of my bed, I stared out the open bay windows and at the rolling lawns. The multitude of puncture wounds lining my limbs had already begun to heal, largely in part to Vora's excellent suturing skills and a blend of Ever magical remedies and mine. We likely could've forgone the balm I'd suggested, but I wanted control over *something*. Vora must've sensed that because she didn't argue. And when she peeled away the salve-coated linens this morning, a surprised huff had escaped her lips. The wounds were shiny and pink with fresh skin, as if her sutures had been in place for a week instead of a night. With the lightest of touch, I fingered one on my upper arm. Perhaps there was something to combining Ever magic and my cures.

A quiet knock sounded from my door. "Edira?"

I shifted to stare at Orin as he entered. He hesitated as his worried gaze searched my face. It was the first time I'd seen him since the incident, and all the questions I'd buried during the time of our escape came frothing to the surface of my mind.

"Come in," I said, voice even. I didn't know how to feel about his haggard expression. Tension riddled his frame as he swiftly crossed the room in a handful of strides. He gestured toward the open space on the sofa beside me, and I nodded.

"How are you feeling? Vora tells me the wounds are healing well."

"She's right." I rested my hands in my lap as I angled my body toward him. "I'm mostly fine."

"Mostly?" His brows scrunched together.

"I'm having a difficult time grappling with my thoughts," I said. "Do you have blight?" I looked at him without flinching, letting the full weight of my inquiry settle against him. It was a question, and yet it wasn't. And Orin knew. A moment of panic flickered through his stare, but it was quickly replaced with a deep sadness that affected all his features. His lips downturned, and he braided his fingers together as he spoke to the floor.

"Yes."

"And everyone else here?"

"The same."

"And your land? This whole estate? It's glamoured to hide the blight, isn't it?" I asked.

He finally met my gaze. "Yes."

For a moment, nothing was said. Anger rose in me with a fury unlike any I'd known. I struggled to keep myself sitting, to not storm out of the room and barricade myself in my brothers' quarters. But that would've solved nothing, and technically, Orin hadn't broken our agreement. I'd entered into his employment in exchange for my brothers' lives. There hadn't been time to hash out details, to truly understand what he'd needed from me.

"This changes nothing," he said quietly.

My answer was sharper than a blade. "Doesn't it? What were your words, exactly? *Just say you'll work with me?* For how long, Orin? Who do I have to cure to get out of this mess?"

"Mavis." He clasped his hands together. "Just Mavis, and I'll consider your work done."

I wasn't sure I could believe him. "Why not tell me the truth, then?"

At that, he raised a brow. "That all Evers are infected with blight?" A dry, unexpected laugh rushed from his lips. "Edira, your distaste for my kind is obvious. If I told you that we were all slated to die, would you still help us? Or would you be thrilled to rid the world of our existence?"

Not the answer I was expecting. I blinked as I stared at him, which only acknowledged that everything he'd said was truth. I wouldn't have cared in the slightest had my brothers not been involved.

"You can speak freely, you know." His words were soft. Too soft. I hated it.

I blew out a breath. "It's hard not to feel like I've been tricked into losing while you stand to gain everything."

"No." His hands shot out to clasp mine. "I admit not telling you about the gravity of our situation was an egregious misstep, but the trade in my mind was always Mavis for your brothers. Not the rest of us."

"You'd forsake your own kin for mine?" I asked. "Why?"

Orin's stare bored into me. "We have time. Mavis does not. If you were to find a way to save her, we could document it. Learn from it. And, hopefully, find a way to use our magic to cure the rest of our family and, eventually, our kind." He inched closer so our knees grazed each other. "I never meant for this to happen. I never wanted you to carry my burden."

What was happening? My pulse climbed higher as I stared into the endless depths of his green eyes. I wore their crest, but I was hardly their family. They needed my powers. Not me specifically. They could've found another threadmender, gone through the same motions again and again. I didn't know what to take as truth, which meant the only person I could trust was myself.

*Trust no one.*

"I'll clarify my evervow if it will give you solace. Trust me, Edira. Please."

*Trust . . .*

And then he dropped his glamour. All of it. Every layer, every woven thread of magic. He was completely bare before me, and yet somehow, in spite of the blight creeping across his form and the stench of decay clinging to his aura, he was resplendent. Perhaps because this was the true version of him—and he believed in me enough to share it.

"I promise the extent of your duty as a threadmender to the Fernglove house extends only to curing Mavis of her blight. No one else."

Power throbbed outward with every syllable he uttered, clashing into me in rhythmic waves until it was almost too much to bear. It cracked the foundation of my resolve. Evers were self-absorbed. Vain. Arrogant. Orin was none of those things.

Silence wrapped around us as he waited for me to speak. A small, indignant flicker of warmth sparked in my chest—the same one he'd ignited and doused, only to rouse again. I didn't know what to do with him, but the magic of his promise couldn't be denied. His words, his vows, were a security I couldn't get anywhere else.

"Edira?" Orin prompted, allowing his glamour to fall back

into place so that his blight was once again hidden from view. "If you agree, the vow takes hold."

"I agree, but"—I swallowed as the rush of magic settled around us, solidifying the vow—"why me? You could've found another threadmender without having to make all these extraneous promises."

"The promises are worth it," he said.

A strange yet delicious prickling raced over my skin as I looked at Orin again. It took me two swallows to find my voice. "To you? Or the family?"

I wanted him to say it. To say something honest and true, something that couldn't be misconstrued. Something he could bind with magic. Instead, he did so much more. He pulled my face toward his until our lips were only a breath apart. He hesitated for a beat, giving me a chance to pull back, but when I didn't retreat, he slanted his mouth across mine. Warmth purled through my limbs as my lips parted for him. I'd almost forgotten what it was like to be touched. To be wanted.

And gods, was it delicious. I couldn't—*wouldn't*—examine why. Not when Evers were immortal and humans lived for no more than a handful of decades. My existence would be just a passing breath, a faint memory, and yet he pressed against me like he wanted something more. Something bigger.

When he finally broke away, we were both breathless. I rested my forehead against his, drinking in the sensation of his skin against mine.

"My glamour acts like a bandage for the blight." He swallowed thickly, and the rough timbre of his voice lit a fire in my veins. "You're safe, if you were worried about that."

"I remember," I said softly. He knew just as well as I did that I couldn't be infected, and yet he was still concerned for my well-being. I gripped his shirt hard and pulled him against me again.

I caught his moan with my mouth and breathed it in deep. I was straddling his lap before I knew it, and my grasp on his clothes tightened. His hands found my waist, and the pressure of his fingers was downright sinful.

Something unfamiliar and heated had taken control of my limbs, my thoughts. I'd never been one to shy away from a dalliance, but this sudden, near-insatiable desire was unlike anything I could have prepared for. It wouldn't sway me. It wouldn't change my opinion or make me forgo my brothers' safety. But I didn't want to deny it, either. We could both enjoy each other's company. Assuming he felt the same pull as me.

"Is this some strange magic of yours causing me to throw caution to the wind?"

Orin raised a brow. "Is that what you need to tell yourself to explain your attraction to an Ever?"

A sliver of shame burned through me, after everything he'd just bared, after the promise he'd made. "Some things are difficult to unlearn."

He gripped either side of my face and spoke against my lips. "There is no magic forcing you to act."

The burn of his words sent a delicious hum racing through my body, and I shuddered in his grasp.

"But"—he let his hands fall away—"we should stop."

"Oh? What happened to finishing what I started? Or was that the wine?"

He laughed. "Hardly."

I slid my hands down his chest, savoring the feel of his sturdy frame while I still could. "I just thought that we could enjoy each other without the pretense or pressure of something more. Because you've watched hundreds of lives pass, because you have no expectation for me to be anything lasting."

He was so still that if it weren't for my hands upon his chest, detecting the subtle rise and fall of his breath, I would've assumed he'd turned to stone.

I skewered my lower lip with my teeth as the ratcheting tension between us blossomed into something so agonizing that I couldn't take it anymore. I made a move to shift off his lap, and the action spurred him into motion. With tender gentleness, he settled me against him and parted my lips with his tongue. He was all I could taste, all I could feel, and even as his grip tightened with desire, there was a softness to his embrace, a care to every touch. When he eased me to my back and braced himself above me, he kept his full weight from pressing against my body.

"I didn't stop because I cared about pretense." He placed a kiss on my neck, and heat began to gather between my legs. "I stopped"—he shifted and brought his lips to one of the bandages on my arms—"because even though you said you were fine, I was inclined to let you heal fully before I take you as mine."

My nipples pearled against the fabric of my shirt, and his hungry gaze slanted to the slopes of my breasts. He bit out another curse. Then he ran one hand beneath my blouse. His fingers toyed with the edge of my undergarment.

"Orin . . ." I tried to slide farther down, to guide his hand along the curve of my breast. But he abandoned his teasing with a growl and pinned me in place with his arm.

"Not yet." He placed a light kiss on the base of my throat that defied every ounce of pure desire in his eyes. "I'm not sure you understand. When I want something, I get it, and I don't let it go."

Something solid formed in my throat. "Even if it's fleeting?"

"All the more reason to hold on tighter."

This time, his kiss was full of promise. And as our tongues intertwined and heat bloomed between us, I felt confident I could convince him to throw away this ridiculous notion of "later." His hands roved along my sides, seeking purchase in the soft flesh of my hips, and I wrenched my fingers in his hair and yanked his head back. With his neck exposed, I peppered the length of his throat with kisses and nipped at his skin.

A guttural hiss slipped through his teeth, and I swore he was about to give in when a firm knock came from the door.

"Not now," he ground out in answer as he fisted the fabric of my linen pants. Again he kissed me senseless, and again the knock sounded. More insistent this time and followed by a stern voice I recognized as Vora's.

"It's Jules. She's in the foyer." Vora's tension-filled words were quite possibly the only thing that could've dampened the moment, and all at once we both slackened in each other's grasp.

"We'll be down shortly." Carefully, he slid off me and straightened his shirt.

"We will? Both of us?" I stood and brushed my hands along my clothes, though the action did nothing to smooth the wrinkles Orin's iron grip had formed. "Are you sure?"

He raised a single brow at the question before extending his arm. "Of course I'm sure. You have nothing to fear when it comes to Jules, and she needs to know the error of her family's ways." He guided us toward the door, and a tendon near his temple flared as ire settled into his gaze. "No one touches you, Edira. Not like that."

The wet gurgle of Dagas's final breath flooded my ears as an image of Rorik holding Dagas's throat flashed before my eyes. I could still see the way the blood oozed between Rorik's fingers, still hear the sickening, soft thump of Dagas's larynx hitting the floor. As horrifying as that moment had been, a dark part of my soul was thankful he'd never have the chance to kidnap me again. I hadn't seen what'd become of Zelyria and Briar. I imagined it was just as brutal.

When Orin and I arrived in the foyer, the air was already thick with unfettered rage. Lydia and Clesian were leaning against the banister of the stairs, keenly watching Jules scream at Seville without any signs of intervening. Fortunately, Amalyss and Tasia were nowhere to be seen, but I doubt that meant they weren't listening somehow. Mavis was as absent as the girls, and Rorik was missing, too—which seemed to be the main point of Jules's rampage, at least what snippets I could gather from the barrage of curses and foul language. Seville weathered the brunt of her verbal attack with a practiced look of disdain, but there was a twitch to her manicured brows that suggested her patience was wearing thin.

Thankfully, Orin seemed to notice that as well, and he released my hand to step in front of his sister and glower at the screaming Ever in his entryway. "Jules. You're not welcome here."

"You," she spat. "Haven't you done enough?"

She went toe-to-toe with him, and if she was scared, she didn't show it. Or maybe she simply didn't have the emotional capacity to do so. Her eyes were puffy and red, the color intensifying the violet shade of her irises and giving her a panicked, unhinged appearance. Her dark hair was unkempt and tangled with leaves. She still wore the same gown from the fete, and the edges were caked in a reddish brown that could only be dried blood. I spied patches of it on her fingers and smeared along her neck. As if she'd screamed in horror after trying to hold her family close, only to come away with the stench of loss.

She reeked of death. She didn't care one damn bit. "Where is he? Your *dog?*"

"My dog?" Orin asked.

Beside him, Seville chuckled darkly. "You mean *your* lover. The one *you* shouldn't have trusted."

Jules only had eyes for Orin. "I smelled him all over the place. I know he does your bidding. You and your sick—"

"Silence." Orin's voice boomed with the kind of authority one would expect from a king. And damn if he didn't command the room like one. The candles lining the hall tables wavered as magic flooded the space, and Orin drew himself to his full height. The angles of his face sharpened, and he took one menacing step toward her. I expected her to cower, to buckle under the weight of his presence.

Instead, she met his eye. A single tear streaked down her cheek. "Go ahead. I have nothing left to lose."

"Oh, let her be, Orin." Lydia sighed, and it was the most demeaning sound I'd ever heard. "Your prize is safe, and they've more than paid the price."

*Prize.* I knew that's what I was to Lydia and Clesian, and while none of them knew about the intimate moment Orin and I just shared, it chafed just the same. It must've bothered Orin, too, because he pivoted in place and delivered Lydia a lethal glare that would've made normal people crumble.

That shift in Orin's attention was enough to break Jules's focus, and she peered around his wide frame to look at me. A flurry of emotions raced through her expression, each one more terrifying than the last. Stars began to fester around her fingers, and they snapped with a magical energy that promised to singe the very skin off my bones. With bared fangs, she took several steps in my direction before lunging in the air.

But Orin was faster. He barred her progression with a clean sweep of his arm, and she went flying into the wall. The wooden planks splintered from the impact and showered the space in a spray of shards. She howled as she slumped to the floor, but the magic in her hands never wavered.

"I'll kill you!" she screamed. Her gaze bounced between Orin and me, and I couldn't tell if she was cursing Orin's existence or threatening mine. Either way, he snarled. He crouched as if he were about to pounce and pummel her into oblivion when sharp, heated footsteps sounded at our backs.

"Jules." Rorik prowled into the space as if he owned it. His boots crunched against the debris, and he kicked aside a rather large piece of wood that skittered across the floor until it crashed into the opposite wall. "What are you doing here?"

"What am I doing here?" she sputtered. "You expect me not to come for retribution after what you did?"

Rorik appeared positively bored. "If you're here to challenge me, then I accept. You'll lose, though, and you know it."

"I don't care!" she howled. Then she sneered up at him from her place on the floor. "At least I'll hurt you as much as I can before I go."

He flexed his hand by his side, and all I could see was blood dribbling through his fingers. Ringing his knuckles. Coating his nails. As if he'd already forcibly removed an organ from her body. I imagined him tossing it loosely to the side with the same bored efficiency as he'd kicked the stray piece of broken wood.

*She doesn't deserve that.*

I was moving before the rational part of my brain could step in and tell me to stop. When I pushed myself in front of Rorik and turned my back on Jules, on the very person who wanted to shove a knife between my shoulder blades, I nearly shocked myself into silence.

Rorik blinked as he looked down at me, and Orin went incredibly still. His gaze bounced between me and the collapsed Ever at my feet. Seville's mouth had dropped open, and Clesian and Lydia . . . dreadful, wide-eyed fascination.

"Don't." It was all I could say as I focused on Rorik's bewildered face. Then, softly: "Please."

Pain flashed through his steely eyes, and he actually stepped back. Stepped back from *me*, as if I were an Ever with the ability to bring him to his knees. His lips parted as he studied every inch of my expression, and I willed myself to keep my breathing steady. The agony in his stare suddenly became so immense and vast that it went far, far beyond that moment. I saw want and ache in his eyes, and it rocked me to my core.

And then it was gone, schooled into place with practiced ease. Gently, he pushed me aside in the direction of Orin. I tried to dig in my heels, but Orin's hand found my wrist, and he yanked me against him.

"Fine," he whispered in my ear. Then he raised his head and spoke to the room. "Jules is free to go, so long as she never sets foot on our lands again."

Throughout it all, Jules stared only at me. "Why?"

I had the feeling she wasn't speaking to Orin, but he answered regardless. "Because it's as Lydia said. Enough is enough."

"I'll escort her out," Rorik said. "Seems like a job for the *dog*." A touch of venom filled his words as he glared at Jules, but something was off. Something not quite as dark and malevolent as I'd expected or witnessed. His mask was nearly perfect—perhaps good enough to convince his family—but maybe because I'd witnessed a different Rorik while we danced beneath the stars, I knew otherwise. I could feel it.

Orin stiffened against my back. "No. Seville will do it."

I couldn't help but frown at Orin's terse reaction. Why did it matter if Rorik got to spend one last minute with someone he obviously cared about?

Rorik merely lifted his shoulder. "Fine by me. I have better things to do."

"Do it now, Seville." Orin shook his head. "We're done here."

Rorik strolled down the hall back in the direction he'd came. He didn't even spare Jules a final glance or goodbye as he rounded the corner and disappeared. Jules had deflated entirely, the last of her anger leaving her in a slump. Seville grumbled in disgust as she yanked Jules up by the arm and turned her toward the door. Her shuffling feet were a hollow, echoing sound that reverberated through the foyer and filled my heart with sadness. I couldn't fathom that ache in my soul, that total feeling of loneliness. And

I knew in my core it was what I would face if I didn't save my brothers.

Orin let out a soft sigh of relief as Lydia and Clesian sauntered upstairs. "You won't have to deal with her again." His brows scrunched together as his grip on my wrist finally loosened. "Why did you come to her aid?"

My shoulders relaxed, and I exhaled deeply. "She'd been through enough. Plus, I trusted you'd be there if in fact I had made an error in judgment."

A droll smile claimed his lips. "Oh, your judgment is far from sound, but"—he stroked my cheek before shaking his head—"you were at least right to count on me."

That was yet to be seen, but the resistance I'd felt toward him was waning faster than I'd anticipated. I glanced around at the debris, gaze halting when I noticed the influx of attendants rushing to help clean the mess.

"What happened with the fete?" I asked.

Orin's expression turned to one of reluctance. "As you can imagine, the festivities ended rather abruptly when I noticed your absence. Quite a few families are still here on our lands for the time being. I need to orchestrate their transport back to Willowfell, as well as smooth over a few things." Then he turned to me fully and brushed his knuckles softly along my jaw. "Please, rest. Take a couple days off training. Research if you must, but nothing too taxing until you're fully healed."

"I'm assuming that includes any shared activities with you."

His grin was tantalizing. "That would be incredibly taxing, I can assure you." He broke away with a slight nod and headed straight for his study. As appealing as the idea of sharing a bed with him was, I couldn't deny the exhaustion that had crept into my limbs. My healing was progressing quickly, but there was little that could replace the effectiveness of a good sleep.

As I climbed the stairs to my room, I felt the weight of someone's eyes on my back. The hairs along my neck rose to the heavens, and I turned in place to find nothing. Again. The space was painfully empty, the only muffled sounds coming from the kitchen as the staff began preparations for dinner. Unease trickled down my spine. The heady stare followed me the entire way to my quarters, but no matter how many times I turned in place, I couldn't find anyone. I rushed into my room, thankful, at least, that the feeling evaporated the moment I shut the doors.

# SEVENTEEN

The following morning, I headed straight for the library. A night of fitful dreams coated with blight had left me on edge, and even though I knew rest was important, I couldn't convince myself to stay hidden away. Not after I'd unearthed the truth about the Ferngloves' sickness. I dove back into the tomes with a new understanding of what was happening, hoping that some piece of their history or some rare plant was the answer. I'd brought my apothecary cases with me, undid the brass clasps and watched as the drawers jumped outward and vials clanked together. I didn't need to heal anything, but I wanted my remedies nearby as I cross-checked ingredients between my tinctures and the flora Evers used in their own magical blends.

There was something to combining our abilities and strengths. My freshly healed wounds were a testament to that. I wasn't quite ready to broach the topic of a heartbond just yet, but researching ways to meld Ever magic with my own creations felt like a real start.

I worked for two more days like that in quiet solitude while my body recovered, and Orin dealt with the aftermath of the fete.

I hadn't thought much about the townsfolk in the wake of my terrorizing evening, but Orin had plenty to do.

"Hard at work?" he called, and I looked up from my notes to find him standing in the open doorway with a tray of coffee and pastries. "I thought you might need some caffeine."

I stretched my neck from side to side before straightening and then smiled. "That sounds lovely. Thank you."

He crossed the room in a handful of easy strides and set the tray down beside my cases. As he handed me my cup, he tilted his head toward the stacks of tomes. "Any luck yet? None of the former threadmenders had knowledge of plants and herbs like you do. I'm hoping that helps."

"Me, too." I blew gently over the steaming mug. "I want to try blending remedies, but there's no way of knowing whether that will work without threadmending."

"Are you ready for that?" He took a careful sip, his gaze never leaving my face. "I know the remedies you and Vora came up with have worked wonders for your body, but I don't want to push you."

"I don't really have a choice." I dragged my finger along the rim of my cup. "Basic threadmending can't save my brothers, but perhaps this will work." Of course I wished I had more concrete proof that I wouldn't be wasting my life's threads for nothing, but we were pioneering into uncharted territory.

"Tomorrow, then." With a gentle finger, Orin grazed my cheek. "I'll be with you throughout the entire process. I promise."

"Everything is handled from the fete?"

He nodded. "The people of Willowfell were more than understanding. I promised to plan a supplemental event in the near future, and they were more than happy with that."

He didn't mention the Starglens. Or, I guess, *Starglen*. Only Jules remained. I took a careful sip of my coffee, trying to wash away the chill that overcame my body. Blight had turned them wild like savage animals fighting for their lives. Survival was all that mattered. And despite nearly dying, I couldn't fault them for their actions—or Orin's swift reaction.

"Edira." Orin's voice was quiet, and I tilted my head toward his. "I'm okay."

Slowly, he pressed his mouth against mine. It was soft, questioning, and yet at the same time the most reassuring thing I'd felt since our last private moment. A slow-moving heat began to gather in my veins. His kiss deepened before he broke away, but his hand remained on my waist.

"I was supposed to conduct lessons today." He pressed his forehead to mine. "But I'm inclined to cancel just to spend time with you."

I breathed in deep and bit my lower lip, looking up at him through the tops of my lashes. His gaze was intense, and his throat bobbed as his eyes dropped to my mouth.

A firm cough interrupted our embrace, and Orin pulled back to spear Tasia with an annoyed look. She stood shoulder to shoulder with Amalyss, and the two of them were stiff as they glanced between us.

"Yes?" Orin prompted when neither of them was brave enough to speak first.

Amalyss's throat bobbed. "We were wondering if Edira needed to be escorted to training before our lessons. Rorik mentioned at breakfast that they'd start up again today."

Training. I blew out a sigh. In the wake of everything that had happened with the Starglens, I'd assumed Rorik would wait longer to resume our sessions. Apparently I was wrong.

"Fine, fine," Orin said with a tense exhale. "Wait for Edira outside. She'll join you momentarily."

They hesitated, as if searching for a reason to linger. Amalyss dipped her head as she began to leave, but Tasia offered a final, weighted look in my direction before following her sister out.

"Tomorrow will be just us." With one last gentle squeeze, Orin pressed a feathery kiss to my forehead. "No interruptions."

Excitement hummed through my bones at the prospect, and we began to gather the materials I'd stacked around the table. He handed me tomes that I neatly slid onto their respective shelves until only the journals remained. His gaze hardened as he rubbed his thumbs along their spines.

"If only they had been more informative."

*Perhaps she was.*

Swallowing my doubt, I cleared my throat. "I noticed a missing page in Rowena's journal. Do you know anything about that?"

For a moment, his expression hardened. A glimmer of . . . distaste? Frustration? Whatever it was, it flashed through his gaze and was gone in an instant, replaced with a more sorrowful look. "She often wrote poems in her spare time. Perhaps she wrote one here but felt like it didn't belong with her research."

That I could believe. Maybe it was one of these fabled letters Seville had mentioned. If she didn't want others knowing about their relationship, or whatever it was, she wouldn't have left it for others to find.

"She was very protective of her work," I said, shelving the journal. "But that aside, we still have a path forward. I'd like to start with using some of the Ever medicine in addition to my own magic to see if that helps with the process of curing blight."

He nodded. "For tomorrow, is there anything you require?"

"I wrote down a list." I pointed toward the table and the scrap of paper full of cramped writing near my apothecary cases. "If you could have those things ready, that would be great."

Orin picked it up and scoured the sheet. "I can have a few things easily by the morning. The others might be a day or two out. Is that enough to start?"

"Yes." A seed of hope began to bloom in my chest. "There are a few different tactics I'd like to try."

"Good. We'll start with one of the infected stags." Orin came around to brush his fingers once more across my cheek. "I can't wait to see what you do."

At that, he slipped his hand into mine and walked with me to the courtyard where Amalyss and Tasia were waiting, the Waterstones a few feet behind them. I'd expected Flix, given Orin's comment about lessons. But Issa and her mother? Ossanna stood with her back pressed against a tree, a careful smirk on full display. And Issa's eager stare found Orin immediately, lingering for a fraction too long before sliding to me. I frowned at the trio of dark-haired Evers, and beside me, Orin's gait stiffened. Then he sighed.

"Ossanna must be concerned about her son's attendance after what happened with Briar." With a curt wave, he signaled for Amalyss and Tasia, and they closed the distance between us. "Take her to Rorik. We'll start lessons when you return."

My stomach tightened. Did Ossanna truly fear Orin would threaten her son?

"Of course," Tasia said as she looped her arm through mine. She started walking without waiting for me to comply, and Amalyss was quick to take up my other arm. I cast one last glance over my shoulder at Orin and the Waterstones. He nodded to Ossanna before placing his hand between Issa's shoulders, speaking into her ear. Her laugh carried toward us on the soft breeze, and a prickling discomfort skittered down my back.

"Don't worry about the Waterstones," Amalyss said under her breath, her eyes cast to the ground. "Orin won't let them near you."

I'd thought the same about the Starglens, but clearly no one had anticipated that.

"Things between the families are . . ." Tasia struggled for a moment, opening her mouth to summon words but somehow struggling to get them out. She wrinkled her nose in frustration before blowing out a hard breath. "Let's just say they're always tense."

*We will* not *drag the past into this.* The memory of Orin's warning—and the heated display of power that came with it—surfaced in my mind. Maybe the girls were too scared to reveal anything about their feud with the Starglens.

"Because of Lorelai?" I asked. In the wake of the Starglens' attack, I'd been too overwhelmed by the truth of blight's reach to ask about anything else. Dagas's daughter had been the furthest thing from my mind, and only now with the tension so obviously rekindling did I remember her name.

Amalyss stumbled as we strolled down the hill, but she recovered quickly. "How do you know about her?"

"I overheard some attendants talking about her." I glanced between them. "What happened? Is she why the Starglens were so mad at Orin?"

Tasia and Amalyss shared a weighted glance before the former slowly exhaled. "She was Orin's heartbond decades ago."

"She died," Amalyss said a breath later. "Orin said it was blight."

"Oh." I looked over my shoulder, but Orin and the Waterstones were nowhere to be found. "Why were they so mad at him, then? It's not like anyone has been able to find a cure."

"True, but Dagas never got over it. Especially since she deteriorated after moving here." Amalyss scratched the side of her neck, and I imagined blight-ridden pustules bursting with the action. Thank the gods for glamour. She never met my gaze, only studied her fingernails for a moment before letting her hand fall lax by her side.

*Deteriorated?* From what I'd gleaned, Evers' blight seemed like a slow, painful progression. Plus, with their glamour acting as a bandage to contain the spread, they managed to last years, whereas humans died within minutes. My mind whirred.

"Orin has . . . a lot of magic." Tasia's words felt strangled, and she frowned at nothing in particular as she cleared her throat. "He's powerful."

"I'd gathered as much," I said with a hum as I recalled the cocoon of magic blanketing my brothers and preserving their very lives. Still, it wasn't enough to cure them. Not yet. I chewed on my lip as I looked between the girls. Tomorrow, I would try blending our remedies. But if that didn't work . . .

*Speak it into existence and it just might happen.*

Seville's words were either an omen or a blessing. Either way, they felt like my undoing. But before I could consider it further, we'd found our way to Rorik and the ancestor tree. With Ywena perched on his shoulder, he nodded to Amalyss and Tasia by way of dismissal before rounding on me. They both gave my arm a squeeze and left without another word. I watched them go as I sifted through the morning's events.

Rorik cleared his throat. "Ywena." He held out his hand, and Ywena fluttered to his open palm and danced about his fingers. "Please go back to Edira."

As I stared at the creature waiting to rejoin me, the fete came flooding back to the forefront of my mind. My dance with Rorik and the way he'd asked me to lie. The feel of his hand on the small of my back, and the unfamiliar twinge of irritation at the sight of it on someone else's waist. That same hand drenched in Dagas's blood hours later.

*You're beautiful.*

His exclamation was a safe truth that meant nothing and everything. He'd used me that night for his own amusement, like a pawn in a game I didn't understand. I was tired of being his toy. I was here to train. Nothing more.

Gently, I beckoned to Ywena and welcomed her delicate feet against my skin. She lingered on my fingers for a breath before returning to her preferred perch in the crook of my neck. I brushed aside my locks to give her space, and I swore I heard her sigh.

"Welcome back," I muttered to her.

"Don't lose her again." Rorik stared at her for a long moment before finally dragging his gaze to my face. "Understood?"

"I didn't lose her." A flicker of indignation sparked in my chest.

He slipped his hands in the pockets of his pants as he leaned against the base of the tree. "You started the night with her and ended it without her. I'd call that losing her."

"Orin was responsible for that." I glared at him.

His answering stare hammered into me with far more intensity than I expected. "I know."

I threw up my hands in frustration as I blew out a sharp breath. "You're impossible."

"Not as impossible as you."

"What are you, ten?" I side-eyed him as I pulled back my hair, neatly tying it in preparation for my warm-up run around the estate. "That's the kind of retort I'd expect from a child."

He didn't bother to deny the accusation. "No running today. I need to assess where you're at."

I stilled. "Assess?"

"Yes. Sit."

His frame was tense as he gestured to the empty space before him. My brows drew together as I sank to the ground and crossed my legs. I watched as he stiffly circled me twice before crouching behind me to place his hand between my shoulder blades.

"Tell me how you feel."

"What?" I shifted to look at him over my shoulder, and he nudged me back into position.

"Tell. Me. How. You. Feel."

"Repeating it word for word doesn't change my question," I bit back. "I'm *fine.*"

"Are you?" The pressure of his fingers against my spine intensified.

"Yes. Are you all right? You're acting strange." My muscles shifted without thought, and I found myself leaning into him. I expected him to force me to straighten my back, to bark out some condescending remark about my "posture," but he only continued to work.

"You're grating as always. I suppose that's a good sign." His words lacked their usual sting.

"Rorik, seriously—"

"Do you have any idea . . ." He swallowed hard enough for me to hear, as if he could somehow bite back the emotion clawing at his words. Emotion that sounded an awful lot like concern. He exhaled forcefully. "Just breathe. *Quietly.*"

I snorted. "What better way to keep me in line than to take my voice?" All at once I thought of Mavis and her stillness, and I shuddered.

"Your voice is only part of the problem."

Even though he couldn't see it, I rolled my eyes. "Yes, well, gods forbid I exist."

"It is problematic." Something shifted in his tone as his fingers moved to the knotted muscles along my shoulder blade. "You're tense." He tested a few spaces with gentle prods before isolating an errant tendon and digging his thumb deep into my back. I lurched forward at the same time Ywena shot a familiar jolt of electricity through to my extremities.

Pivoting in place, I finally escaped his touch and shot him a glare. "Of course I'm tense. You just told me my existence is problematic. And on top of that, I was just *attacked*, in case you forgot."

"As if I could forget." He let his hand fall away as he raised a brow. "Is that all?"

There was something so nonchalant, so boorish, about his response that all the emotions I'd been suppressing at the sight of him came frothing to the surface. Anger for the way he'd toyed with me to further his agenda. Longing for the way his fingers felt on my skin. Confusion and pain for wanting more, especially when I knew I could seek comfort in Orin's arms. And fear. Fear that Rorik could be so lethal, so devastatingly horrific, and still it wasn't enough to send me running.

"Why is it so hard for you to be nice?" I seethed. He went stock-still as I turned fully and leaned close enough for our breaths to intermingle. "All I've done since coming here is try to help, and for what? For you to be a colossal ass every time we meet? It's any wonder the rest of the family looks down upon you. The only time I've ever heard a nice thing out of that damn mouth of yours is when you were drunk."

He stared at me with scrunched brows, and a flicker of wonder passed through his gaze as his careful veil of feigned indifference slipped away. Pressing his lips together, he studied my face with enough intensity to bring a flush to my cheeks.

Finally, *finally*, he tipped his head forward as his lips curled into a sinful grin. "You've been thinking about my mouth?"

I blinked as the raging emotions inside me stalled. And then I let out a groan as I pulled back and pinched my nose between my forefinger and thumb. "Impossible."

"Indeed. Now, turn around." I didn't fight him as he went back to kneading tiny circles down the length of my spine. Better to look anywhere but at his face. Gods, he was a thorn in my side that somehow wormed itself deeper with each passing day. Still, it was hard to complain when my body couldn't get enough of his touch. Each aching tendon begged for the release his fingers brought, and I bit back a moan to keep him from gaining any satisfaction from the sound.

*The only pain I'd ever intentionally inflict on you is the agony of making you wait to feel the pleasure of release.*

Gooseflesh rippled across my skin from head to toe, and while I couldn't see Rorik's expression, there was an infinitesimal twitch to his fingers.

"Hit a nerve?" he asked, voice low.

Did he ever. "No. I'm fine."

The silence that followed was unbearable as unspoken words hung in the space between us. An eternity passed as he trailed indecipherable patterns down my back, until finally he deemed me relaxed enough to work. I expected him to pull away, but instead he leaned forward and spoke softly against my neck. "Let's just work on breathing today."

"Why?" I wanted to crane my head over my shoulder, but that would undo the glorious work he'd just performed on my muscles. It was amazing I was still sitting upright when the tendons holding me together had transformed into butter. I'd molded to his touch so much that I hadn't realized how close we'd gotten, not until he kicked out his legs, cradling me on either side. My pulse spiked as he guided my back against his chest with two firm fingers against my shoulder.

He hesitated for a breath before his soft words floated through the air. "Because your body has been through enough."

Awareness prickled at my senses, and the hesitation, the *guilt*, was suddenly so apparent in Rorik's words that I failed to find my own. I hadn't thought about his place in all this. But I did remember the way he looked at me strung up on that tree. The fury and ire in his pupil-less gaze. The tension in his fists.

Rorik cleared his throat when I didn't respond. "And it's important to learn how to preserve your breath specifically while using your magic." The thrum of his words reverberated down the column of my spine. "Once you've gained that kind of control over your body, perhaps you'll be able to better choose how much power to use when working with blight. The only reason you managed to do so with your brothers was because Orin got to you in time."

"And you know that because?"

He stiffened for a moment, then let out a curt laugh. "Orin told me. How else would I know?"

"I still don't understand how you expect me to do anything

with you right up against me." I forced a hard swallow as I stared at the ancestor tree and the sun creeping toward the horizon.

"Well, first, I *expect* you to kick on your magic. Unless you struggle to do that as well."

My body was glowing with moonlit power before the terse words could fly out of my mouth. "Of course I can do that."

"Good. Now, feel the rise and fall of my chest. The beat of my heart." His breath was warm against my skin as he lowered his head to my shoulder. "Will your body to match it. I'll slow my breathing and my heartbeat every few minutes or so. Let's see how long you can keep up—and don't let your power slip. Focus on maintaining both at the same time."

My glow sharpened and receded with my emotions. My heart was cantering like a wild horse, and Rorik's quiet chuckle told me that he knew. Because of course he could hear it. Of course this exercise would be beyond easy for him. My magic paled in comparison to Evers'. I couldn't see in the dark or hear a pin drop a room away. If I tried to hold my own against one of them, I'd lose—as evidenced by my recent bout with the Starglens. Breathwork wouldn't save me if something like that happened again.

"You know," Rorik said, his words barely more than a whisper, "it's easier to match my pace if you can keep your mind from racing."

"That's an impossible feat," I muttered, pitching my voice in the same tone as his.

I could practically hear his smile. "Busy thinking about my body against yours?" He shifted a fraction, somehow bringing himself closer. "I am quite distracting. All the more reason to keep at this. If you can ignore me, then you've mastered something no one else has been able to do."

"Your arrogance knows no bounds." My heart hammered against my throat, but my glow remained steady. "I thought we were training so I'd be better at threadmending."

"I'm training you to survive."

"Why?"

The rise and fall of his rib cage slowed, and I forced myself to match his breathing pattern. He waited until I'd settled into the new pace before finally answering.

"Because you deserve to live."

So damn soft. His words were barely a whisper on the evening breeze, and yet they settled against me like weights.

"The issue isn't whether or not I deserve it. I'm bound to die in a matter of years if I mend. Hopefully, I'll cure a few people before I go."

He scoffed. "The only people you should cure are your brothers, and that's only if it doesn't affect your lifespan."

My breath caught in my lungs. Ywena responded with a jolt of electricity that felt far gentler than normal. Or perhaps my shock dulled the sensation of her power. Either way, a ripple, like the aftereffects of a stone skipping over water, fluttered through my light until once again everything smoothed.

It took me several moments to find my voice. "That is the exact opposite of why I am here. Your family—"

Rorik cut me off before I could finish. "If we're supposed to die, then we die. I've lived enough. Seen enough. This obsession with immortality, that's the real sickness." He swallowed thickly, and the action caused a more defined rise and fall to his breath. One that my body instinctively matched. "None of us are really *living*."

For a long while, we said nothing. Instead, we listened to the lilting chirps of insects and watched the sun dip beneath the horizon, leaving behind an indigo sky awash with twinkling stars. I sat with his words, with the decreasing frequency of his inhales and exhales, with the steady beat of his heart knocking against my back. I didn't know what to say to him, largely in part because I'd thought there was a sickness in their home that went beyond blight—and his words confirmed it. A deep pang settled into my heart as I watched the night sky grow darker.

Gods, I missed my brothers. I missed the family I had. The one where my mother and father were still alive and our days were filled with laughter. There wasn't much of that now. There wasn't any of that within the walls of Fernglove Manor.

"You're brighter than the moon and just as steady." Rorik rested his chin on my shoulder as he spoke into the crook of my neck. "Even with me touching you, you've managed to maintain your breath. Nice work."

I laughed quietly, unwilling to let go of this strange sliver of peace we'd unearthed. Buttery-yellow lights were bleeding to life one by one through the manor's windows. Any minute now, and we'd be expected for dinner. "Glad I passed your assessment."

After a beat of silence, he whispered, "I wasn't drunk."

"What?" I asked as I failed to follow his train of thought.

"At the fete. You said I was drunk."

"Oh." I didn't know where he was going, and I was afraid to look back at my memories of the night and unpack his actions as if he had been sober. Some were tantalizing. Some were infuriating. Some were painful. All were dangerous as hell. Slowly, I scooted out of his loose embrace and let the cool evening air settle against my back. I called off my power with a mere thought, and the world darkened around us. He watched me closely, studying every movement.

Everything that happened during our training session felt too raw and personal, as if this was more than just a lesson. As if this moment was bound to live with me for the rest of my days. Suddenly, I felt powerless. I couldn't breathe in his space for a second longer, and I swallowed thick emotion as a peculiar heat pricked at the backs of my eyes.

"I'm sorry about Jules," I said.

It was a reminder for both of us. Something wild and fierce

flashed in his gaze. It was too easy to fall prey to his taunts. I had work to do. People and Evers to save, even if he didn't see value in their lives.

"Edira, there are things . . ." His throat bobbed, and he winced. After squeezing his eyes shut and forcing out a harsh breath, he once again leveled me with his molten stare. "I carry the weight of unspoken burdens in my bones."

I hated that it sounded like an apology. Earlier, I would have asked him to explain. Now, I was just tired.

"Me, too, Rorik." I stood and brushed dirt from my pants. "Me, too."

As I walked away from him, I shouldered the weight of my life—a life of unfilled dreams and heartache, of unspoken truths and burdens—without looking back. Because unlike him, that's what I had to do to survive.

That night, I skipped dinner and went straight to my brothers' room. And as I lay on the ground at the foot of their coffins, I thought about nothing more than inhaling and exhaling, because at least Rorik was right about one thing: I deserved to live.

# EIGHTEEN

My training with Rorik was a hazy memory by the time I woke the next morning. There was no sense in unpacking the hidden meaning in his words when I didn't understand his motivation. He'd toyed with my emotions one too many times. I had better things to do, like ready myself for my work with Orin. A quiet smile pulled at my lips. With him by my side, it felt like I could do anything.

The manor was quiet, creaking, as I laid out my clothes. The very walls seemed to watch me as I moved, as if they knew that I might find a way to cure the matriarch resting within her room. Expectation was thick in the air, and I prayed I didn't disappoint.

I ran my hand over the ivy-green blouse and tan pants—along with a more subdued, cream-colored bralette from my day with Seville—just as Vora knocked on the door. She entered without waiting for me to respond, glancing briefly at the clothes before veering into the attached washroom to draw a bath. I let her bathe and dress me without speaking. It wasn't until she sat me before the vanity and dragged a bone-colored comb through my hair that she talked.

"You were missed at dinner last night."

I raised a brow. "By whom?"

"Orin. He expects the family to dine together, but he understands if you need space."

"I was tired after training with Rorik." I waved off her words as I kept my breathing steady. Ywena had crawled onto my lap while Vora worked, giving her room to tame my locks.

"I gathered as much." She tugged harder than necessary, and I frowned at her through the mirror. "He and Orin got into a disagreement at dinner."

And Rorik thought I was problematic. "Dare I ask why?"

Vora let her hands fall away. "Rorik found out you were going to threadmend today, and he got angry. Said you weren't ready, that you could barely even maintain your power while distracted. Orin disagreed."

*You're brighter than the moon and just as steady.*

Thank gods I was already sitting, because Rorik's betrayal felt like he'd swiped my legs clean out from under me. My body went impossibly stiff as an ache swelled in my throat. After that personal moment we shared, he still didn't think I was good enough? Heat purled through my veins, and I fisted the fabric of my pants. What was he getting at? I steeled my rising anger by channeling more focus to my breath, taking satisfaction in the fact that Ywena hadn't shocked me once.

"Rorik should keep his thoughts to himself." I stood abruptly, pushing away from the vanity and resisting the urge to knock the perfumed bottles off their tiered pedestal. Ywena fluttered about the crown of my head for a moment before once again settling against my neck. "I'm done training with him."

"Edira." Vora rushed to stand before me, and she gently rested her hands on my arms. "Please."

"Please what?" I brushed her off and headed for the door. "It's fine. I have more important things to do with my time."

I let the door close behind me with a definitive thud and stormed down the stairs. I didn't bother with the dining room, either, or the breakfast platters waiting on the table. Largely because I didn't want to engage in conversation with Lydia or Clesian, and they watched me pass with rapt curiosity. Their girls, too, tipped their heads in confusion as I headed into the kitchen. The room was full of bustling attendants swarming from one station to the next, preparing food and drink and delicate treats as if they were about to host a fete and not just a breakfast. When they noticed me, the room came to a standstill.

"Don't mind me." I waved them off, hoping the action was commanding enough. I turned toward a freshly baked loaf of bread and cut away a slice, slathering it with hazelnut butter. One by one they went back to work, eyeing me over polished kitchenware. The heat of the stoves was too sweltering for me to linger, and I walked off my frustration while I ate. My feet, of course, led me to Orin's study.

*I'll show Rorik what I can do.*

Wiping the last of my quick breakfast off my lips, I knocked softly on Orin's door.

"Come in," he called over the shuffling of papers.

I breezed into the room like I'd seen Seville do, claiming the space with each footstep as I moved toward Orin. His eyes widened as he looked up from his stack of papers and absently let his pen fall to the desk. We hadn't set a time for our work, but I didn't care. I just wanted to feel his arms around me. Orin leaned back in his chair as I rounded his desk, and without waiting for him to speak, I climbed atop his lap and grabbed his face with both hands. My mouth was on his in an instant, and his lips parted easily as my tongue twined with his. Every inch of my skin lit up as I pressed myself closer.

He moaned and gripped my hips tight, only pulling away after nipping at my bottom lip. "To what do I owe this greeting?"

"Call it excitement for what today could bring." I peppered the length of his throat with light kisses. Rolling my hips into his, I sat back and smiled down at him as heat flared in his green eyes.

"How am I supposed to focus when I'll be thinking of this all day?" He palmed my cheek, then let his hand fall to the nape of my neck where his fingers wove through my hair. With restrained force, he guided my mouth to his and held me there, a breath away from pleasure.

Warmth pooled in my lower abdomen at the thought of being with him. Ywena's shocks weren't enough to curb my want, either, but Orin's gaze slid to her as he dragged his lips across mine. Annoyance raced through his expression. It was there and gone in a flash, leaving behind a tremor of something heated and dangerous. With soft fingers, I smoothed an errant tendon feathering down his jaw.

"Are you all right?"

He sighed, but his smile was genuine. "Yes. I just hope that when the time comes, we won't have an audience." Tilting his head slightly, he nodded toward Ywena.

Nicking his ear with my teeth, I whispered, "You can send her away."

"Of course I could." His pleased growl simmered from somewhere deep in his chest. "But the stags are already waiting."

"Later then," I mused, masking my disappointment with the same efficiency I used to regain control of my breath. My heartbeat.

Orin held my stare. "Absolutely."

He eased to his feet, sweeping me up with him, before placing a kiss on my forehead and setting me on the ground. He never let go of my hand. A mixture of excitement and fear fused in my core, sending a strange, electric sensation purling through my limbs.

The old me would've avoided threadmending like the death sentence that it was. But Edira of Fernglove? I squeezed Orin's fingers, my body brimming with a confidence only he could give. She had power.

And I would be the one to put an end to blight.

We made our way out of the study together. We didn't bother to speak to Lydia or Clesian as they stood in the parlor with their daughters. They must've known what was about to happen. Their stares were hungry, but layered beneath was a thread of hope I recognized all too well, for it was the same ribbon unfurling in my veins. I inclined my head to Amalyss and Tasia by way of greeting. If I decided to be kind enough to cure anyone in this household beyond Mavis, it would be them.

And Orin.

Rorik's tight expression flashed in my mind, and I quickly pushed it away. I was ready. I would be everything he didn't think I could be.

The morning lawns were quiet, the woods still. The very air around us seemed to hold its breath as we came upon the stables. The farmhands were nowhere to be found, but the creatures were fed, their stalls pristinely cleaned. Like the rest of the estate's residents, the beasts watched us approach with an intense focus full of anticipation. Orin unlatched the wooden pen door leading to a lone stag, standing tall over a heaping mound of hay.

The beast looked as magnificent as it had the day it'd pulled the carriage toward Fernglove Estate. Easily twenty hands tall, it peered at me with glowing pale eyes. Its rack was massive and covered in ivy that seemed to sprout from the base of each horn. I ached to run my fingers along its mossy hide, to lightly touch the flowers blooming between tufts of fur. By all accounts, it seemed healthy.

"This is Zotakoss. He's one of the magical beasts we've been able to domesticate." Orin reached for the beast and placed a soft hand on its snout. "You can call him Zota for short. He has been with us for many years."

Zota chuffed in response. Steam curled from his nostrils and intermingled with the dripping strands of foliage wreathing his head like a mane.

"Hello, Zota." I extended my hand and let it hover in the space before his snout.

His focus swiveled to me, and he inhaled deeply before thrusting his nose against my fingers. A smile claimed my lips as I gently pet the length of his muzzle.

"He won't startle easily. Oh, and here's this." Orin slipped a hand into one of the pockets of his trousers, extracting a small, shallow jar full of an off-white cream. "One of the concoctions you wanted to try."

I grinned as I took it and untwisted the lid. I was hit with the familiar scent of one of my tinctures for pain relief and a foreign, floral scent. Ground petals from a white tear flower, a special bloom that grew in response to Evers using earthly magic. Fortunately, the Ferngloves were at the forefront on that ability, and Orin had easily coaxed one from the earth under the light of the moon just the night before.

"Thank you," I said as I coated my hands in the balm and let it soak into my skin. I hoped it would lessen the effect of blight's ailments as I mended Zota's threads.

"Just take your time and begin whenever you're ready." Orin retreated a few steps to lean against the wood paneling of Zota's stall. Crossing his arms, he nodded once to the creature before shifting his attention to the space where my hands hovered near Zota's snout.

I leaned in close and spoke softly against his nose. "I'm going to try and help you."

Prior to coming to Fernglove, I'd only ever heard horror stories about magical creatures and their violent natures. I doubted any of those myths were based off Zota, because one look into his eyes won me over. While he could crush me beneath the weight of his massive body, there was something gentle and kind about his presence. He fervently ducked his head several times over, as if understanding my words and agreeing to accept my help.

Leaning my forehead against his muzzle, I closed my eyes. My breathing slowed as I centered myself and drew on the power lying dormant in my veins. It ignited with ease, flaring to life and speeding through me as a pleasing, rippling current of energy flooded my fingertips. When I opened my eyes, I felt magic gloss over them at the same time a soothing white light ensconced my fingers.

The faint scent of Orin's power filled the air, and I realized he was removing the glamour from Zota's appearance. In less than a breath, I was faced with the reality of the beast's condition.

He was little more than bone and sinew. Gone was his lustrous hide, and in its place was a patchwork display of dried, leathery skin on the verge of flaking away. Zota's rib cage was exposed, and his head was hardly more than a skull with cracked bones protruding in a crude attempt at a rack. Where his eyes should have been were hollowed-out holes that were lifeless and cold. Blight rimmed every opening, and sickening yellow pustules dotted the expanse of his body. My hand shook as I stared at the space where my fingers met his muzzle. The slimy texture of muscle and puss coated my skin, and I forced bile down with a hard swallow. Tears pricked the backs of my eyes as the stench of death wrapped me in a suffocating cocoon.

How Zota was still alive was beyond me.

My chest heaved in protest as I forced myself to keep breathing. I couldn't falter. Not now.

"I'll keep his glamour removed while you work." Out of the corner of my eye, I caught Orin studying me.

I nodded, and the power drenching my fingers sharpened to a near-blinding light. "Let's take a closer look."

Zota's life threads bloomed from his center mass and limply fell about his frame. There was hardly any movement to his tar-soaked strands. A few had already petrified and were on the verge of dusting into oblivion. But there was hope. There were still glimpses of color beneath the encroaching blight. I marveled at the threads, pausing as I took in the curious muted teal shade.

*She embedded parts of ancient beasts into her being and gained additional strength and power in return.*

The first Ever had taken from Zota's ancestors. It seemed that bestial magic and power shifted the very hue and makeup of Evers' threads. If I could mend Zota's threads, then there had to be a way to cure Mavis. And most certainly my brothers.

At first, I did nothing but breathe. Slowly. Evenly. Maybe Rorik was right. I loathed the idea of giving him any credit, but there was something to channeling my breath to strengthen my magic. Time slowed as my heartbeat became nothing more than a quiet thump stretched out over eternity.

Magic pulsed through me heady and strong as I reached for one of Zota's strands. Gently, I wrapped one around my hand and draped it between my fingers. I knew better than to try to wipe away the putrid liquid. Doing so with my brothers' strands had resulted in immediate repercussions that hit with a force I couldn't withstand. What I didn't comprehend, though, was why blight affected Evers so differently. Mortals who became infected died swiftly. With Evers, it was as if the poison was designed to linger, to eat away at their beings with deliberate slowness so they felt every inch of themselves fading away.

I hadn't started mending Zota's threads, but I could already feel the blight prickling against my skin. It sunk deeper and deeper into my muscles and bones with every steady inhale, and with it came a throbbing ache that enveloped me so wholly I couldn't tell where it started and ended. Black dots danced across my vision as I studied the strand. The sludge bubbled and frothed as it slid across my fingers, steaming as it kissed my skin. Breathing helped me weather the storm as I fought against wave after wave of churning sickness forming in my gut.

Slowly, I cupped my hands around Zota's strand and willed my power to increase. A blinding orb of light fractured between my fingers, chasing away every hint of a shadow. But the tar remained, save for the spaces where my flesh made direct contact with the life thread. A sizzling met my ears as pain bloomed behind my eyes. Somehow, I held it together long enough to watch the sludge cook away. It re-formed within the span of a few breaths, but for a moment, I'd seen nothing but muted teal between my fingers.

Excitement pushed back against the rising ailments, and I extended both of my arms. Zota's strands answered by wrapping my limbs entirely, and for a moment, nothing happened.

And then my power faltered under the presence of Zota's unrelenting blight, or perhaps the magically crafted balm had worn off—likely both. In less than a breath, I was wrapped in his threads with no sharp glow to burn away the blight, and the sickness hit me with an animalistic ferocity I couldn't have trained for. The gut-roiling stench of decay and mulch filled the stall, and I tasted the brackish flavor of it on my tongue as I gasped for air. Each breath was erratic and sharp, like blades slicing away at my lungs. My bones throbbed with a pain that pulsed in time with my heart. But even as my stomach was churning, preparing to heave my meager breakfast, I caught sight of Zota's threads now retreating as I reined in my magic.

His teal threads.

Hope sparked for the span of one harrowing breath, then was crushed with absolute certainty as I watched the blight easily regain the ground it'd lost. Tar coated the resplendent threads a tacky black, and they slowly curled toward Zota's center like withering leaves.

"Edira!" Orin shouted.

I'd nearly forgotten he was there. Slumping fully to the ground, I sought purchase in the dirt and hay at Zota's feet as I let my power fade away completely. Orin was there, yanking me back toward the stall wall and cradling me in his arms. The movement was enough to send me reeling again, and I pressed my eyes shut until the swaying stopped.

*Breathe.*

Everything was heavy. My hands. My limbs. My thoughts. I pulled what strength I could from the warmth of Orin's embrace, but his arms were iron grips against my bruising muscles. His heartbeat was as loud as the town's bell toll; his breath a turbulent wind that threatened to carry me away with it. It took everything in me to peel open my eyes. Somehow, I managed. I picked a spot in the stall—Zota's water trough—and focused only on it. It became my anchor, the object of all my attention, while my senses settled. Once the world finally returned to its normal axis and the nausea in my belly stalled, I braved a glance at Orin.

"What happened?" he asked, tucking a strand of sweat-dampened hair behind my ear.

"I couldn't do it," I croaked.

"It's all right." His brows crawled together as he pressed his forehead against mine. "I still believe in you."

Exhaustion settled deep into my bones. "I'll try again. I just need to rest."

"Okay." With a tender kiss, he pressed his lips to mine and then scooped me up in his arms. I didn't want to fall prey to my subconscious, but I couldn't fight the darkness blooming across the edges of my vision. The fact that I'd lasted this long was a testament to my training and the combination of Ever remedies and my magic. My eyes drifted closed of their own accord, and I sighed. I didn't remember the trek back to the manor or Orin placing me in my bed. I didn't remember anything beyond the sound of his feet thudding against the earth as he ran.

## NINETEEN

Two days passed before I tried to threadmend Zota again. And again, I failed. It went on like that for days—me attempting to threadmend under Orin's careful watch, and me failing every time, despite the variety of balms I had made and slathered across my skin. The only solace was that each dance with blight left me a little stronger. A little more hardened. After the third time, I needed only a day to recuperate. The fifth, six hours. Of course, Orin insisted I continue to rest and eat normally to give my body every opportunity to replenish itself. Most threadmenders under his care were unable to work again after five or six encounters with Zota. I was faring better, but we had no way of knowing what kind of long-term damage I was incurring.

By the seventh time we'd run out of all my initial ideas for blending magical ingredients with my own tinctures. Every medicine had a shelf life, and nothing lasted long enough for me to fully eradicate Zota's sickness. I even visited the library after one of my failed attempts to snag *A Collection of Rare Flora* and *Sloan's Guide to Curses and Poisons* in an attempt to brew something entirely unheard of. Orin sent Vora to retrieve the rare herbs and ingredients, and it took her a week by ley line to acquire what I needed. After, Orin and I worked together to craft a thick salve that stuck to my body like a second skin.

The blight destroyed it within minutes.

Throughout it all, I hardly saw anyone else in Fernglove outside of my brothers. But everyone else I avoided out of an abundance of caution. I went straight to my quarters to bathe myself after each attempt at threadmending and bagged my soiled clothes. If I was too weak to handle it immediately, Orin would cast a layer of glamour over me to keep any traces of it from spreading. The last thing I wanted was to unintentionally infect an attendant.

While the Ferngloves weren't at risk, I still didn't see them. I suspected that was intentional—Orin's way of making sure I was free to work as I pleased—but I found myself missing the sharp, scrutinizing looks from Seville. The laughter of Amalyss and Tasia. Even Rorik's incessant teasing. Instead, my days were full of Orin and his words of encouragement. The warmth of his touch, the soft feeling of his lips against mine, the steady reassurance I felt each time I gripped his hand tight. It was enough to keep me going. The only other person I saw was Vora. She visited after I was clean to slather on medicine and grumble about lasting repercussions.

She wasn't wrong, either. So far, I couldn't see any hints of sickness marring my appearance, but I could feel it. There was a sluggishness to my actions as if I were forcing my limbs through mud. A perma-fog had crept over my brain, and I often found myself reading the same lines in my books over and over again before fully understanding the words. I was beginning to wonder if this was what happened to my aunt. I had Vora bring her journal to my bedside and reread it every night, feeling more kinship with her stilted language as my mind began to wane. While none of her entries compared to the poems she used to pen, there was a distinct shift in quality from her early days to her last. Everything became blunt. Harsh. As if she had energy only for the facts and nothing else.

But I had to keep going. I didn't have a choice. It was as if the blight knew I was coming, too, because it'd started to eat away at my brothers with more fervor. I didn't notice right away, but after visiting several nights in a row, I started to spy new wounds forming along their arms and necks.

Time was running out.

After my tenth failed attempt at healing Zota, something changed. Not in me, but in Orin. He'd endured so much, watching me try again and again, only to bottle up his hope and bury it back down each and every time. I saw his disappointment in the way his eyes fell when he stared at my trembling fingers. Felt it in the hollowness of his touch. It must've been agonizing for him to watch on levels I couldn't begin to understand.

"This is hopeless," he muttered as he sat beside me, not touching my sweat-soaked body.

I ached to feel the warmth of his embrace. "I'm close. I know it." I couldn't tell if it was a lie or a truth or if it mattered at all.

Orin looked away. "Am I failing you?"

"What?" I straightened, ignoring the pain that came with the sudden action. At least that was one-sided. Zota remained largely unaffected by our sessions and often ended up resting on the ground with his head propped against a hay bale, like he was now.

"Have I pushed you too far?" Orin sighed as he shook his head at nothing.

I scooted toward him so our hands were touching. "Orin, you have nothing to do with this."

"You're not holding back just to spite me, are you?" He met my gaze, and I saw fear in his eyes. Rubbing his jaw, he studied me as if he'd forgotten about all our moments together. About the heat that had blossomed between us. About the unnamed emotion that drove me to consider saving his life. The fact that he questioned all that . . . A painful tightness settled in my throat.

"How can you even ask that." It was meant to be a question, but there was no inflection to my voice.

"No one wants to die." He dropped his gaze to our hands.

"That may be true, but if I fail you, then I also fail my brothers." Slowly, firmly, I threaded my fingers with his. "And I don't want you to die, either."

Silence enveloped us. For a long moment he said nothing, and then he heaved a sigh that carried with it the weight of the world. Pinning his chin with my fingers, I angled his face so I could force him to meet my gaze.

"Orin, I . . ."

I didn't know what to say. If I told him I cared for him . . . that I *loved* him . . . My insides squirmed. There were too many other things in the way. The length of my quickly shortening life. The blight all around us. My brothers. His family.

Gently, I kissed him. "I'm close. I promise."

Finally, he smiled. It was soft and hardly the wide grin I'd grown accustomed to, but it was a start. He dragged his thumb over my cheek. "I didn't mean to doubt you. I just wish there was some way to make this easier for you."

*Speak it into existence and it just might happen.*

There it was again. That damning, tantalizing thought. Would it be so bad to share my power with him? Would he balk at sharing his magic with me? I didn't think so.

The sound of footsteps met our ears, and Vora rounded the corner of the stables before coming to a halt several feet away from Zota's stall. She didn't look my way once.

"Sorry to interrupt, but Ossanna is here. She requests your presence."

Orin sighed as he stood. "Ossanna? Why?"

"She didn't say," Vora said. She brushed stiff hands along her apron as she glanced back toward the manor. "You know her. Always angling for something."

Orin's eyes narrowed. "Indeed." Then, to me: "Don't tax yourself anymore today. You deserve a break." Leaning down, he trailed his fingers along my jaw before kissing me deeply on the mouth. Relief bloomed in my chest at the feel of his lips on mine, and I nodded with a smile as he and Vora returned to the manor.

His kiss lingered on my mind far longer than I anticipated, and as I sat in the stall beside a slumbering Zota—his snores were the perfect, soothing backdrop to the quiet chirps of insects—I turned over the possibility of sharing a heartbond with Orin. There were worse things in the world than being tied to him. It was strange to think that not too long ago I'd flinched at the idea of being seen with Seville at market. Now I was contemplating permanently tying myself to her brother.

My body protested as I stood, but I couldn't sit any longer. While I'd learned how to better grapple with the consequences of threadmending over the past several weeks, there was still an undercurrent of pain that accompanied each step I took. The only thing that somewhat alleviated it was managing my breath. At least Rorik had finally taught me something useful. As I willed my heartbeat to slow, the pain ebbed away. I'd become mindful of where my oxygen was going, diverting it to the places where my body ached most.

I crept along the quiet paths of the courtyard, moving without really thinking about anything beyond bathing and then falling into bed. When I opened the door, the house was eerily quiet, the halls devoid of sound and movement. The few candles that were still lit suggested that most had turned in for the night, and there were more shadows spilling across the polished floors than bright spots. As I moved through the darkness, a low growl rumbled through the air. My gaze snapped toward a thin shaft of harsh light cutting across the floor. Orin's study.

"I told you to dispose of them," Orin seethed. The heat and ire in his words were so uncharacteristic that I couldn't bring myself to move. Curiosity and dread had rooted me to the ground like the great ancestor tree outside.

"I did," Rorik said. Footsteps sounded, and then chair legs scraped against the floorboards, as if someone was taking a seat. "Dispose. Not kill."

Orin slammed his hands on his desk, and I heard the angry rush of scattered papers being tossed into the air. "It was implied."

"Implications are more like suggestions. I only do what you force me to do." Rorik's bored voice carried easily, and I couldn't help but picture him lazily leaning into his seat with his head tipped to the ceiling. "Zelyria and Briar are long gone. Jules, too. She caught wind of their whereabouts after her outburst here. Is this why you summoned me?"

Shock nearly caused me to gasp, but I caught myself before my breathing could stutter. I hadn't seen Briar's and Zelyria's deaths, just assumed them, but Rorik had let them go. A strange, unexpected warmth stemmed from my chest.

"*Jules caught wind.*" The words were scathing as they dripped from Orin's lips. "No doubt you were responsible for that, too. You deliberately defied me. I wouldn't have even known had Ossanna not seen them crossing her lands."

Magic rolled from the study in palpable waves that filled the hall, and I instinctively slowed my breathing to just the shallowest, most infrequent cadence. I was hidden in shadows, obscured by the statues and potted plants. I made no sound. No movement. I'd never felt something so heady, so all-consuming, as Orin's power. It was smothering in its oppressiveness, and it hung in the air like a summer storm about to unload. Warning bells crashed in my ears. If this was just the surface of his magic, could I even handle it? Could I even become his heartbond, welcome his power into my body, and use it to help my family?

"Ossanna," Rorik scoffed. "What a nuisance. Still, she doesn't concern me."

"Don't test me, Rorik." Orin's voice was deadly calm. "There's too much at stake."

The conversation stalled, and I was about to leave in case one of them caught me eavesdropping when Ywena suddenly started. She'd been still against my collarbone until then, but now was craning her head in the direction of the door. She let out the faintest chitter—a quiet creak that could've been the house settling in for the night. Then she flattened herself to my chest, as if telling me to stay put.

Rorik's voice seemed a touch louder than before. "Testing you is my favorite pastime. Even Father couldn't put a stop to that."

A low growl simmered through the air. "His evervow was meant to protect us, and yet you still find ways to put us at risk just to spite him. Think before you act, or I'll take matters into my own hands."

"No, you won't." Someone stood then and moved before the door. Rorik. His broad back filled the small crack, but I could just glimpse the fringes of his burnished locks. The heat of his words filled the hall. "You know you can't do that."

"One day, I will find a way around it," Orin said.

A chill crept down my spine at Orin's words. He spoke them with such lethal surety that it took me a moment to process what he said. An evervow? Left by their father? What did it even entail? And why?

Rorik chuckled darkly. "We'll see."

The hairs on the back of my neck rose. This conversation felt far too personal, steeped in too much history. I could still taste Orin's barely contained rage in the air. A shiver ran across my skin as I slowly inched away, and Orin's insult trailed after me.

"Go back to your insects and the filth they live in. It suits you."

My heart thudded in my ears, but my feet didn't make a sound.

Even my breath was nothing more than an errant current drifting through the house from one of the many open windows. I willed myself to stay calm, to keep moving and remain out of sight until I reached the safe confines of my quarters. But just as I rounded the stairs and was about to let out a sigh of relief, a glimmer of pale skin and the whisper of light feet over the carpeted runner made me freeze in place.

But there was nothing, no one, to be found.

*Fuck this house.* If it wasn't some Ever's magic rooting me to the floor, it was a spirit flying through the halls. Had anyone here ever known peace? Quiet? Ease? I seriously doubted it. After staring into nothing for a solid minute and confirming that I was, in fact, alone in the hall, I crept up the stairs and made a beeline for my room.

I closed the door and locked it, though I doubted that mattered.

I bathed quickly and then dragged myself to bed. Thankfully, sleep took me swiftly. I dreamed of Zota's desiccated body covered in golden beetles. Of a tar-black thread of blight binding Orin and Rorik to the decaying manor at their backs. Of Seville's haughty laugh and the whisper of the word *evervow* that came from nowhere and everywhere all at once. Of a ghost with billowing clothes and heavy eyes that wormed into my very soul.

And me drowning in the chaos of it all but powerless to save anyone. Including myself.

# TWENTY

The next morning, I sat alone in Zota's stall, picking at a muffin laden with blueberries and sugar. Orin was already awake and working when I stopped by his study, and he promised to join me the moment he wrapped up a letter he was penning. Before I left, he'd pinpointed his gaze on some indistinct spot, and a rush of warm magic had filled the space. It disappeared as quickly as it came, and then Orin nodded. He'd removed Zota's glamour so I could study his threads, but he begged me to wait for any actual threadmending. Even so, I had yet to ignite my power. Instead, I just sat. Everything was quiet. The manor. The lawns. The stables. Fernglove was holding its breath, waiting to see what I'd do next. And I didn't know.

Before checking on Orin and grabbing breakfast, I'd stopped by my brothers' quarters to once again find that their blight was accelerating. More wounds, more damning pustules, more rivers of black sludge in their veins. Their pale skin was glossy and damp, as if they'd freshly bathed, but I knew better. Their bodies were cooking them alive. I checked on their threads, too, and I wasn't surprised to find them limp and covered in tar, loosely writhing about their frames.

Sighing, I set the muffin down, largely untouched, and stretched my hands to the sky. I had to figure something out. Fast.

Zota chuffed and eagerly threw his head as he targeted my abandoned breakfast. A smile tugged at my lips. At the very least, our sessions hadn't drained his personality. I couldn't help but wonder how spry he'd be without the blight eating away at his body. I scooped the muffin up and offered it to him, and he ate it without hesitation straight from my palm. I brushed saliva and crumbs from my hands, and Ywena shifted against my neck as the collar of my blouse rubbed her wing.

"Sorry about that," I murmured, flicking back my hair and offering her two fingers as a perch. "Are you hungry? What do you even eat?"

She kneaded my shoulder for a moment, as if ensuring my breathing was steady before abandoning her post, and then she fluttered to my hand. A needle-thin tongue uncurled from her mouth to graze a smeared streak of blueberry. Rorik had never instructed me to feed her, and she rarely left her post. After a few more ticklish laps from her tongue, she took flight and danced about my head before dropping to the earth near a cluster of white flowers.

I watched quietly as she peeled back the petals with her feet and then dipped her tongue deep into the flower's center, searching for nectar. A low sigh pushed through my pursed lips. I doubted she'd get much from the dying plant. It was glamoured to look beautiful, just like the rest of the estate, but if what Orin said was true, then it was as blight-ridden as the inhabitants who lived here. Still Ywena . . .

A memory bloomed in my mind.

*Blight seems to have altered their biology, but instead of killing them, it allows them to feed on diseased plants.*

I nearly kicked Zota as I clambered onto my knees and brought myself closer to Ywena. She stalled in response and tilted her head in my direction.

"Go on. Keep eating."

If a moth could narrow her eyes, Ywena did. But she eventually relented, once again drinking deeply from the flower's core. Rorik's words hung in the air as I ignited my power and allowed my threadmending magic to blossom around me. Like Zota's, Ywena's threads were a muted teal, but there wasn't a single trace of black tar marring their beautiful shade. At least, not at first. But then Ywena must have finally secured the sliver of remaining life from the flower, because she curled her tongue back into her mouth and ingested whatever she brought with it.

Black droplets formed on one of her wayward strands, quickly dousing the entire thread in a sticky, tarlike substance that halted its lazy twirling. For a moment, nothing else happened. Ywena went about scrubbing her face with her front legs and showed no additional signs of illness. Her other threads were still wild and free, darting dangerously close to the infected strand. This couldn't have been the first flower she'd snacked on, so how?

A shudder passed through Ywena as if a cool breeze had tickled her wings. The infected thread twitched. And then suddenly it was writhing, wrapping itself around every wayward strand until they were all tangled together and knotted with blight. I gasped and covered my mouth as numbness flooded my fingers. The creeping ink-black sickness spread to the rest of her strands until every single thread was covered.

*Not Ywena.* Scrambling toward her, I cupped my hands on either side of her body, not touching her strands but bringing my shaking fingertips close. She'd become a constant for me. I'd grown accustomed to her gentle shocks, the feel of her feet lightly kissing my neck, her wings fluttering in my ear. I didn't want to be without her.

A white light formed between my fingers, and I was about to thrust myself into threadmending once more when Ywena cracked one eye open as if to say, *Wait*.

I froze as the tar on her strands shifted to something beautiful. Instead of tacky sludge or cracked dust drifting away on the breeze, the blight had transformed into a shimmering ink that streamed toward her center. The cascading blight was draining into her body, flowing like fast-moving rivers down the threads of her lifespan. One moment her threads were dark; the next they were completely free of blight.

I never would have seen it if my power hadn't been active.

"Ywena," I whispered. It was all I could manage. She'd ingested the blight and become one with the disease, and she was perfectly fine. As if to hammer that truth home, she took flight and danced about the crown of my head before settling against my neck.

I jerked my head toward Zota. With my magic still intact, I stared at his blight-ridden strands. My heart pounded in my ears. He wasn't able to siphon the sickness, to draw it from his threads and expel the illness. But Ywena could. *I* could. Instead of searching for an impossible thread to restitch for an illness that seemed to stem from everywhere, what if I just took it? Drained away blight from Zota like Ywena had with the flower? Could I take it all? How much of my life would I lose in the process?

*You deserve to live.*

Rorik was insistent even in my memories. Pushing aside his words, I turned my focus to Zota. For now, I had to see if my theory was correct.

"Ywena," I said, speaking to her without breaking my gaze with Zota, "perch somewhere else. For your own safety."

She must have sensed my purpose, because she didn't hesitate. With a few beats of her wings she was off, searching for a suitable place to land along the wood railing of the stall. Even without her pressed against my skin, I couldn't forget Rorik's teachings. He'd seared them into my brain, into my very lungs, so that each breath was filled with power. Magic. Alabaster light grew around me, and I willed it to coat my entire body. Every inch. I'd become a seam of moonlight itself, and the world fell away as I focused solely on Zota's dying threads.

With a steadying breath, I opened my arms wide and welcomed the blight. "Come."

His diseased strands slunk toward me with deadly efficiency, sliding around my legs and arms like snakes eager to deliver their venom. My mind rewound to one of the threadmenders' journals, with a note about pinching and refining threads to force them to take certain shapes.

It'd been his final entry, but something about it felt right.

Pinching one strand between my forefinger and thumb, I shaped it like a needle and thrusted it deep into my skin. Pain erupted as it broke through with ease, and I winced at the sharp, metallic tang of magic that scorched the air. I stitched Zota's thread into my arm, weaving sickness into my skin and tying my existence to his. As soon as I'd coaxed the first thread into my veins, the remaining tendrils dove in after without prompting. The sharp pricks of thousands of needles ravaged my limbs as blight was sutured deep into my bones. Those tar-soaked tendrils tied me to Zota as if I were his puppeteer, coaxing the blight to move from him to me.

My throat tightened as I struggled to breathe. A fist had grabbed my insides and was violently twisting them into knots, and an uncontrollable tremor took hold of my body. Pain exploded from my bones the longer I worked, but I couldn't stop. It splintered and ruptured through my arms, my legs, my ribs. There was nothing but the smell of sour mulch and decay and a heat that cooked my blood. Heady ringing filled my ears so that all other sounds fell away. Panic set in as my vision went.

*Why did I think I could do this?* My chest shuddered as my knees cracked against the ground.

*My brothers . . .* my brain screamed as a fog settled over my thoughts, taking away their names and my memories.

I was nothing. Nothing . . .

*Breathe.*

A subtle warmth bloomed between my shoulder blades, as if a hand was gently resting against my back.

*Breathe.*

Slowly. Intentionally. I clenched my jaw tight as I forced a heavy inhale through my nose and held it. Then loosed it. The pressure in my chest lessened a fraction.

*Again.*

Tipping my head back, I imagined inviting the energy of the world in with my breath. I imagined life flooding into my lungs with the sweet, floral-tinged breeze of the Willowfell countryside. I imagined the taste of fresh coffee shared in tin mugs between family members. Brothers. I let the buzzing of insects fill my ears as I remembered the feeling of warm arms holding me tight. Protecting me.

My vision returned with the sounds of the estate, but I didn't stop focusing on the sensations of my life. I'd kneeled before Zota and braced my palms against the earth, seeking purchase in the cool ground of his stall. And while I vaguely realized my breaths were laborious and my limbs riddled with pain, I didn't stop.

Because it was working.

I watched in morbid fascination as the blight was leeched from Zota's threads. Gone was the tacky, suffocating substance. The blight had liquefied into peaceful rivers of black ink sliding down his threads and into my veins. The moment Zota's strands were cleansed, they retreated to twirl about his body, blissfully free of sickness and painfully exquisite. My throat clogged at the sight of Zota's beauty returning. The hollowness of his face began to fill out, the scraps of loose skin falling to the earth like leaves. Fresh skin formed over muscles and tendons that now bulged with life. His hide was lustrous, and his mane was glossy. He was a stag of myth and beauty, and if it weren't for the blight now running rampant in my body, I would never have guessed that he'd been sick.

Throughout it all, Zota had been still, but now he stood to his full height and let out a long, low-pitched grunt full of warmth and joy. Tears rolled down my cheeks, and when I went to wipe them away, I stilled at the sight of my fingers. My body was still drenched in a void of black night, but minuscule dots of blinding white light were blooming across the expanse of my skin. Stars. I was the cosmos incarnate as my magic began to eat away the blight. My blackened fingertips were the last to go until, like Zota, I was cleansed.

My power was doused an instant after that, and I collapsed fully to the ground as the weight of what I'd done slammed into my body. But no matter how much I ached, no matter how much the splintering pain in my skull continued to grow, no matter how much the world spun or how exhaustion was already pulling me under, there was only joy.

I'd done it. I'd sacrificed gods only knew how many of my threads in the process, but I'd cured something of blight.

Even though the very action felt like a blade carving into the muscles of my face, I smiled. I smiled because, so long as I woke up, there was a chance I could save my brothers. Save Mavis. And maybe, *maybe*, even Orin.

The last thing I saw as the world faded to black was Ywena flying away. Orin would come. He always did.

# TWENTY-ONE

I'd really grown tired of waking up with no concept of how much time I'd lost. Everything felt stiff and my thoughts were muddled—that much I could tell—but at least I was waking up. I shifted beneath smooth sheets as I peeled open my eyes. My room was quiet, the curtains drawn. A mug with an empty vial beside it sat on my nightstand, and as I propped myself up on my elbows to get a better look, I found there wasn't any liquid left to be had. An incessant scratch tickled my throat, and I spied a pitcher of water a few feet away on the dresser.

"Of course," I grumbled, eyeing the distance. As comfortable as the sheets were, though, the idea of quenching my thirst was more enticing. Bracing myself with a long breath, I prepared for an onslaught of pain as I forced myself to move. And found none. Frowning, I sat upright in bed and swung my feet over the side, surprised by the ease of the movement. I wiggled my toes. My fingers. Rotated my wrists and stretched my neck from side to side. Nothing. Gingerly, I stood. The world stayed on its axis. Nothing happened.

Unease wound through me. How long had I been out? Immediately, the need for water was tabled as Noam and Nohr surfaced in my mind. If I was this healthy after curing blight . . . It could've been months. *Months.* I spun toward the door and made it halfway before Vora strode into the room. She paused, took one look at my panicked expression, and then rolled her eyes.

"It's been a week. They're still alive." She set down a tray of food on the coffee table before moving to the curtains. With a forceful yank, she thrust them open. "I'd hoped you'd sleep longer."

"A week is plenty long." My gaze bounced between her and the door. *Alive.*

"Yes, well, you didn't see you." Vora snatched the pitcher of water and strode to the nightstand, snagging the mug and filling it with practiced ease. She handed me the drink. "I thought you were dead."

I drained the water in one fell swoop and held it out for her to refill. "That bad?"

She nodded. "Cold as the night. Drenched in sweat. Barely any pulse."

"And Zota?"

"Is that all you're concerned about right now? Honestly." She filled my glass and then set the pitcher down with more force than necessary. "Zota is fine. Cured. Orin was beside himself. Giddy as a young boy."

Her flat voice did little to sway the building excitement in me. "I knew I could do it."

"But at what cost?" Vora turned away and headed for the coffee table, where she arranged a small plate of bread, cheese, and meat and gestured for me to sit. "I cannot stress enough how bad your condition was."

"It doesn't feel like it." I sank onto the settee and picked up the plate. A ravenous hunger gnawed at my insides, and I shoved a thick piece of sourdough bread into my mouth.

"That's because I drugged you." She didn't bat an eye. "I used a mixture of your tinctures and Ever medicine to brew a sleeping aid to keep you under."

*My tinctures.* I chewed slowly, wondering what blend of medicine I would need to keep on hand if I intended to cure more people of blight. "What did you use?"

"Valerian, lavender, one of your vials titled 'slumber.' At least your naming conventions are clear. And then some rare herbs and magic to mix it all together."

I'd have to get a list of those rare herbs at a later date. "Thanks."

Her eyes narrowed as she watched me eat. "Don't thank me. It was my lord . . ." She winced as if the phrase had tumbled from her lips by accident before continuing. "He insisted you stay under for your own safety. And to keep anyone from demanding you threadmend again too soon."

Orin. Heat bloomed in my chest. "Who else knows about Zota?"

"Everyone does." She pursed her lips. "If they knew you were awake, they'd—"

It was as if that very thought summoned him, and Orin quietly opened the door to peek his head into the room. He stilled when he saw me sitting beside the unlit fire, food in hand, and then beamed. He was by my side in an instant, and I was overcome by the boyish charm of his features, the sheer excitement in his endless green eyes.

"Edira," he murmured.

My name was breathless on his lips, and my heart skipped a beat. "Hi."

"Leave us," Orin said to Vora without breaking eye contact with me. He'd kneeled before me and clasped my knees with his hands, and damn if I didn't feel like a queen. Like someone worthy of this devotion and admiration. I set aside my food and placed my hands over his. Squeezed them tight.

Vora pursed her lips. "Orin, I don't think—"

"*Lord* Orin," he cut in quickly, his grip tightening on me a sliver. My brows crept together. He caught me staring, and his expression softened. "Apologies, Vora. I've been on edge waiting for Edira to wake. Can we please have some privacy?"

"Of course," Vora said. She hesitated for a beat, and remorse flickered through her eyes. I barely had a chance to glimpse it before she hid it away behind a dutiful facade of obedience. While I couldn't fathom why such sadness had marred her face, especially in the wake of my recent discovery, it stuck with me. It was a splinter worming beneath my skin that lodged itself deep in my muscles, just out of reach. I frowned at her back as she left, closing the door behind her with a soft click.

"Are you all right?" Orin cupped my face, and I brought my gaze back to him. Back to warmth and joy and hope. It was enough to burn away the doubt Vora had seeded, and I settled into his touch.

"I did it."

His eyes twinkled. "I know. Edira, you . . . you are incredible. Tell me everything."

And I did. I told him about what I'd witnessed with Ywena—who had yet to return, likely thanks to Orin demanding I rest—and how I'd applied that theory to my own magic. How I stitched Zota's blight into my body and drew it in, cleansing the sickness from his threads. How I'd nearly slipped into oblivion, but still managed to pull myself back. I told him how beautiful Zota's threads were.

"And soon Mavis's, too," I said quietly as I met his gaze. "And Noam's and Nohr's. I can't wait to talk to them again."

"And you will." Orin's full-blown smile had me melting into him, and he chuckled as he pulled me into his arms. He felt so safe and warm, and I nuzzled his neck.

He lifted me with ease and carried me to bed, tucking me

against his side. "I think I'll ask them about the time you attacked that child in defense of Noam." Mirth filled his eyes as he stroked my cheek. "I'm dying to know what they thought of their sister in that moment."

I rolled my lower lip into my mouth as I grinned. "They'll probably say I was out of line."

"So volatile," he murmured. He rested his forehead against mine. "You and I have that in common."

"Oh?" I rubbed my nose against his. "How so?"

His exhale was warm against my lips. "In that moment, all you wanted to do was protect your own. You were consumed by this desire to act. I know it because I feel it every time I look at my grandmother. I'm so afraid she'll die that sometimes I just lose myself."

My chest tightened with emotion, and all at once I understood. That shared look of hunger in his family's eyes stemmed from their fear of death. From the fear of losing someone they cared for with every fiber of their being. It was the same way I felt when I checked on my brothers.

"I understand." With light fingers, I grazed the length of Orin's jaw, then ghosted them over his lips. He pressed featherlight kisses against each finger, and a growing warmth flickered to life in the pit of my belly. I angled his mouth to mine.

He kissed me gently, his hands palming the sides of my face, and I parted my lips to let his tongue slide in. A low groan thrummed from the back of his throat. Orin tipped my head back and deepened our kiss as my entire body arched toward him.

"I've been waiting to do that for a week," he said softly, keeping his mouth poised over mine.

Chills raced down my arms. "Good thing you don't have to wait any longer."

Before he could say anything else, I kissed him hard. I swallowed his words and gave no room for argument. He hesitated for only a breath, and then he answered with a fire that sent pleasure racing through my veins. He wrapped his fingers in my hair and gave a heavenly tug. The only thing that mattered was the hungry scrape of his teeth against my lips, his tongue melding with mine. A heady warmth brewed between my legs, and I swear to the gods he could tell. Something fierce and wild simmered from the back of his throat, and he eased over me. His hands slipped beneath my loose, thigh-length sleeping gown, teasing the soft skin of my abdomen and the hemline of my undergarments.

"Orin," I managed through a heavy groan.

"Are you well enough?" he asked, his hand palming my breast. It was all I could focus on. I should've been depleted and weak, but Vora's concoction and Orin's want filled me with a vigor like I'd never known. Now, all I desired was him. And I wouldn't be satisfied until I had it.

"I am," I whispered.

"Do you remember when I told you that I get what I want?" Heat ravaged his gaze, and he pressed bruising kisses against my neck. My collarbone. The top of my cleavage. Shivers raced down my spine.

"Yes," I managed. He did things to my senses that defied all logic.

His words were more of a growl as he deliberately dragged his lips across my skin, stopping at the shell of my ear. "I want you."

I turned and caught his mouth with mine, inviting him in and dragging my fingers down his back. Nothing else was said between us. He unbuttoned his shirt and removed his clothes with aching slowness and a wicked, self-assured smile. And then he shredded my gown and yanked off my underthings. The raw desire in his stare set light to a wildfire across my skin, and every inch of me burned to be touched by him.

And he didn't deny me. His tongue traced the length of my

body, sparking a deep-seated desire that ached to be relieved. His mouth consumed me in a way I'd never been devoured before, and when he finally pressed his lips to my crease, my hips bucked into him. He licked, and my back arched as delicious pleasure raced through my spine. A guttural moan escaped from somewhere deep in my chest.

He pushed me to the edge of oblivion with that glorious tongue of his, and my entire world narrowed to the feel of his breath, the warmth of his exhale. As I let out another whimper, he looked up at me without stopping, and then he drove two fingers deep into my core.

"Fuck," I cried, rhythmically grinding against him, begging him to move faster. Deeper. He did no such thing. Instead, he slowed his pace and abandoned my clit, biting at the soft flesh of my hips. I was about to combust if he didn't give me what my body so clearly needed. I rolled beneath him, trying to shift his attention back to my obvious craving, but all he did was chuckle.

Only when he was satisfied with my writhing want did he finally shift. Crawling up my body to position himself over me, he stole my breath with his lips and swallowed my moan. His impressive length, velvet smooth and yet harder than granite, slipped along my crease. Painfully, sinfully slow. I watched with rapt fascination as he slid through my folds, trying and failing to angle my hips to drive him in.

And then he sheathed himself in me. I barked out a curse as he held himself there, letting me adjust, and then began thrusting in earnest. Brilliant, wondrous pain shifted to pure longing as we moved in unison, a tangled mess of limbs and heat. I lost all sense of myself as he wrenched pure desire from somewhere deep in me, someplace I never knew existed.

"I want you to let go," he whispered, his voice low and gravelly. His words were an added layer of pleasure, and the coil of need in the pit of my belly wound tighter in anticipation. A glimmer of magic coursed through his eyes as he pushed in deeper, and suddenly thin, wispy clouds stretched over us. Stars drizzled from them in a lazy, winking descent. Each tiny particle of magic was bloated with his power, with his passion, and their gossamer touch against my skin was more like a bolt of unfiltered desire straight to my bones. I was enveloped in the sensation of his want, and it did me in completely. I shattered around him, and he let out a roar that felt like a claim. His release followed mine, and for a moment we simply remained joined together. With his head pressed against my forehead, he gazed into my eyes and smiled. Softly. Lovingly. Slowly, he rolled to the side and pulled me against his chest.

"That was . . ." I could hardly think of the words. They hadn't been written into existence. Nothing could explain the way he'd made my body feel.

He chuckled, drawing idle circles on my back as he stared up at the rafters. "I know."

My skin tingled as another flurry of stardust settled against my arms. Already want began to stir in my belly. "I'm a fan of this magic."

"I am, too." He held out his hand, and a few particles landed in his palm. Visible gooseflesh trailed down his arm, and I tracked its progression until I spied the Fernglove crest on his neck.

With gentle fingers, I traced the broken sword and insects, then stilled when a sudden flare of icy cold nipped at the tip of my finger, right at the blade's severed point. It was there and gone in a flash, and I flinched without thinking. Magic? Maybe, but it hadn't felt like Orin's power. He was warmth. Summer rain and spring flowers. This was sharp, like the chilled bite of a freezing winter night.

Orin turned to frown at me. "Everything all right?"

"Yes, must've just been a spasm." I flexed my fingers. Gently, I resumed my tracing of his tattoo, feeling nothing but warm, sweat-slicked skin.

His hand clasped mine before I could reach the tip of the sword again. "Promise?"

I hated the look of doubt, of worry, so soon after our lovemaking. Extracting my hand from his grasp, I smoothed his brow and chased away the canyons forming across his forehead. I let my fingers wander through his hair and gave his locks a gentle tug. Then I kissed his lips. Deeply. When I felt his tension loosen and his hands gripped my waist, I pulled back. "See? Everything is fine."

"Good." He kissed me again, and I gave way to his touch. His magic, his presence—everything about him stole the very breath from my lungs. We made love again, leisurely, tenderly, and I lost track of the hours. Of how many times I moaned his name. I reveled in the sensations he coaxed from my body and in the way that he made me feel wanted. In all my previous dalliances, I'd never been so lavished in affection. I wanted to lose myself for as long as he'd allow, until we were fully sated and our energy exhausted.

When the last of his magic dispersed, he pressed a light kiss to the crown of my sweat-dampened hair. "You make it difficult to want to do anything else with my time."

"I fail to see how that's a problem."

He laughed, and the sound echoed through my bones. "It's not. Or rather, it won't be as soon as we get this place back in order."

Right. The blight. My brothers. Mavis. Nuzzling my head against his neck, I sighed. "I'd like to try and cure my brothers first. If that's all right."

Our bargain hadn't dictated who I had to threadmend first, Mavis or them. Had Orin's hands not been resting against the small of my back, I might not have felt the subtle twitch of his fingers. He watched me closely, his features stiff. The smile he wore was hard, as if it'd been hammered into place by words.

"If my recovery rate stays the same, I'll have Mavis cured in no time." Unease made my tongue loose as I fought to reassure him. "My brothers just don't have as long. You know how quickly blight works against mortals. It's been progressing faster and faster. The last few times I visited them, I found more signs of illness. And you said yourself you didn't know how long your magic would hold."

He pressed a finger to my mouth, effectively silencing me. "Edira. It's fine. I was thinking of *your* health. If you're in fact well enough to try."

Oh. I rolled my lower lip into my mouth as I lowered my gaze. "Sorry."

"You don't need to apologize." He slipped a finger beneath my chin and pulled my focus to him. There was a sadness to his smile that softened his features and properly chastised me for rushing to conclusions. I nodded, and he brushed a strand of hair away from my face. "Get some rest. We'll see how you feel in the morning."

He planted a gentle kiss on my cheek and then slipped out of bed. I blinked at the sudden absence of his presence, at the cool nip of air against my skin, and I pulled the sheets tight around my chest. "You can't stay?"

"If I do, you won't sleep." He shot me a smirk as he pulled on his pants.

"Again, I fail to see how that's a problem."

"Edira." He came back to the bed and leaned over me. Just the nearness of him, of his glorious bare chest, was enough to make my mouth water. "Rest. You're still human. Give your body a break."

I'd never wanted to be an Ever more than in that moment. In fact, I'd never really thought about being immortal at all. But the idea of recuperating faster, of living longer . . . Suddenly I was all too aware of my shortened lifespan and the few opportunities I'd have to enjoy what I'd just unearthed with Orin.

I didn't want to die. Not yet. Not anytime soon.

Orin placed one last kiss on my forehead before bidding me good night. I hadn't realized how much time we'd spent together. One look out the windows, though, confirmed it was already late. I'd gained so much in the span of a handful of hours, and already the day was lost. And I only had so many left. A chill trickled through my limbs as I watched Orin close the door behind him.

*You're still human.* Lucky me. I blew out a frustrated breath. I couldn't bring myself to sleep just yet. I moved toward the attached bathroom, stopping by my apothecary cases to snag a few salts and oils, and then made for the claw-footed tub. I'd do as Orin said. Rest. Recuperate. Give my body a break. And then, when the morning came, I'd see to my brothers.

A smile tugged at my lips as the water began to fill before my eyes. I couldn't wait to show Noam and Nohr all the things I'd accomplished. I couldn't wait to show them what I'd become.

## TWENTY-TWO

I rose with the sun the following morning. In a matter of minutes, I'd dressed, scrubbed my face, and braided my hair back, and the manor was just beginning to stir. But try as I might, I couldn't still my nerves or convince myself to stay put. I'd spent most of the night staring at the ceiling, wondering whether to cure Noam or Nohr first, and settled on Nohr. Then I'd written a letter explaining the situation and begging him to behave while I recovered. I wasn't sure how long I'd be out, and while I knew Orin would look after him, there was no telling what the other family members would do. With his letter in hand, I exited my room and entered their quarters. I placed it on the nightstand beside them before glancing at their slumbering forms, and hope swelled in my chest.

"Soon," I murmured as I rested my hands on their caskets. I couldn't wait to see their eyes light up again, to hear the timbre of their voices as they balked at everything that'd happened since they fell ill. My eyes traveled over Nohr's face before sliding to his chest. And then I went stock-still.

"Nohr?" I knew he couldn't hear me, but his name fell from my lips just the same. The blight had increased tenfold in the span of a day, and black veins were wrapping his neck like a stranglehold that threatened to choke him. Fresh pustules had formed and ruptured across his sternum, and there were several places where gaping wounds had carved divots right out of his muscles. Blight birthed from his bones and spilled across his skin in the form of yellow loam and black sludge, and my gut churned at the sight.

I needed to cure him *now*.

Turning on my heel, I raced from the room and bolted down the stairs. I passed a few wide-eyed attendants who were opening windows and setting the table for breakfast. Every minute felt like an eternity as I searched for Orin. I ran through the halls and burst into his study, only to find his chair empty.

"Orin!" I shouted, whirling in place as panic clawed at my throat. Where was he? Why was this happening now?

I sprinted back the way I came until I finally found him in the library with Rorik. They were locked in a low conversation, each one of them glaring at the other, and they both snapped their gazes to me as I skidded to a halt.

"Edira?" Orin tilted his head to the side. "What's going on?"

"It's Nohr. He's dying." I didn't wait to see if he'd follow. I simply took off up the stairs and headed for my brothers' quarters. Both Orin and Rorik followed, their rushed footsteps pounding against the floor until we all came to a collective stop inside Noam and Nohr's room. With a shaky hand, I pointed to Nohr. "Look."

Orin gently moved me to the side and stood before my brother. He narrowed his eyes as he inspected him from head to toe. Sadness crept into Orin's features with every passing breath, and I wanted both to hear him speak and for him to stay silent. Because in that moment, everything was fine. Manageable. Nohr was alive, and I could cure him. Nohr was still here. Nohr. A quiet, strangled sob fractured my chest.

Rorik's hand found the small of my back. "Breathe."

I wanted to tear that word up and burn it from his mind so he could never speak it again.

But he did, just to spite me. "Breathe, Edira."

With a shuddering inhale, I did as he said. It did nothing to alleviate the fear gnawing at my gut, but the tingling in my fingers subsided, if only a little. Pursing my lips together, I forced another deep breath through my nose. The ringing in my ears dulled. Slowly, I looked up at him. His features were tight, his expression masked. The only thing he couldn't keep hidden was the emotion in his eyes. They raged with fear and anger and despair and so many things at once that I wondered how he kept it all together. How he managed to breathe his way through that kind of maelstrom. Only when his gaze softened did he pull his hand away. He brought it to his shoulder where Ywena was perched, and she crawled over his fingers. Gingerly, he brought her to me.

"For comfort, not training."

I could barely hold back the tears as I welcomed Ywena's gentle touch. She nestled in the crook of my neck, and something about her presence grounded me. I was able to wrangle the last of my fear and grip it tight as I waited for Orin to speak. When he finally turned his attention to us, his gaze slid first to Ywena. Something hardened in his eyes before he met my stare.

"He's alive but deteriorating quickly." Orin gripped the back of his neck. "Edira, I know you want to cure him, but—"

All the panic I'd battled into submission sprang up again, and I took a quick step forward. "No. You have to help me. Get rid of the barrier."

"Edira . . ." He stepped between me and Nohr.

"No!" I shouted, banging my fists against Orin's chest. "Move! You have to let me try. Let me save him. Do it, Orin, or . . ." My thoughts were wild, my breath hard and fast. Ywena didn't shock me. At least one Ever here was true to his word. "If they die, the bargain is void. I'll leave without helping Mavis. Without helping any of you." The words tasted like ash on my tongue, and my heart revolted at the idea of condemning Orin to death after the day we'd spent tangled in bed. But nothing could keep my anger at bay. He couldn't stop me, not now. Not when I had a chance. Not when he made me feel whole and important and wanted.

"You heard her, Orin." Rorik's voice was dangerous. Low. It was full of heat and threat that matched the fire burning in my veins, and I was thankful to have Rorik by my side. "Better let her try. It's peculiar how quickly his condition has worsened."

Orin spat venom with his response. "Quiet." Then, to me, much softer and full of remorse: "I can't let you. Not yet."

"You promised!" I saw red. It didn't matter how deeply I'd come to care for him, how kind he'd been to me all this time. If he didn't let me cure Nohr, I'd let blight destroy them all. Every last Fernglove.

"Please." Orin kneeled before me and gripped my hands. It took everything in me not to rip them out of his grasp. "Listen. I'm not saying you can't threadmend him. I'll lift the veil right now if you demand it."

My breath caught as I clung to his every word.

"But before you try, I want you to be aware of what could happen." His thumb brushed over the back of my hand. "As Rorik pointed out, his condition is worse than expected. If I dispel the barrier, there's no telling how much time you'd have to threadmend him. Minutes, maybe less. Right now, my magic is still working. He's not going anywhere today, so long as that barrier remains intact. Neither of them are." He dropped his gaze and spoke to the floor. "All I want is for you to cure him. But what if you're not ready and he dies? You've succeeded on a beast, but never a person. What if it takes more time to remove their blight? More time than they have to give?"

"I can't watch them die," I said, voice cracking.

Orin's grip tightened a fraction. "If this had been yesterday, even, when he showed some iota of health, I wouldn't stop you. Because I *believe* you can do it."

My throat swelled with emotion as tears lined my eyes. "What am I supposed to do?"

"Perfect the method first. Try it on one of us." He gestured between himself and Rorik, and the latter raised his brows. "Our bodies are meant to endure more. We're not as sick as them or even Mavis. Adjust your technique as many times as you must in order to get it right. And once you have it, because I know you'll get there, you can cure Nohr without worry. And Noam."

My heart thundered in my ears. He was right. I hated that he was, but I couldn't deny his reasoning, no matter how badly I wanted to save my brother. I'd believed that I was ready with every fiber of my being, but what evidence did I really have? Because I'd cured a stag? Noam and Nohr were *fragile*. So very, very fragile. It was evident in the way the blight was progressing. If they'd been Evers, we would've had more time. If I'd been stronger, it wouldn't have mattered at all. I would've cured them before we ended up here.

I couldn't give up. Not now. Not yet. Not ever.

"Let me try, then."

Orin's face fell. "If you insist."

"Not on Nohr." I gave his hands a gentle squeeze. It was the most I could handle after the swing in emotions from rage and fear to resigned understanding and despair. Hopefully it was enough. He looked up at me, a question burning in his eyes. "On you."

"Edira." He stood and twined our fingers together. "Are you certain?"

"I don't think that's a good idea." Rorik hadn't moved from his spot against the wall, but when I turned to glance at him, it was as if a monster had taken his place. Parts of his glamour had slipped away to reveal his ink-black eyes and pointed fangs. His sharpened onyx horns. Before, his arms had hung loosely by his sides; now, there was nothing relaxed about them. I could see every hardened, stiff muscle and practically feel the knots forming beneath the surface of his skin. His hands had curled into white-knuckled fists, and he barely breathed as he glowered at us.

"You can leave," Orin hissed, drawing me close.

"Not on your life." Gold flashed through his stare. "Rather, not on hers. She shouldn't do this."

"Know your place, brother." Orin closed the space between them until they were within striking distance of each other. "Unless you want me to leave you to rot."

"Better me than her." Rorik didn't flinch beneath the weight of Orin's glare.

"You don't know what's best for her." Orin growled as his own glamour rippled away. But he didn't stop with revealing only a few of his features—he let his entire mirage fade. He didn't care about the blight marring his skin. He didn't care about anything other than staring down his brother. His tail unfurled behind him and snapped through the air at the same time his crown pushed through his forehead. The stench of death and decay filled the small room, but nothing was more suffocating than the power he displayed. It was nothing like the stardust I'd enjoyed the day before. This was invisible and yet somehow tangible, a raw current of pure energy that charged the air like the moments before lightning struck.

"And you do?" Rorik leaned into his space. "She wouldn't be the first—"

Orin struck him hard and fast, and the sound of his fist cracking against Rorik's cheekbone reverberated against the walls. I expected Rorik to crumble, but all he did was tip his head back toward his brother with a saccharine smile. Blood gathered at the corner of his lip, and his tongue darted out to wipe it away. He towered above Orin as he pushed off the wall and bared his teeth.

"Enough!" I didn't know where I found the courage to move, but I did. I shoved my way between their bodies and pressed my hands firmly against their chests. At the same time, I uncorked the power dormant in my veins and let it flood outward in a vibrant display of moonlight. It came easily, willingly, as if it sensed the presence of their blight and wanted to rid the space of its infestation. My power gave me strength, and I didn't budge as I held my ground between Rorik and Orin. Neither one seemed pleased I'd found myself there, but Rorik relented first. His glamour easily slid back into place as he reclined against the wall. The only thing that remained were his endless black eyes that roved over my body.

Finally, Orin stepped back. "I'm sorry, Edira."

I let my hands fall to my sides, but I didn't cap my power. Instead, I let it flare with anger. "I don't know what kind of history you two have, but this decision is *mine*." I shot a glare at Rorik before rounding my gaze on Orin. "I am ready to try. And I'm happy to do it."

A haughty, satisfied smile claimed Orin's lips as he looked over my head to gloat at his brother. Fortunately, Rorik didn't take the bait. He continued to focus only on me.

"Go on then," he said, voice surprisingly soft. I hated the way it made me question everything. He motioned for Ywena to join him, and I tried to ignore the sudden cold her absence invited.

Orin held out his hand to me. "Whenever you're ready."

For a long moment, I studied his fingers.

"You won't be able to see it," I said as I let my power grow. The life strands wrapping his body uncurled in response, reaching toward the light. "But if I succeed, you'll know."

He nodded, and the all-consuming hunger in his stare sharpened. I understood why it was there—especially after our private moment together—but something about it unnerved me. I wanted it gone. I wanted his soft smiles and warm looks. His easy laughter, unbridled by this fear of death. I wanted him to be free.

I beckoned to Orin's threads with a slight curl of my fingers, and they flew to me with ease. In a matter of seconds, they'd wrapped around my arms, my legs, my stomach. Like before, I took a single thread and began stitching the blight into my body, but the pain was excruciating. I'd been able to tolerate the prick of needles with Zota, but this felt like white-hot blades carving away at my skin. The blight that seeped into my muscles brought with it a horrific sickness that immediately took me to my knees. Pain arced through my limbs, and my body began to tremble. Dots bloomed across my vision. Every breath was a battle, each inhale full of glass and each exhale riddled with salt. I couldn't stop the burn, couldn't douse the flames cooking me from the inside out. I bit my lip to hold back a scream and tasted the brackish, coppery tinge of blood.

With what little energy I had left, I focused on one of Orin's threads. His blight wasn't just a sickness; it was a starving beast willing to eat anything and everything in its path. The black tar bubbled and frothed as it oozed from his threads to my skin. I could've been delirious from the pain or perhaps it was magic, but I swore each bubble was a tiny maw with jagged teeth. As it crawled over my limbs, it tore at my skin. Drank in my blood. Settled in my bones. My light battered relentlessly against it, but I was drowning in a sea of tar and yellow loam, and nothing was strong enough to pierce it.

I didn't know where I was anymore, if I'd already died or if I was somewhere in between. The blight was cooking my mind and my blood, and my vision swam out of focus. There was nothing but the heavy aroma of sour mulch and rotting flesh.

A quiet memory of Alec teased the edge of my thoughts. He'd started to hallucinate when the blight took over, too. Vaguely, I wondered what I looked like to Rorik and Orin. If I was writhing on the floor, suffering through an invisible pain they couldn't abate. Or maybe I'd slipped into a slumber and was completely unreachable.

It was surreal to be lost in blight. At some point, the pain had faded and all I was left with was this unbearable sense of knowing that I was about to meet my end.

A flicker of awareness bloomed from somewhere in the depths of my mind. An itch I couldn't quite reach. I didn't know what it was, but it gave me pause. I shifted and watched as, for the first time, one of my own moonlit life threads appeared before my eyes. I froze as it drifted like a ribbon in the air, dancing about my body without the weight of blight. I'd never been able to see my threads before. Was it all a hallucination? An invisible breeze carried it close to my face, and a frayed end threatened to pull away from the core. With a sudden twist, it splintered off, no larger than a strand of hair but somehow still bright and resplendent and full of power.

*You're dying.* The realization hit me hard as I watched the strand float away. How many of those tiny threads had I shed throughout the years? How many did I have left? I tried in vain to crane my head and once again glimpse the life threads twirling around me. But each time I caught sight of their moonlit ends, they'd shift and jerk away out of sight.

The itch in my mind was growing more and more insistent by the second. It wasn't just an errant thought, but a voice. Someone calling my name. Someone bringing me back. The fabric of the hallucination trembled as it tried to keep me buried. Blight surged and frothed around me, pinning my limbs and tipping my head back. I could feel it creeping around the orifices of my face. My ears. My eyes. My nose.

*Breathe.* Was that my thought or someone's shout? They coalesced into one single command that shook the blight's hold on my mind. Suddenly the pain returned. Horrific, unending agony as sharp as knives cutting away at my organs. And with that, the rest of my senses came flying back. First there was sound. An earsplitting scream that threatened to shatter glass. My scream. And then there was the taste of blood—a mouthful of it—and I gagged as I managed to tilt my head just enough to feel its tacky warmth flood over my cheek. Finally, my vision. Orin's strand was still stitched into my arm, and I was still siphoning sickness from his body. My gut churned at the sight of only one clear aquamarine thread. I'd hardly taken anything. Rorik and Orin were screaming, though I couldn't tell what, as they waited on either side of my body. Orin was looking away, yelling at something or someone out of sight. But Rorik looked only at me.

"Edira, stop this," he said when he noticed my eyes had cracked open. Or maybe they'd never closed. I couldn't tell. Someone had dumped sand into them, and every blink was a rough scrape. Still, Rorik realized I was back. Somehow, he knew. His hand was pressed between my shoulder blades, and I wondered if his command to breathe had returned me to my senses. He'd ingrained that word into my body with every training session to the point it'd become an intrinsic response. An undeniable order to catch myself, to assess. I coughed, and another rush of blood flowed from my mouth to coat my blouse. With what little control I'd salvaged, I shut off my power and watched with relief as Orin's thread was forcibly thrust from my body.

Rorik's other hand was on my shoulder, and his grip tightened. "It's all right. You're all right."

I tried to smile and failed. "Liar."

"Edira!" At the sound of my hoarse voice, Orin rounded on us and quickly pulled me into his lap. "Thank the gods."

Rorik stared at the space where I used to be in his arms. I'd gotten blood on his hands, but he didn't bother to wipe it away. He'd become a statue, and the only movement that came from him was the ragged, uneven rise and fall of his chest.

"Why didn't you stop sooner?" Orin pressed me close, and my body screamed in pain. I bit my lip and winced.

"I couldn't." My head throbbed as the world began to spin. "I couldn't." I forced a swallow and then vomited at the overwhelming presence of blood. The sudden retching sent another torturous wave of pain through to my toes. "Vora."

"She's already preparing the remedy." Orin smoothed my hair with a shaky hand. He was covered in remnants of my blood and vomit, but he didn't complain. He caged me in his arms and stood without faltering before heading out the door. With my cheek pressed against his shoulder, I caught one last glimpse of Rorik before we left. He still hadn't moved.

Orin swept me into my quarters and headed for the bathroom, commanding the bath to fill with his silent magic the moment we entered. With gentle fingers, he freed me of my clothes and eased me into the copper basin. The once-clear liquid instantly shifted to something pink and murky.

The world tilted from left to right as I fought against sleep. Even with heavy-lidded eyes, I could still see the more prominent effects of my failed threadmending attempt. My skin was ashen and peeling in places, and my nails had turned a brittle yellow. Bruises blossomed across my legs and arms. Somehow, my muscles had lost all definition, and I was nothing but loose skin draped over bones. It was horrifying, and yet I couldn't feel any fear. The only sensation that riddled my being was exhaustion. And gods, did I want to succumb to it. It would be so peaceful . . .

"Medicine first, then you can sleep." Orin's voice shook me, and I startled in the tub. Vora had entered the bathroom at some point, though she'd froze at the entrance. Her face was parchment pale, her lips parted and eyes wide. She blinked several times before handing it to Orin, and he pressed a mug of something thick and warm against my lips.

I drank it all.

"Make sure you've got her. She's about to go under."

With Vora's words came a beautiful nothingness, and I slipped away to the feel of Orin's hands sliding beneath my arms.

## TWENTY-THREE

This time when I woke, I didn't rush to get out of bed. My body felt better than it did before I'd taken Vora's remedy, and while the fullness had returned to my muscles and the bruises had vanished from my skin, my mind was still too far gone. I'd been fighting and training for so damn long just to fail in the end. What was the point of it all? Why be gifted with a magic meant to heal, only to be faced with an incurable sickness? The pain of that truth was far greater than any physical ailment I'd experienced, and I curled in on myself beneath the sheets and hid from the world. From my brothers. From their deaths.

Vora and Orin checked on me frequently, but I didn't have the strength to speak. It felt like admitting failure would permanently cement my brothers' fates into existence. My mind was constantly flickering through all my encounters with blight. I went back to the start of it all, exhuming the memory of my parents' death. It was a fog, a mirage on the horizon, but I wanted to relive every instance and glean as much information as possible.

Sighing, I leaned my head against the windowpane and stared out at the pristine lawns. I'd taken up the bench seating by the bay window in my room, a tray of cooled tea and biscuits untouched beside me. Vora would be back any minute now to clear it. Ten days. Ten days had passed, and I was incapable of doing anything to save my family.

A soft knock sounded from the door, and Vora entered quietly. She looked as disheartened as I felt, her eyes downcast. She barely spoke while I recovered, and I was grateful for that. When Orin visited, he tried to soothe me with promises of future attempts and the knowledge that my brothers were still alive. I knew that. The only time I left my room was to lie on the floor by their coffins and cry. But I'd dried the last of my tears a handful of days ago and was growing weary of Orin's reassurances.

"No tea today?" Vora asked quietly as she came to my side and picked up the tray.

I shook my head. Outside, a farmhand was ushering the stags into an open field. Zota stood out from the rest. His movements were lithe and strong, and he frequently pranced about as if begging the others to play with him. I wondered how old he was, if his age had anything to do with the success of my cure. I doubted it, but I was grasping at straws to try to find an answer.

"Orin requested you join him for a walk."

Vora's gaze traveled over my body, searching for something. I'd bathed and dressed on my own in the hopes some action would alleviate the ache in my mind. Maybe a walk would help.

Vora's stare softened. "Or I can tell him you're sleeping."

I looked at her out of the corner of my eye. "No, it's all right."

She settled on the window bench beside me. "You carry too much weight."

"Not by choice." I returned my focus to the window and Zota. His innate bestial magic, plus the glamour bandage from Orin, had kept him alive despite the scale of his infection. Blight was swift when it came to claiming the life of a mortal, but when blight attacked an Ever it was a deliberate, prolonged assault. Something meant to last years, until the suffering finally became too much.

I wasn't sure how it would be to try to mend Nohr or Noam, if my reaction would be as visceral. Fear snaked through my gut. If I failed and one of them died in my arms, I'd never survive.

"I'm sorry, Edira. I wish I could've done more to help." Vora toyed with the teapot. "If only the medicines we blended together worked half as well on blight as they did on you."

*Blended.* I reflected on combining Ever cures with my own tinctures. There was something about melding the two healing practices together that . . .

A rush of adrenaline coursed through my limbs. "Vora, where is Orin?"

"In the courtyard." She watched me closely.

"I have to go." I jumped to my feet and turned in a circle as I searched for my shoes. Prickling awareness danced over my skin. I knew the answer. Power sharing. Heartbond. I'd waited long enough. All this time I'd been hesitant because I didn't truly know, didn't truly trust, but not anymore. Warmth purled from my chest. I loved him. I had been too afraid to admit it. Too afraid to acknowledge something that would last only a short while with my death looming nearer.

*All the more reason to hold on tighter.*

Orin's words filled my mind, my soul, and the fears that had been plaguing me for days drifted away. We could find a way to get rid of blight together. If we combined our magic, we could take on anything. Including blight.

"What's gotten into you?" Vora set down the tray and stood. Her eyes tracked my movements as I whirled about the room, finally finding my shoes and quickly securing them in place.

"I'm going to ask Orin to be my heartbond."

"What?" She froze for a moment, only her stare trailing after me. Then she moved between me and the door and placed her hands on my shoulders. "Please." She opened her mouth to speak and then forced a hard swallow. "Ask every question. Be absolutely certain."

"Vora." I placed my hands over hers. "I *am* certain. I'm certain this is the only way." I stepped out of her grip and into the hall, quickly taking the stairs to the first floor. Vora called my name as I went, but I didn't stop. I pushed through the double doors leading to the courtyard, and I found Orin sitting on a stone bench cradling a small book in one hand. My heart fluttered at the sight.

My feet pounded against the cobblestone, and he glanced up from the pages at my approach. Relief and shock blended in his features until he smiled. "Edira?"

I sank to the bench before him and closed his book over his fingers. "I know what to do."

He frowned. "About?"

"The blight."

His eyes grew wide, his smile brilliant. I could barely contain my excitement, and his response only fueled my resolve.

"What do we do?"

*We.* I bit my lip as I shifted to hold his hands in mine. Nerves tingled in the pit of my belly. It was strange to suddenly be hit with a burst of anxiety when every other interaction with him had been so easy. Natural. Yet something about asking him to be my heartbond, to tie him to me, changed everything. I loved this man, this Ever. We were already a team.

"I want to be your heartbond." I said the words in a rush before I could take them back. "I know I don't have as much to offer in terms of power sharing as some other Evers, but—"

"Yes." He crushed his lips over mine and kissed me hard. I blinked as his sudden answer settled over me. I'd expected to explain more, to make him understand why I wanted to tap into his power. I hadn't been prepared for his eager agreement, and that only made me surer of my decision. A tear slipped down my cheek as I wrapped my arms around his neck and kissed him deeply.

After a beat, he pulled away to rest his forehead against mine. "Give me a day to get everything in order."

I brushed my nose against his. "I don't need a ceremony. I just need you."

"Just us." He brushed his fingers against the strand of moonlight hair dangling near my cheek. "Still, there are a few things needed for the bond to be successful. I'll get them, and then we'll be together."

"And then hopefully I can cure you. And Mavis. And my brothers." I searched his eyes for any sign of hesitation and found none. He believed I could do it. He believed in me. Heat bloomed in my chest, and I kissed him again.

"By blending our magic," he murmured against my lips, and I nodded.

"Yes."

He brought his hands to my face and cupped my cheeks. "I knew you were special from the moment I met you."

After another round of deep kisses, he excused himself to begin preparations, and I watched him go with a smile. With hope. It sparked in me and grew like a wildfire, consuming every waking thought and burning doubt to ash. Yet, as I walked back to the house, a chill swept down my spine. I glanced up at the manor to find Mavis standing on her balcony with her gaze locked on me. All the giddiness swelling through my body evaporated in a solitary moment, and I froze as I held her silent stare. She never moved. Only watched. I waited until my ratcheted pulse returned to normal, and then slowly, I walked toward the house. She was stiff against the balcony railing, and while she was immobile, her gaze continued to follow my every step. Her eyes inked a target into my skin so that even when I passed out of her line of sight, I could still feel their mark.

*What the hell?* I ran my hands over my arms, but the chill remained. I couldn't help but wonder about all the things she saw but never spoke of. What secrets lay beyond the quiet trappings of her blight-filled existence?

# TWENTY-FOUR

Our ceremony would be private, but that didn't stop everyone at Fernglove from finding out Orin's and my plan to become heartbonds. Moments after I'd escaped Mavis's weighted stare, Seville found me in the foyer and dragged me away with a smirk. She'd been the one to spark the idea back in Mrs. Marlow's shop. I wondered if she knew I would come around to the notion all along.

Yet there was a hard glint to her eyes that hinted at anger beyond her signature, arrogant smirk. Rather than voice it, she fell effortlessly into the role of doting attendant. She led me to her private quarters, where we perused her closet until she found a flowing gown covered in winking crystals. She let out a disdainful sigh, as if it weren't the most beautiful thing I'd ever seen, and deemed it suitable enough. Time didn't allow for more custom creations. After she'd set aside my dress, we were interrupted by Tasia and Amalyss, who came bounding into the room with wide grins and mischief etched into their expressions. And wine in their hands. Much to my surprise, Seville actually squealed.

"This will do," she said, eyes bright. In that moment, she was carefree and young and beautiful. She looked like a morning star eager to greet the day, and my breath caught at the sight. At all of them. They were feeding off the hope I'd created, and for once they were simply . . . them. No riddles or threats. No unkind gestures. They poured wine in crystal goblets and linked arms as they danced in a circle and laughed.

And I realized, in that moment, I wanted to cure them, too.

Apparently, heartbond ceremonies typically involved more grandeur and preparation—because they were Evers and everything was a spectacle—but they complied with Orin's demands and made do with what was available. The most cherished prerequisite was a weeklong bath at a hidden Ever hot spring where no one packed clothes and they simply let their skin drink in the moonlight. Instead, attendants dragged in four copper basins, and the magic of the manor filled them to the brim with milky water. And as we eased our bodies into the tubs, we let go of everything. The fear. The doubt. Together, we almost felt like a family.

We talked the night away and shared stories of dalliances. Tasia and Amalyss had none, but Seville didn't let that stop her from sharing every glorified detail of her most recent encounter with someone at the fete, though she refused to name the woman. They were all horrified to learn my first romantic encounter had been less than pleasing, and they cursed the man who left me wanting. Not being lavished on was the greatest slight for an Ever, and I chuckled privately to myself at the thought.

After the bath, they fell asleep naked on soft hides before a low-burning fire. For a while, I simply lay unclothed beside them. I'd never been one to turn a cheek at a bare body, but I was surprised how easy it was to feel comfortable in my skin around them. I was surprised how comfortable they'd come to be with me.

For the first time, I imagined a life outside of the one I left behind in Willowfell.

*What about your brothers?* Certainly Orin would allow them to stay here, if I asked. If they wanted. And if they didn't, that would be fine, too. We all deserved to live.

Rorik's devilish grin filled my mind. Insufferable know-it-all.

Unlike Amalyss, Tasia, and Seville, sleep evaded me. So, when the fire was nothing more than embers and their snores grew too loud to stand, I found my clothes and quietly left Seville's quarters. The halls were dark as I crept across the second floor. There was no one about, which was unsurprising, given the hour, but I picked up the pace regardless.

A deep groan rumbled through the air as the manor settled, and my stomach tightened.

*It's just an old house.*

The walls gave another indignant creak.

Ringing crested in my ears, and my wide eyes burned from staring hard into the dark. There was nothing behind or in front of me, and yet I could feel needles prickling against my skin as the heady weight of eyes once again burrowed deep into my back. I whirled in place to catch a slip of something white in my peripheral vision: an ivory curtain fluttering on an invisible breeze, or . . . My gaze sharpened.

There, standing alone at the bend of the hall, was a petite woman with unblinking, doe-like eyes that bored right into my soul. A scream threatened to split my throat, but as my lips parted the ghost pressed a single, dainty finger to her lips. No, not a ghost. Mavis. My shriek died on my tongue, but I still couldn't bring myself to move. Her hair flowed around her in waves, starkly contrasting the white muslin nightgown clinging to her thin frame. The cut of the hemline above her breasts was low enough to reveal the signature pommel of the Fernglove crest, and she absently trailed a single finger along its hilt. And then she took that same finger and curled it toward me, beckoning me to join her. It was the most I'd ever seen her move without the help of one of her family members.

Unless she'd been the one lingering just out of sight, studying me with those relentless, harrowing eyes all this time.

"You," I whispered as I quickly came to stand before her. "You've been watching me from the moment I got here. Why? What are you doing?" I glanced around, expecting to find Seville or Lydia nearby. Mavis was utterly alone.

She scowled at me and once again pressed her finger to her lips. Silence, then. She was tiny in comparison to the rest of the family, as if aging ushered her toward childhood instead of the grave. But I knew what lay beneath that artful glamour. I'd yet to glimpse it, but I knew just the same.

Turning her back to me, she moved with a steady gait that defied all my preconceived notions about her health. Only after a few steps did I notice a heavier rise and fall to her chest, a slight sheen to her forehead. How much energy had she stored in preparation for this moment? What did she want? I opened my mouth to ask, but she shot me a stern glare before the words could fully form. She paused before a set of double doors I recognized as the entrance to her room, and she gestured for me to open them.

Hairs lifted along the nape of my neck. My fingers hesitated above the knob as I glanced at her. For a brief moment, I contemplated simply walking away. But something in her eyes kept me from leaving. She looked at me as if I were her last hope. Her only shot. Mavis was scared. Her infection was by far the worst in the family, and likely she knew I'd been working with Orin to successfully cure blight. She wanted me to try.

My lips turned down as I rested my hand on the worn metal knob. "I can't cure you yet. But if you just wait a little longer, I'll try."

She blinked. Then shook her head and once again pointed to the door.

"All right." I sighed as I let us in. I wasn't entirely convinced she'd understood me, anyway. I'd get her safely to bed and then let someone know she'd been walking around on her own. As we shuffled inside, I glanced around the dimly lit space. Her quarters were surprisingly tame in comparison to the more ornate rooms that made up the manor. There was a small sitting area with two high-backed chairs next to a low coffee table. Before that, a quiet hearth full of fresh logs. The mantel was decorated with long-stemmed roses and a handful of precious stones—some raw and uncut; others pristinely polished and awaiting the perfect setting.

One stole my attention entirely. It was no bigger than a marble but as brilliant as a full moon with an inner shimmering light that seemed to throb like a heart. An everjewel. My mouth fell open as I inched toward it.

*Everjewels are special to my kind.*

Orin's words rang through my head as Mavis paused to follow my gaze and then shuffled toward it. With shaking fingers, she picked it up and pressed it against her wrist. The glow sharpened for a fraction of a second and then began to diminish.

"Is something wrong with it?" I asked.

Mavis only stared at me with her brows drawn sharply together. Then, without breaking her gaze, she grabbed a nearby letter opener from the mantel and tore open the underside of her forearm. With one easy motion, she slipped the stone inside the cut. Blood circled her wrist like a bracelet, but she never yelped. Not once. Invisible magic filled the space about her with the creeping chill of a winter's fog until the wound sealed, and then the everjewel was gone, as if it had never existed in the first place.

*They help keep us, well, us.*

Again, Orin's words filled my mind as I stared in horror at the blood splatter on the floor.

Mavis grimaced at my slack jaw and thrust her wrist toward me once more for effect. Then she grabbed my hand and pressed my fingers against the now healed line. A sudden rush of cold nipped at my skin, and I flinched. The longer my touch lingered, the more painful it became. It was like grasping a metal pole in the depths of winter, and just when I thought frostbite would claim my fingers, the pulsing cold abated. The stone seemed to shift between muscle and sinew, and its icy kiss ebbed away. When it fully dispersed, Mavis released me.

"Do all everjewels feel like that?" I rubbed my hands together, sparking what warmth I could.

She held my gaze for several breaths before turning away. Slowly, she moved toward a small, freestanding writing desk complete with a multitude of drawers with brass handles. When I didn't immediately follow, she beckoned to me with a weak wave.

Carefully, I moved to her side, and my gaze snagged on an oversized painting in a gilded frame. There were several Evers all standing together around a woman seated on a throne. There was something familiar about her stature, small but strong. Lustrous, wheat-colored hair fell over her shoulders like a blanket, and her smile was wide. Bright. Realization dawned on me as I took in her features.

"This is your family."

Mavis glanced between me and the painting and nodded. With a shaky finger, she pointed to the Ever seated on the throne.

"That's you," I said in awe. I saw it now as I glanced between them. It wasn't that Mavis didn't resemble her depiction; it was just that the painting of her, of who she used to be, was so much more vivid and alive. I looked at the rest of the Evers with new appreciation. Beside Mavis's chair was a woman with hair the same color as hers, but her eyes were as fresh and vibrant as spring grass. Her rosy skin was flushed, her lips full and glistening. A small girl stood before her, and on one side, two boys.

Seville, Orin, and Rorik. The woman was their mother, Mavis's daughter. I hardly recognized Lydia. She stood on the opposite side of Mavis's chair and was wrapped in Clesian's arms, the picture of joy and tenderness as she leaned against his broad chest. Her smile was resplendent and entirely foreign. Rounding out the portrait were two men I hadn't seen before, and I brought myself closer to inspect their visages. Mavis reached out then and trailed a light finger over the Ever standing between her and Lydia. He had chestnut-colored hair and warm brown eyes, and his smile seemed to fill every inch of his expression. Mavis gently brushed his face before pulling back to graze the space above her breast. Heartbond. She didn't have to say it for me to know. I could tell by the look in her eyes. By the very love that seemed to emanate from her core.

"I wish I could've met him," I said, tipping my head to hold her stare for a moment. With a nod, she turned toward her desk. She waved her hand over one of the drawers, and I heard a lock click. Gently, she tugged on the brass handle until the drawer gave way to reveal stacks of loose paper. As she riffled through her things, I gave the painting one last look. The only individual left was an Ever with oak-brown hair and deep emerald eyes. Seville, Orin, and Rorik's father. He had to be. Those emerald eyes were the same as Orin's, and his lips were curled in the same sharp, condescending grin that Seville often wielded. I leaned forward an inch, squinting as I studied the painting. Rorik stood slightly apart from the rest, and his expression was tight. There weren't any similarities to be found between him and his father, who had one hand on Orin's shoulder and the other on their mother's. A prickling awareness sprouted in the recesses of my mind, and I dragged my attention back to Rorik.

The artist had paid special care to his burnished locks, as if there weren't enough colors in his palette to accurately depict all the varying coppery hues that made up his hair. His eyes were crafted with such perfection, with such intention, that they might as well have been real. And their shade was uniquely his. He shared only one attribute—the sharp cut of his cheekbones—with his mother.

A sharp poke pulled my focus, and I shifted to find Mavis had jabbed the back of my arm with a paper that had been folded into the shape of an envelope.

"For me?" I took it without thinking. A wax seal the color of maple syrup held it closed, an elegant *F* stamped into its center. Above it in small, looping handwriting:

*Open alone.*

Dread filled my limbs as a cool sweat formed at the base of my neck. After a thick swallow, I met Mavis's gaze. "What is this?"

She only wrapped my fingers tighter around the envelope.

I never wanted to drop something more in my life. And yet there was an insistent, almost fearful nature to Mavis's pleading stare. She worked her throat as if trying to speak, but nothing came out. A glassy sheen covered her eyes until a single tear escaped and bisected her cheek.

"Mavis," I whispered, gripping the paper tighter. "What's going on?"

Her lips parted. Closed. Parted again. A strangled sound, like her words were being choked in a vise grip, crawled out.

"No time. Open."

My hairs were on end, my breath hitting hard and erratic, and I didn't have Ywena to shock me into normalcy. The croak of Mavis's voice flooded my ears and set my heart racing. My fingers traced the ridges and grooves of the seal. *Open alone.* What if it was a trick, like the bargain Amalyss and Tasia had played when I'd first arrived? What dangerous thing would I unleash—alone—with no one around to come to my aid? A small piece of wax flaked away as I ran my finger beneath the lip of the fold.

My world winnowed to that space. I was a breath away from

doing something that couldn't be undone. I felt that truth in my bones. My gaze drifted back to the portrait. To the happy family that no longer existed.

*Be careful who you trust in this place.*

It'd been a long time since Vora's warning had surfaced in my mind, but it did its job. I pulled my finger away from the seal. Just as I opened my mouth to speak, the bedroom door swung inward, and Lydia strolled into the room. Her nightgown was wrinkled, her eyes heavy-lidded. There was a sadness to her expression that I'd never once witnessed, and she seemed to shuffle rather than walk into Mavis's room.

"Mother, are you awake? I—" Lydia froze when she saw me.

I blinked, and Mavis had shifted. It wasn't much, just an infinitesimal step in front of me to obscure my hands with her body, but she did it with such speed that it appeared as if she'd always been standing between me and the door. And then her life force seemed to evaporate into the night. A chill swept over me as I stared at the ghostly Ever before me. Her once-probing stare was now lifeless and vacant. Her trembling frame showed none of its former vigor, however fleeting. Her power, her soul, was simply gone.

And it turned my world on its axis. The prickle of the paper against my palm suddenly felt like a blade, and I crossed my hands behind my back to hide them from view.

"What are you doing here?" Lydia asked, her words sharp. She'd regained her composure within the same time Mavis had moved, and all traces of sadness were hidden with the same effectiveness as glamour.

"Mavis's door was open." I moved my hand slowly, slipping it beneath the back of my blouse to tuck the envelope in the waistband of my pants. "I thought she might need help."

Lydia's eyes narrowed as she looked between Mavis and me. "The only thing she needs is a cure for blight. And until you've gained access to Orin's power, I don't think you'll be able to provide that."

"Right." I came up beside Mavis and placed a gentle hand on her shoulder. She didn't react. Not even when I bade her good night and strolled passed Lydia. Once I entered the hall, she slammed the door behind me. I turned away without looking back and walked as quickly as I could to my quarters. Only when I'd locked the doors and checked the latches twice did I dare to extract Mavis's gift from my waistband.

I rubbed it gently between my fingers, once again studying the scrawl of ink. I trailed my finger over the seal once. And then broke it.

I'd expected a wave of magic, or a sound, or some sort of elaborate spell that would take hold the moment the wax snapped in half. But nothing happened. The only change I noticed was a subtle aroma of leaves that seemed to be infused in the paper.

But as my finger ran along the jagged edge that had initially been folded in, I knew what I was holding—even before I spied the familiar, neat handwriting of my aunt.

My throat tightened as I read her note.

*I've figured it out. They need everjewels to remain immortal. I'm not sure why, but the blight has weakened their effect. They bury them in their bodies to try to stop the spread. That's why Orin wants my power. He's trying to convince me to heartbond with him, because he needs something stronger—and I'm not the first one he's tried to convince. I'd sooner die than let him take my magic, and I fear that's coming.*

*I've left this note with Mavis. The others are too closely watched. She'll give this to you when she believes you can find Orin's everjewel without raising suspicion. The stone's power is similar to ours and reacts to our magic. I don't have enough time left. You must find it and*

*destroy it. If you need help from someone in the house, you'll need to
break the family's evervow first. I don't know much about it, just that it
exists. I wish I could tell you more—help you more.*

*I don't even know whom I'm writing to, but, Edira, if you've found
yourself here, know that I love you. I believe in you.*

*Save yourself.*

All sounds dulled to a monotone static, and I dropped the letter. *Rowena.* A shuddering breath wrenched itself free from my
lungs, as a nettling sensation raced over my skin. She chose death
over Orin. *Death.* And even now, beyond the grave, she was trying
to save me from that fate.

*Find Orin's everjewel.* My heart hammered against my throat as
I remembered the sharp, icy kiss I'd felt against my fingers while
trailing his tattoo. The whisper of cold that had filled Mavis's wrist
after she'd shoved the stone into her arm.

Panic settled into the marrow of my bones. Everything I'd just
agreed to with Orin . . .

My vision blurred as tears filled my eyes. I thought he'd
cared. Pain flared through my chest, spiderwebbing out from
my heart, along with a red-hot shame that flooded my limbs. I'd
*trusted* him.

I combed through every memory of Orin and me. Every shared
moment, every subtle look or reassuring hand squeeze. The brush
of his fingers against my cheek, the sound of his warm words, the
feel of his lips. I wanted to scream. It couldn't be true. Rowena had
to be wrong.

*Save yourself.*

I retrieved the note and reread her words. My mind whirled.
Even if this was all true, how was I supposed to destroy an everjewel encased within Orin's body? My lessons with Rorik never
could have prepared me for this. What was this familial evervow?

And my brothers. Their life-sustaining caskets had been a balm for my aching worry, but now their coffins were unbreakable prisons. Orin was the only one with the key.

I sank to the floor and let out a silent, agonizing shriek. What the fuck was I supposed to do? I wanted—*needed*—answers, but whom could I trust? Orin had been spinning up stories since the moment he met me. He'd been the creator of our shared narrative, the one who cautiously laid the groundwork for me to fall headfirst into his arms.

Because what did it matter if he threw the town a little more coin? He had plenty to spare.

Keeping my brothers alive? The spell hardly seemed to drain his expansive power.

Every kind action. Every carefully orchestrated moment.

He was a fucking Ever, and I should've known from the beginning. He wanted my power, not me. Just like he wanted my aunt's and every threadmender's before us. We were expendable pawns.

I nearly balled up the paper, but as the crinkling pulled my focus, I glimpsed a few more lines beneath Rowena's note written in a different hand.

> I'm sorry I didn't trust Rowena sooner. I didn't know until it was too late.
>
> My daughter gave her life for this, but none of us can speak it.
>
> Zeverin Ignatus Embergrave.
>
> We all want to be free.

The moment I read the name a weight pounded into my bones, and the metallic tang of magic singed the air. It was only a name, but the letters seemed to burn into the backs of my eyelids, so that even when I squeezed my eyes shut to chase away the lingering magic, I could still see it perfectly. What the fuck was going on in this gods-forsaken manor?

I couldn't trust anyone outside of myself.

That truth settled me, and the swirling emotions subsided. I couldn't break. Not now, not when I was so close to curing my brothers.

I had to go through with the heartbond. I had to keep my shit together long enough to help Noam and Nohr. Even now, with my mind so absolutely shattered with the knowledge my aunt left behind, my heart ached at the notion that Orin was anything other than good. What if he and Rowena just didn't get along? What if that was an act of desperation on his part, but now he'd become something more? Something better?

A brittle laugh escaped my lips at my fragile logic. I wanted it to be true, but I doubted it was. I forced myself to stand and then headed for the bathroom.

When I stood before the copper bathtub, I closed my eyes and centered myself with a long breath.

*Zeverin Ignatus Embergrave.*

The name rasped through my mind like dying leaves scraping against cobblestone. It felt important. Powerful. I found a match in my apothecary case and dropped it on top of Rowena's final words. And possibly Mavis's.

Only when it had been reduced to ash did I move. I willed the basin to fill with water, and I watched as the remains dissolved and drained away.

# TWENTY-FIVE

I had only a few hours before Orin would return and the ceremony would begin. He'd told me he needed to complete a ritual of his own before we could become heartbonds, but he hadn't elaborated on what that entailed. Whatever it was, I was glad I had some time to school my emotions into place. And to find answers. Of course not a single book I'd read included anything about everjewels other than brief mentions of their existence; it seemed their magic was safeguarded above all else. I doubted I could trust anyone in this manor, but perhaps I could trick them with innocent conversation into revealing hidden truths.

As I left my room and headed for the stairs, I weighed my options.

Mavis was off the table. She'd already expended what little energy she had left to deliver the letter, and I doubted Lydia would leave Mavis alone after finding me in her room.

Which of course meant Lydia was out of the question—unsurprisingly, I wouldn't have started with that raging Ever, anyway—and by proxy Clesian. Amalyss and Tasia, maybe. But if they were within their parents' reach, then definitely not.

I could ask Vora, but she was devoted to her lord. I couldn't risk her letting Orin know anything before I was ready to confront him. Seville or Rorik, then. My feet hit the foyer and I paused, glancing through the windows at the dawn light cresting over the quiet forest. Seville had spoken so fondly about Rowena during our trip to Willowfell. But what if Seville had tricked Rowena in the way Orin had tricked me? I'd never seen Seville so much as raise her voice at Orin.

*I don't love either of my brothers, but I know which one not to piss off.*

The burn behind her words, even through the fog of my memory, couldn't be denied. Not Seville, then.

My gaze crossed the hall to Orin's study. The door was open, the lights doused. The empty room was like the maw of a cave with a whispering, rattling inhalation that sent a chill up my spine.

*His evervow was meant to protect us, and yet you still find ways to put us at risk just to spite him.*

Awareness crested in me at the ghost of Orin's words. The familial evervow. He'd been discussing it with Rorik. That's where I had to start. It was no secret Rorik detested his brother, but I had no idea if that disgust had any impact on loyalty.

*We all want to be free.*

I hoped Mavis was fucking right.

The brisk air greeted me as I pushed through the double doors to the courtyard. The morning was quiet, the sleepy lawns just barely awakening with the faint streams of daylight peeking over the surrounding forest.

My boots thudded against the grass as I abandoned the polished pathways for the manicured lawns. I'd heard once from the gossiping attendants that Rorik rose with the sun to train alone beneath the ancestor tree. While I wanted to storm down the hill and pin him against the writhing bark and demand he speak plainly for once, I doubted that was the best way forward. Knowing him, he'd probably like it.

A soft grunt pulled my focus, and I looked up from the ground. Rorik had draped his shirt over one of the low-hanging limbs of the tree and was bare-skinned, holding a sword in one hand. He swung it through the air in an artful, sweeping arc and halted his thrust just before the tip came crashing into the earth. Every muscle on his back was taut, his shoulders defined and broad, the Fernglove crest emblazoned on his spine. The broken sword was perfectly poised in the center, and the surrounding insects flared out over his shoulder blades. With every harsh movement as he went through his drills, they took flight across his muscles. Danced along his tendons. Moved when he moved.

I wondered if he'd stab Orin through the heart for me if I asked.

"Get an eyeful while you can." Rorik spoke without turning to face me and continued to thrust his sword through the air. "Soon, you won't be able to do so without repercussion."

My temper was a hair trigger away from becoming full-blown, unfettered rage, and he had no idea how close I was to combusting. I bit the inside of my cheek for a moment before speaking. "Repercussion? And what would that entail?"

"How would I know? Ask your heartbond."

There was a bite to his words I couldn't ignore, one that matched my own hidden anger, and I pressed my lips into a hard line. "Do you have a problem with what I'm doing?"

With a definitive thud, he sank his sword into the earth and rounded on me. It was impossible not to gape at the defined planes of his chest, at the contours and grooves along his stomach and waist. He was absolutely gorgeous, and while there had been a moment of strained frustration in his gaze, it evaporated when he caught me staring. A different heat filled his smoldering gaze, and his lips curled to reveal pointed canines.

"I have lots of problems where you're concerned." He closed the gap between us so there was hardly any room to breathe. A bead of sweat rolled down his sternum, and he absently brushed it away.

I tracked the motion and remembered the feel of his fingers exploring my waist while we danced. The gentle brush of his touch along my jaw before he pinned my chin and threatened to kiss me without saying anything at all. Then all the anger and heartache that had been building from the moment I opened Rowena's letter came splintering to the forefront, and I spat venom at his feet.

"What the fuck is wrong with you and this mess of a family?"

"Everything." His brow tightened as he scoured my face, searching. I'd never felt more scrutinized in my life than in that moment. His golden gaze was heavy against my skin, and it only caused more heat to surge through my veins. "You have no idea what you've gotten yourself into."

"And how could I?" I snapped. "Tell me, Rorik, how the fuck was I ever supposed to survive this place?" I filled every word with menace, never once backing down. "No one here is honest. You want me to save you? Save the family? Why the hell would I? I can't trust any of you!"

"And you shouldn't!" he roared. His expression tore through my anger, because it didn't make sense. There was rage, certainly. But there was also desperation. Anguish. The muscles of his neck strained against his skin as he stared me down. "And I never asked you to save any of us. If anything, I told you to live."

I'd already opened my mouth to argue, but at that my words died, because he was right. From the moment I set foot in Fern-glove, he'd treated me not as a threadmender but as a person. He was rough and callous, sure, but he didn't give a damn about what

I cured. He didn't praise me when I succeeded, either. To him, every use of my power was a waste of my life.

A quiet sense of resolve filled my bones, and my words came out soft. "Tell me what you and Orin were talking about the other night in his study."

A bolt of lightning struck Rorik's spine, all anger fleeing in less than a breath. His eyes were wide. "I knew I sensed you."

"I was curious." I watched his throat work as if he wanted to speak but couldn't. Instead, he clenched and unclenched his jaw. Swallowed thickly. When his conversation with Orin had lulled, Ywena had reacted. Rorik must've communicated with her somehow, urging her to get me to stay. He'd wanted me to hear that conversation. Could I trust him?

"Ask me whatever you want, Edira." The intensity of his gaze hammered into my bones. "Please."

It was that single word that did me in. The strained plea full of so much weight, so much emotion. Rorik never asked for anything, but he asked for this.

And I obliged.

"What's the evervow? The one Orin mentioned?"

There were no visible ties holding Rorik back, but there was an immediate release that raced through his form and loosened his muscles.

*I carry the weight of unspoken burdens in my bones.*

Apparently, there was someone who'd been more bound in this manor than me. And now he was free.

"Finally." He rubbed his hand over his throat. "I wasn't sure you'd ever get there. The evervow prevents us from directly speaking about it to anyone unless they already know of its existence. Over the years, a few have found out in similar ways."

"That's why Ywena wanted me to stay. To listen." Hope began to bloom in my chest. If Rorik was willing to share this family secret with me, then maybe we could break it. Maybe he could help me save my brothers. "What does the vow entail?"

"No Fernglove can seriously hurt another. We can't leave our lands for more than a few months at a time, either. And finally, no one can outwardly oppose the head of house, which used to be my father and is now Orin." Rorik scowled at the manor. "If Orin wills something for the good of the family, we must obey."

"And you all agreed to this?" I raised an incredulous brow.

"Not intentionally." Rorik's lips curled in distaste. "My father was excellent at wording contracts. He enjoyed binding people to his will, and he was powerful. Not powerful enough to stop the blight from eating him alive, though." A gleam of satisfaction flared in his amber eyes.

"He seems delightful," I muttered. "Why on earth would your father make a vow like that?"

Rorik gripped the back of his neck as his gaze darkened. "Family name. *Honor.* My father cared about order and appearances above all, and his obsession with hiding my mother's *transgression* led to the evervow."

"Transgression?"

"I am not my father's blood. Seville and Orin are my half-siblings. I am a Fernglove only because my father hated the idea of anyone learning of my mother's dalliance. I was expected to act as his son even though, behind closed doors, he refused to acknowledge me. His disgust was palpable, and my siblings took it upon themselves to follow in his stead. There was little peace. Lots of pain.

"But outside the walls of our home"—Rorik flexed his hands as he stared at one of the tree limbs—"they pretended like everything was fine. I couldn't take it. I lashed out often, until my father created the evervow to keep his deteriorating family ties, the precious Fernglove name, intact."

I followed his gaze to a thick limb that branched from the trunk. I had no way of knowing which appendage belonged to which deceased family member, but there was an unmistakable air of malice that grew from him the longer he stared at that arm. After a weighted pause, he shook his head and retrieved his shirt, easily slipping it back into place.

"Rorik." I failed to find words as I saw decades of pain etched into his gaze. I couldn't imagine growing up in a loveless home, not to mention my siblings betraying me. If Noam or Nohr ever abandoned me the way Seville and Orin did . . .

As horrific as his past was, his story revealed a truth I couldn't deny: he held no love for this place. I pored over the words of Rowena's letter in my mind. If I wanted Rorik's help, we needed to break the vow.

"Is there a way out of it?" I asked.

"I don't know. Evervows aren't meant to be broken. My mother tried to find a way, but I'm not sure if she succeeded."

A heady sense of knowing filled my limbs. The name. It had to be the key.

"Rorik"—I grasped his forearms—"I might have a way. But we need to do this carefully."

"What are you talking about?" His eyes flicked between my hands and my face. "How?"

My words came out in a tight rush. "Rowena left me a message. I think I can do it, but not yet. I still need to heartbond with Orin, so I—"

Rorik took a sharp step back, as if I'd slapped him across the face. "Heartbond. After everything I just told you, you still want to be with him?" He hissed as he adjusted the collar of his shirt, giving it a harsh yank. "Do you even know where he is right now?"

"No, I don't, but that's not what I'm trying to say. I just need—"

"He's with Ossanna. And Issa."

I stalled as I pictured Issa and her sweeping dark hair. She'd been quiet the last time I saw her, standing with her mother and brother on the lawns outside Fernglove. She had no need to attend lessons, but that didn't keep her from stopping by.

"Why?"

Rorik glowered at me. "He's reassuring Ossanna about the terms of their agreement. Issa was meant to be his heartbond in a few years." His eyes scoured my face before dropping to my heart. "He'll be sure to tell them of your shortened lifespan and how it has little impact on his promise."

A smaller, weaker part of me was thrust under another wave of hurt. Given everything, I shouldn't have been surprised. But heat still pricked behind my eyes. Yesterday, we'd shared a hopeful bliss, and now . . . none of that mattered.

Thoughts fell into place like sink weights in water.

First, Seville's words:

*I met someone years ago who could summon stars that dusted into diamond-like particles. It was beautiful.*

Then the black-haired attendant in the foyer:

*She did pass rather quickly after, well, you know.*

And of course, Amalyss:

*Especially since she deteriorated after moving here.*

My breath hit harder, faster. I'd known that Lorelai had been Orin's former heartbond, but I hadn't connected the dots. The stars. The magic he'd used while we'd come together. A brackish substance flooded my tongue, and I forced it back down with a hard swallow. Lorelai Starglen had bonded with Orin, and she'd died soon after.

*Not the first time, either.*

I fisted my hands by my sides as the whispered words of the attendant surfaced in my mind. Orin was a black widow that no one could control, and I'd fallen into his web. How many other powers did he have stored away? Rorik was right. I had no fucking idea what I was getting into.

But I wouldn't be Orin's unwitting pawn any longer.

"As vomit-inducing as all this information is," I said after steeling myself with a breath, "it still doesn't change anything. I need to heartbond with him." Rorik opened his mouth to argue, and I shot him a hard glare. "*Not* because I care. But because he has my brothers, and if I'm going to break open their caskets and save their lives, then I need Ever magic."

Rorik had the good sense to hold back whatever ire-filled retort he had initially prepared. Instead, he ran a hand through his hair, tugging slightly on the ends. "And you think Orin would just let that happen?"

"He won't have a choice if I destroy his everjewel."

Silence. Rorik was still, calculating. His tight gaze lingered on my face, as if he were turning over the validity of my words and determining if they had merit. "And you know where he keeps it?"

"Yes." I'd never forget the sharp bite of ice against my fingers. "But even with his magic, I'm not sure I'd be strong enough to take him down."

"You wouldn't." His brows drew together.

"Normally I would take offense to your obvious slight, but in this case, you're right." Slowly, I took a step forward and closed the distance he'd put between us. "But if I release you from the evervow . . ."

I held my breath as I waited for him to respond. It was one thing to ask him to defy his brother's wishes, and another thing entirely for me to make a bargain for murder. His eyes filled with a look of pure sadness. "It won't work. You *need* to find a way out of this place, Edira. If you heartbond with him, you'll be a Fernglove, which means—"

A harrowing rip split the air like the forceful tearing of a seam. It emanated from the manor and filled the quiet estate, setting the hairs on the back of my neck on end. A mottled scent of decay carried to us on a chilled breeze, and with it came a deep, knowing sense of wrong. My power erupted from my center without my command. Soft light enveloped Rorik and me as we stood in open-mouthed silence.

Then we pivoted toward the house. I knew this feeling. I'd encountered it three times over. First with my parents, then with Alec.

Death was here.

# TWENTY-SIX

The manor's glamour was sloughing off like withered, curling wallpaper. Each strip that fell away was an eerie tear on the breeze, and gooseflesh ravaged my skin at the sight.

I'd known they'd magicked their estate to hide all traces of blight, but I hadn't expected . . . *this*. Rotting, putrid vines climbed the walls and tore away at the crumbling facade. Instead of mortar, a bubbling ooze the color of curdled milk dripped from between the bricks. Pools of frothing loam surrounded the building like a moat, eating away at the soft earth and preparing the manor for an early grave. The stench of decay and sour mulch was so thick that I gagged. Without warning, a handful of spores near the grand entrance burst, showering the air around the steps in a fine spray of mustard-yellow particles.

And that was only the manor. The entire state was a putrefied mess as the glamour that had been so painstakingly layered simply dusted away. The grounds were leached of color, the grass beneath our feet now golden brown. The neatly trimmed hedges were nothing more than thorny skeletons where leaves had once thrived. The flowers? Gone. No blooms. No stalks reaching toward the sun. Just an expanse of decay and disease that unfurled across the lands and into the forest, where the trees had been transformed into barren bones that speared the cloudless sky like knives.

I could barely find my voice. "What's happening?"

Rorik's eyes were wild. "I don't know."

He bolted toward the manor, leaving me to sprint after him. I tried to force my magic to settle, tried to dampen the power surging through my veins in reaction to the absolute grave that Fernglove had become, but I couldn't. So I let it pulse from me with every heartbeat, taking what comfort I could in the alabaster light coating my limbs. We didn't have to go far. The moment Rorik and I burst through the double doors leading to the entry foyer, we found someone crumpled on the floor. She'd folded in on herself, pulling her knees to her chest and wrapping her arms around them tight. Her brittle hair splayed out behind her, and her skin was covered with wounds. Blight festered from every hole and crawled over her entire body. Her fingers twitched. Her breath was a high-pitched, shuddering wheeze.

"Grandmother," Seville sobbed as she kneeled beside the near-lifeless form.

Mavis. It was Mavis. She was a desiccated shell of the vivacious woman I'd spied in the painting. She had maybe minutes left. With my power fully intact, I could see a solitary thread still attached to her center. There wasn't an inch of it that wasn't covered in tar, and already it was hardening to an impenetrable surface. Soon, it would simply dust away.

"She just collapsed. I tried to encase her, but her body rejected it," Seville said through her tears.

*Encase her.* Immediately I pictured my brothers in their floating coffins, and I prayed to the gods they were safe, that whatever magic Seville used to try to save Mavis hadn't affected their barriers.

Seville's hands aimlessly fluttered around Mavis's head. Lydia and Clesian were there, too. They'd wrapped their arms around their daughters, pressing their bodies flush to their sides. Amalyss and Tasia stared in wide-eyed, open-mouthed terror.

Rorik swallowed thickly as he set his jaw tight. "Seville, you need to stop siphoning. You've already pulled every ounce of magic from the estate. You'll drain yourself next."

"No!" she screamed, and she flung herself over Mavis's trembling form. I hadn't noticed the aura of magic surrounding her until now. It was the same shade as the caskets housing my brothers, but try as Seville might to direct that green mist to Mavis, nothing stuck. Seville's power ate away at her glamour—at all their glamours—and suddenly she was laid bare before me. A gasp caught in my chest. Seville had always looked youthful. Flawless. Now, she looked startlingly similar to the dying matriarch in her arms. Full of blight and fear and a heated rage in her stare. I glanced at Rorik and stilled.

Gods. I'd seen some of his magical features before: the glossy wings with the golden underside, the sable horns and pointed fangs. The endless depth of emotion in his ink-black stare. But there was more, so much more, to his being. An iridescent sheen coated his skin like a golden-hued exoskeleton, and he had daggerlike nails that were as dark as his eyes. Blight ate away at the carved muscles along his arms and bloomed against his cheek. Yellow loam and pustules sprouted from beneath his collarbone and spread toward his throat like the limbs of a tree. Seeing Rorik covered in death made my heart tremble.

It wasn't the fact that he was already drenched in sickness; it was the fact that he didn't seem to care at all. There was nothing but resignation in his gaze as he stared at his dying grandmother.

A chill swept over my skin. He wanted this. Maybe not for the others, but certainly for himself.

"You," Seville said, turning her sharp gaze toward me. "Save her. Please."

A hollow ache grew in my chest. "I can't. Not yet."

"Liar!" she screamed. "You can help her. You just won't." She spat at my feet as tears bisected her cheeks. They streamed over the edge of a wound stretched across her jaw, and the foaming blight seemed to writhe with pleasure as it caught her tears. As if it took joy in her sadness, her pain.

"Seville, look around you." Rorik's words were soft but full of authority as he gestured to the manor. Everything was rotting from the inside out. Blight was a patchwork design of black and yellow crawling across the ceiling, dripping from the rafters, seeping into the furniture. The air was thick with yellow dust that settled against everything like a weighted sheet. There was no escaping what they'd become. The collective glamour they used to hide from it all couldn't obscure the truth any longer. Seville had destroyed it in her search for any scrap of power she could use to help her grandmother.

"There isn't any time left," Rorik said. "Edira can only do so much."

At the sound of my name, Mavis's eyes flew open. With a forceful wheeze, she struggled to turn her head and meet my gaze. "Come."

Everyone stilled. Time slowed as the weight of her dying request filled the air, and I bit the inside of my cheek. I glanced at the family and blissfully found their expressions free of suspicion. Only Rorik's brows drew together as he watched me drop to Mavis's side.

"I'm here." I knew I couldn't cure her, but I'd ease her passing just the same. My light covered us in a gentle barrier that blocked the drifting spores. Soft hisses filled the space as the yellow snowflakes drifted to their demise and burned away against my skin. I pushed soothing energy through to my fingertips and willed it to transfer to Mavis, to take away her pain. Her gaze never softened.

"Speak."

It was the last thing she said before her eyes slipped closed and her breathing stopped. And as her last thread disappeared into nothing, my magic finally receded.

"Grandmother." Seville ran light fingers along Mavis's brow.

"What did she mean? *Speak?*" Clesian asked as Lydia stepped out of his embrace to take a cautious step forward. Tears filled her eyes as her breath hit harder. Faster.

"People tend to lose their grips on reality in the end." I pitched my voice low and kept my pulse steady. Not yet. Not until I had the power to save my brothers. "I'm not sure what she meant."

Lydia's eyes narrowed. She opened her mouth as if to probe further but never got the chance. Just then, Orin sped into the room. As he crossed the threshold from the outside world into the blight-ridden house, his glamour fell. Seville's power stole whatever magic it could, sharpening suddenly with Orin's presence, but he didn't flinch. Instead, he silently scanned the surroundings, taking in the display of blight and his grandmother's corpse on the floor.

"Seville, that's enough. She's gone. Take her body to the tree so she may join the others," he said quietly.

She complied with one last shuddering sob. Capping her power, she slipped her arms beneath her grandmother. She trembled when part of Mavis's body disintegrated in her hold, but she steeled herself by pressing her lips tightly together. As they walked away, they left a gray-and-yellow trail of ashes and blight.

"Lydia, Clesian, I need you . . ." Orin swallowed as his voice broke, and he pinched his eyes shut. His nostrils flared as he took a long, heavy breath through his nose.

His pain was so *believable*. It made me want to puke. But rather than show my distaste and let him in on my budding plan, I kept quiet. Still. Beside me, Rorik's expression hardened, and a tendon strained against his neck.

When he regained his composure, Orin straightened and once again met his family's gazes. "Gather what's needed for the ceremony. We'll join you later."

Like Seville, the four of them left without saying another word.

"Ceremony?" I blurted. So much for poise. The ceremony was exactly what I wanted—needed—but in the aftermath of Mavis's death it just felt wrong. "What about Mavis?"

"Seville will bury her. She may not make the ceremony, but that's all right. She needs to grieve." Orin came to my side, and he palmed my cheek with a gentle hand before letting it fall to my waist. Anger clawed beneath the surface of my skin at his touch, but I didn't wrench his hand away and spit in it. Yet.

My tongue, however, was not as easy to hold back. "And you don't?"

His eyes dropped to my mouth, and he exhaled so deeply it seemed to stem from his bones. "I will miss my grandmother. But I can't change what happened, only prevent this from happening to anyone else. *We* can prevent this."

I hated how, even now, his syrupy words made me question my resolve. "Mavis is gone. What happens to our bargain? Are my brothers safe?"

Orin had the smarts to look appalled. "Edira, I would never harm them. Mavis may have been the reason you came here, but she's not the reason I'm asking you to stay now." He tucked a strand of moonlit hair behind my ear before brushing his knuckle along my jaw. "You know that."

At that, Rorik scoffed. A nocturnal sheen passed over his gaze, and all at once I was reminded that he was a killer. The reflective gold flash was a threat aimed directly at his brother, and I believed in my core that if I broke the vow, he'd rail against Orin—not for me, but for himself. And that was enough reassurance for me.

"As if you're actually *asking* her to stay." Rorik's grin was feral, his words tight.

Orin didn't respond as he inched closer to me. Claiming me. His fingers on my waist tightened like the shackles of the evervow that held everyone's collective rage at bay.

Rorik tilted his head toward me but kept his gaze on his brother. "Edira, leave while you can. I know you don't want to, but it's the only way. Do it now while you're not bound to anyone here."

"I have her brothers," Orin seethed, taking a small step forward. His eyes widened a fraction at his own outburst, at the glimmer of his true intentions finally rising to the surface.

"You *have* my brothers?" My gut churned as I twisted out of his grip. "What does that mean, Orin?"

His gaze turned pleading, but I could see it now: the tension straining the sides of his emerald eyes, the twitch to his brow, and the uneasy shift of his weight from one foot to the other. "I'm sorry, Edira. I didn't mean it like that. A lot has happened in such a short amount of time, and I'm not handling this well. Once we do the ceremony—"

"You'll be a *Fernglove*," Rorik interjected. His eyes shone with so much heat and despair that I couldn't help but freeze. "The vow, Edira. Even with his power, you'd still answer to him."

My knees went weak at his words. This fucking *evervow*. I needed Orin's power to save my brothers, but I couldn't get that without heartbonding to him. And then I'd be beholden to the vow and unable to speak the fucking name to break the damn thing.

But if I played my hand now and shouted the name, Rorik would be free to act as he wished, to pummel Orin into oblivion like he so obviously desired. But to what end? I'd have no magic to save my brothers. Their caskets would be nothing but a memory the moment I acted against Orin's wishes, and the blight feasting on their bones would finally finish its meal.

As I spiraled in silence, Orin went impossibly still. He stood there, unmoving, long enough for me to question whether he had mastered a way to erase his breath entirely. And then rage crashed over his expression as he pulled back his lips in a vicious snarl. He pushed me behind him to seethe at Rorik.

"You told her. How?"

"*You* told her." A dangerous, fang-clad smile filled Rorik's face. "She overheard you the other night, when we were discussing the Starglens."

Orin's fingers twitched. "You've manipulated her for far too long."

"Have I now?" Anger glinted in Rorik's eyes. "That's fascinating."

"How much do you know?" Orin leveled me with his stare. The manor trembled beneath our feet as roots shot through the floorboards and tangled in an intricate web. Thorns pushed through the bark and surrounded us like daggers.

Fear spiked in my throat at the violent display of power. "I know enough."

"I'm guessing this wasn't part of your elaborate plan." Rorik grinned. "Pity."

"Silence!" Orin roared. He stepped into the mess of still-growing roots, not caring that the barbs tore at his pants and nicked his skin. "I will end you."

"You can try." Rorik seemed to delight in Orin's rage, and he only uncrossed his arms to thrust them wide. "I'm right here."

That was the only invitation Orin needed. He moved so fast I barely caught the movement. One moment he was there, and the next he'd slammed into Rorik with such force that they went crashing into the wall. The house groaned at the sudden impact, and rotted debris began to crumble around them.

"Edira!" Rorik shouted from beneath his brother's form. "Get out!"

I couldn't glimpse either of their faces. The house had started to collapse, and plumes of yellow dust filled the air and my lungs. All around us the walls caved in. Picture frames crashed to the floor and glass shards skittered against the wood. Screams crested from somewhere outside the manor, and through one of the now empty window frames I saw attendants fleeing across the trembling lawns. They'd likely all left when Seville first tore away the glamour and were waiting to return, but now with the ground caving in, they were racing away from it all. Only one person ran into the foyer, into the thick of the blight and Orin's raging magic. Vora.

"We need to get my brothers!" I shouted, and she spurred into motion in the direction of their quarters. I took off after her to help, but a wayward root covered in sharp barbs erupted from the ground to decimate the stairs behind her. I only prayed she'd get there before the whole manor fell. All around me, vines writhed and thrashed as if they were beasts. They lashed into me, leaving welts and bloody scrapes along my skin. With each biting slap I winced in pain, but the creaking whine of the house was all that mattered.

I stumbled over the puckered roots and fell into a bed of thorns. They wormed into the soft flesh of my stomach and punctured my arms, my legs. Even one of my cheeks. Pain arced through my body as I forced myself up. One thorn broke off and remained lodged in my thigh, and I dragged my leg behind me. There had to be another way upstairs, another way to get to my brothers. But already the ceiling was crumbling, and I froze as a chandelier came loose from the rafters just above my head.

I didn't know where Rorik came from. Just that he'd somehow thrown Orin off him and wrapped a single arm around my waist, yanking me out of the way. The chandelier exploded in a violent spray of crystal shards, and Rorik rushed us outside through a hole in the wall. The entryway crashed behind us, and he lunged several feet away from the crumbling manor. A flicker of relief touched his eyes as he scoured my face.

And then Orin slammed his fist into Rorik's temple.

Rorik flew back, but he found his feet quickly and tore toward Orin. They collided with unrestricted violence, both of them snarling as their fists connected with flesh.

"Stop!" I screamed, but they didn't hear me. No one could hear anything over the collapse of the manor. Bony trees stripped of color and leaves punctured the earth and sliced into the house like blades. Windows shattered as their jagged limbs kept growing, and the roof cracked as one monstrous, barren oak punctured the beams and climbed toward the sun. Fissures splintered the earth and blight poured out in a flood, coating everything in loam and sludge. I stared in horror as Rorik and Orin continued to pummel each other.

They couldn't seriously harm each other. The evervow wouldn't let them. But how long would this go on before the magic kicked in? My heart pounded as I ran. Blood spilled from the wound in my thigh, but I ignored the burning rush of pain and the dots blooming across my vision.

I got to Orin first and threw myself at him. He pushed me aside as if I were no more than a stubborn cattail battering against his calf in a mild breeze. I hit the ground and rolled, drenching myself in blight and coughing as spores filled my lungs.

"Edira!" Rorik was at my side, hoisting me up.

"Get away from her!" Orin snarled. Anger fueled the blight at his feet, and ripples formed across the bubbling surface as if he were the center of a storm. "You should've stayed away. You've ruined enough."

"You think I want to be here? Surrounded by people I loathe?" Rorik refused to move from my side. Cuts lined his biceps and blood oozed from a gash on his chest. But not for long. Blight saw an opportunity to strike, and it didn't hesitate. The hungry maws of the tar-like substance crawled over his skin and settled in the gashes. And from it birthed yellow loam and pustules poised to erupt and spread more sickness. If Rorik was in pain, he didn't show it.

In my peripheral vision, I spotted Vora off the side of the house, my brothers' floating caskets before her. She was pushing them away from the debris, and adrenaline surged through me at the sight. I raced toward her as quickly as my injured leg would allow and thrust my body weight against Noam's coffin. Vora nodded but said nothing as she focused on moving Nohr. How she'd managed to get them down the gloomy, tight staircase at the back of the house baffled me, but I was grateful she did.

Tears spilled from my eyes as I pushed. Noam was so close. I could see him, see his weakened body and sallow face. Nohr, too. I glanced between them, resolve forming in my bones as we finally came to a stop.

Rowena's hatred for Orin was already my own, but I needed him. I needed him in a way she could never have understood, because there'd been no one he'd used as collateral. She'd had no family to protect. I looked at Vora, tears lining my eyes, and her own gaze was thick with sadness.

"Thank you." I squeezed her arm once and then took off, heading back into the wreckage where Orin and Rorik still raged. Orin had thrown Rorik into a tree, and the splintering crack reverberated over the lawns. His chest heaved as he glared at his brother, and I took that moment to come to his side.

"Orin, I can fix this. Fix all of it," I begged. Rage and fear mingled in his eyes as I placed my hands on his chest. I couldn't give up on the small hope that he would still let me cure my brothers.

He could have my power, do whatever he wanted, so long as they were safe. "Please. We can do the ceremony now. Call me your heartbond, grant me your power, and—"

"You can't seriously still want that," Rorik hissed, and I turned to see him staring daggers at me.

"Do not talk to my heartbond that way," Orin seethed. His hand found mine and gripped it tight. "You will rot. I might not be able to kill you, but I will never heal you—and neither will she. And I'll celebrate the day blight finally rids us of your stain."

The rest of the family waited on the fringes of Orin and Rorik's war. Even Seville had returned, her body racked with anguish but her gaze full of malice. Not one of them seemed surprised that it'd come to this. They only watched and waited. The attendants had long since fled. The glamour had protected them from the affliction, but now? In a land riddled with disease? One cut and they'd be gone, and it was obvious Orin didn't care.

The only one who remained was Vora. She'd risked her life to save my brothers. She hadn't even thought twice when I asked for her help. But why? Her gaze was pinned on Rorik, and she clasped her hands tight before her as fear gathered in her eyes.

*I've worked for my lord for years.*

Every interaction I had with her blended together and spread out before my eyes. All the times she'd gently warned me without going against Orin's commands. Her hesitation surrounding my decision to become his heartbond. The way she said "my lord" with reverence but spat Orin's name with vehemence. The way she kept me sleeping to keep him at bay, to keep him from pushing in when my body, my mind, needed rest.

Rorik. He was the reason she worked at Fernglove. She'd been tasked to watch over me at his behest, not Orin's.

"Don't let Rorik get under your skin." Orin's hold on me tightened. "The deal was Mavis for them, and look." He gestured to where Vora sat with my brothers by her side, as if he'd been the one to orchestrate their safe escape from the manor. "They're still safe. I could've let them die the moment she did."

I marveled at his nonanswer, draped in a threat, when he could've set everything right with just a simple phrase.

"Tell me, were you ever going to let me cure them?" All the pent-up rage fractured through me and seeped into my words. "Or were you going to command me to mend only those you deemed fit?"

"You think I'm the bad one here?" He rounded on Rorik with venom in his glare. "You trust him?"

Rorik stilled.

"Trust?" It was my turn to laugh. It was strange and maniacal and on the verge of breaking, but I couldn't stop it. "I don't trust any of you. How can I? At least Rorik didn't lie to me."

Orin's answering smile was ice straight to the veins. "Ask him about your brothers. Ask him how he knew about everything. Ask. Don't worry. He'll respond. The evervow commands he follow my will."

"Edira." My name on his lips was a breathy plea. "Don't."

The world began to shift beneath my feet. "What does he mean, Rorik?"

"I'll tell you what I mean." Orin released me and strode forward to grab Rorik by the neck. Slowly, Orin lifted him, so Rorik's toes just barely skated over the grass. "His affinity for insects. His control over them. It really is handy, because no one gives a damn about them." Orin's grip tightened, and Rorik wheezed. "Funny how one golden beetle can keep tabs on everything. The best part, though? Insects aren't bothered by blight. The spores can cling to their legs and transfer with ease to other people. Like Noam and Nohr."

My heart hammered in my throat. Sounds faded in a howl of nothingness. Noam. Nohr. Tears flooded my eyes as I stared at Rorik. He never once brought his hands up to try to wrench free of Orin's hold. Instead, he only looked at me. He couldn't speak, but it didn't matter. His empty eyes told me everything I needed to know.

Everything had been planned from the start.

"Why?" I barely found my voice. "They didn't do anything to you."

"You wouldn't have come otherwise," Orin said with a shrug. "Mavis was on her way out. The rest of us aren't far behind. We needed a cure."

*I get what I want.*

"You planned this from the beginning," I said in a whisper. Tears spilled over as I looked at Orin. "I thought . . ."

"You thought wrong."

I'd thought I'd known anger and heartache before. The moment I'd read Rowena's warning, I'd been consumed with a heated ire that threatened to spill over at every moment. But this. *This.* A numbness took hold of my limbs as an endless roaring churned in my ears. My heart slammed against my rib cage like a beating war drum, and my ratcheting breath carried the acrid taste of bile. Time slowed. My vision blurred as tears threatened to take over, and then every breath, every sound, every thought, sharpened on Orin.

This was fury. And I wanted to see him, all of them, burn.

*My daughter gave her life for this, but none of us can speak it.*

Mavis's note was tinder to the flames raging in my body. I wouldn't give anyone my power. But I would destroy Orin's.

"Zeverin . . ."

Lightning struck the spines of Orin and Rorik, and they stilled. The word was barely a whisper on my lips, but the power of it filled the air with tension.

Orin's grip on Rorik loosened. "What did you say?"

". . . Ignatus . . ."

"Edira, what are you doing?" Orin took a step toward me.

What was I doing? Whatever was necessary so I could carve that everjewel from his neck and end his sorry existence.

"... Embergrave."

The sound of metal clanking against metal sang through the air, as if shackles had been cast off and thrown against stone. A swell of electricity bubbled between us and then exploded. It rushed outward in a gust of wind that knocked everyone off their feet, and an eerie quiet settled over the estate.

"You removed the evervow." Orin scrambled to his feet first. "How?" He stared at me with unbridled wrath, and I couldn't help but smile. Good. Let him feel loss. Let him lose control of everything he cherished.

"Mavis." I pulled myself up and bit back a curse at the pain. "You're far from beloved, Orin. I can't wait to watch you fall."

"You don't know what you've done," Orin bristled at me. Then his gaze shifted to Rorik, and he stilled.

Murder filled Rorik's stare, and he stood slowly. He rolled his head from side to side, then flexed his hands. Behind him, his wings flared out, stretching wide before settling against his back. He raised one hand to the air, as if grazing the invisible currents of magic still lingering around us. A smirk tugged at his lips.

"Who would've thought," he murmured. "Mother, you actually did it. You outsmarted Father. Your *lover's* name."

Something fierce flashed in Orin's eyes. "He is *not* your father."

Rorik's grin was pure evil. "I know."

And then he lunged. He closed the distance between them in a breath and slammed his fist into Orin's face. Blood spurted from Orin's nose, and the sickening crunch of a broken bone filled my ears. Orin tumbled backward but was upright in a matter of seconds. The earth rumbled as roots began to erupt through the soil at his feet. A thorny branch burst from the ground and speared Rorik's arm. It went clean through, but Rorik didn't falter. He only broke it off with a sweep from his hand and cast it to the side.

I hardly recognized the Ever standing before me. His features were sharper, his gaze violent and full of hatred. Rorik was a predator unchained. The evervow that had bound him to Orin's will, gone.

Rorik moved with lethal accuracy as he slammed into his brother again. Orin went flying until his back cracked against a pile of debris from the manor. But he was strong, too, and he whipped around after securing a slab of stone and hurled it in our direction. It blocked out the sun as it arced toward us. No, not toward us. Toward me.

Time slowed as I watched it fall. It'd crush me with ease, and I didn't have a chance to escape.

At least I'd be done with this family. This mess.

Rorik jumped in front of me and braced his arms across his face. The slab crashed into him, and debris showered around us. He stumbled back and fell to one knee, just inches away from me. His shoulders rolled forward as he caught his breath. I could hardly stand to look at him. It didn't matter that he'd just saved me from death. All I could see were my brothers' sick faces, their blight-ridden forms. It may have been at Orin's command, but Rorik was responsible for Noam and Nohr's condition. He alone delivered blight straight to their veins. He was why I was here.

"I don't want your help," I said, my voice a deadly whisper.

He didn't look at me. "I know. But I'm giving it anyway. Tell me where his everjewel is."

My brows drew together. I hadn't expected that response, but I would take it. I would take an opportunity for revenge. I stared past him at Orin, and anger swelled beneath the surface of my skin. "In his neck. The tip of the sword. Destroy it."

"With pleasure." Rorik lunged like a savage beast and sliced into the flesh of Orin's side with his nails. Orin howled in response and then ripped Rorik off him. He landed on his feet a few yards away, teeth bared.

They came together like two mountains crashing, and the

open clearing rumbled with the force of their hits. Rorik drove his talon-like nails toward Orin's jugular, but Orin moved with the fluidity of water. Gone in an instant and then behind Rorik's back, driving a fist straight into his kidney. Rorik went flying, and Orin tipped his head back to laugh.

"You won't last against me," Orin spat as he stalked toward Rorik. Streams of iridescent magic dripped from Orin's fingers, splashing against the blight and sending quakes through the ground.

Rorik moved like the hunter I'd always known him to be, and rage burned in his eyes as he set Orin in his sights. That look was enough to chill me to my core, but I silently urged him on. Rorik lunged, and this time, he met his mark. His fingers clawed at the soft flesh of Orin's neck, and with one harrowing rip, he extracted the hidden everjewel and then leaped away.

And then he crushed it between his fingers.

Relief sang through me at the sight. Orin was done. I'd accomplished what Rowena had set out for me, and he would be no more. I hadn't saved everyone, but at least this wretched being would be gone forever.

Throughout it all, Orin never moved. And then out of nowhere, he laughed. The action caused blood to spurt from his wound, but he didn't even bother to clap his hand over the gash. An aura of magic began to pulse from his body, and he pointed two fingers directly at Rorik.

"You think that was my only jewel? I have more hidden in me, and you'll never find them." His stare was wild, his words a booming cascade of dread. Roots erupted around Rorik and chained him to the ground. He roared at the thick trunks burying him in the earth, but he was pinned in a matter of seconds. The blight stemming from the land surged in earnest, coating his body and covering him in a thick layer of black sludge.

Orin chuckled. "Pity, I was looking forward to a more satisfying brawl after putting up with your insulting presence all these years."

Wild, uncontained fury raced through Rorik's expression, and his muscles bulged against Orin's hold. "I'll kill you."

"I suppose you can now, if you're strong enough. And speaking of death . . ." Orin turned his attention to me. "In case you forgot." He raised one hand and snapped his fingers. The sound was more like a thunderclap, and it reverberated through the air and rattled my bones. A wisp of glittering green magic streamed toward his hand and absorbed into his skin.

Vora screamed.

I jerked my head toward her, toward my brothers, and watched as their tombs evaporated and they fell to the ground.

A panicked cry ripped through my throat as I ran. I didn't care about the pain in my leg or the burn of my breath. I didn't care about anything except getting to Noam and Nohr.

Somewhere, Orin laughed. "I will get what I want."

I would die before I gave him anything. Moonlight coated my entire body as I uncorked my power. When my magic doused my eyes, Noam's and Nohr's threads came into view.

There wasn't any color left to their strands. Just thick tar on the verge of solidifying and dusting to ash.

"No!" I shrieked.

"It won't work." Orin's voice was amplified with his magic and filled the entire clearing. "Not without me."

When I reached my brothers, I slid to my knees. The muck of loam coated my legs and arms, and my chest threatened to cave in. My frantic gaze raced over their forms. Consciousness slowly returned to their faces, followed immediately by harrowed looks of agony. Then mania. Their deranged chuckles and nonsensical speech bubbled around me.

"No," I sobbed as I reached for their threads. I took one from each of them, pinching them into needles and thrusting them directly into my arms. The moment their blight-ridden threads made contact with my body, the rest of their infected strands burrowed into me. Pain exploded behind my eyes as blight from two separate sources flowed into my core. Burning tears cascaded over my cheeks.

*Save them. Save them. Please, just take me instead.*

Adrenaline surged through me, staving off some of the pain as I held my brothers close. They didn't even register that I was there. Vora joined me on the ground and ran her hands through their hair. Her eyes were full and glassy, and she forced a swallow as she looked at me.

The blight on their strands liquefied and streamed into me like endless black rivers, and my body cooked from the inside out. My light waned. My vision swam. I didn't have enough power to save them both.

My brothers were about to die.

"Give me what I want, Edira, and I just might spare them." Orin strode closer, and he beckoned to Rorik with two fingers: "Wouldn't want you to miss this." The branches chaining him in place thrust from the ground, carrying Rorik with them. Shards of bark splintered off and fractured around Rorik as he rallied against their hold. But each time he managed to break free, more vines and roots shot from the earth to bind him tight.

*Might.* Orin would never save them.

The last dredges of my power bloomed from my center and pushed outward, coating my brothers in a soothing white light. Their blight still moved through their threads into me, but adrenaline was a magic all its own that somehow kept me from succumbing to the agonizing pain riddling my frame. If I couldn't cure them, I hoped I went with them.

Vora looked beyond me to Rorik. Her lips pursed together. Slowly, she rounded her gaze back to me. Her words were no more than a whisper: "I know you don't trust me or him, but if you want to save you brothers, let it happen."

A subtle shift in the loam drew my focus. It was slight, like the churning of soil in preparation for planting seeds, and then a ribbon of magic so clear and beautiful broke through the surface. It was the color of shined gold, glittering and full of promise. The hue of the beetle that'd set my life on this path. My gaze riveted to Rorik. His fingers had curled to obscure his palm, and the magic easily slid from his hand. I followed its trail down his leg and into the earth. To the ribbon now gingerly waiting by my fingertips. Slowly, it wrapped around my forearm without touching my skin.

It hovered there as if waiting for permission.

*Heartbond.* I didn't know how I knew, but I did. I looked at Rorik, at his clouded expression. I looked at his life threads dancing about his frame, drenched in the same sickness that infected my brothers. The death sentence he'd delivered.

"I don't want him," I said to Vora without breaking his gaze.

"He knows," Vora said to my back. "He doesn't care. He'll give you what you want and leave you be."

Orin took a few more steps in my direction and smiled. He was so sure he'd won. "Well, Edira? What is your decision?"

"I accept." But it wasn't for him. And somehow, Rorik knew.

The golden ribbon of magic tightened against my skin and went taut between us, casting off loam and blight as it burned with otherworldly brilliance. At the same time, my brothers' threads pulled out of my veins at the sudden influx of power, and they hovered before me half drained of blight. Orin froze. He glanced from Rorik to me, as if sensing the solidified magic of our heartbond. Realization slammed into him, and he roared as he turned toward Rorik.

Time slowed as the magic seeped into my skin. A sense of awareness snapped into place, and suddenly we were tethered. I could feel the tension in Rorik's muscles, the anxiety racking his mind as he prayed I'd accept what he had to offer. And the magic. The *magic*. It swelled through my limbs and turned my veins gold, and the light surrounding my body was dusted with glittering, gilded flecks.

And then, for the first time, my life threads bloomed to life around me in a visible display of power. They writhed with energy. With Rorik's magic. With *purpose*. I narrowed my focus to Orin, and they split into hundreds of smaller strands and shot outward in a rush. Several drove into the ground and pushed my body upward so I floated in the sky above the blight and sickness. The rest slammed into the family. Into Seville and Lydia and Clesian and their daughters.

My brothers.

Even Rorik. But not Orin. Never Orin.

And then my veins drained them of their blight.

Black tar was siphoned from their bodies, from their life threads, from the very earth beneath us, and it flowed down my strands like I'd broken a dam. Everyone watched in rapt horror and fascination. My body was cooking with the sudden onslaught of disease, with the arcing pain lancing through my limbs as wave after wave of blight crested against me. The edges of my vision blurred as my breath became harsh. I vaguely registered that Rorik was calling my name, but my head had tipped back to the heavens and tears fell from my cheeks to dampen my blouse.

Not tears. Blood. The ruby-red droplets looked like gems in the light of my magic.

A sickening splash of liquid met my ears, and I tilted my head enough to see Orin had summoned a root and sent it straight through Rorik's abdomen. Blood flowed from him with the same efficiency as the blight flowed into me. His hands immediately went to his stomach, and they came away red. Then he looked at me and smiled as the color of his eyes dulled.

I felt his life flicker both through our bond and my threads, and I screamed. I screamed with everything I had. I screamed because Orin had stolen so much, and while I didn't understand why it mattered if he stole Rorik, too, I wouldn't allow it.

Vengeance filled me to the brim and chased away the pain, and I cast my arm to the side as I commanded one of my threads to slam into Orin. It pinned him to the ground, and I willed my magic to bring my feet back to the earth. Slowly, I walked toward him.

"You wanted my power." I hardly recognized the timbre of my voice. It was heady and deep and riddled with magic. "Take it."

With one hand, I summoned several more threads and aimed them at various points in his body. At the faintly glowing gems hiding beneath the surface. I recognized the likeness of my magic in the everjewels, and they throbbed with recognition. Orin couldn't hide them from me. Not anymore.

I flicked my wrist, and the strands drove into his flesh. I channeled everything I had into them and redirected the blight I'd drained from his family. From my brothers. From everyone who'd ever been a by-product of his schemes. I wanted Orin to have it all. To suffer like we had.

The jewels shattered in an instant, and Orin screamed.

Black liquid surged into his being as the wounds along his skin festered in the presence of more blight. Pustules formed and erupted across the expanse of his chest, and his eyes rolled to the back of his head. And then yellow loam frothed in his mouth and coated his teeth. He gagged as sickness slid down his throat. Tar leaked from his eyes. His ears. His nostrils. Gone was the resplendent Ever with power and beauty fit for a king. He was nothing more than a grave.

A full-body tremble overcame him, and he gave one last gargled gasp. Then he stilled. He disintegrated before our eyes, leaving behind nothing but bones. He'd have no chance to join the ancestor tree. He didn't deserve it. The blight that remained hardened and dusted to ash, and a quiet breeze carried it away. Gone.

"Goodbye, Orin." I would've said more, would've cursed him to the ends of the earth, but my power crashed and, with it, so did I. I hit the ground hard as my vision went black, but before my senses dispersed, I swore I caught the sound of Noam's and Nohr's confused voices.

Alive. I'd done enough.

# TWENTY-SEVEN

# RORIK

dira was utterly still beneath the woven blanket. Her head was propped on a pillow, her eyes closed, her lips slightly parted. It was a sight I couldn't bear to look at, and yet I couldn't bring myself to leave. Not when I was the one responsible for everything.

Once Edira had passed out on the lawns, Vora sprang into action. She tore through the debris of the manor, and when my family simply gaped at her, she screamed at them to help. I'd never seen Lydia move so fast in all my life. Together with Clesian and her daughters, they built a ramshackle shelter for Edira. Their earthly magic, shockingly calm and gentle in the wake of what we'd just witnessed, birthed a tree that hollowed and surrounded Edira's still form. Moss crept over the rich bark and softened the ground beneath her body, and I watched in muted shock as Amalyss and Tasia flicked their wrists and urged pebble-sized white flowers to bloom by her side.

It'd taken me several painful minutes to move. The wound Orin had left in my abdomen was weeping blood, and I'd peeled off my shirt to tightly bandage it around my stomach. Later, I'd properly dress and care for it, but all I wanted in that moment was to get to Edira. Adrenaline did the rest of the work, numbing the pain to a dull throb, and I rushed to Vora's side to help her secure one of Edira's apothecary cases that'd been pinned beneath a beam. A breath later, Vora was kneeling beside Edira, and her fingers maneuvered deftly between vials as she secured tinctures and muttered ingredients aloud. Seville unloaded a blanket and pillow from her arms before returning to help Lydia sort through the mess of Fernglove.

Days passed and Edira still hadn't moved. Neither had I. I stayed in the small, hollowed-out tree and watched through the open archway as my family summoned magics to slowly clear away the debris. The manor was destroyed beyond recognition, and while many of the surrounding buildings also suffered massive damage, they were at least still standing. Lydia and Clesian were quick to dole out orders, and I was surprised to see Seville take them without argument. But her gaze was distant, always snagging on the horizon even long after the sun had set.

After a week of working with Lydia and Clesian, Seville finally approached Edira's shelter. Her throat bobbed as she stepped inside, and I wondered if she'd stayed away for the same reason I refused to leave: guilt.

"How is she?" she asked.

"No change." I glanced at Edira's still form.

Seville studied me for a long moment. "At least she looks better."

She did, thank the gods for that. At first, her body had been withered, her skin peeled off in layers, and her breath was hitched and shallow. But each day, her body recuperated. Muscle definition and color slowly returned to her sleeping form. I was far from patient, and every hour, every minute, felt like an agonizing eternity.

"Why?" Seville asked, and I rounded my gaze on her.

"Why what?"

"Why do you care?"

It was the very question I'd been asking myself since Orin first commanded me to spy on her. Maybe it was because of how deeply she cared for her brothers—something I'd never experienced and could hardly fathom. Maybe it was because of the way she'd looked at me the day I brought her to Fernglove. Like I fucking mattered, like I was someone—something—to be marveled at. Or maybe it was her cunning mind and the way she analyzed absolutely everything at the dinner table that evening. Or maybe it was when she'd told me skirts wouldn't stop her from stabbing me. Or the day she tried to strike me. I'd never met anyone quite like her, and I'd spent lifetimes encountering all sorts of people. She'd intrigued me from the start.

But I didn't care to share any of that with Seville, so I settled on something tamer. "I was tired of the suffering."

"Right." Seville stared right through me with the same sense of knowing as our mother. I hated it. "Well, if she doesn't eat you alive upon waking, tell her I said thanks."

My gaze shifted back to Edira. "You won't be here when she does?"

"Should I be? I don't think so. One Ever lording over her while she tries to recover is plenty." She snorted to herself before shaking her head. "After all, I doubt Edira will want much to do with us given what she just went through."

"I wouldn't, either," I said as I folded my arms across my chest. "Though I'm surprised you didn't try to save him."

It'd always been them against me for as long as I could remember. The true heirs versus the mistake. I was the reason for our mother's death. Even now, Seville glowered, but she shifted her weight from one foot to the other. Calculating. Her thin brows pulled together as she gathered her thoughts, and then she finally relented with a sigh.

"Lorelai was . . ." She pressed her lips together and shook her head, as if convincing herself it was safe to continue. "I wanted to be her heartbond. I cared for Rowena, too."

Lorelai Starglen, one of Orin's many former heartbonds. A hazy memory began to unfold before my eyes: Seville, all those years ago, stiff with rage and lips so thin they'd nearly disappeared, standing silent at Lorelai and Orin's heartbond ceremony. And then the single, heart-wrenching cry I'd heard through the halls the night of Lorelai's death. It'd been the only time in my life I'd considered knocking on Seville's door. I'd kept walking.

And Rowena. My shoulders slackened. "I didn't know."

"I didn't want anyone to know. It was safer that way. Orin still found out, though. He always did." Ire filled her ice-green stare, and I wondered if the anger she always wielded had nothing to do with me, or our history, at all. She shuddered, hiding away whatever emotion she was too cautious to show, and allowed a smirk to claim her lips. "Though it looks like you're the one collecting heartbonds now."

"A means to an end." The words burned like ash against my tongue, but they were true. I hardly knew Edira. We'd never had the chance to speak freely with each other, and now she'd never want to. Not after what I did to her brothers. I glanced past Seville to find Noam and Nohr helping Vora forage for herbs. With the collapse of the estate, the majority of her wares were destroyed, and Edira needed a constant supply to help keep her body from failing. We'd been filling them in about Edira's work here and there, answering their questions without reservations. We owed them the truth, and we had no reason to hide it. Not anymore.

"And her end will be sooner than most." Seville's words were harsh, but her tone was not. The gentleness of her voice gave me pause, and I shifted my attention back to her. She watched Edira with a subtle warmth, almost as if they were friends.

When I didn't say anything, she leveled me with a weighted look. "What are you going to do?"

"About Edira?" I asked.

"Edira, the estate, the mines." Seville glanced at the grounds where Lydia was marking the land as if determining the layout of some new structure. Somewhere, Clesian and his daughters were helping track down the stags that had bolted in fear into the woods. They'd fallen into a routine without missing a beat when they simply could've left. But still, they remained.

"Fuck the mines." I scowled at nothing as I pictured the blight-ridden earth surrounding the cavernous maws filled with tantalizing gems. "We have enough everjewels for the family and we no longer have blight. Plus, we have more money than we know what to do with. If the townsfolk want to mine them at their own risk for their own profit, then that's on them."

"I suppose that's a call you could make as head of the estate," Seville hedged.

"Not for me." I bristled at the title. "I think Lydia and Clesian would be happy to run the place."

"Maybe in your stead, but not permanently," Seville said as she tucked a strand of hair behind her ear. "Shocking, I know."

"*My* stead?" It was impossible not to balk. "I don't want this place. If not them, then certainly you."

"I think it's pretty clear who Mother would've wanted to be in charge. Lydia has already mentioned honoring her wishes." There wasn't an ounce of disdain in Seville's words. If anything, there was a sliver of remorse that made her tone waver. "That aside, what do you think will happen when more Evers learn of Edira's ability to cure blight? Our attendants fled the moment the glamour fell. A few have started to return, but not all of them. Her talents are bound to get out."

An involuntary snarl ripped from somewhere deep in my chest, and my canines sharpened to snag on the soft flesh of my lips. "I won't let them touch her. She's done enough."

"I know, but the fact remains. They will come for her." She loosed a heavy breath, as if she didn't want to keep going. But she did anyway. "Especially the Embergraves."

My pulse climbed higher, and I formed fists by my sides. Anger brewed in my gut as my lips curled. Zeverin. All these years, we'd never been able to talk about him or even whisper his name. I knew little about my real father. But all Evers knew just how bloodthirsty and horrendous the Embergraves were. They were dangerous and had sway over a multitude of smaller Ever families throughout Glaes. No one stood up against them, but I would. For Edira, I would burn their estate to the ground.

I let my glamour fall away in a ripple. Magic crackled in the space between us. "I don't care what kind of power they possess. I don't care about their family or how many they have under their control. I will kill them all. No one touches her."

Before Seville could respond, a flicker of awareness sparked in my chest, and my world froze. It was small, like the first star winking to life in the presence of dusk, but brilliant just the same. And with it came a soothing warmth that beat through my limbs in time with my heart. My breath caught in my lungs. Slowly, I turned my gaze to Edira. And then she moaned. I'd felt her awaken through our shared bond before the soft sound filled the air. My power left in a rush, and my glamour slipped back into place as Seville straightened. She glanced around me to look at Edira, and the fear that had crested in her eyes dissipated.

"Okay, Rorik. Together, then." She placed a soft hand on my

shoulder, completely upending everything I knew about our sibling relationship, and then waved goodbye. I didn't have time to process her words, and I didn't care to. Because in that moment, my entire fucking world winnowed to Edira and her now parted eyes.

She blinked several times over, working her mouth for a few moments. Finally, she spoke. "Water."

I was on my knees in seconds, gingerly placing a calfskin canteen to her mouth. Water spilled over Edira's lips, and she drank deeply until she turned her chin. I capped the canteen and set it beside her.

"How are you feeling?"

She stared at me for a harrowing minute, and I swore I saw the moment all the memories came flooding back to her mind. The cloudiness in her eyes evaporated in a breath, and she scowled at me with a cold, distant fury that chilled me to the bone.

"I'll be fine. Where are my brothers?"

"Helping Vora gather herbs for your medicine. They'll be back shortly, I promise."

"Promise? I'm tired of Ever promises." A brittle laugh scraped from the back of her throat, and she pressed her head into the pillow to stare up at the ceiling. She frowned at the sprawling, interconnected tree limbs and ivy strands. "Where am I?"

"Vora refused to move you. You're outside Fernglove in a makeshift shelter. Now that you're awake, though, we can get you out of here."

"Good. I never want to see this place again."

While I could understand why, her words burned unexpectedly. If she detested the idea of remaining at Fernglove this much, then she undoubtedly felt the same way about me. An unfamiliar twinge of despair twisted through me, stemming directly from my heart.

*Heartbond.*

Her eyes widened, too, and suddenly she was glaring at me. "I don't want this. I don't want to *feel* you."

"You won't know I'm there unless you come looking. I swear it." I would shield every emotion from her, distance myself both in mind and body, to keep her from dealing with the aftermath of me.

"More promises." She looked away, but the absence of her ire-filled stare did nothing to assuage the guilt ravaging my throat.

"Edira, I'm sorry."

She didn't meet my gaze.

"I know that those words will never be enough. And that no explanation, no matter how true, will ever make up for what I did." I wanted to beg for her forgiveness. I'd never felt more alive than when she targeted me with her dove-gray eyes. They tore right through me each and every time, and I didn't care one bit if they left me bare and wanting.

A glassy sheen covered her irises, and the air in my lungs came to a screeching halt. She barely had the strength to move, and I didn't dare touch her, so all I could do was watch as a single tear slipped free and slowly descended her cheek. It broke me entirely.

When she finally spoke, her words were barely a whisper. "Thank you, Rorik. For helping me save my brothers."

That damn tear moved so fucking slow. My fingers burned to wipe it away. "You're welcome."

"But that doesn't change what happened." Slowly, she turned to look at me once more. "I'll never be able to forgive you for what you did. You're the reason they were sick to begin with."

My heart thundered in my throat. She'd saved me from my brother's wrath, and, heartbond aside, I would do anything to grant her peace throughout her final days. Even if it meant staying away. *Especially* if it meant staying away.

"I'll get Vora and your brothers." I turned to go, pausing only for a moment at the threshold of her shelter. I gave her one last chance to say anything she wanted. One last opportunity for there to be something besides anger and remorse traveling down this heartbond of ours.

She said nothing.

I left without looking back.

## TWENTY-EIGHT

The freshly upholstered couch in our living room was my new favorite piece of furniture. I guessed Mrs. Marlow decided to use higher-quality fabric after seeing me with Seville, but she didn't know I no longer had any contact with the Ferngloves. No one did. Sighing, I reclined onto the cushions and lightly dragged my finger along the rich indigo material.

Two months. I'd spent two months of my life with the Ferngloves. More, if I counted the weeks following Orin's death. I'd been unconscious for days as my body recovered from the aftermath of ingesting blight on such a colossal scale. Apparently, Vora had refused to let anyone move me until I was healthy enough to do so on my own. Only when I regained consciousness long enough to send Rorik away did she allow me to be placed on an elevated cot instead of the strangely soft bed of moss.

It took another two weeks for me to stay awake for more than a few hours, and as such, my memories were hazy. The only thing I knew for certain was that after our initial conversation, Rorik wasn't in any of them. He'd held true to his word and disappeared, leaving me in Vora's capable hands. Between her and my brothers, I was more than cared for. They never left my side while I recovered, and as much as I'd appreciated their help, their constant worry had grown tiresome. So, I demanded we return home. Back to our lives. Neither Vora nor my brothers argued with that.

I still struggled to move on my own for more than a few feet, and I tired easily. I'd told Vora time and time again to get on with her life, to leave me to Noam and Nohr, but she refused. Instead, she bustled away in the kitchen and served me meals and tinctures to aid my health. She promised she'd go one day, but not yet. I found I wasn't in a rush to send her away.

My brothers quit their jobs in the mines and turned their focuses to other trades. Turns out, Noam always wanted to be a woodworker like our father. Nohr was interested in horses. We had all been burying our wants to keep the family afloat. Now, we didn't have to. My deal with Orin had never involved money, but that didn't stop Lydia and Clesian from loading several hefty bags of coins into the carriage when I left.

"For my daughters," Lydia had said, and I'd understood. They had a chance now, too.

The amount was obscene, and we'd have enough to keep our family and our children's families—if it ever came to that— thriving for years.

Vora made several trips early on between our house and Fernglove, and on her final visit to what was left of the estate, she brought back a small parcel wrapped in twine and a letter. Ywena had also returned with her, and my heart twisted at the sight. She'd fluttered to me with ease on an invisible current and then nestled in the crook of my neck.

I'd stowed the small package and letter in my dresser, unopened. It was unmarked and plain, which told me enough. There was no way Seville would've gifted something without using some elaborate, florid signature.

I didn't ask about Rorik. If I wanted to know where he was, I had a feeling he wouldn't be hard to find.

A flicker of warmth stemmed from my chest, and I absently brushed my fingers over my sternum. The heartbond was still intact. I could feel him, as if he were standing at the end of a bridge some great distance away. But he wasn't looking at me, and I wasn't looking at him. One day soon, when Death was finally ready to welcome me home, our connection would disappear, and he could move on with his life. Maybe find a heartbond for real. His magic was the only reason I was still alive. As much as I loathed him for everything he put me through, I could at least thank him for that. I'd been granted a few more years. Enough time to watch my brothers grow into their own.

A knock sounded from the front door, and I leaned the back of my head against the frame of the couch. "Vora? Can you get that?"

No answer. Ywena shifted against my neck, and I offered her my finger. She skittered onto it and flapped her wings once.

"Not here?" I mused as I studied her eyes. I'd hardly needed Rorik's power to communicate with Ywena before, but now her thoughts—more like a series of images moving at a rapid pace in my mind—were plain as day. Vora had gone out to gather some herbs and pick up meat from the butcher. Noam and Nohr were lounging in the fields.

With a quiet groan, I pushed myself off the couch. Every bone creaked. "I'm coming."

I shuffled toward the door and pulled it open. Mrs. Marlow stood in the entryway with a bright smile stretched across her face and a package in her hands wrapped in thin white paper. She handed it to me.

"I'd hoped to deliver it to Seville directly, but since she ordered it for you . . ." She shrugged. "It's already paid for. Hope you like it."

"Thank you," I said as I took the parcel. It was light in my hands and tied with a pale pink ribbon.

"Please send her my way when you see her next. I have some new pieces I think she'll love," she said with an eager smile.

The townsfolk assumed I was still employed by the Ferngloves, and I wasn't keen on correcting them. If my power was reserved for my Ever lords and ladies, it was not accessible to them. I didn't want to deal with the passive-aggressive pleas for threadmending. They could continue to buy tonics and tinctures like they always had. My magic was my own to use.

Mrs. Marlow tipped her head slightly by way of goodbye. Her son was waiting for her at the gate, and he waved when he saw me. Toman. At least his nose was still straight. I smiled and waved before slipping back inside.

Ywena fluttered about my head before landing on my hair.

"I'll open it, sheesh." I pulled at the ribbon. "You're impatient."

I let the wrapping fall away, and my fingers stilled. It'd been a lifetime since I'd stood in Mrs. Marlow's shop and let Seville outfit me in armor. The gilded, silken fabric moved over my fingers like liquid, and I grazed the black lace and onyx crystals. Something heavy lodged in my throat. It was the same sheen as the golden beetle that had derailed my entire life.

*Rorik.*

The tether between us tightened at the thought of his name. Ywena shifted to my shoulder, her feet a gentle kiss against my bare skin. She shared nothing with me, and yet I felt sadness blooming from her touch. She missed him. Part of me did, too.

Slowly, I made my way to the bedroom and shut the door. I set the undergarments on my bed and turned to the dresser. A tightness formed in my throat as I opened the drawer and pulled out the plainly wrapped parcel and letter.

I unfolded the parchment first and studied Rorik's cramped handwriting.

YWENA WANTED TO STAY WITH YOU. I SHOULD HAVE
GIVEN THE GIFT TO YOU SOONER.

Setting the note aside, I stared at the package. My breath caught in my chest, and I almost wished Ywena would shock me. I needed her to help me move, to guide me and push me toward whatever it was that Rorik left for me.

Slowly, I undid the twine and peeled back the wrapping to reveal a polished mahogany box with a golden clasp. My fingers hesitated over the cool metal.

"You have any idea what this is?" I asked Ywena.

No, she didn't. But she wanted me to open it and find out.

Undoing the clasp, I flipped open the lid and found a piece of leather resting in the silk-lined box. The breath left my body.

With a trembling finger, I traced the embroidered flower stitched into the worn hide. My mother's work. The piece of leather I thought had been burned to ashes with the rest of my clothes before traveling to Fernglove.

The memory of that night crashed into me, and I remembered standing above the basin in the kitchen as I looked out at the night, rubbing the piece of leather between my forefinger and thumb. I'd been boiling water for Noam's and Nohr's baths, staring out at the moon. Later, I'd seen the golden beetle clinging to the rafters while I'd bargained with Orin to save their lives.

Rorik's beetle.

He'd been watching before we'd even met, and it'd taken him no time at all to understand how important that piece of my past was to me—and to keep it from being destroyed.

Tears flowed over my cheeks, and I held my mother's leather tight. A quiet sob racked my chest. It hurt to hate him. It hurt more to care. I pressed the hide to my heart and closed my eyes, clearly seeing the golden bond stretched between us.

I thought about grazing it and letting him know I was there. I didn't know how I'd react if he showed up at my door. But I wanted to find out.

Just as I was about to prod the strained bond between us, a glimmer of something dark snared my focus. Slithering in the golden river, like a viper waiting to strike, was a slimy thread of black tar. I watched in horror as tiny maws formed and lazily gnawed away at the magic. Panic raced through my mind.

I thought I'd cured him. I thought I'd cured them all.

But as the blight continued to creep along our bond, I realized that it was one thing to chase away the illness, and another thing entirely to root out and eliminate the cause.

This was a sickness that wouldn't stop coming. And even with Rorik's magic pulsing through my body, I wasn't sure I would ever be strong enough to prevent it from surfacing again.

# ACKNOWLEDGMENTS

THESE PAST FEW YEARS HAVE been trying for me, both personally and professionally, and I wouldn't be here today without the love and support of so many people.

Apparently the triangle is the strongest form, and I believe that wholeheartedly thanks to Alexa Martin and Lindsay Landgraff Hess. We're a cult of three, and I love it.

Alexa, thank you. Thank you from the absolute bottom of my heart. You listened to me cry and vent and spiral endlessly as I made huge leaps of faith throughout this process, and you never once doubted me (if anything, you encouraged me to jump farther). I can't thank you enough for your honesty and support and for not thinking I'd completely lost my mind (just partially!).

Lindsay, you're everything I hope to be when I grow up. I'm eternally grateful to have you shouting at the top of your lungs, supporting my work, and encouraging me to step out of my comfort zone. You're an absolute gem and the first person I'd want beside me in any tussle. Thank you for believing in my words even when I didn't.

Piper J. Drake, thank you for being my sounding board and writing sprint companion. You're a fantastic shoulder to lean on and a talented writer. I'm thankful I can count you as my friend, and not only because you know how to order the best dishes at any restaurant.

Stefani Sloma, don't ever leave me. You're stuck with me for life. You've championed me and supported me and pushed me to honor myself and my words in a way no one else has. You deserve all the pretty rocks in the world.

Kimberly Whalen, you're a rockstar agent and an awesome human being. Thank you for taking a chance on this book and seeing its potential from the start. Your immediate faith in me and my work is something I will never forget.

To Ariana Sinclair and the entire Harper Voyager team, thank you! I wouldn't be here without any of you, and the support you've given this book makes me teary-eyed and emotional (in the best way!).

To my readers new and old, thank you for choosing to spend your precious time with my books. I write these stories for you. I hope you find joy in the worlds I create, and your continued support is the reason I sit down to write with a smile on my face.

To my family and friends, thank you. Thank you for your understanding while I lock myself away for days—weeks—at a time and forget to communicate with y'all. Thank you for being my OG support system and for proudly telling anyone who will listen that I am an author.

And of course, to my husband, Jacob, and our two darling toddlers, the biggest of thank-yous. I love our little family, and the joy you bring me fills my cup in a way nothing else can. Thank you for giving me the space to chase after this crazy dream of mine and for being patient during those long nights of drafting and editing. You are my rocks and my inspiration.

# ABOUT THE AUTHOR

MAXYM M. MARTINEAU IS AN associate creative director by day and a fantasy author by night. She earned her bachelor's degree in English literature from ASU, and currently lives in Arizona with her husband and two wild kids. When she's not drafting her latest novel, she enjoys playing video games, binge-watching television shows, and of course, reading.